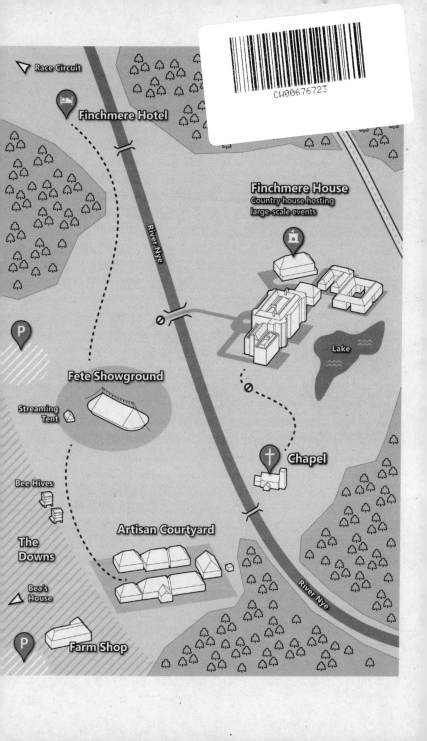

A Swarm of Butterflies

Sarah Yarwood-Lovett

embla
books

First published in Great Britain in 2024 by

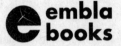

Bonnier Books UK Limited
4th Floor, Victoria House, Bloomsbury Square, London, WC1B 4DA
Owned by Bonnier Books
Sveavägen 56, Stockholm, Sweden

A CIP catalogue record for this book is available from the British Library.

ISBN: 9781471416422

1

This book is typeset using Atomik ePublisher.

Printed and bound in Great Britain by Clays Ltd, Elcograf S.p.A.

Embla Books is an imprint of Bonnier Books UK.
www.bonnierbooks.co.uk

For Granny and Granddad, Violet and Stuart.

Organisers of fetes, winners of most of the fete's prizes –
with definitely no connection between those two facts.

For your creativity, curiosity and humour.

Chapter 1

DI James Clark was breaking a few speed limits, rushing to Finchmere House: it was too much to hope that Sylvia's fears about their friend, Dr Nell Ward, were unfounded.

He knew Sylvia Shawcross well by now, ever since her brave testimony helped to sentence a killer. She was too worldly, too level-headed to catastrophise. If she was asking him over to discuss a potential threat to Nell, he *had* to take it seriously.

Speeding along the country lanes from the market town of Pendlebury, he saw that the next turn would take him towards Cookingdean – and Nell's house. He might catch her before she and Rav left for Finchmere, her parents' estate, to prepare for the upcoming Finchmere Fete. The chance to gauge her mood, to see if she was aware of any risk, before he met Sylvia, was worth a detour.

Under arching leafy boughs gilded with early light, he opened his car window to drink in the crisp air. Then, his inhale dragged in the alarming, thick, noxious stench of burning.

It should have prepared him for the sight of it – the sheer devastation of it – but it didn't. When he pulled up at Nell's gates, horror punched him in the gut.

Keying in the code urgently, glad he was one of the few who had it, the gates opened to reveal the awful scene. Nausea churned in his stomach; he was already feeling sick from the acrid air.

The fire had torn through Nell's house, the flint wall blackened, windows shattered.

The roof had slumped in, its jagged charred beams exposed. Underneath the collapsed mess, the ceiling and upper floor had caved in. Right where Nell's bedroom would be.

Inside, Nell's home was melted and misshapen, smothered with the smoggy snow of soggy charred ash.

This wasn't the first house fire James had seen – but it was one of the worst: the place was a ravaged ruin. He fought the panic as he tried to think, to assess.

But all that was running through his mind was: *how the hell could Nell or Rav, in his wheelchair, have gotten out of this?*

Wednesday 5th July – 8 a.m.

The previous day

As the golden rays of morning sun filtered through the summer-bright leaves of the beech canopy, Nell crept towards the sinewy hornbeam, stealthily, as she hunted for the tiny species. It was crucial not to forewarn these creatures, or she'd send them scattering into the thicket.

Beside her, Rav – Dr Aravindan Kashyap – was just as quiet, despite manoeuvring on crutches over the mossy forest floor, until excitement made him whisper, 'This place is doing *so* well, isn't it? The hazel and blackthorn have really taken – they'll be great food reserves.'

Nell was pleased to agree. This part of the rewilding project at Finchmere, her family's downland estate, had been under his professional supervision. He'd been determined to manage this survey, initially by all-terrain wheelchair, as he gradually recovered from that awful car crash. It had taken two years of painstaking, pain*ful* hours of therapy to get this far.

After seeing him lose his sense of purpose at the start of his recovery, Nell had always tried to make sure he felt valued. She needn't have worried: Rav had become a presenting superstar. Their *Following Finchmere* YouTube channel – where they presented sustainable activities across the historic estate – had been an unprecedented success. They'd employed a videographer and levelled up their content, and the stratospheric number of subscribers had spurred advertising and sponsorship deals, generating marketing prospects for Sylvia and additional income for projects.

Rav's determination to recover had won as many hearts as his devotion to ecology had. It was inevitable that his charm on camera would attract swarms of admirers, leaving gushing comments. Nell's own star power wasn't burning quite as brightly: the positive comments meant a lot to her, but they were notably fewer, and she couldn't really relax in front of a camera, given how past events had made her retreat and minimise her profile.

With Rav revelling in the attention, she'd tried – repeatedly – not to feel jealous of his success. But she did feel a bit elbowed out of her own project, at her own home.

Yet, they were partners in this endeavour. They'd wanted good publicity, and they – or Rav – had certainly got it. And she was pleased for him. *Honestly*. It was just that some days, she wished they were more . . . in it together. She felt left behind, somehow.

Now, though, his focus on how well his project was doing was a real joy. So what if she was a bit sidelined next to his soaring popularity? Her ego wasn't his problem. He was making a real success of this – the work *and* the filming – and the impact this was having on his recovery reminded her of what really mattered.

Around them, the woodland echoed with morning birdsong. A treecreeper hopped up an oak's gnarled trunk, seeking insects; a distant hammering told her a woodpecker was doing the same, with more brute force. By transferring the strain from head to body, this bird could withstand ten times the impact of a sixty mile-per-hour, head-on car crash. The thought – so close to recalling Rav's recovery – made Nell shiver.

He leaned his crutches against the tree and opened the large clear polythene bag, as she reached for the small wooden box, which had no obvious hole, wired to the hornbeam's trunk. She placed the rubber bung in the hidden hole that faced the trunk, at the back of the box, then opened the sloping lid a crack. *A nest!*

'We've got one!' Nell whispered, looking for clues of the resident. 'Grapefruit-size, no obvious way in – so not a harvest mouse or wren nest. The roof and leaves are woven, with stripped honeysuckle bark, so not a wood mouse or yellow-necked mouse nest, either.'

Rav gaped at her. 'So . . .?'

'*Dormouse* nest!' Nell was thrilled to confirm it and see Rav's excitement shine in his dark eyes. But finding a nest was easy – seeing an elusive dormouse in the fur, quite another.

'Anyone in?' he asked, tilting forward, reaching for his phone.

'I'd look . . .' Nell closed the lid and unhooked the box from the tree, then placed it inside the polythene bag to contain the resident. 'But that's your job, isn't it?'

His eyes widened in delight. He opened the lid, gasping as a pink snuffly nose and pair of dark eyes appeared. He cupped the warm body in his hand and, with a quick, apologetic check of the genital papilla, deftly transferred the male into a weighing bag. 'Only nineteen grams. Maybe this little chap has used up his calories enticing a mate. At least there's plenty of food here to fatten him up.' The indignant-looking dormouse squirmed. 'Sorry, fella, breeding season will put you in full territorial mode. Let me pop you back home.'

As Rav put him back, another little furry face blinked up from the nest. 'No *way*!' He looked at Nell. 'You know what this means. You take her – you're more dextrous than me.'

With great care, Nell scooped out the plump, golden dormouse, who showed no signs of stress and instantly curled up, fluffy tail over nose, and snoozed.

Nell gazed at her, captivated, as Rav took a photo. Weighing her, Nell said, 'Twenty-three grams. You're right, they're a breeding pair and she must be pregnant.' Reuniting the mates in their nest, Nell deftly reattached the box and unblocked the trunk-side entrance.

Rav shook his head in delighted disbelief. 'I can't believe they're *breeding* here!'

'*You* connected the habitat and improved their food resources.' Nell kissed him. 'We should film an update. We'd better keep the cattle out of the woods in winter, though, or the dormice will be trampled to death when they hibernate on the ground. We'd better make sure their home is safe.'

Rav nodded. 'I'll go to the office now and organise some temporary fencing. I don't want that to get forgotten with all the craziness of the fete.'

* * *

Back at Finchmere's offices, they were collared for a few hundred other jobs as the estate team went into overdrive, preparing for the massive fete in two days' time. Rav hoped Nell hadn't forgotten their plan to escape for a pub lunch and afternoon off.

It was quite a gesture from her. Thousands were coming, over the three days when Finchmere Fete was on, in celebration of all things rewilding, putting immense pressure on Nell to make it a success. They had a long week ahead of them, but he was hoping to steal a couple of hours with her before he went to see his parents in London tonight and tomorrow.

So, when she nudged him, impishness dancing in her amber-flecked eyes, he didn't hesitate to down tools and follow. Even so, he hated relying on Nell to drive him everywhere, after all this time. It was that, or racking up a ridiculous amount on Ubers, or getting an adapted car, which he'd insisted would be a waste for a temporary need. At least now that he could manage most of the day on crutches, she looked more convinced by that.

Winding along high-banked lanes, frothing with cow parsley, to Cookingdean, they reached The Mill pub. Eating club sandwiches, and chips too hot to pick up with their fingers, they'd soaked up the view of the cricket green and the Nye River beyond.

For the millionth time, Rav wished he could hold Nell's hand and stroll along the bank, under the arching willow boughs, past ducks dabbling in the shallows. He still couldn't manage it on crutches – but he had a plan, which he repeated like a mantra: *recover, walk again, propose.*

They drove on, past the village church, down the leafy lane to Nell's flint barn. Within the gates, she pulled up in front of the house. Since she'd be taking him to the train station later, she didn't bother to park in the triple garage, a former stable block that was now – like the converted barn – spilling over with a flowering green roof buzzing with insects.

Limping to the front door, Rav noted that the wheelchair ramp still made life easier on crutches. Inside, Nell's antique rugs had been rehomed at Finchmere, so he could traverse the patinaed flagstone floor unimpeded. He hated the stairlift, gouged in the stunning flint-faced wall. But Nell hadn't hesitated to make her home accessible, so he could reach the bathroom and bedroom upstairs, in the half of the barn that wasn't open to the vaulted ceiling.

While he made coffee in the handcrafted navy-and-copper kitchen, Nell strode past bookcases that groaned with books and boxes of ecological finds, dividing the study – with its wide desk orderly with microscopes and samples – from the stylish living and dining areas. She threw open the bifold doors to the garden and Rav caught the sweet scent of sun-drenched honeysuckle, before the rich aroma of coffee curled around him.

As he poured their drinks, Nell arranged cushions and throws on the chairs around the garden table, angling them in the dappled shade so they could enjoy the downland view. When she took out her laptop and opened it, Rav bit back a fond smile, knowing she'd be revising the questions for the expert panel they'd be hosting for a select audience on Friday's Rewilding Champions day. With the mini-conference being live-streamed, there'd be nowhere to hide if they made a hash of it.

Taking the milk out of the fridge, Rav caught his reflection in the custom polished-copper finish, and practised his surprised-delighted face as he rehearsed his opening comments: 'I hear your rewilding work hasn't only supported rare species, but it's attracted visitors like the black stork, whose populations have declined over many years in western Europe.'

As Nell came in for the drinks, she caught him. For a moment, he thought she was rolling her eyes, but she laughed. 'Rav has such fascinating facts at his fingertips,' she teased, quoting one of his fans' comments from a recent YouTube video. Then she asked, 'Do you think they'd be disappointed to know how much research goes into those off-the-cuff comments?'

'Nah.' He grinned. 'Kat likes the bite-sized facts. She says they're more memorable.' He paused, putting on his sunglasses, then searched his rucksack. 'Have you seen my travel mug? I thought I left it here, in my bag. I was going to take it with me later.'

'Didn't you take it with you this morning?'

'No. I always have it in my bag, with my sunglasses. I wanted to take a coffee with me to the station. Have you moved it? Or used it?'

'No. It's probably just been left in an office back at Finchmere.'

He wasn't convinced, but he shrugged and followed Nell outside. As she settled in her seat, in front of her open laptop, she shot him a sheepish glance. 'I'm as keen as you are to make sure we have those facts at our fingertips.'

'I *think* the hard work may be paying off. I'm starting to feel like we may be prepared for the big day on Friday.' He eased into the seat beside her, savouring the coffee, the view, the chattering acrobatic swallows swooping around them. 'And tomorrow should be fun.'

'Oh, yes.' Nell clicked on her emails, bringing up the schedule that Kat, their one-woman videographer and producer, had put together for their filming. 'Interviews with our artisans, so we can weave that in between the live-stream footage of the fete over Friday, Saturday and Sunday.'

'As you might expect, I'm prepared.' Rav saluted. 'Got all the questions ready for our beekeeper, woodworker, vintner and food producers. But it's low pressure, we can always start again if anything goes wrong. Unlike our live chat with the panel of experts on Friday.'

'Oh, that'll be a friendly crowd.' Nell's tone was reassuring this time, so his nerves must be showing. 'They're either involved in rewilding one way or another, or they want to be, so they're already onside. And we've got our talking points and questions ready. Oh!' Nell glanced at him. 'D'you want to share the success story of our dormice?'

'We could, couldn't we!' Rav pulled Nell's laptop towards him. 'Do we have any photos showing the progression of the woodland management?'

Finding the organised pictures, he made a quick presentation, ending with the photo of the dormouse from this morning. Knowing Nell wouldn't resist making a few final touches, Rav took advantage of her focus while he packed.

When she drove him to the station, he asked innocently, 'What'll you do for dinner?'

'No idea, now my favourite chef is away.' She grinned. 'I'll have toast or something.'

As he kissed her goodbye, he whispered, 'Lucky I've left you a surprise, then.'

As Nell pulled into her drive, about to open the gates, a car drew up with her. She frowned. This area was quiet, and she guarded her private space fiercely. Were they turning around?

But the car stopped and the driver got out, dressed head to toe in black, as if blending into the shadows. Nell froze. After assisting the police with solving a string of murders, her natural caution had developed a side effect of suspicion.

When the stranger opened the back door of his car, reaching in for something, Nell felt sweat slick down her back. The warm, close evening grew oppressive behind the windscreen. She fumbled in the glove compartment for her pepper spray.

He walked towards her, clutching a paper bag, then called out, 'Takeaway? For Rav?'

Nell's legs turned to jelly in relief. With a wobbly exhale, she opened the window. 'Thanks.' She took the bag, still gripping the canister in her other hand, wary of . . . anything.

But he simply handed her the dinner that Rav must have ordered for her, and walked away with a cheery wave. Only when he'd returned to his car and driven away did Nell put back the spray and press the button for her solid wood, seven-foot-high gates to slide silently open.

Driving in, she closed the gates. When noting the cameras, the garage's coded lock, home alarm system and deadbolt, she admitted her overkill approach to security – and her overreaction to the delivery man. She'd thought her instincts had sharpened; perhaps it was her imagination.

While serving the aromatic bhuna and cardamom rice in the kitchen, her growling stomach made her concern melt. Taking her meal to the sofa, she spied the parcel that Rav had left on the coffee table: a cute card with his sketch of a snoozy dormouse, scented candles, the promise of her favourite takeaway on its way – *ha!* – and Finchmere rosé wine in an ice bucket. She poured the wine, lit candles and chose a film, curling her feet up as Jezebel purred beside her.

By the time her cat insisted on being fed – sitting upright on the sofa, blinking wide golden eyes at Nell – the candles had burned low and the bottle of wine was empty.

After feeding Jezebel, Nell checked that the windows left ajar were locked, leaving only the small one above her study area open. It was far too hot to close it, even at this late hour. She took up her laptop, drew the curtains as she cleaned her teeth, ditched her duvet in favour of a crisp, cool sheet, and then changed into a pair of Rav's boxers and a T-shirt.

After good food and wine, she fell asleep fast. But the heat made her slumber restless.

When Jezebel patted her awake with a velvety paw on her face, Nell gently pushed her away, needing more rest. *It can't be morning yet.* But Jezebel patted her cheek again.

Rousing, Nell sighed – and the air she drew in was tinged with an acrid smell.

Bolting upright, Nell's pulse quickened, just as the smoke alarm began *screeching*. She sniffed, taking a second to register the hot, chemical stench of smoke.

She darted to the bedroom door, opening it – the sheer heat and the clouding smoke from below hit her like a wall.

Paralysed with shock on the landing, she saw her living room filling with dark, rolling plumes of black, billowing smoke. It filled her nostrils, coated the back of her mouth.

She couldn't believe the spread of the bright yellow, white-hot blaze, the speed of it, the *roar* of it. There was no escape downstairs. *Thank God I don't have any rescue bats in, or they'd be trapped in the utility room.*

Already, she felt light-headed as the fire sucked the oxygen from the air. Sprinting to the bedroom, she slammed the door, stuffing a dressing gown along the bottom to reduce the amount of smoke getting in. Turning to the bed, she looked for Jezebel. There was no sign of her.

She checked the duvet piled up on the floor, in case her cat was hiding there. Nothing.

Frantic, Nell kneeled, searching under the bed. In the middle, pressed against the back wall, Jezebel was quaking. She was just out of reach, and Nell had to squirm under the bed, pushing herself with her knees, to reach her.

As her fingertips met Jezebel's fur, her terrified cat hissed and backed away.

'Come on, poppet.' Nell tried to sound calm and reassuring, but her words were no match for the screaming, relentless shriek of the alarm. 'I know it's scary. Come with me.'

As Nell edged closer, jamming herself under the bed, Jezebel hissed and lashed out with a devastatingly accurate, lacerating set of claws.

Holding back swear words, Nell wriggled out and used all her strength to shove the king-size bed aside, then dropped to her knees to try again.

Jezebel backed away, but not quickly enough and Nell grabbed her by her haunches.

'I know, poppet. But you can't stay here.' She tried to drag Jezebel towards her, battling her cat's resistance.

The alarm's scream might be piercing, but her system meant that the fire service would be called automatically; she didn't need to phone while she tried to deal with this.

As Jezebel slackened her grip on the thick carpet, to lash out again in an attempt to make Nell back away, Nell used the chance to pull her in. As needle-like claws raked her arms, she felt hot blood trickle. But she'd got her, even if the cat in her arms was unrecognisable. Jezebel yowled in pure fear, lashing out in terror, hissing in protest, her instincts to protect herself overriding everything.

Nell held her, trying to sound calm. 'OK, poppet. It's OK.' But her pounding heartbeat contradicted her words, and spoke the language Jezebel understood.

Black smoke curled through minute gaps around the door, the smell making Jezebel thrash. Nell feared for her cat's little lungs; she wouldn't last long once the smoke got in.

The screech of the alarm was making her own ears ring; Nell could only imagine how awful it must be for much more sensitive feline ears.

Grabbing her site bag, she one-handedly tipped out the contents, shoved her laptop, chargers and phone into the side pocket, then wrestled Jezebel into the main part of the rucksack. Jezebel did not agree with the plan.

Seeing smoke pluming through the door fired enough desperation in Nell to ignore Jezebel's defensive attack, even as her arms were being sliced with more frantic scratches. She eased the zip up at every inch gained, until Jezebel was contained inside. The bag thrashed while Nell gently put it on her back, then opened the bedroom's French window.

She could get out to the balcony – but climbing down was another matter. With no time to plan, she scissored her legs over the wrought-iron side rail, gripping the top as her body weight dropped into her shoulders. Her bare feet flailed towards the wall of the house as she moved one shaking hand from the top of the rail to one of the iron poles, then the other.

Clinging on for dear life, she tried to find a foothold, her sweaty grip sliding.

Frantic, Nell tried to steady herself. Her toes found cold, sharp flint, but no footing.

Jezebel's writhing inside the backpack made it impossible to balance and she felt her grip strength waning. There was only four feet to fall. She'd jump it in a climbing gym without thinking twice – but there, she'd fall on a crash mat, not unforgiving gravel.

She knew *how* to fall, how to roll to take the force out of it. If only she didn't have her beloved, furious cat on her back.

With a deep breath, Nell bent her legs, exhaled – and let go. As she met the ground, she let her legs fold, rolling onto her hip, her breath juddering through her. She thrust out her hands to stop tumbling onto her back and hurting Jezebel.

Scrabbling to her knees, ignoring the bruising pebbles, Nell slid the rucksack off and unzipped it an inch, seeing Jezebel's baleful golden eyes staring up at her. Nell kissed her soft forehead. 'We're OK, poppet. We're OK.'

But – as Nell heaved a sobbing sigh of relief, the dark night sky above her exploded with bright light, making Nell leap up as the inferno tore through her bedroom and burst through her window.

Hugging the bag – *Jezebel* – tight against her heart, she backed away in horror, and watched her home burn.

Chapter 2

Thursday 6th July – 4 a.m.

Nell had shivered as the firefighters fought the blaze. She'd raced to open the gates as soon as she'd heard the siren, and then it had taken hours to put the fire out. Everything around her was ashy, blackened, choked with smoke, and drenched.

It was a miserable sight of loss, after the raging roar of the fire. Nell tried not to think of the treasures destroyed, the meaningful things from Rav that had been swallowed up, the horrible, unnecessary destruction. It was her own fault – and could have been so much worse.

What if I'd been just as careless any other night and couldn't get Rav out safely?

Despite the near miss she and clever, brave, brilliant Jezebel had just had, she couldn't help thinking of all the even more awful alternatives.

The paramedic had arrived later, and now wrapped her in a foil blanket as she cleaned Nell's arms. 'Can you call anyone? Do you need to use my phone once you're warm?'

Her chattering teeth made Nell stammer. 'I-I've got my p-phone here, and there's some c-clothes in my car.' The small gesture of kindness undammed the emotional tsunami, and all Nell's fear and grief flooded out of her.

The paramedic hugged her, her green uniform infused with woodsmoke. As she released Nell and nodded, Nell went to the garage. Unlocking her electric RS Audi with her phone, she was glad of her habit of keeping a change of site clothes in the boot and pulled on the combats and hoodie. She hoped for socks stuffed into her boots. No such luck, but she could manage. Sinking into the car seat, trembling, she called Rav.

'Mmmf?' Then, 'Nell? Are you OK?'

'Not . . . Not really.' Her words came out in juddering gasps. 'I'm s-sorry to call. B-but our house . . . Our house just b-burned down.' She sobbed at the words, but they were only sinking in around the edges. It couldn't be real. But the smell, the sight, the glimpse of the amazingly capable people who knew how to handle this devastating calamity were actively confirming it.

'What?' She heard his bed creak as he sat up. '*How?* Are you OK? Jezebel, is she—?'

'W-we're OK.' Nell hurried to reassure him as she cuddled Jezebel through the backpack. 'I'm just so . . . s-sorry.'

'How did it happen?' At her whimper, he added, 'Look, don't worry about it. I'm coming. I'll be there as soon as I can.'

'OK. Th-thank you. I'm sorry.' Nell's voice wobbled but then the firefighter gestured that he needed to talk to her. 'I have to speak to the officer now. I'll call later. Love you.'

The firefighter glanced at her phone. 'You all OK for somewhere to go?'

'Yes, my parents live nearby.'

'Good.' He took Nell's contact details, then asked, 'Any idea how the fire started?'

Nell forced herself to admit it. 'I must have left a candle alight downstairs.' Misery engulfed her. 'That . . . That *blaze* was just so *fast*. I never imagined it could all go up like that. But of course, it's all wooden beams. I can't believe I was so careless. I'd had a bottle of wine.' She pulled the bag against her chest. 'I nearly killed Jezebel.'

Startled, the officer spun round to the ruins. 'But we accounted for everyone—?'

'No, she's my cat. She's in here.' Obligingly, Jezebel wiggled within the bag.

'Thank God.' He smiled in relief. 'There'll be an investigation, for the insurance.'

'It'll be void. It was my fault.' Nell stared at her home in despair, her teeth chattering.

The officer patted her arm. 'Don't make any assumptions yet.

13

You'll need to take photos of the damage, which I'll help you with now, and you'll need to send them to your insurance company today. They'll recommend a cleaning company, who can dispose of anything safely if needed, and surveyors. You won't be able to come back until the inspector says it's safe, so you'll need to leave the place secure.'

More shakily than she wanted to admit, Nell took photos of her burned, water-damaged home. She tried to detach herself from the wreckage of it, but small, silly things pierced her heart. The slumped stairlift that Rav had been so close to no longer needing, marking how they were building towards something together, made sobs well in her chest.

As the officers left, Nell secured the gates behind her. With Jezebel contained in the partly open bag, she drove to the on-call vet. Despite her driving talents, she unerringly found every pothole on the way to Pendlebury, the journey as jangling as her nerves.

The cloying disinfectant of the surgery table nauseated Nell's already roiling stomach. Poor Jezebel seemed to find that the check-up added insult to (thankfully no) injury. Her eyes weren't red or irritated, her lungs were clear and her breathing was normal, with no wheezing or coughing. No signs of burns on her skin or mouth; no lethargy, weakness, odd behaviour or vomiting.

Nell felt weak with relief as Jezebel was given a clean bill of health. She snuggled her close, smushing her chin against the cat's forehead. 'You lovely poppet. You saved us both.'

The enormity of it welled inside her like a tide, tears brimming as she cuddled her clever cat. Jezebel tucked her head in against Nell's chest, smushed against her arm, sharing the ordeal they'd overcome – and the gratitude of escape.

As Nell headed to Finchmere, she realised she'd arrive in time to see her parents at breakfast. As she drove up the copper-beech-lined drive, the sun golden and low over the misting downs, she dreaded breaking the news.

She needn't have worried. As she reached the refectory, stumbling with tiredness and aftershock, reeking of smoke and smutted with soot, her parents froze, both with toast mid-way to their mouths.

'What's happened?' Her mother Imelda was on her feet immediately, assessing Nell and the unusually clingy Jezebel still in her arms.

'I'm . . . I-I'm really sorry. It's all my fault—' A shuddering breath snatched her words away. 'There was a fire. The barn has . . . burned down.' The awfulness of it was beginning to leech through the shield of shock.

'What?' Hugo was on his feet too now, toast forgotten as he stared at his daughter.

Imelda's appraising gaze swept over her. 'Are you OK? Have you had a check-up?' As Nell nodded, Imelda's hand flew to her throat. 'Oh, dear God, where's Rav?'

'Fine. He's fine. He was staying with his family last night.'

'And Jezebel's OK?'

'Yes. Jezebel woke me. If she hadn't—' Nell trembled. She'd escaped just minutes before the fire had ravaged her bedroom. If Jezebel hadn't woken her . . .

'Stay here. For as long as you all need,' Imelda said. 'I'll even let Jezebel steal my slippers.' Her voice softened as she fussed Jezebel's chin. 'Gorgeous little hero.'

As Hugo poured her a coffee and marmaladed a thick slice of sourdough, Nell sat and sent Rav a text: *Jezebel's been checked by a vet and is fine, we're at my folks'. Next is the insurance inspection, but the fire was my fault, so we can't expect anything there.*

She felt sick at ruining almost everything Rav owned. As she forced herself to eat, Jezebel curled up beside her, eyes wide as she settled, one paw resting against Nell.

Once Nell had eaten breakfast, she took a long shower, scrubbing the clinging smell of smoke from her. As she towel-dried her pixie-cut hair, she spotted a text from Sylvia, Finchmere's Marketing Manager: *Sorry for short notice, sweetie, can we meet at 6.30 a.m.?'*

Dressing hurriedly, Nell gulped the last of her coffee, then rushed to meet Sylvia. The early time and lack of warning weren't typical, but a catch-up would be handy; she'd have to postpone today's meetings, and she knew Sylvia would help.

Climbing the stairs to the second floor of Finchmere House, her feet were leaden. Yesterday, she'd been pleased to see the new lease of life that the rewilding work had given this formerly unused part of the house, repurposing the rooms as estate offices; today, she felt numb. *Is it shock?*

Her phone buzzed and, as she answered his call, Rav asked, 'Hi, how are you doing?'

'I feel awful, Rav, I'm so sorry—'

'Stop saying sorry. As long as you and Jezebel are OK, it's all fine. I'm on my way. Everyone wanted to come and make sure you're OK, but I fended them off. I thought it might be a bit overwhelming right now, but Mum, Dad and Aanya all send their love. And Mum has sent an industrial supply of Patisa, to cheer you up.'

'That's so kind.' Nell was touched. 'You're right: as lovely as it would be to see them, I'm not up to it. I just want to distract myself with work, and deal with the necessities. But pass on my thanks, especially to your mum, I love her baking. Sorry I disrupted your plans with them.'

Her guilt warred with buoyant relief that he'd be back soon, and the clamour of jobs to do: the paperwork, insurance requirements (pointless though they'd be), cleaning services, picking through the wreckage in case anything was salvageable, replacing everything . . .

Rav interrupted her churning thoughts. 'I know there's a lot to do. But I'll cover the most important thing: I've got hugs.'

'Oh. Bragging now, are you?' It was a weak attempt at teasing, as she tried to deflect how much she needed exactly that: there was nothing she wanted more than his arms around her, blocking out the world.

'Too right. I'm your hug sommelier. For this occasion, I have a warm, wrapped-up hug, smushed up close. The kind of hug that says it will all be OK.'

Nell managed a smile, but it was wobbly. 'Perfect. I could do with that. That, and nothing else going wrong today would be nice.'

As they ended the call, she heard the door along the hall open. 'Nell! Thanks for coming. I'm so glad you could meet at short notice. We've got a problem.'

Thursday 6th July – 6.30 a.m.

As James walked around Nell's wrecked barn, he couldn't bear to call the hospital to ask if she had been admitted. But her number seemed permanently engaged. *Is that a bad sign?*

He tried again – and nearly jumped out of his skin when she answered. 'Nell? Are you OK? Where are you?'

'I'm OK. Had quite a morning. Me and Jezebel are moving into Finchmere for a bit—'

'Then . . . Rav?'

'He's at his folks.'

'Oh, thank God for that.' His sigh buffeted down the line as he let out the tension and fear he'd been holding in.

'So, you know,' Nell said.

'Yeah, I'm at your place.' His shoes crunched over broken glass and the blanket of sodden ash as he walked around what was left of the barn. He stared in disbelief through the frame of the exploded bifold doors, at the soot-soaked dereliction of the scorched room. 'I don't know how you got out of this. I'll come by and see you.'

As he hung up, he squinted into the room, wishing he could recall the signs to read. But he didn't need to be a fire expert to know something here wasn't right.

Nell was too careful, too conscious of everything all the time.

This couldn't have been an accident.

Ending her call with James, Nell turned to Sylvia, who was immaculate as ever in a scarlet power suit, despite how worried she looked. 'Sorry. You said there's a problem?'

Sylvia's shrewd eyes widened as she took in Nell's state, even post-shower and with shirt sleeves that covered Jezebel's frightened reaction. '*You* look like you're weighed down with problems today, sweetie. What's happened? Come in. I'll make tea.'

Sylvia swept Nell into her new office, ushering her towards a seat as she made drinks. Nell looked out at the view of the downs, feeling a little calmer. 'Thanks, Sylv. Your radar's accurate as usual. I've had . . . the worst night.' Her voice cracked. 'I . . . I can't go through it all again.' She clamped her lips, shaking her head, making Syvia pause, appraising her.

When Nell could speak, she said, 'I could do with your help in clearing my diary today, though. I've got meetings with Ryan Goldstein and Chuck Garrod from Napa Val—'

'Consider it done. I'll move all your meetings until after the fete.'

'Thanks, Sylv.' Nell leaned back in the chair, closing her eyes as she felt some tension lift. 'And James will give you the full low-down when he gets here. I'm not holding out on you – I just can't bear to go through it all again.'

'Well, I wanted to discuss something else with James.' Sylvia pressed a mug of tea into Nell's hands. 'But maybe it can wait . . .' Her eyes darted to the generous oak desk in front of the wide window.

Nell followed her gaze and registered the piles of post. 'What's all this?'

The sleek computer and curving screen had been pushed back to make room for the rows *and rows* of letters. About thirty of them, each in its own clear plastic bag, so the contents were readable without anyone having to touch the page, as if they were evidence. Sylvia wouldn't have done all this for nothing. 'Is this the problem you mentioned?'

As Sylvia nodded, Nell scanned the letters, her skin prickling.

Your work's so fascinating – you're an inspiration.

'Fan mail?' She glanced up. 'Why is this a problem?'

'Read them *all*.' Sylvia's emphatic nod made her short blonde curls bounce. 'They're all from one sender – the letters and envelopes are the same. They start out admiring the rewilding on *Following Finchmere*. Then it becomes *obsessive*.'

Studying the postmarks, Nell realised the sender had posted the letters from their local village of Cookingdean, not even sending them from Pendlebury, the nearby market town, for more anonymity. Why take such a risk? Was it to make a point?

In date order, the messages within the typed letters ramped up. *You're gorgeous on screen. What's the point of Sidekick Nell? You'd be better on your own. You'd be better with me. We'd get on so well. Oh! Was that a hint of a lover's tiff today? I'll be here for you. I'll always be here.*

Skimming, Nell plucked out more lines. *Got loads of fans, now – remember* I'm *the one who's been with you from the start.*

The next one made Nell gasp. *We'll meet soon. Then you'll know we were meant to be together.* The following letter confirmed a meeting had taken place: *Oh! You're even more delicious in the flesh!*

'Jeez.' She sank into Sylvia's ergonomic chair. 'They've *been* here?' She glanced at the postmark of the last letter. March: when *Following Finchmere* was rising in popularity.

Sylvia, who'd honed their stories, had been delighted with its success, and how the estate had benefitted from the new income. It had paid for the refurbishing of the barns near the farm shop, which formed a courtyard where some artisans had moved in in May, after being selected in March. They were food producers who used Finchmere's harvests, craftspeople and a new vintner for *Finchmere Estate Vineyards* – and these were the artisans that Nell and Rav were due to interview today for their channel.

'If these letters are dated from four months ago, why have we only found them now?'

Sylvia nodded at a crate, bursting with letters, assorted teddy bears holding hearts, embroidered statements of love, hand-knitted scarves and other crafted items. 'Those arrived yesterday. The accumulated letters *to date* fill that storeroom.' She thumbed it. 'We only looked for any odd letters because Conor's security team did a spot check ahead of the fete.'

'Of course Conor would think of it,' Nell said. As the ex-SAS security detail for her controversial MP mother, he'd be on high alert for the event.

'Once they came across one letter that sounded concerning, one of his team worked through the night to collate as many as they could find, with the same envelope, writing style and postmark. And all these are still just a dent in the mountains of letters we have.'

Now, Nell realised there was someone still in the storeroom, shuffling quietly – presumably Conor's security guard continuing the search – while Sylvia updated her.

'What did he advise?' Now that Conor and Sylvia were married – brought together over an attempted murder – Nell knew her chances of dissuading them from their recommended course of action would be nil.

'Police. Immediately. Hence, me arranging the letters like evidence. James asked me to assemble them, and he'll be here soon to review things.'

'Isn't that a waste of police resources?' Nell had a feeling she'd already needlessly taken up James's time this morning. *What can he do about an anonymous letter writer, anyway?* 'Isn't this just part of what we have to deal with for putting ourselves out there?'

'No, it certainly isn't.' Sylvia's gaze was determined. 'In fact, we need to think about making some adjustments there. Such as how wise it would be to continue with the fete, and throwing your home open to everyone this weekend.'

Nell gaped at her. 'You're not suggesting we *cancel* it, are you? We *can't* do that! It's been so much work. This is just some over-involved loner.' Indignation rose. She wouldn't let her home burning down stop her work commitments – and she certainly wasn't going to let a few obsessive letters derail the immense efforts of the whole team.

Given how many were invested in its success, Nell had been delighted when thousands of tickets sold out in two days; but now that meant too much was at stake to cancel.

'Really?' Pursing her scarlet lips, Sylvia made her disagreement clear. She'd put more work than anyone into the upcoming event – and Sylvia had a worldly-wise head on her glamorous shoulders; if she was serious about the nuclear option of cancelling just the day before the three-day event, she'd have good reason.

When the soft knock on the door made Nell jump, Sylvia invited in the team member bearing a massive post sack. Conor's security officer emerged from the storeroom to pour the sack's contents onto Sylvia's desk. Scanning for the familiar envelope, he spotted two.

Nell's blood ran cold.

Pulling on latex gloves, the guard bagged the letters, not even giving Nell the chance to see what was written. *Probably for the best . . .*

As he headed to the door, Sylvia piled up the other newly arrived parcels to put into storage. Then Nell caught an odd smell. 'What's that? Can you smell it? Am I imagining it?'

Sylvia's nose twitched. 'Is it my perfume?'

'No. It's definitely *not* perfume.' Fear unfurled as Nell's instincts recognised it before her brain would acknowledge it. It was the rancid, fear-spiking stench of death.

Seizing the parcels from Sylvia, the guard opened the first box. A knitted version of Rufus, their Highland calf, tumbled out. 'Adorable!' Sylvia laughed in unexpected delight. 'Kat was right to focus more attention on our calf, wasn't she? He's had our highest ratings.'

As the security guard took the second box, the offensive odour ripened. The base of the box bowed, as if liquid was pooling within and about to seep.

'*Ugh.* What *is* that?' Sylvia grimaced.

Opening the box, the high, hot stench of decay hit them – and a swarm of flies emerged, right into Nell's face as she peered in and regretted her curiosity.

'Oh! What's *in* there?' Sylvia darted to open the window.

As Nell took in the close-up photo of herself – her eyes viciously scored and ripped out – she had to cover her mouth and nose, so she didn't gag.

Her mutilated picture was skewered with a metal spike to a dead, glassy-eyed rat, its shocked stare above the frozen grimace of yellowed, sharp teeth.

Its guts had been ripped open, spilling out blackening blood, lurid pink and greying entrails, and the putrid stink of disembowelment. The rat was heaving with maggots gorging on organs, churning under the flesh.

Chapter 3

Thursday 6th July – 10 a.m.

Reaching Finchmere, James dashed through the familiar hall to the refectory, a chunky oak and glass extension to the Regency house.

Huddled at the end of a long table, Nell looked exhausted, her hands wrapped around a mug of coffee. There were cubes of flaky pastry treats in front of her, which James guessed were from Rav's family. With his arm protectively around Nell, Rav looked full of worry.

'Nell, it's so good to see you. You have no idea.' James pulled her into a hug, as relief that she was OK surged through him. He studied her in concern, especially since Sylvia's phone call, updating him on the delights of this morning's post. 'How are you doing?'

'I'm fine. I've even had a care package from Rav's parents.' Her smile didn't meet her eyes; she looked shaken.

James appraised her with narrowed eyes. He and Nell had briefly been a couple and then salvaged an enduring friendship – he knew better than most that Nell tended to brush things off. He glanced at Rav. 'How is she really?'

'Worn out and upset but I'm pretty sure we'll be in the indignant phase soon.'

'And then we'll really need to look out,' James joined the teasing, winning wan but rallying smiles. 'How are you, mate?' He nodded at the crutches. 'Do I detect progress?'

'Some. Early days. Don't want to jinx it.' Rav tapped the oak table, then his head.

Despite wanting to talk to them in a more private space, James didn't have the heart to ask them to move. Sitting down, he eyed the passing estate workers who grabbed coffees and muffins, most of them eating on the go and rushing off through the bifold doors to the grounds beyond the rose garden, lake, and grassland that stretched into woodland.

As James wondered how to broach the subject of their stalker, Rav asked, 'Are you here about the fire? And what the investigation will involve?'

Rav's question crystallised the fear that had been building as James had driven to see them. *Surely, it's too much of a coincidence for Rav to have a stalker, and for Nell's house to burn down . . . ?*

His professional reason warned him to remain open-minded, not to make assumptions. He'd need the expert opinion of the fire investigation team before he could discuss that with Nell and Rav. But any advice he gave them now could take that additional risk into account.

So, he nodded. 'Yes. The fire, and your stalker.'

Rav frowned. 'Stalker?' His eyes fixed on Nell as concern shock-waved over his face and his body. 'Are you OK? What's happened? What have they done?'

'Not me, Rav. *You're* the one with the stalker.'

He gave a short laugh. 'What? Some girl with a crush? That's no big deal, is it?' He ruffled her chestnut pixie-cut hair, making light of it. 'That's one less thing to worry about.'

'It could be a man or a woman,' James said. 'And stalking is one area where women can be as dangerous as men.' His colleague, psychology specialist DI Ashley Hollis, had prepared him for the likely questions, and even given him a bingo card of likely rebuffs she'd expected Rav to make. James had just mentally dabbed out two. 'And it's already escalated.'

Rav frowned, and Nell explained, 'Over the past nine months that we've been presenting *Following Finchmere*, you've had fan mail, Rav, which became obsessive, then referenced meeting you in person. And . . . I've had, well, hate mail, I suppose you'd call it.'

'Yeah, I'd call skewering your defaced picture to a dead rat hate mail,' James said.

Rav gaped, staring at Nell. 'Jeez, Nell. That's . . . unhinged, isn't it? Are they likely to *harm* you? Do you think they'd go that far? Is it jealousy, or something?'

James trod carefully, steering them towards making the connection. 'Yes. That's *exactly* the issue. When we know the perpetrator, we can try to anticipate how things will develop – but we don't know who this is, or what they'll do. If we even knew their sex, it would help, because different tactics apply. Male stalkers tend to be narcissistic – it's all about them. Female stalkers tend to use deceit. As you rightly hypothesised, Nell may be the focus of their jealousy. And then there's always the classic: "If I can't have him, no one can."'

As they absorbed the information, Rav pushed his hand through his dark, wavy hair, telling James how agitated he felt. His unsettled gaze studied Nell. 'Is . . . Is it a coincidence that your house just burned down?'

Nell gaped at him. 'What? *How?* That was my fault—'

'Let's all wait for the results of the investigation,' James said gently. 'No assumptions, no recriminations, OK?' He met Nell's gaze, making her nod. 'But I *can* factor the potential risk level into our response.'

This new horror made Nell's eyes widen. 'B-but s-someone would be an idiot to try to burn the place down. How could they? I've got cameras—'

'Yes, you have, but only at the front of the house. It wouldn't be impossible for someone to gain access via the fields at the back and through the hedge, if they were determined enough.'

Panic flickered across Nell's face. 'But . . . hardly anyone knows my address.'

'That may help to narrow down suspects. But anyone can find pretty much anything online, if they look hard enough.'

Nell spoke slowly, as the peril sunk in. 'You really think . . . Rav's stalker just . . . tried to kill me?'

'Or both of us,' Rav said. 'How could they have known I wasn't home?'

'Excellent question. Who *would* know? That may also help to narrow things down.'

'Only if the stalker knows we live together,' Nell pointed out. 'If they found my address online, everything there would be in my name only.'

'Given the danger,' James said, 'you have a series of decisions to make. How do we make sure you're *both* safe? How do we handle a fete that starts *tomorrow*, which will grant access to any member of the public who bought a ticket?'

'Well, we cancel it. Right now.' Rav's look at Nell was full of fear and determination. 'I'm not risking anything happening to you.'

Nell shook her head. 'If the stalker is a threat,' she reasoned, 'then they're a threat whatever we do. No point ruining an event that will undo so many other people's work.'

James knew Nell would react like this. *Too damn pragmatic for her own good.*

Ignoring Rav as he threw up his hands in disbelief, Nell asked, 'So, what *can* we do, James?' Despite her practicality, her face drained of colour.

'You're sure you want to go ahead with the event?' James checked. He couldn't disagree with Nell's logic: they'd still need a plan, fete or no fete.

Looking at Rav's worried face, Nell leaned forward and took his hand again. 'Yes.'

'Then I'll talk to Conor about stepping up security for the house. Not just more officers, but keeping everything, including windows, locked, restricting access. He and his team will be experienced in dealing with this: as security for high-profile clients, like MPs, they'll be familiar with exactly this type of risk. As for you two, the best thing you can do is keep vigilant.'

Rav nodded and gripped Nell's hand.

'You're both . . . *unusually* observant,' James continued. 'Look for patterns, anything that might distinguish who this person is, from things they say or do. See if anyone around you gives any indications of having obsessive feelings. Though I warn you, women excel at masking. The most unassuming, approachable type can be harbouring the deepest, darkest obsessive thoughts – *and* act on them.'

'Oh, great.' Rav winced.

With rising concern, James realised that Rav hadn't taken on board any of the risks to himself. His eyes were full of worry for Nell.

Leaning forward, James said, 'Rav, can we be realistic for a moment? You're still . . .' He nodded towards Rav's crutches. 'Recovering. And

I can see how well you're doing, mate. But it doesn't mean I like your chances if someone decides to get . . . physical.'

'I think I can defend myself against someone with a crush.'

'How long have you been out of the wheelchair and on crutches?' James asked. Rav would hate him for asking, but they knew each other well enough by now. He'd weather a bit of acrimony, for a bit of sense. He thought too much of Rav not to.

'Since . . .' Rav's hot gaze dropped. 'For the past few months I've used crutches almost all day. If I overdo it, I know about it. I'd rather use the chair and be out and about, than not.'

'That's incredible, Rav. And it's a great starting point for putting practicalities in place. Think about any areas that are harder to get around, and try to avoid them if you can.' He turned to Nell. 'Are you using the Land Rovers? To get around the fete?'

'Yes. All-electric fleet now. The same key works for all of them, so we can all carry duplicate keys and use any of the Landys.'

'How fancy.' James turned back to Rav. 'Always have a key on you, so you can use one whenever one's to hand. Just think a few situations through and equip yourself. OK?'

Nell's quick glance at Rav, who masked his fleeting flinch, made James wonder if his suggestion was unfeasible. The way Rav was recovering, driving an automatic seemed possible. Unless he wasn't ready to get behind a wheel again . . . *Ah.* James nearly winced at his insensitivity. But Rav was nodding, as if James's advice was sound.

As she appraised Rav, Nell asked, 'Can you send out a team? You know, for extra eyes on things?'

James had to hide another wince. 'Ideally, yes. But it's always trickier than it should be to resource pre-emptive action. How*ever* . . .' He shot Nell a hopeful smile. 'If you can swing a ticket for Hesha, and maybe Ashley, I happen to know this is where they wanted to spend their weekend off.'

'Done.' Nell smiled, the tension across her face lessening. 'You should have said.'

'We'll also need some intel. Spotting someone in a crowd is an outside chance, so I'll check in with you early tomorrow morning, before your fete opens.'

'Oh, that would be great. We have a breakfast meeting at 7 a.m. tomorrow.'

'I'll be there.' James smiled. 'And I'll ask DC Ed Baker to pick up the letters and the rest of your post today, and we'll check through all of it.'

'Sylvia bagged the ones she found; they're with all the post in a locked storeroom.'

'I'd expect nothing less. What will you be doing in the lead-up to tomorrow's opening?'

'We're interviewing our artisans – which we're actually late for, now.' Nell grimaced.

'Watch out,' Rav warned. 'Kat'll appear any minute to get us back on schedule.'

'That's to give us footage for Kat to edit in between the live streams from the fete on Friday, Saturday and Sunday. Our Rewilding Champions day, tomorrow, will be quieter – only a few hundred coming, instead of the few thousand who have tickets for the weekend.'

'Oh? Why's that?'

'The champions are a select audience who are – or want to be – involved in rewilding, like practitioners, researchers, ecologists, school teachers, enthusiasts. It's a mini-conference, detailed Q&A and activities.'

As she chewed her lip, James waited for the admission. 'But . . . those *enthusiasts* – they're our keener followers, who've entered a competition to attend. Sylvia's been calling them our superfans.' She winced at the word.

So did James. 'Perfect. Do you have a big neon sign that says: "Stalkers, This Way"?'

'If it helps,' Rav said, 'the conference and Q&A will be live-streamed, so the experts presenting their findings have some exposure on our channel. Will that make it safer?'

'Don't assume anything, and *always* be on your guard.' James looked up at the woman hurrying over from the doorway. She seemed deliberately officious, like she wanted to mark out her professional place: dark blonde hair tied up, crisp white shirt under a teal jacket, sleeves folded back to reveal a flash of floral lining. Her sharp blue eyes made her look intelligent, observant. Every movement was quick, like she had no time to waste.

Nell pushed herself to her feet and mustered a bright smile. 'Sorry, Kat, we got chatting and lost track of time. We're coming.'

Rav stood, assembled his crutches, then looked at her. 'Ready, Kat. Sorry.'

'No need to apologise.' Kat smiled at Rav, then Nell, as she frowned and said, 'Though we *are* behind schedule now, so it would be great to get going. Cameras are ready, sound checks are done. So . . .?' Her quizzical gaze scanned the tight knot James, Rav and Nell had become as they'd leaned in to discuss the issues. 'Could we get started?'

'Yes. Of course. Thanks, James.'

As they rushed off, and more team members wandered in for coffee, James prickled with uneasy awareness of the hundreds of new or temporary staff that were swarming the place. It would be so easy for anyone to gain access now – for any reason.

Listening to the fading conversation as Nell, Rav and Kat walked away, he heard Kat say, 'You'll be *so* pleased with the Champions event. Double the numbers we expected. And the competition results are in. There are some seriously diehard fans out there . . .'

His blood running cold, James sent Nell and Rav a text: *PLEASE – keep your wits about you. There are so many people at Finchmere. Your stalker's probably already here.*

Chapter 4

Thursday 6th July – 11.15 a.m.

Rav limped alongside Nell and Kat outside Finchmere House, to the Land Rover, fretting about Nell, and wondering how he could stop her worrying about him.

The thought of someone sending her revolting hate mail was one thing, but someone burning her house down – while she was *in* it – was another. It was so horrific that he knew his brain was actively rejecting it. He was *trying* to grasp it but the enormity of it . . . just hadn't sunk in.

He could tell that Nell was in the same state; she was coping by addressing the practicalities, the jobs, the things she could do something about – while totally sidelining the risk, the danger, the things outside of her control.

Despite all that, *somehow* they both had to keep their mind on work. Kat was oblivious, chattering on, outlining the interviews as they piled into the Landy and she bounced them over the fields to the Artisan Courtyard. Rav knew this team of artisans. He'd worked with them a few times to do previous pieces. But today everything was different.

Is one of them really my stalker? And are they actively trying to harm Nell?

Rav looked towards their destination, recalling when the artisans had moved in, about two months ago. They'd breathed life into Nell's restoration of the scruffy, derelict barns, which had originally formed WWII barracks and a pillbox, when the armed services had requisitioned Finchmere. Now, the smart horseshoe of flint buildings enclosed three sides of the replanted courtyard, and reflected the crafts and produce of the residents.

Kat steered them to a table set up in the centre of the courtyard, so that her pre-set camera took in the downland view beyond. 'Right, where's Zeus got to?'

She turned to the three barns that flanked one side of the horseshoe and housed *Finchmere Estate Vineyards*, overseen by the talented vintner Zeus Peacock. The furthest barn presented only a flint wall to the courtyard, as the large doors at the other end opened for the delivery of the harvested grapes to be pressed and processed. Beyond the barn, the south-east-facing downland slopes were filled with neat lines of vines. The next barn along housed the winery, where the wine was created, refined and aged – and where Zeus's technological recommendations had streamlined the process. The nearest barn, with its glass bifold doors to the courtyard, formed the stylish tasting room.

Kat approached the doors, calling, 'Zeus? Can you join us?'

A voice from within suggested he was on his way, and Kat strode to the opposite side of the courtyard, where *Graze!* took up another three barns, occupied by Noah and Gigi. In similar style to the winery, two of these barns also presented flint-faced walls to the courtyard, opening on the other side for deliveries – one for cheesemaking and one for charcuterie, where prime cuts were aged, hung and smoked. These barns were Noah's spiritual home.

The third barn along this side was Gigi's bakery, with a welcoming café and shop at the front, from which maddening aromas of freshly baked bread wafted over the bistro-style tables and chairs arranged across the courtyard. Kat peered inside and waved.

As she rejoined them, Rav caught the sound of rasping from Holly's woodworking barn, which formed the horseshoe's third side, leaving the fourth open to the downland view. Small, squat and square, Holly's flint building had wide windows along the sides, with a smaller one at the front, allowing room for a double-width door. After a moment, the rasping stopped and the young woman emerged.

'Sorry, lost track of time, Kat. I'm ready for the briefing.'

When Holly yawned, Rav's assessing gaze fixed on her. She was in her late twenties, wearing a leather apron over T-shirt and jeans, which were loose on her willowy frame. Her blonde hair was always in a messy bun, skewered with a pencil, artful wisps framing her face. She struck him as permanently Insta-ready. Yet, she was always asking him for advice about her own YouTube channel, *Holly: The Wood Whisperer*.

'Hi, Nell.' Holly's smile at her was tight but it widened as she turned to him. 'Hey, Rav! Thanks for your suggestion to use time-lapse filming to show a fast transformation as I work. It's going well! I've called the segment "Trunk to Treasure".'

'Oh great!' Rav forced a smile. Yesterday, he would have been delighted for her. Today, he was only aware of the tense glances she was darting towards Nell.

'The analytics show it's an audience winner. I can even see which bits are paused or rewatched, so I can make more of the things that get the most interest.'

'I'm glad it's going so well.'

'Yeah, my subscriber numbers have doubled over the past month.' She beamed at him. 'I definitely owe you that drink!'

When Gigi and Noah approached, bickering, Holly seemed to shrink into her chair.

Gigi's retort to Noah became audible as they drew near. 'It makes no difference whether I am at 'ome or not.' Her indignation made her French accent more pronounced. 'Why pretend you care?'

'That's not . . . That's . . . *ugh*.' Noah threw his hands in the air, glancing at the nearby company. 'We don't have to make this everyone's business, y'know?' His New Zealand twang was weighed down with exasperation.

'*Salut*, Nell!' Gigi greeted her with enthusiasm. '*Mon Dieu*, we are booming.' Her fingers flared out like an explosion. 'We have so many orders for our picnic hampers for tomorrow. And supplies for the café here and in the food hall. This event is inspired, truly. We are all benefitting.' She sank elegantly into the seat next to Rav, fanning her face. 'But, boy, I cannot wait for it all to be over!'

When Gigi smiled at him, Rav knew it was intended to infuriate her husband. 'And you are our superstar, eh, Rav?' Gigi said. 'Are you ready to meet your adoring fans?'

As her musky perfume wafted towards him, he spotted heavy concealer under her eyes. Gigi didn't usually wear makeup. She was one of those women blessed with flawless skin, effortless style and incredible cheekbones, set off with chignoned dark-blonde hair that was silvering like highlights. She oozed charisma, and relished her pastries and Zeus's fine wine without guilt about carbs or alcohol intake – and Rav sensed she was well-versed in the temptations of life.

Noah, by contrast, always looked like he'd just been wrestling a bear. Well-built and permanently dishevelled from the physical side of his work, he mostly looked worn out and not entirely satisfied with life. He and his wife may both be in their early forties, but they seemed to have little else in common.

Now, Noah was definitely needled by Gigi's attention towards Rav.

Thankfully, Zeus's arrival sliced through the awkward atmosphere, his Texan drawl full of bonhomie. 'Hey, folks! Are we all ready for our close-ups? Gigi, honey, you're always ready.' He kissed her on both cheeks, the cerise lining of his cobalt tweed suit flashing. 'Hey, Noah. We need to talk cheese. I have a few pairing ideas that'll blow your mind.'

'Awesome.' Noah forced a smile, still bristling at his wife.

'Holly, I'm so glad to see you taking a break! I've heard you workin' all hours in there, girl!' Zeus took one of her hands in his, critically appraising it. 'Spa day, stat. Y'hear what I'm sayin'?' He chuckled. 'Hope I'm not goin' *against the grain* there?'

At the eyerolls and grins, Kat took charge. 'Right, we have a lot to get through today, and I know you're all busy with last-minute preparations for the fete, so I'm aiming to keep this efficient and painless for all of us.' She smiled. 'Me included.'

Gesturing at the carefully positioned table and camera, she added, 'I've set this spot up so we could have a tasting session, Zeus, with a couple of wines you want to highlight, paired with some of the food from *Graze!* on one of Holly's charcuterie boards, please. Gigi and Noah, I'd like you to join this interview, and talk produce. Please have your soundbites ready, and I'll make sure Rav and Nell have a closing line. Then we'll come to your workshop, Holly.'

Everyone nodded.

'You'll have time to get the table ready while I whisk Nell and Rav away to do some filming at the wildflower meadow, also already scoped out, so we'll be quick. Then I'll come back for this interview, and then Holly's, and I'll spend the rest of the afternoon taking some shots for B-roll. Sounds good?' She didn't wait for a reply. 'Great. Let's go.'

The wildflower meadow was a short walk – or, for Rav, limp – away. It overlooked the main area of the fete, where Rav saw vehicles and heavy equipment setting up the marquees and vintage fairground. Since working at the estate with Nell, Rav had seen a few events being set up. It was usually a time of optimism, but now unease flared at knowing how many people were growing closer – and at Nell being the fete's public face.

She'd have to introduce displays and present awards to winners in the central massive event tent. He knew she'd also make the effort to thank everyone: the artists, potters and farriers of the craft quarter, the local producers in the food hall, and the volunteers on the smaller wildlife stands that orbited the main tent, with fascinating presentations from the Mammal Society, Wildlife Trust, British Trust for Ornithology, Moth and Butterfly Group, Woodland Trust and Bat Conservation Trust. They were all usually trusted partners. But now, he was questioning everyone.

'Your live-stream tent is nearly ready.' Kat pointed uphill: one part an enclosed wall of tech, monitors and cables, attached to an array of solar panels; one part an open-sided canopy – this was where he'd film live updates over the day. Kat had positioned it perfectly for a backdrop of the colourful fete and Finchmere House, nestled in the downland's patchwork of green and gold fields.

The plan, for him and Nell to divide up the coverage, had seemed ideal. Now, Rav feared Nell would be out there, alone and vulnerable. Nausea churned.

'Looks good.' Rav managed to sound enthusiastic. 'But we might need to review the programme. Nell and I should do more together, so I'll take a look and add some notes.'

A flicker crossed Kat's face.

'Sorry, I know last-minute changes aren't ideal. Think of them as minor tweaks.' What he was suggesting wasn't a tweak, so he didn't blame Kat for being annoyed.

But she nodded. 'Sure, let me know what you're thinking, and we'll make it happen. I'm sorry I didn't anticipate that. I should have.'

He hid his relieved sigh, glancing away, downhill. There, by the lakes and woodland, Finchmere's *reWild Side* Safari team had designed a tour of the rewilding successes. The tour was even better than expected, since the Land Rovers had all been converted to become fully electric, by specialist mechanics Mark and Cassie. The silent vehicles immersed you in nature, spooking fewer species, giving a better chance of spotting the flourishing, yet elusive, wildlife.

With wildlife impossible to guarantee, though, the Highland cattle, with their auburn fringes and gentle manner, were always a hit. They roamed freely and grazed on the chalk grassland, near the riot of wildflowers with aromatic wild thyme that had resulted in a spectacular swarm of large blue butterflies. It was towards this field that he, Nell and Kat were hurrying.

A couple of weeks ago, the sight of fluttering blue butterflies over the thyme had been epic, but Kat had prioritised filming with him to build anticipation for the fete, and hadn't understood Nell's excitement about the rarity of the species, nor how fleeting this swarm was.

As they approached Kat's camera set-up, pointing across the chalk grassland, he caught the herby aroma of the thyme. The wholesome scent was settling, somehow, a direct connection to nature. As his inhales deepened, his shoulders loosened a little.

There were barely any butterflies today, though. *We're too late.* He felt a pang of regret that his pieces had taken priority and lost them the opportunity to film the impressive clouds of large blues. *Nell must be thinking the same.*

'I can still do the butterfly story, Kat. Though the footage won't be quite so dramatic.'

'It looks good to me,' Kat said, framing up the view through the camera. 'Although Bea is supposed to be here already for her piece.' She squinted past Rav and tutted. 'She does know we're doing her a favour, doesn't she? This will boost her ratings for her *Bea's Bees* YouTube channel. And bees are supposed to be busy, aren't they? Do you think she could be persuaded to kindly get a move on?'

Rav turned and saw resident beekeeper Bea – Beatrice Camberwell – across the field, in animated conversation with the parish vicar, the Reverend Louise Brimstone. As Bea threw her hands up, Rav frowned. *Are they arguing?* 'I'll get her,' he offered, curious about the disagreement, 'while Nell does her piece.'

As he limped across the field towards Bea, he soaked up the glorious view: the wildflowers blazed across the chalk downland to the coastline beyond, with pink pyramidal orchids spiking between mauve pincushions of scabious, regal purple-fringed knapweed and buttery spears of agrimony. The hum of insects feeding lazily in the summer sun was ever-present.

A wave of nostalgia hit Rav. This was just like those endless golden childhood holidays. But that carefree freedom, when you had time to notice bees bumbling from bloom to blossom, feel the cool grass under your bare feet, drink in that high, sweet note of summer-warm flowers, seemed to belong to an alien world now.

As he approached, Bea stopped talking and stared at the ground. Rev Louise Brimstone twisted round so fast that her white surplice fanned out, showing her running leggings over her sinewy frame. With a wide beam, she said, 'Ah, Rav! Our very favourite superstar!'

'Hi, Rev Brimstone—'

'Lou! Please! Especially *now*!'

Rav's gaze slid to Bea, hoping that the local vicar wouldn't give away why he'd been speaking to her lately. Part of his plan – *recover, walk, propose* – involved understanding the unknown world of banns and other wedding mysteries. Nell, he was sure, would want a ceremony here. This place was in her heart. But if Nell said yes, and they told their families, he knew his eagerly awaiting mother – who had a ticking clock on Number One Son's marriage – would go into overdrive.

Unfortunately, Bea didn't miss Louise's familiar tone, and her surprised gaze flicked between them. The slump of her shoulders suggested to Rav that she was used to being a little out of the loop, and gave her an air of melancholy.

Rushing to smooth over the awkwardness, he beamed at her. 'Great to see you, Bea! We're excited to interview you – Kat's all set up over there, ready and waiting.'

If Bea didn't get the hint to hurry, Lou certainly did.

'Fab!' She speed-walked in her neon trainers. 'I'd *love* to see you in action.'

Catching Bea's daggered look at her, Rav tried to be encouraging. 'This is exactly the right time to film your bees, isn't it? All golden sunshine and hazy insects up on the wildflower meadow. Kat has a great eye.'

He smiled, hoping Bea would be eager to meet Kat and benefit from her knack for framing stunning footage with a crisp soundbite, which was so popular with viewers.

But Bea still didn't pick up her pace. She studied the flowers around her, her dark hair gleaming as she checked the bees' activity. Her face was flushed and Rav wondered why. Even though she was pushing a loaded wheelbarrow, it only had a few items in it. Beekeepers' suits, mostly. She was hardly exerting herself.

As they reached Kat and Nell, Rav marvelled at how immune Bea was to Kat's rattling energy to get going. Seeing the set-up, a slow smile spread across Bea's face, lighting up her dark eyes. Her unhurried air gave her a calm demeanour, which, from the way Nell was twitching, didn't translate to everyone. Like Kat, Nell was ruled by the clock, and the many things she always had to get done.

'Hi, Nell,' said Bea. 'Thanks again for letting me site the hives here. Kat, I've got a couple of ideas for things we can film today. I thought something hands-on would be interesting.'

'We were hoping to see the honey-making process,' Kat said, gesturing to the set-up.

'Ye-es.' Bea squirmed at the taskmaster tone. 'I can't do that here, though. This is the second nectar flow—'

'Save it for the camera,' Kat said, staring through the lens.

Rav shot a mock-grimace at Bea and Nell, making Bea giggle, flush again, and then straighten her face when Kat glared at her.

'I've got us all beekeeper suits – I'll open a hive and see if any frames are ready to remove, so I can take them away and extract the honey.' Bea smiled.

'I'd like you to step into shot, Bea . . . That's right,' said Kat, 'and then give us a quick intro on how the bees here are doing . . . and then say exactly that. We'll keep rolling when you put the suits on. It can be quite funny to speed that up, then we can pick up your commentary again when you start to open a hive. OK?'

'Er . . . Great.' Bea fidgeted as Kat mouthed the countdown and Lou made a helpful thumbs-up sign at Rav.

After a few takes, Kat announced that she was satisfied and that they could return to the courtyard for the next piece.

As they climbed out of their beekeeper suits, Rav said, 'I'd love to see how you extract the honey from the frames we've taken from the hives today. Could you give us a demo some time?'

'Er . . . Of course.' Bea's glance at Rav averted to the ground as she reclaimed the suits.

He frowned, wondering if he'd been too pushy. But his interest was sincere; he'd be fascinated to see the process. When he glanced back, though, his concerns eased as he spotted a beam spreading across Bea's face. As she turned away, folding the suits on top of the precious cargo of honeyed frames in her wheelbarrow, he wondered if she was just shy.

'It would be easy for you to pop by,' she said. 'I live just a minute or two down the road. I walk here, unless I have a lot of equipment to bring. There's a shortcut over the fields if you can manage a chestnut paling fence? There's a spot where I can get this through.' She hefted the wheelbarrow handles before continuing, 'So I think you'd be OK?'

'Any ecologist worth their salt can manage any fence,' Rav joked. 'Just let me know when suits you.'

Bea flushed, looking delighted – but then her face changed, like a summer's day clouding over, as Lou strode towards them.

'Bea! That was great!' Lou said. 'But we still need to talk.' She grimaced then mouthed, 'About your Gran's *funeral*?'

A shadow crossed Bea's face, her eyes darting to Rav before she muttered, 'I thought we had.'

Lou crossed her arms, her head on one side.

With a huff, Bea nodded. Her 'Fine' was clipped, irritated.

'Oh, *terrif*!' Impervious to her tone, Louise beamed and steered Bea away, back towards the courtyard.

As Nell, Rav and Kat packed up the equipment, Rav couldn't help catching Louise's words once she imagined they were out of earshot.

'As you well know, Bea, while I was writing my sermon for her, I referred back to my notes about your mother's funeral. You know, I'm concerned. And now I also hope you know that I simply cannot let this go . . .'

Chapter 5

Nell was trying to hang back as Kat route-marched her and Rav to the courtyard once again, aware that Bea and Lou were locked in an awkward conversation and probably wanted some space.

Kat either didn't realise or didn't care, as she lugged her kit. To be honest, now Nell felt the weight of some of the equipment, she didn't want to dawdle, either. As they overtook them, Bea and Lou's hissed conversation silenced.

Fortunately, the prepared table won a smile from Kat: spalted charcuterie boards laden with meats, cheeses, olives, pickles, nuts, sliced figs, apples and grapes; silver Finchmere-crested ice buckets bearing selected wines. 'This is just what I wanted. Perfect!'

'Oh, yes.' Lou joined her, appraising the view beyond. 'You do have a knack for framing a shot, Kat. I should get you to speak to my good friend, Rev Woodwhite. He dabbled with social media for a bit, but he's been out of action for a while. Poor man. He's popping in to see me for the gen on how to relate to the youth, now he's back in Ambledown again.'

'Sure.' Kat's smile was unconvincing, and she added, 'Schedule allowing.'

'Have we passed muster?' Noah asked, looking more cheerful as he brought out a loaded cheese board. 'We had help.' He nodded at the winery. 'Your young friend, Rav.'

Rav turned to see, just as Erin walked out with a tray of glasses.

Frowning, Nell wondered why Erin was here. She used to work with her, Rav and Sylvia at EcoLogical Solutions. Now that the three of them had moved on to work on rewilding Finchmere, Erin occasionally came out for some training. She'd been Nell's mentee, but the relationship had been fractious: Erin had always held a candle for Rav, and still flirted with him as a way of covering her bruised ego.

Rav had been all too aware that by dating Nell – her colleague – Erin had been forced to see their relationship blossom as they worked, so he had tolerated more than he should. Nell had to hope a stalker would be sufficient incentive for Rav to be clearer with Erin *and* with his boundaries.

Setting the tray on the table, Erin flicked her long dark hair, letting it shimmer down her back, and challenged Rav. 'You stood me up! I missed breakfast and haven't had a chance for any lunch yet because I've been waiting in the woods all morning!'

'We're not surveying today, Erin.'

Nell saw the awkwardness that Rav tried to conceal. He didn't bother reaching to check his phone: he'd turned it off since they'd spoken to James. 'We cancelled today, remember? Because there's so much to do for the fete.'

'Well, lucky I'm versatile, then, isn't it?' She smiled. 'What are we filming?'

Erin *had* helped to film some pieces, when they related to the ecology work she was training for, but not the wider estate work. Her presumption irritated Nell. But she needed Rav to speak up on this. As she waited, bright birdsong and the sound of sanding from Holly's workshop cut the uncomfortable silence.

Trying to hide her annoyance at Rav being lost for words, Nell sat at the table. She smiled across at Zeus, who was lovingly swathing the wines in the solid silver Finchmere-crested ice buckets with pristine linen. Noah and Gigi joined them, and Noah seemed to be turning the tables on his wife. He was practically salivating over Erin. Gigi's lip curled.

Rav took the last seat, next to Nell. 'OK, Kat, we're ready.'

Under the table, he caught Nell's hand. She squeezed his back, though she was now annoyed at filming with a live audience. Lou was watching Kat at work, while Bea sized up Erin, who seemed to be clinging like a limpet to the hope that Rav would include her in the interviews.

'We'll be ready to go in five, four . . .' Kat mouthed the remaining, 'three, two, one.'

And, right then, Nell's phone beeped.

'Ohhhh!' The collective groans turned into a chuckle.

'So sorry. I can't afford to turn it off on a day like today.' Nell glanced at the message. Shock at what she read made the words swim. She pushed her chair away from the table. 'I . . . er . . . I think this is urgent. I have to . . .' She gestured towards the main tent down the hill, and Rav stared at her, in wide-eyed concern. 'It's fine. Just a health and safety thing on the main site. But I have to go now.'

'You're not leaving, Nell?' Kat was saying, sounding exasperated. 'We're all framed-up here. Can't you go afterwards?'

'Rav can handle the interviews,' Nell replied. 'I might even be back for Holly's. Depends how long this takes to sort out. I'll be as quick as I can.'

'I can manage on my own, Kat. It's fine.' Rav spoke up in support of her. 'Nell has a lot to cover, so we'll all have to lean in today. We can just rearrange the table quickly—'

'No need!' Erin slid into Nell's vacated seat with a smile. 'I said I could help.'

Nell knew Rav wouldn't turn her down. He couldn't, without embarrassing her. And, true to form, he nodded, though he did add a caveat. 'We're on a tight schedule, Erin, so let's try one and see how it goes, OK?'

As Nell staggered away, she realised her breathing was ragged with panic. Rounding the corner of the barns, she leaned against the wall, dragging air into her lungs.

She read the message again. The unknown number had made her dread squirm before she'd opened it. Then, the sheer bitterness had burned off the screen.

He's too good for you. Everyone sees it. When will you back off & leave him alone?

She glanced around, uneasy. This was all too close for comfort.

Phoning James, Nell gave him the number.

'OK, thanks, Nell. I'll get the team onto it. Chin up, OK?'

It didn't reassure her. Fear spread through her like decay: she'd almost started to believe that the stalker was likely to be one of the artisans. The timings, the growing relationship – all seemed to fit. But she hadn't seen anyone sending a text.

Could I have missed it? Could they have hidden it? If it's not one of them, is it someone I haven't even considered? Is someone else here? Watching me?

Thursday 6th July – 1.30 p.m.

Rav was trying to help everyone feel at ease, so he could get this filming over with – and go and find out what had upset Nell.

Erin moved her seat closer to Rav's, making Kat sigh. 'Pull your chair back a few inches, Erin, I've got the view behind framed up.'

While Erin sulkily obeyed, Zeus made light of it, framing Rav up and peering at him through his squared-up hands. 'Surely, the view's all about our *superstar*? No wonder the camera loves you, sweetcheeks. Gorgeous on screen, even more so in the flesh. Mmm-*hmm*.'

Kat's countdown saved Rav from answering, but he'd noticed sweat sheening Zeus's bald head. He was either sweltering in his country-gent attire – and Rav knew enough about suits these days to recognise made-to-measure when he saw it – or he was more nervous than he was trying to appear. Rav would be surprised to discover that the handsome Texan – who had honed his craft in Napa Valley, before bringing his impressive résumé to Finchmere – found this climate warm. He watched him, wondering why he might be on edge.

But Zeus was already dazzling into the camera like he was born to it.

'Delighted to join y'all on *Following Finchmere* from the very heart of the estate's core producers. As the vintner in residence at *Finchmere Estate Vineyards*, I work closely with my colleagues over in *Graze!*' He made a sweeping gesture at Gigi and Noah. 'We create pairings that delight.'

Reaching to seize a bottle from the ice bucket, Zeus grinned. 'I can always be relied upon to bring a bit of sparkle to any occasion.

Since we're celebrating the success of Finchmere's rewilding work, as well as the upcoming fete, what could be better than our Classic Reserve?'

Right on cue, he popped the cork, allowing a hint of foam to appear as he expertly directed the effervescent fragrant wine into the coupes.

'Now, *this* is how to start an interview!' Rav laughed.

The light gold liquid fizzed in the sunshine as the group around the table all raised their glasses.

'As you taste this, I want you to think of the *terroir*. Our South Downs geology here shares the same chalk as you'll find in the premium Chardonnay areas of the Côte des Blancs, in Champagne.'

As approving nods and murmurs rippled round the table, Zeus didn't pause before pouring crisp white wine for them all. 'So I want you to notice how these wines taste alongside our local cheese and bread and meat.'

He pushed the generous charcuterie and cheese board towards them, and Rav couldn't resist selecting some delicious morsels. Erin looked like she wanted to, but held back.

'That unique flavour, the drink, the food, all from one soil, then savoured in the same air – that's *terroir*. That's when it all tastes its best. And that's why I work so closely with Gigi and Noah.'

Hastily chewing and swallowing, Rav nodded. 'All this definitely makes for a heavenly picnic. Your hampers for the fete will sell like your hot cakes, Gigi!'

'It's all because Finchmere is about heavenly *produce*,' Gigi said. 'Nothing is farmed, in the intensive sense. Everything 'as lived a good life, and tastes better for it.'

'That might make our produce *unpredictable*,' Noah said. 'But that *inspires* us to be more *inventive*. If Finchmere's land manager culls a deer, we'll feature top-grade venison. Once a year, we have the sought-after Highland cattle milk, when the calves are weaned, to make our limited edition, award-winning Finchmere Gold cheese. And a spring glut of nettles from our beekeeper's wild garden had us experimenting with a yarg-like nettle-wrapped herby cheese.'

At her mention, Bea's head jerked up, as if surprised Noah would credit her. Lou shot her a sidelong look, frowning. But her expression conveyed concern, not criticism.

'And we have some special treats for the fete, of course,' Gigi said. 'Finchmere's wildflower honey cake, from our resident beekeeper, is to die for.' She gave a chef's kiss.

Was that aimed at me . . . or the camera? And did I imagine Noah's glare? Rav shook himself for being an idiot, and noticed Bea's second gratified smile. Beside Lou, she sat up a little straighter.

'That's why we're called *Graze!*.' Noah beamed. 'We're all about giving the right *grazer* the right food *to graze*. Whether you're livestock or human.' He turned his palms up. 'Am I right?'

Gigi groaned. 'You are cheesier than our famous boards. Speaking of which . . .' As she described each type of cheese they supplied, Zeus suggested a wine. Of course, everyone duly tasted both cheese and wine, then charcuterie and wine, and finally dessert and wine. And Zeus believed in generous samples.

There was no way Rav was going to indulge. Keeping on his guard, he tried to get away with smelling the wine, or just letting it touch his lips in a pretence of a sip.

Erin, however, showed far less restraint. When she noticed Rav was being abstemious, she finished his drinks, too. With Zeus being quick to provide refills, or offer a comparison wine, it wasn't long before Erin was more than a little light-headed. She grew more fluttery with each glass, nudging Rav, complimenting him, leaning against him.

While awkwardly trying not to encourage her, Rav had to keep smiling through the interview – otherwise he'd run the gauntlet of retakes.

With Erin obviously believing she was increasingly hilarious as time went on, Rav was relieved at how deftly Zeus managed her, while playing the ebullient, generous host.

'. . . And the rewilding work here is a real attraction,' Zeus said. 'I love anything that celebrates our pollinators. Ain't getting any wine without them little suckers. This natural approach going on here makes all the difference.'

'Damn straight,' Noah agreed. 'I was a sheep farmer out in New Zealand. But I was looking for an adventure. I wanted something new, but I still needed to satisfy that call to the wild, deep in my soul. So this rewilding is right up my alley. I love those Highland cattle. I can see what they're doing for the ecology. It's a positive loop. Everyone wins. *We* take that positive loop to the next step – like our friend Zeus says, it all tastes best when you enjoy local produce together. And that's what we're all about at Finchmere: perfect pairings.'

They all held their smiles and Rav caught Gigi's acerbic whisper under her rictus grin, '*Vraiment, huh?*'

'Cut. That was great, thanks,' Kat said, to collective sighs. 'We're done.'

Beside Rav, Erin woozed, leaning back in her seat. 'Oof. I don't think I can feel my arms,' she slurred. 'They've gone all floopy on the inside! Help me, Rav! You've got all the biceps!' Erin reached for him, but could only manage to flap her hand at Rav's muscles.

'I think you may have had enough,' Rav suggested, pushing the nearest bottle just out of Erin's reach. 'I should get you some strong coffee and find someone to take you safely home.'

'Ah, our handsome devil is, in fact, chivalry personified,' Zeus approved.

Rav frowned, unsure if he was reading too much into Zeus's flippant comments.

'Oh!' Erin's eyes widened as she leaned forward. 'Ohhhhhhh . . .'
Her face slicked with sweat, and Rav knew what was coming.

So did Kat, who darted from behind the camera to throw out the water from a redundant ice bucket and thrust it under Erin's chin in time to catch her rancid puke. Placing the bucket away from the table, Kat stroked Erin's hair back from her face. But, behind her back, Kat pulled a face at Rav and whispered, 'I don't think Erin's interview material, do you? Best not put her in this position again.'

Rav winced, and then saw how concerned Zeus looked. 'Oh, man. I shoulda given her one of our new alcohol-free cordials,' he fussed, shooting worried glances at Erin. 'Our elderflower, from Bea's garden, has been outta-this-world popular.'

'Yes, well, bit late now,' Kat said. 'Sorry about this. Very unprofessional.' A glare at Erin. 'We'd best call it a day. I'll take her to the bathroom and get her cleaned up.'

'Use mine, please.' Zeus gestured towards his tasting room. 'Least I can do.'

'I'll bring over coffee and something to eat,' Noah offered. 'Soak up all that vino.'

Following Zeus, Kat steered Erin through the tasting room to the bathroom, and Noah and Gigi headed to their café.

As people scattered, Rav gazed in the direction Nell had gone, wondering if she was OK. He switched his phone on to send her a text, ignoring the flurry of messages from Erin.

As Lou strode towards the winery, Bea tiptoed towards him. 'Um . . . Rav? I made this special batch for you.' She held out a jar of golden honey. 'Some honeys have wonderful healing properties and I know that your recovery has been incredible, but . . . Well, you don't need it, I know. I just thought . . . every little thing can help.' She gave an awkward smile as she put it on the table, then relief flooded through her as her phone rang, and she stepped away to answer it.

'Thanks!' Rav held up the jar and smiled at her as she waved and backed away, heading towards a distant table to talk to her caller.

Now, Rav caught Louise's strident tones coming from the winery. The conversation sounded . . . combative. Sensing they wouldn't want to be overheard, Rav turned away, engrossed in his phone. That wasn't hard, given his desperation for a reply from Nell.

Louise sounded furious. 'You can't carry on like this, Zeus. If you don't take responsibility and address this, then I will.'

'If you're saying what I think you're saying, *honey*, that's a very bad idea.'

Rav chanced squinting across the courtyard, watching Louise and Zeus's apparent stand-off. With the slam of a door, further inside, Kat rushed across from Zeus's storeroom, clutching a packet of paper towels. She froze for a second as Zeus and Louise stared at her.

As Louise strode off, Kat turned towards the bathroom. 'Oh, Erin! You look better! I found some towels.' She walked towards her. 'Let's go back in and finish sorting you out.'

Rav saw that Louise had paused in the shadows between the charcuterie barn and the fromagerie. She leaned on one arm against the wall, drawing calming breaths. She was clearly angry, or worried, or shaken – and Rav wondered what Zeus had, or hadn't, done to cause that reaction.

A little further along, inside the café, Noah and Gigi were also arguing.

As Rav wondered if the heat, wine and event pressure were getting to everyone, he watched as an unfeasibly good-looking barista with a man-bun and designer stubble placed the coffees he'd made on a tray on the counter.

Noah grabbed the tray to take it across to Erin, but Gigi blocked his path to the door, her hand on his chest pushing him back.

Through the open window, he caught Gigi's accusing tone, and the mention of 'young girls' and 'menace'. And Rav began to understand what her concern was.

Before Rav could intercede, though, the barista walked past Gigi and Noah, picked up the tray and walked across the courtyard, towards Erin.

Glowering, Gigi watched him from the window. Noah looked even less impressed and started following him outside, standing at the café door, hands on hips, before striding off to the charcuterie barn. Noah was so busy glaring at his employee that he nearly collided with Lou.

As she staggered out of his way, Lou seemed to realise why he'd been distracted. She shook her head. 'Seriously? Temptation might come in many forms, but you've really got a one-track mind in that area, Noah. I've warned you before about your lack of boundaries.'

'It's only coffee—' Noah's protest sounded more whiny than convincing.

'We both know it isn't, Noah. It's predatory. Keep it up, and I'll make a formal complaint. Understand?'

Chapter 6

Since Sylvia had called him earlier, and he'd seen that revolting parcel of the disembowelled rat, James had been pushing every line of inquiry he could think of. He'd called the fire investigation team, and had their assurance they'd fast-track their assessment.

Now, he was following up with the tech team every half hour. He was desperate to get the location of the phone that was sending Nell the texts.

Well-versed in the hurdles of the mobile-phone companies, he'd anticipated the first request: *You can't apply for the data without a warrant.* He may have used up all his favours with Val, his Chief Constable, but he'd got the warrant expedited and sent.

The next message from the phone company was equally expected: *Thank you for your data application; we'll need time to investigate. Yours is one of many such requests and we thank you for your patience.*

As soon as he received it, James dashed back to Val's office, knocking on her door and framing his argument.

If they couldn't get the phone company to prioritise their request today, they'd have no hope of hearing anything useful until tomorrow – or maybe even later the following week.

He just couldn't afford to lose time. If this stalker had already escalated to arson, they were a critical risk, and he needed something – anything – to help identify who they were dealing with.

Before it escalated to something even more deadly.

As Rav tried to help Kat seat Erin at the shady bistro table, the barista duly followed with her coffee. Gigi also headed over, bringing a pie and some pastries from the café to help soak up the alcohol.

'Rav?' Kat asked. 'While Erin has something to eat and drink, do you think we could film our final piece and get the interview with Holly in the can?'

'Oh . . . um . . .' Rav looked at Erin in concern. She seemed a little better, but that wasn't saying much.

'I'll take my lunch break now, keep an eye on her.' The barista pulled out a chair and sat down, flashing a charismatic grin at Erin, and Gigi's sympathetic expression flickered with irritation.

'Oh?' Erin straightened up a little, her face brightening.

As Rav shot a glance at Erin, checking she'd be OK, he heard Kat clear her throat and hurried to follow.

Inside, he caught the warm, clean, almost spiced-nut scent of woodwork; the fresh, sweet warmth of sawdust; and the honey-rich aroma of beeswax.

Holly stood up from her seat at the bench, brushing off her hands on her leather apron. 'Hi! Welcome to my workshop.'

The space was the perfect mix of order and chaos. Through ever-present dust motes, a wall of tools showed those missing in active duty by the pencilled outlines of planes, hammers, wrenches, screwdrivers and chisels on the pinboard. Below, the wide, wooden bench was scattered with offcuts and little mounds of wood curls. Vices of every conceivable size were attached to the edge, some clamping layered work or joints of furniture.

From behind the camera, Kat was muttering, tweaking a connector. 'Hmm . . . I think I need to replace this cable. I'll be right back.'

As she left, Rav turned to Holly. 'This place is brilliant. I haven't seen it since you moved in. It's great to see your incredible work in the flesh . . . Well, grain.'

Pieces had been lovingly stacked on the massive table, for sanding and waxing.

'Wow, what's this?' A striking curving purplish piece of wood, at the far end of the bench, had a few carvings picked out, beginning to resemble twining flowers.

'Yew. Amazing colour, isn't it? Giving me some inspiration. Not quite sure where it's going yet, though. It's from Bea's garden.'

Rav freed his hand from his crutches so he could trace the lines of it; then he couldn't resist stroking a large polished walnut sculpture. Other pieces of furniture filled the space, with free-standing shelving units stacked with smaller items. Attached tags noted the commissions' details.

Moving aside as Kat came in and replaced the faulty cable, he gestured at all the work around him. 'This place is filling up so fast. Lucky you've got the cellar.' He nodded at the iron hatch in the centre of the workshop that led to it.

'Yeah, I *seriously* lucked out, didn't I? I can't believe I got the barn above the famous bat hibernaculum. I saw how you and Nell made sure it wouldn't be disturbed when you refurbished the barns here.'

'Well, they'll be in the pillbox next door, and in the cellar under there, now that we've bricked up where the two cellars join. That way, you get some storage that you can use without disturbing the bats, and they get a whole deluxe area to themselves.'

'Yes, I saw that episode. Well, I've seen every episode! I thought that was clever. Everyone gets the best of both worlds.'

'OK.' Kat took charge. 'I'd like to start with you, Holly, in action. Then, you can join her, Rav – see your mark on the floor, there? – and we'll proceed with intros, and talk about the work and the fete.'

As they did exactly that, nailing it in one take, Rav noticed that despite Holly's apparent nerves, she was a natural performer.

Once Kat had dismantled the kit and taken it outside, Holly tapped Rav's arm. 'Could . . . Could I ask you for some advice?' She glanced at the door, checking no one was coming in.

'I can spare a minute or two,' Rav said, cautious.

'I . . . Well . . . I just want to know what your "secret sauce" is.' She gave a laugh of embarrassment. 'You've had such *incredible* success with your channel. I'm having some interest now, but I don't know how to get to the next level. Where you are . . .' She shot him a sidelong look, hopeful eyes under long dark lashes. 'Do you . . . Do you think it has anything to do with how open you've been about personal stuff? Like your recovery?'

Frowning, he wondered how to answer, and shrugged. 'Maybe.' Given he'd started out presenting in a wheelchair, sharing his progress had been unavoidable. 'It wasn't exactly planned, though. It was just my situation.'

Her sidelong glance narrowed, giving her a sly look. '*I* think it made you look magnanimous, as well as incredibly determined.'

'Magnanimous? Why?' He knew he was falling into a trap as he asked it.

'Well, you know. Given *the accident* happened *here* . . . even though the inquiry into it absolved Nell's family of all responsibility.'

He tried not to react as her comments prodded a painful spot in his and Nell's relationship and their families' histories. But if Holly knew about the crash – especially the details of the inquiry – then she'd done her fair share of cyberstalking.

'If you've read the inquiry results, then you'll know the fault was mine. They're a lovely family. You can't have too many reservations about them, since you've rented workspace from them.' Rav kept his voice level. 'And use free timber from their woodland.'

Her flush of embarrassment gave him a twinge of satisfaction. Then he felt mean as she raised her sad eyes to meet his and apologised. 'Sorry. I was *trying* to say that I really admire how open you've been. I think it generates trust. I'm trying to work out how to build that same type of connection with my viewers. But it takes courage, to put yourself out there like that. Don't you ever worry what people will think?'

Edging towards the door, he tried to draw the conversation to an end. 'Look, share what you're comfortable sharing. You can't control people's reactions. Usually, they say more about them than about you, anyway.'

He hurried outside, glad of the sunshine, only to spot Lou, still looking unsettled from her earlier exchanges with Zeus and Noah. From across the courtyard, he could see that she was muttering to herself, as if rehearsing an argument, rolling her shoulders and bouncing on the balls of her feet, like a boxer about to take on the next round.

Turning, she saw him and her intent frown cleared into a wide smile as she strode over. 'Rav! Now you're a free agent, I thought we could . . .' she tilted her head, 'have that *chat*.' She raised her eyebrows. 'The one you asked for.'

'Oh, thanks, Lou.' Rav limped to the side, making her follow, so they were some way from Holly and Kat. He lowered his voice and turned away from their curious glances. 'I *do* need to speak to you, but this is a hectic week. Are you free later?'

'For you, always!' Lou beamed. 'I can't tell you how delighted I am with your plans. Of course, we can keep it to ourselves for now. I'll be here, getting everything shipshape for the big day, or running around the parish. Literally.' Her sudden, demonstrative lunge was deep. 'Healthy body, sharp mind, pure heart, and all that. You can call me anytime.' She rubbed his arm fondly. 'I'll always make time for you.'

As she jogged off, Rav checked his phone for a message from Nell. Still nothing. Aching to find her, he called, 'Kat, are you done with me for today?'

'Yes. I want to shoot some extra B-roll, then I can focus tomorrow on checking footage and editing. We've got some great shots. You always make the edit easy!'

'That's all you and your talent, Kat!' Rav gave her a mock salute.

With a grin, Kat glanced beyond him, at Erin waving.

'Rav! Ravvie? Are you finished? Please, will you take me home? I need my bed.'

'I . . . er . . .' With a flutter of panic at the thought of driving, Rav looked around, hoping to see a member of the team who might be free to take her. But there was no one.

Kat grimaced. 'I can join you if you need reinforcements? Or a chaperone?'

He didn't need an audience. Swallowing, he said, 'I'll manage. Erin and I have been friends for a long time.' Turning, he called with a voice he marvelled at for not shaking, 'OK, Erin, I'll drive you home.'

As he spotted a Landy, he checked his pockets for the key, which he'd kept at the ready, as James had advised. After all, an imperfect plan was better than no plan. But his heart pounded at the prospect of his first drive . . . since the accident.

He wasn't just concerned about his ability. The new use of his legs, waking up different parts of his muscles, would be welcome. It was the thought of sitting behind a wheel that made clammy nausea roll.

Overcoming that barrier of nerves and trauma, the memory of the world tumbling as the car rolled . . . He heaved and his pulse raced through shallow breaths, as sweat trickled down his back.

'Can you help me up?' Erin reached for him.

'One sec.' It wasn't just the wave of sudden dread that made him phone Nell. She hadn't replied to him, and he was worried.

'Nell? Hi. Everything OK?'

'Sort of. I'm with Sylvia, running through the health and safety reports. I . . . just wanted to be somewhere I didn't feel . . . watched.'

'What's happened?' His hackles rose.

'I'm getting texts. From our mysterious friend—'

'Hold on.' Rav blinked. 'How? How is that happening? Have you told—'

'James? Yes, he's working on the triangulation as we speak.' He heard a muffled huff as she shivered. 'So, I've decided to turn my phone off and then I can turn it on when I need to use it, so I'm braced to see them all in one go, instead of their words seeping in like poison. I just turned it on now because I wanted to see how you are. Do you want to come up and help? I have loads to do here—'

'Sure. Let me come up in about forty-five minutes. I . . . I have to take Erin back. Zeus's samples got her tipsy and I said I'd drive her home.'

He paused, wondering if she'd picked up that this would be his first time driving since he crashed her father's classic Alfa on their racecourse.

'*You're* taking *Erin* home because she got *drunk*?' Her voice rose an octave in outrage.

She hadn't registered it. He couldn't really blame her, though, with everything else going on. *Even so* . . .

'Rav, seriously, anyone can take her. Can't you please just . . . not go anywhere? Today of all bloody days.'

'For God's sake. It's not far, I won't be long. There isn't anyone else to take her. And then, yes, I'll come back and help. But I kind of feel . . . guilty.'

'Your bloody guilt complex about Erin has got to have run its course by now,' Nell retorted. 'She exploits it, you know she does.

And please, Rav. I don't really want to be alone today. And I don't say that lightly, you know I don't. I've waited while you've interviewed everyone else, knowing full well one of them could be the person threatening me. Please.'

'I'm not asking for a day. I'm not even asking for an hour. We're taking more time arguing than me actually doing it,' Rav reasoned.

'Fine.' She hung up, and he started, then stared at his phone.

'Rav?' Erin nagged. She tried to stand, but wobbled, and Rav dropped everything, crutches clattering to the ground, as he staggered to help her. As she weaved towards the Landy, he grappled for his crutches, and hurried to follow.

He was still fuming from Nell's stinging words. *Guilt complex and being exploited, indeed!*

They needled, he realised, because they were true. And if Erin could twist him around her little finger, what could someone with more manipulative, more malicious intent do?

As his irritability subsided, he acknowledged that Nell was right. He should try harder to find someone else to take Erin home. But the courtyard was empty now, and the event team were flat out . . . There was no one *to* ask.

Gripping the wheel, he prayed for a peaceful journey. Maybe Erin would be too sleepy to be trouble. She climbed in and slumped in her seat, and he had to reach past her to pull her door shut.

His optimism was dashed as she beamed at him. 'Zeus was right. You're *so* chiv'rous.'

It was only when he was halfway to Erin's flat, in Pendlebury, that he realised he'd dropped his phone back at the courtyard.

Chapter 7

Since he'd persuaded Val to make that crucial tactical call to the phone company, James had unashamedly badgered colleagues for any emails arriving in their inbox, in case it was the vital intel appearing.

With no hint of apology, James knocked on the tech officer's door for the millionth time, glad that Ashley had joined him now. It might help to make the point that this was urgent. 'Anything yet?'

The tech officer he'd been hounding deadpanned, 'Yeah. I've been waiting all day for you to follow up. What kept you?' But, when he shook his head, James knew he was in for a disappointment. 'All it confirms is that it's a burner phone, so I've got no helpful name for you.' He handed James a printed list. 'But you said the text was received by the target at Finchmere, didn't you?'

James nodded, with a rising sense that he wasn't going to like what was coming.

'That's exactly where the text was sent *from*. Someone on, or near, the Finchmere estate.'

With his stomach churning, James tried to find a positive in the situation. 'So that means Nell may know or be close enough to the stalker to stand a chance of observing their behaviour?'

Ashley shook her head, her brown afro swaying. 'Not if they're good at masking. And they could be geographically close, without being known to Nell. Think how many workers are on that site right now. And all the ways to get near the house, via footpaths, through woods, over fields, the hotel, the farm shop—'

'OK. But if someone's sending texts, they may be looking for her reaction?' James knew he was clutching at straws. 'They may send a message when they're nearby? If Nell keeps vigilant, she may spot them.'

'Never heard of send-delay apps, Detective?' the tech officer asked. 'Your stalker could write a day's worth of messages and stack them up, to be sent at set times. They could be standing right next to Nell when – *boom!* – message arrives. They don't give themselves away by touching their phone – yet they get to see *exactly* how it affects her.'

In Sylvia's office, Nell was feeling twitchy.

She wished she hadn't argued with Rav. That was exactly what his stalker wanted, wasn't it? They were playing right into her or his hands, and she hated it.

Despite finding it difficult to settle, the time had flown, as she'd had so many last-minute fete-related tasks to help with. When she'd checked her phone and spoken to Rav, the extensive insurance forms had landed in her inbox, and she'd spent the last hour completing them as best she could.

As she itemised the losses they'd suffered from everything burning in the house, Nell was mired in guilt and grief again. Until the fire investigation said otherwise, she still felt horribly responsible. Yet the threat of an arsonist, someone willing to *attack* her, bubbled just under the surface. She kept thinking about it, like prodding a bruise, to try to make James's warnings – the danger – feel real.

Her lack of sleep and the pressure of the work she still had to keep pace with made the peril seem surreal, like the disorientating sense of an awful nightmare. But the fire had been too real, and James was deadly serious about warding off their stalker.

Hoping Rav would come straight to her when he got back, Nell knew they'd make up for snapping at one another. It was natural, really, given the unsettling, tense uncertainty making them brittle with irritation. But she *wished* Rav would be more circumspect.

Sylvia glanced up from her desk. 'Well, our artisan website is live. It's rather fabulous, if I do say so myself. Want to see?'

Nell walked over to Sylvia's desk and watched as she clicked through the bios and photos.

'I had them all in here yesterday, throughout the day, for mini-interviews so I could write these lovely descriptions of their work and their backgrounds. What do you think?'

'It looks terrific, Sylv. Thanks.' Nell managed enough enthusiasm for Sylvia to give a gratified smile.

'Thank you, sweetie. Now, I was thinking of getting away early, since it's been busy and we have some long days ahead. Would you like to do something? Maybe a walk?'

'No.' Nell shivered. 'No, you go, enjoy your evening. And thank you.'

'Want a coffee before I leave?'

Nell shook her head, and Sylvia slipped off, taking the lift.

As she watched the clock, Nell paced, restless, then leaned over the desk to close and lock the sash window.

She ached for company, for Rav's reassurance. He'd probably be back already.

Stumbling downstairs, she headed to the refectory. If he wasn't there, she'd run the gauntlet of turning on her phone to call him. It would be more practical to just block the stalker's number, but she didn't know if James needed more examples to help trace the texter.

Nell turned into the room, expecting to see Rav – but he wasn't there.

Sagging onto a bench, she turned on her phone.

The texts piled in. She tried to ignore them, but fleeting words on the screen took root in her brain, gorging on her self-doubt.

Your accident of birth was lucky – you wouldn't be here if you had to rely on talent, would you?

Do you think Rav wants you – or Finchmere?

It was a relief when Rav's voicemail flashed over the texts.

As she listened, she checked his location. *What's he doing in the Artisan Courtyard?*

Hey, Nell, I'm doing some extra filming with Holly in her workshop. Some of the footage didn't record well. Can you join me? Don't worry if not, I can try to do it without you. I'd just rather wrap it up with you if you're free?

Huh. No 'sorry', no reference to their argument. And even though she'd alluded to how hard she'd found the filming, there he was, redoing it instead of coming over to see her.

But . . . he had asked for her to come and help. And this was all to put Finchmere in the best light, so Nell couldn't complain – and she couldn't *not* show up.

Kat had warned them there may be retakes once she'd checked the footage.

With a sigh, Nell hurried out and got into a Landy to drive to the courtyard.

The place was unusually quiet. *Graze!* and *Finchmere Estate Vineyards* had closed for the day. Everyone seemed to be making the most of the calm before the storm. Holly's workshop also seemed empty.

Nell crept over to the open door, her neck prickling with apprehension.

Before she went inside, she scanned the space. No one was there. No Holly, no Kat, no film equipment – and no Rav.

Glancing around, she saw no one waiting in the courtyard, or hiding in the shadows. Her pulse thumped as fear for him grew.

Where is *he?*

Nell had been in enough scrapes by now to know she needed to forewarn someone. Opting for someone who would cascade the message, she texted Sylvia.

Had a weird call from Rav asking me to do some filming at the Artisan Courtyard. He's not here, neither is anyone else. I'm worried about him. Can you ask Conor to send security, and call James to ask him to attend if he can?

Urgency made her fingers fumble over the words, and it took a while to type. Once she'd sent the text, she looked around. The area seemed to have grown colder. Shivering, she pulled her shirt around her – then thought she caught a sound from inside the workshop.

Rav? She didn't say his name aloud, afraid he'd somehow got hurt.

Looking around, Nell jittered as she waited for security or James to arrive. Knowing they'd be on their way in seconds, and here within minutes, made her feel a little safer . . .

So – tentatively – one step at a time, she tiptoed inside.

Her whole body tingled, alert to every sound, heart thudding, veins surging with adrenaline. Her rapid breaths filled her lungs with the scent of sawdust.

A distant knocking drew Nell further in. She passed a claw hammer on the workbench, and picked it up, hefting it in her hand as she crept on.

Approaching a tall, free-standing shelving unit, she raised the hammer. She held her breath as she peered around the large piece of furniture.

No one.

Scanning the space again, she still couldn't see anyone. But it was impossible to see around every large piece and be certain. Hot fear rolled over her. Her clammy grip slipped on the hammer's handle.

Then she saw it: the iron hatch door to the cellar was open.

Instinctively, Nell stepped back. Then another sound drew her closer.

Is Rav down there? Is he stuck? Has he been pushed?

Her worry for him drove her forward.

She looked for any sign that he'd been there. But the place was deserted. The sawdust on the floor wasn't disturbed, so there were no traces of a scuffle.

Reaching the cellar door, Nell crouched, squinting into the dark space.

Damp, cold air wafted her face.

'Rav?' Her voice sounded small, fearful, questioning.

Nothing.

'Rav?' Her voice was bolder now, and she leaned in, looking, listening.

She didn't expect the hard shove, plummeting her down the six concrete steps into darkness.

The fall was fast.

She folded herself with the experience of a climber who'd fallen off the bouldering wall a lot: head tucked, and rolling.

But the concrete steps were still cruel. Her elbow, head, knee . . . *Argh!* Her ankle smashed against the sharp edges, crushed and twisted under her own body weight. The crunch of gristle sent flashes of hot nausea through her. She heard the bright ding of metal as the dropped claw hammer clattered to the side.

Momentum made her land heavily on her left leg, her hip aching, her ankle on fire.

Stunned, her head throbbed and her body seemed to be injured everywhere. Nell crumpled on the cellar floor, in the darkness.

She didn't know how long she'd lain there for, as she began to come round.

Collapsed amongst the concrete grit on the ground, with her body battered, she was too winded to breathe. Shocked, Nell blinked at the square of light from the hatch above her.

Is anyone there?

For a long moment, she couldn't move. She was afraid to try. She ached everywhere.

Wincing at the pounding in her head, she gradually tested her hands, arms, legs – all bruised and painful – and then feet . . . *Aargh!*

She tried to push herself up, but her leg gave way underneath her, burning. She tested her left foot, sensing something was broken, or at least sprained. Putting the tiniest pressure on it made her stomach queasy.

The sickness only swelled when she peered up again at the square of light above her, and the hatch – her only way out – was slammed shut.

Chapter 8

James had his accelerator slammed to the floor as he blue-lit to Finchmere. Sylvia had been full of apologies for not noticing the message sooner, but she'd been enjoying a walk and some rare peace.

Now, half an hour had passed since Nell had sent the message, and no one could get hold of her. Her phone was dead.

James couldn't help the grim thought: *hopefully* only *her phone was.*

'We'll be there soon. I'm calling for backup.' At least Hesha sounded calm. 'Do we know what we're walking into?'

'No. So keep alert. With luck, though, Conor will have got someone there even quicker.'

James knew this wasn't stacking up well. This wasn't a strategy. It was blind hope.

Nell pulled her phone from her pocket, the screen crazed and cracked from the fall. She wasn't surprised to see that there was no signal in this underground cellar.

Turning on the torch, she squinted at the sudden bright white light. Her foot hurt like hell, but that could easily be a sprain and not a break. But either would cause it to swell, and if she took off her boot and sock to look at it now, there was every chance she wouldn't be able to bear putting them back on again. Instead, she pointed the torchlight at the hatch.

Her body still throbbed, her head ached, her arms were bruised and pain was shooting along her legs. Adrenaline was surging through her, colliding with shock and nausea, making her shake.

She tried to kneel. 'Ahhh!' Her ankle flamed as she bent it, a wave of sickness flooding her at the pressure against her foot. She gritted her teeth against it, and forced herself onwards. Crawling on her knees, she dragged herself up a couple of the stone steps and pushed the hatch.

Unable to make it move a millimetre, she shoved again. It refused to budge. Shifting to get better purchase, Nell drove all of her strength through her shoulders and *heaved*.

Nothing.

Panic set in, as she realised that whoever had pushed her in had also blocked her route out.

The horror of it engulfed her: her attacker knew there was no way out. This was deliberate: there was no doubt of the intention to harm her – maybe *kill* her.

Am I supposed to starve to death down here?

She pointed the light of her phone into the cellar and looked around.

The area was full of debris: a rogue sack of cement that hadn't been used, a broken wooden ladder that had found its last resting place. An old sledgehammer had also been left behind – and any hope that *that* raised was dashed as Nell saw why it had been discarded: the splintered handle looked like it was on the verge of rotting off.

The small, dark space was stifling; only about four or five feet high. While that had, at least, made the fall blessedly short, it also made it impossible to stand. This was not going to be a pleasant place to stay while someone worked out where she was . . .

A new fear gripped her. *How would anyone know?* Sylvia hadn't reacted very swiftly to her message – what if she hadn't received it for any reason? Even if she had – and even *if* someone came here to find for her – no one would even *think* of looking in the cellar. Nell shared her location with Rav but, as her phone now had no signal, he'd never see where she was.

If she waited overnight, Holly *might* hear her, when she arrived at her workshop. But, with tomorrow being Champions day, Holly would only be in her workshop to lead a demo, and that wouldn't be until the afternoon, with the event easily being noisy enough to drown out Nell's shouts for help – even if she could make herself heard through the thick stone floor and the iron hatch. What if . . . What if Holly didn't hear?

It could be days before anyone even thought of looking here. The swirling sickness at being trapped clouded her thoughts. Fighting it off, Nell took a deep breath of dank air.

Bloody hell. I really am supposed to starve to death. If the fall hadn't knocked me unconscious . . .

The thought of someone weaponising her home hit Nell like a sucker punch. The places where she'd imagined she was safest had become where someone had wheedled their way into her confidence, into her inner circle, with the ruinous intention to destroy what she loved – and maybe her.

Well, they won't. Determined indignation fired her.

She knew this place; she'd been down here before, when she and Rav had helped to brick up the cellar, leaving a small area for storage under the barn, and an area for hibernating bats. Cold, dark, damp. Perfect for over-wintering bats, not so great for humans.

Now, she regretted how carefully they'd done every aspect of the work. This could have been a shonky wall, and she could have stood a chance of knocking it down. Then, she might have made it into the pillbox, and her phone might have got a signal.

She looked again at the sledgehammer, then the wall, wondering . . . hoping . . . she'd stand a chance of bashing it down.

There was no other way out. This underground box had no windows, no holes, no burrows . . .

As she shuffled down the steps on her bottom, saving her battered ankle while she could, her gaze followed the cellar's perimeter, as if she was surveying. She wasn't surprised to register a pile of droppings by the wall – probably bats, from when they'd used the whole cellar space.

But these looked fresher than that and, in the torchlight, had no telltale sparkles of insect elytra to suggest they'd been left by bats.

Nell knew there was one test to prove it: the squidge test. If she squidged the droppings and they crumbled to sparkling dust, they were bats'. At this relatively large size, they'd have to be from serotine or noctule bats.

But if they squidged . . .? For the first time, Nell wanted the test to disprove bats. If these *were* rats, then they'd have to be getting in from outside – and the only way in would be through the pillbox on the other side of the wall, which meant they had been chewing through the brick to get into this sheltered space.

It wasn't out of the question; rats and mice could chew through concrete if they felt so inclined.

Hope flickered.

If they *were* . . . If the wall had been weakened by their activity . . . she might stand the slightest chance of breaking through.

Propping her phone up on the bottom step with a rock, so the light filled the space, she crawled over and picked up a dropping, squeezing it between finger and thumb.

It squidged.

She wanted to leap up, seize the broken hammer, bash her way out. But her ankle – and the ceiling height – stopped her.

Easing herself to her knees, ignoring the pain, she checked the sledgehammer. The handle might hold – *just* – but it would tear her hands to ribbons. She pulled off her shirt, already ripped and bloody from the fall, and wrapped and then tied it tightly around the splintered wood. If this was the only hope she had, she'd make the best of it.

Shuffling painfully on her knees, she followed the worn mammal track from the pile of droppings to the wall, where she spotted the small hole in the corner. Reaching out, she felt the chewed brick, pushing it with her bare hands. The weakened mortar crumbled enough to dislodge a couple of bricks.

Optimism blazed, and she leaned back to regard the wall. With a determined nod, she took off her T-shirt and tied it around her face, covering her nose and mouth.

Gripping the sledgehammer, she squared up to the wall. The swing from her knees and the low target were awkward, and limited the force she could apply. But she'd just have to go for it. Tensing her core, she braced herself for the flash of agony in her ankle as she swung back, then *walloped* the hammer, right near the hole, with all her might.

Dust flew around her, nearly making her cough, despite the T-shirt mask.

When it cleared, she saw that cracks had crept along the mortar.

It sparked enough encouragement to make her secure her grip, and swing again, *bashing* the hammer against the wall with *all* the force she could muster.

The wall caved a little, with another shower of dust.

Nell tested the hammer's handle. The splinter had cracked along the shaft, and she wasn't sure how many more chances she'd have before the hammer fell apart.

Her ankle throbbed in protest, as her swings transferred pressure right into her injury. But Nell *had* to ignore it – she feared this would be her last try, and she *had* to make it count.

Swinging wide, she *whacked* the wall with *every* molecule of strength she had.

As the hammer smashed against the wall, the handle splintered in half, exploding in her grip, the force ricocheting up Nell's arms, like lightning ripping up through her limbs to her shoulders.

She fell backwards, gasping, ankle burning – knowing she was out of chances.

Thursday 6th July – 6 p.m.

James pulled up at the courtyard, leaping out of the car to search the barns. Every one of them was locked: still, silent and dark inside.

Peering through the windows – one by one – he saw no signs of any disturbance.

He tried Nell's phone again as he looked around for Conor's team. *Why the hell weren't they already here?*

At the sound of a Landy's tyres crunching over gravel, James turned. He waited agonising seconds for the driver to appear, and saw that Hesha had her Taser at the ready.

One of Conor's team approached. 'Had to go back for the keys to the barns.'

James bit back the exasperation. He knew it would be shared. Not knowing where Nell was, all he could do was wait while they tried each barn in turn.

Agonising minutes passed. The café, bakery and storeroom at the back were empty. But James's heart was in his mouth as he approached the next two barns, both with large, walk-in chillers for cheese and charcuterie.

Pulling the fromagerie's chiller door open, he weathered the shivering blast as he searched for Nell.

Inside, shelves were stacked high with vast roundels of cheese, their pungent aroma rich even in the cooled air. Finding nothing, he headed back out and checked that the large churning vats were closed. He moved around them, searching, trying not to be spooked by the shadows.

The next barn held an arsenal of knives and hatchets, their sharpened blades glinting in the light, on magnetic wall strips around stainless-steel tables that looked like they were ready for a post-mortem.

He braced himself to open the chiller, and came face to face with the macabre sight of large flanks of meat hanging from the ceiling, salted and cured. Sausages, as fat as his arm, had been expertly strung up, bound with neat coils of knotted butcher's string.

Searching through to the far end, relief surged through James that Nell wasn't there – followed by the sick punch of fear that he still hadn't found her.

Next, they approached the vintner barn. While his security colleague moved on to unlock the last barn, and Hesha searched around the bar and between the barrels of the stylish tasting room, James pushed through to the barn beyond. He stopped dead, confronted with the sight of terrifying viticulture machinery.

A bottling conveyor, glinting with empty glass bottles, blocked his path. Beyond, a uniform, soldier-like row of stainless-steel vats, each large enough to contain a person, stood along the centre of the barn. Sprinting up the steps to the platform overlooking the cylinders, James hurried along each one, trying to ascertain if Nell could possibly be trapped inside any of them. With relief, he saw the openings were too small, and that the vats were connected to the conveyor beyond, where the grapes were pressed . . . The thought made James freeze – then dash back down the steps to peer into the presses' wicked machinery.

Finding nothing, again, blessed relief churned with nausea.

Heading out, he nodded at Hesha and found the security guy outside, fumbling with the door of Holly's barn.

'Having trouble here.' He looked at James. 'They've added a new lock to the woodworking barn. I can't find a key to match it.'

'Then that must be where she is.' James just knew. He looked around for a way to break in.

Hesha tested a window to see if it was locked. But James was already well past that stage. He strode towards the bistro chairs – and paused at the sight of a phone. The distinctive camo case made James certain it was Rav's. He called Rav's number, and the phone in front of him lit up, beeping. James bagged, then pocketed it carefully to give to SOCO to test; his resolve to find Nell – and now maybe Rav, too – only strengthened. Seizing the chair, he flung it through the window, then punched out the glinting shards of glass from the frame.

Pulling up another chair, and making sure his arms and legs were covered, he climbed inside.

The workshop looked sinister in this context: the rows of tools made convenient weapons, the large pieces of furniture and sculptures too easy for someone to hide behind.

Holding his Taser out, he moved methodically through the space, checking under, around and between as he navigated the obstacles. He listened, alert for anything.

But the space was silent. The sawdust and curls of wood shavings on the floor weren't smudged and smeared to suggest there'd been a struggle. But he did wonder if the large sculpture right in the centre had been inconveniently placed. Maybe it was so the woodworker could reach all angles. From the detailed craftsmanship, he saw that would make sense, even if it did present an obstacle to moving around the place.

Not finding her, James couldn't bring himself to admit defeat.

But if Nell isn't here, then where is she?

Climbing back outside, James shrugged. The security guard nodded and spoke into his collar. 'Step up the perimeter search. She's not here.'

Nell had scrambled gently, yet urgently, to her knees again, inspecting the damage to the wall – *hoping, hoping, hoping.*

A handful of bricks had been dislodged, and she pushed them aside, making more dust cloud around her. Her skin and bra were turning orange-red, the abrasive dust scratching her arms and chest, grinding fine grit into the grazes caused by the fall.

Shoving at the weakened mortar, more bricks fell, and Nell's hope bloomed.

It wouldn't take many more bricks before she'd be able to squeeze through.

With gritted teeth, she grabbed the sledgehammer's dislocated head and bashed the bricks around the opening. As they showered free, and Nell pushed them clear of the hole, she guessed – optimistically – that she could slither through.

Shuffling on her knees, she retrieved her phone, then pushed as much debris clear of the hole as possible.

Wincing, she forced her way through the gap. She *had* been optimistic. The bricks showered dust on her as they scraped her bare shoulders and back, and then hips, which were at least protected by her jeans.

As her bottom got wedged in the gap, Nell swore, digging her forearms into the dark, gritty foundations as she tried to pull herself forward. The fiery sting told her she'd skinned both elbows. But she had to keep going.

God, imagine if I die here, like this, because my bum's too big for the bloody gap.

At the glimmer of defeat, a wave of exhaustion rolled over her.

A squeak in the deep darkness told Nell she had company. She couldn't feel entirely unhappy about the presence of rats, since they'd helped her get this far. But she didn't like it when one scampered over her, pinprick claws scuttling over her bare back, scaly tail dragging behind, smearing – *ewwww!* – the hot dribble of urine across her skin.

Falcons may appreciate the incontinence of rodents, so they could hunt them via their wee (fluorescent, via falcon-vision), but Nell did *not*.

It spurred her to drag herself forward, and take the whole damn wall with her, if need be.

As more bricks caved in, smashing onto her legs and her painful ankle, Nell nearly sobbed with the effort it took to drag herself inch . . . by . . . inch . . . to pull free.

Surging forward, she collapsed on the other side, her skin burning, her ankle pulsing.

Pausing to catch her breath, she fumbled on the floor for her phone. As she picked it up and spread its torchlight, she saw the glint of a pair of rodent eyes – level with her on the floor.

Again, she ached to leap up – but couldn't.

With an agonised groan, she realised she'd have to clamber up more stone steps. This time, her injured ankle had been even more battered, she was worn out, and it looked like she'd have to do it, eyeball to beady eyeball, with a rat.

She managed to crawl up two steps before her ankle flamed and she had to take a breather.

I'm nearly halfway. Come on.

Sweat stung her eyes as she gritted her teeth and forced herself up two more steps. She was panting, her head slicked with the exertion. She felt sick and dizzy, and the air was so dank, it felt like her lungs were closing down.

Just two more.

Nearly sobbing with the sheer effort, sheer will, she pushed herself onwards, upwards. She didn't think she could possibly manage the very last one. It just seemed one step too far.

But then a rat scaled up her legs, her naked back, and bit her arm, eyes shining darkly in the torchlight as it turned to face her. Nell shoved the rat away – but it forced her to scramble up the final step.

With no hatch here, thanks to it being removed to allow access for those blessed, lovely hero bats, Nell could crawl straight into the pillbox.

The thin slits along the low roof let in slivers of light, and gloriously delicious fresh air.

And phone signal.

Nearly swooning, Nell pulled her phone from her pocket and texted James.

I'm in the pillbox. Come soon.

Chapter 9

Thursday 6th July – 7.30 p.m.

As Conor's guard dashed off to widen the search for Nell, James's phone beeped.

The relief at seeing Nell's name made him buckle.

The pillbox . . . *Where the bloody hell is the pillbox?*

Her urgent message made him frantic. He yelled after the disappearing security guard, 'Hey! Where's the pillbox?'

But the guard didn't hear. Hesha looked around, as if hoping it would be obvious.

There was nothing James could do but rush back to the house and find someone to ask.

'I'll go,' Hesha said, already sprinting, calling over her shoulder, 'I'll be as quick as I can.'

Helpless, James looked for anything that resembled a small, squat building. As he paced, he saw something that . . . *might* . . . be what he was searching for.

The small, windowless building was smothered with ivy, and tucked behind Holly's workshop, near the woodland edge. As he ran, the view bobbed as he squinted at it – but he spotted the horizontal window slits near the low flat roof.

Yes! He'd found her!

But he still had to walk all around the walls before he found a small hatch in the wall.

Padlocked.

'Nell? Nell?' he yelled through the window slits.

The lack of reply made fear swell through him, but he kept talking, kept his tone positive. 'I'll get you out, OK? I need the key.'

He phoned Hesha. 'Already on it, James,' she puffed. 'I found Rav, and he's giving me a lift back in the Landy with the key. I've called an ambulance.'

The seconds it took them to arrive were agony. James contorted himself to try to see through the awkward-by-design slits, but couldn't make anything out in the gloom, except for a few lumpen shapes.

'Rav's on his way with the key. He'll be here soon.'

At his words, the Landy pulled up and Hesha fired out of the passenger seat like she was in the world's most crucial relay race.

He took the key from her outstretched hand as she skidded to a halt beside him.

His trembling hands managed to turn the key, opening the lock just as Rav limped up.

The creaking hatch clanged open, and James peered inside.

Crawling into the constrained space, he saw her, almost passed out, on the floor.

'Nell? Nell? Can you hear me?'

She was breathing, and just about conscious. He couldn't assess her injuries in this gloomy cave-like space. He had to lift her, and he tried to support her head as best he could.

'Help me get her through the hatch.' He grunted with the effort to move her, while his own movements were so restricted.

Rav threw his crutches aside and flung himself on the ground, arms outstretched to reach Nell and haul her towards him. As he dragged her outside, James followed.

In the sudden, warm sunshine and fresh air, James coughed and wheezed air into his lungs – and so did Nell.

Rav pushed Nell to her side, so she wouldn't choke, supporting her weight. Her battered torso was bright orange with brick dust, her T-shirt looped around her neck; her already scored arms scraped raw. As she squinted in the sunlight, she managed to smile.

'I knew you'd find me. I'm OK.'

Rav recognised the signs of adrenaline draining away, leaving her worn through.

'What the hell happened?'

'I was pushed into the cellar.'

Rav frowned as the questions churned. 'What? The cellar? Who did that? And how did you end up here?'

'I don't know who pushed me. They locked me in. I . . . I had to break the wall down to get out here.'

James gaped, but Rav hugged her to him as love surged through his heart. 'You're such a warrior.' He eyed the hatch they'd dragged her through. 'Thank goodness you wanted to install that so we could monitor the hibernating bats.'

'The voicemail message, asking me to meet out here, was from you.'

'*What?*' Rav shifted so he could stare at her. 'I didn't leave a message.' He looked at James, feeling the need to make the point. 'I didn't!'

James leaned forward to take Nell's phone as she unlocked it. He found the voicemail – from Rav's number – and played it aloud.

Rav felt sick at hearing his own voice say words he'd never spoken, luring Nell to a trap to hurt her – maybe even *kill* her. 'But . . . that's not me! I didn't say that! I didn't phone you!'

Pulling Nell against him once more, blame looped in his mind.

I should have done, though, shouldn't I? I should have said how sorry I felt. I shouldn't have left you – exhausted and grieving and worried – to take Erin home.

He hugged her to his chest, and murmured into her dusty hair, 'I'm so sorry I didn't call you back, or send a text to say sorry. You're right. We need to be more together about . . . all this.' He swallowed. The situation was getting worse. Nell was right in someone's firing line.

If I'd given Nell the care she'd needed, right then, maybe she wouldn't have believed this fake message. Maybe she wouldn't have been attacked . . .

The distant wail of the ambulance cut through his thoughts, and Nell pushed herself to sit up. 'Is that for me? I don't need it. I'm fine. I don't need a medic.'

'Nell, you have to at least let a paramedic check you over,' James advised.

Rav wasn't sure if it was just to distract her, but James played the message again.

'You left your phone in the courtyard,' he told Rav. 'So the stalker could have got hold of it then.'

'Yes. I must have forgotten it, when I was taking Erin home.'

He shot an apologetic sidelong glance at Nell. He was kicking himself for leaving his mobile unguarded for just a few minutes, let alone the couple of hours it had actually – and unexpectedly – taken to wrangle Erin.

'I know, I should have been more careful. *How* did they manage to make it sound like it was from me, though?'

'I can get the tech team to check that it definitely came from your phone, Rav. But there doesn't seem to be any reason to doubt it, given that your number showed up on Nell's phone, and that the message was left while your phone was out of your possession.'

'Yes, but to sound *exactly* like me? To lure her out here and hurt her . . .' He couldn't finish the sentence.

All this, piled on top of his volcanic fear after the fire, was just too much. And James was already making it worse, as he calmly explained how it could be done.

'Anyone can do that. Zero technical expertise needed,' James confirmed, making Rav's stomach sink like a stone. 'Think about it. There's hours of footage of you talking, freely available, on YouTube. Anyone can access it. And all the people here are subscribers.'

'Yes, but surely not everyone would have . . . What? Editing software?'

'They wouldn't need anything nearly so technical.' He glanced at Rav. 'How many apps do you have on your phone? It's as complicated as sending an email: download an AI app, play your video, and any message typed into the app will be said in your voice.'

Rav feared he'd be sick, frantic at what Nell might be sent next. Or . . . *anyone* for that matter. Everyone he loved was in danger. 'I've been stupid enough to let my stalker get hold of my phone – any of the artisans or Finchmere team could have seen me open my phone with my passcode. I do it without thinking twice. And now the stalker – whoever they are – would probably have copies of all my contacts.'

He rubbed his face, willing this all away. 'You'd need to be pretty competent to use an AI app or whatever . . . wouldn't you?' He clutched at the hope.

'Not really.' James didn't look apologetic. 'No point in sugar-coating it, is there? It's no different to downloading any other kind of app. And, honestly, if you wanted to make people think you were less technically competent than you really are, it wouldn't be hard for someone to fake that, to throw you off, would it? So I'll say it again, and this time, *please* pay attention, Rav. You *have* to be more on your guard. I mean it, mate.'

'We *all* need to be more on our guard.' Nell looked mutinous as the ambulance approached and pulled up. 'With *everything*: phones, food, drink, company.'

As the paramedic ran over, Rav watched Nell as she was prodded and checked. Her ankle was badly bruised but luckily not broken or sprained.

'Ice, compression and rest will help,' the paramedic said. Rav knew Nell would ignore the third of those instructions.

'Thanks. I just need to clean myself up, really. Everything else is superficial. Even the rat bite. My tetanus shot will cover that.'

Oh, Nell! Rav squeezed her.

'Here.' The paramedic gave her a card warning of Weil's disease symptoms.

When Nell insisted on just going home, the paramedic, James, Rav and Hesha didn't stop her. But they did insist on taking her straight there.

As Nell took the lift to her room to shower, James waited downstairs as Hesha headed back to the station with Rav's phone for the tech team to investigate.

Settling Nell on a sofa, her swollen foot elevated with an ice pack over the compression bandage, Rav felt nauseous with desperation as he perched beside her, clinging on to her hand. She looked so horribly vulnerable – pale, wan, injured – and all because of him.

'I'm concerned about how this attack fits with the fire at your home.' James didn't mince his words as he fixed Nell with a worried gaze. 'I've asked the fire investigation team to fast-track your case. They'll survey your house tomorrow, and they'll phone when they've finished, so we'll have confirmation then, and we won't need to wait for the report.'

'Thanks, James.'

From Nell's pale face, Rav could see that the thought of arson was too much, and that she still felt responsible. But terror rose within him: if someone had burned the house down, then it was looking increasingly likely that the arsonist knew he'd be away.

'*Please*, Nell,' he heard himself beg, 'surely now, in light of the likely arson and your attack, we *have* to rethink the fete. We'd be idiots not to. Your event team would manage to run it, so we won't need to cancel. But you don't need the pressure of fronting it right now.'

He squeezed her hand, willing her to know how he felt, aching for her to agree. '*Please* take a step back from it all. Everyone would understand. The artisan team is pretty stressed, going by the arguments I saw between Louise, Noah and Zeus.'

'Well, there's a lot of pressure on them right now. But that's not the case for us. This isn't about rebalancing workload. You're suggesting we step back from our actual *life*.'

Nell elbowed to sit up, and Rav knew she really had the bit between her teeth now.

'And then what?' she demanded, the amber flecks in her eyes blazing. 'Will we be too scared to come out of hiding? Too scared of what might happen? We'll *always* be in *exactly* the same position, won't we? Because this person will stay in the shadows unless we flush them out – silently controlling, ruining, eroding *everything*. Not just our *business*. Or my *family home*. But our whole *life* together, Rav. *Forever*.'

'Nell—'

'*That's* what this *means*, Rav! It's everything we have for the rest of our lives. It's bullying of the worst, most pervasive kind. And you don't let the bully take control. You take the fight *right* to them.'

Her shoulders were heaving now, and he knew she wouldn't back down. He hated to admit it, but she had a point. If they gave ground now, they'd be giving more and more by degrees until their life shrank to nothing. They might not even have each other. He'd fight for all he was worth in a heartbeat to prevent that.

'If someone I'm about to eat with *is* trying to threaten me, then *I'll* show them it isn't going to work.'

He took her hand. 'Nell, I'm so sorry. I was totally in the wrong. I should have prioritised you. I was an idiot, and I put you in danger. Again. It won't happen a third time.' He reached out and stroked her pale cheek. 'I promise.'

Swallowing, Nell gave him a wobbly smile. 'So? What are we doing?'

He sighed. 'What do you think?'

He squeezed her hand; he was too afraid to smile, so how terrified must she be? How long could she endure a threat like this? And why should she have to? All because of him. He'd brought all this destructive danger to the woman he loved.

Chapter 10

Nell towelled her hair, desperate for coffee after barely any sleep: the first day of the fete had arrived and – no matter how they both felt – she and Rav had to put on their game faces.

Along with James and Conor, they'd agreed a strategy of business as usual: smiles, no concerns, welcoming demeanour. Easier said than done.

'I have to admit, I hope Erin will be too hungover to come today, after all of Zeus's samples.' Rav grimaced at her as he sat on the bed, pulling on his jeans.

'Hmm . . . Now I know why he asks for such a large hospitality budget. Maybe he should cut back a bit.' She buttoned her summer shirt, hiding the scrapes along her arms.

'I can see why Erin succumbed.' Rav emphasised his own London accent as he teased, 'It's that irresistible Finchmere *terroir*, innit?'

'Careful, marketing will want to get their hands on you next.' She detoured to kiss him, and he caught her, hugging her close, then gazed at her, his face growing serious.

'How are you holding up?'

'Don't.' Nell shook her head. 'I can't afford to think about it. I'm doing everything the insurance company asks. I'm ready for our expert panel, and I'm prepared to go headlong into battle if we have to. And that's about all I can manage.' She shivered and Jezebel, who'd become Nell's shadow, patted her arm with a velvety paw, and nudged her head against her.

As her phone vibrated in her pocket, Nell tried to ignore it. It had become a game of roulette: between the usual last-minute requests for miracles, she'd been bombarded with bile.

Now, she read: *You need to leave him. He's too good for you . . .*
What's wrong with you, are you too stupid to get a hint?

She showed Rav; his shoulders tensed, and his hug around her
tightened.

'Battle it is, then,' she said. 'Are you ready?'

He kissed her. 'For you? Always.'

Heading into the refectory to meet the artisans for breakfast, Nell
was fuelled by defiance. Although someone had put a target on her
back, she was determined not to show the weakness of her bruised
ankle and swollen foot that had restricted her choice of footwear
to old, loosely laced trainers. She needed to look as bulletproof as
possible. If she could have stage-managed a slo-mo walk through
swirling smoke to a dangerous soundtrack, she would have.

But everyone – including Erin, who'd somehow got over the
hangover of the century and found out about the breakfast – was
disarmingly normal: no one seemed astonished to see Nell was
actually alive; they all showed surprise and concern at her injury.

Yet Nell knew that one of them was putting on a façade of
familiarity, while they grubbed their way into the heart of her life,
to wreak destruction.

Holly gestured to a seat and poured her a coffee. 'If everyone's this
early, we must be keen to get going! It's usually just me and Gigi as
the morning larks, first at the courtyard.'

Scanning the busy room, Nell spotted James eating breakfast,
unobtrusive in the corner, apparently engrossed in his phone while
he observed the group. Reassured, Nell managed to smile as the
team helped themselves to breakfast – walnut porridge bubbling
beside chunky chargrilled sourdough with herby avocado, fresh
eggs or apricot jam, and warm nut and seed muffins to be snaffled
away as a snack.

Once everyone was eating, Nell stood up to give the welcome.
'Thanks, all, for being here so early! And for your hard work to get us
to the big day – opening the fete with our Champions.' She swallowed,
about to outline the programme, when Kat stood.

'Thanks, Nell. So, here's the plan and how we're live-streaming.
Our select guests arrive at the courtyard from 8 a.m., with coffee,

pastries, etc. from *Graze!* and time to explore the stands or go to Rav's meet-and-greet at the film tent.'

Noting Kat's brisk tone, how quickly she took the lead, Nell sat back, displaced. She'd *wanted* to delegate some front-facing work today – but it didn't come naturally to defer to someone else, for her own event. Yet everyone was listening, intent on knowing their part.

'We'll go to the event tent at 9.30 a.m.,' Kat continued, 'for our awards and mini-conference – which is *so popular* we've *exceeded* capacity, and will be live-streamed. After lunch, guests can join a *reWild Side* Safari, make a bat box at Holly's workshop or visit the stands, before we say farewell with gift bags. *And then* we can enjoy cocktails at the hotel bar, where Merlin has crafted some artisan-inspired cocktails especially for us, courtesy of Nell.'

At the cheers, Nell smiled at Kat, feeling like she'd unfairly projected her insecurities on her. She needed to be better at accepting help. Especially now.

'Tomorrow and Sunday are busier,' Kat added. 'Rav has set pieces at the film tent—'

Louise's arrival interrupted her. She hurried in, straightening her white surplice over her running gear. Seeing that the company had congregated without her, she stopped short. 'Oh, I'm not late, am I?' She peered at her watch.

'No.' Nell sensed tension ripple around the room. As Zeus darted wary glances at Lou, Nell overcompensated. 'We're all early. Keen to get the fete off to the best start!'

'Indeed! Big day for all of us!' Louise helped herself to a coffee from the cafetière. Shunning the nearest empty spot, beside a glowering Noah and Gigi, Louise clambered into the narrow space between Rav and Holly, making Holly's smile wither on her lips.

Louise nudged Rav. 'I was thinking about you on my run this morning. You're right, we really do need to talk soon. I'm so looking forward to it.'

To Nell's surprise, Rav nodded. 'Me too.'

'So, when do you want me?' Louise turned to Nell. 'For the judging.'

'In good time for the awards at 9.30 a.m., please,' Nell said. 'It's a fun icebreaker to show how anyone can rewild, whether they're at school or retired, with acres or a window box. You're vital for the judging, Lou, as the respected voice of the community. So, you're welcome to stay for lunch or leave if you need to.'

As Kat passed Lou a printed copy of the judging schedule, Nell continued, 'You'll also see the times of the awards on the Saturday, when we'll need you all day—'

'Oh?' Louise snatched the page and studied it. 'At this rate, I'll be coming and going all day. I thought it was just the one stint for all the judging, in the afternoon?'

'Wasn't it *your* brilliant idea, Lou, to divide them all up over the Saturday?' Rav interrupted. 'So we could live-stream them over the day.'

'Oh.' Louise smiled. 'Yes. Of course.'

'So, on Saturday,' Rav qualified, 'you'll start with produce and flower arrangements mid-morning, with Gigi and Noah—'

'Oh, this is ideal. Our judgements are always aligned.' The smiles Gigi bestowed upon Louise and Noah were sweeter than her patisserie, and iced with sarcasm.

'I'll have to leave the tasting to you, Gigi. Sugar's a poison,' Louise said.

'Then crafts and small pets with Holly and Bea, mid-afternoon,' Rav continued. Neither of Louise's co-judges looked happy at the prospect.

'Let's not forget Saturday's main event.' Zeus flashed his wide grin at Louise. 'When we judge the homemade liquor. You get to let your hair down. Now *that*, I'd like to see.'

'Not for me, *thanks*, Zeus. I'll hand out the prizes, but I won't succumb to alcohol.'

Kat tapped her pencil on the table. 'Good. We'll film the awards, and I'll capture the buzz of the day across the fete, the safaris and the fairground. Rav'll live-stream fete updates from the filming tent, interspersed with interviews on VT.' At Louise's frown, Kat clarified, 'Videotape – a legacy term, since it's not tape anymore – of our artisans—'

'Oh? I wasn't interviewed.' Louise looked indignant. 'Was I supposed to have been?'

Kat frowned. 'We focused on Finchmere's rewilding, so we spoke to our food producers who are part of that, or who use the land for crafts or sustainability projects.'

'Oh, count me *in*! I *only* safeguard all the *souls* of this parish! I could talk about the historic churches that need sustainable preservation. The solar panels, wildflower confetti . . .' She nudged Rav. 'This is how I'll engage our younger parishioners. Just like you advised.'

Erin sniggered. Rav ignored her.

Glancing at Rav, Kat said, 'Fine. I'm juggling many schedules for today's filming.' She checked the time. 'Speaking of which, I must collect my time-lapse camera, which I hope caught the sunrise over the fete in this morning's atmospheric mist.' She nodded at Lou. 'I'll squeeze you in this morning. We won't have time for many takes, so please be prepared.'

'Always! I'll be at the chapel, for those who want a few words. Pop in any time.'

'Be warned, Lou,' Rav said. 'If it goes wrong, Kat'll put it on our blooper reel.'

Grinning, Kat poured coffee into her travel mug. 'I'll get going, to fit in the filming.'

Reminded to look for his own mug, Rav picked up his rucksack and rummaged through the survey supplies he always kept to hand. Not finding it, he sighed.

'Everything all right?' Kat asked.

'Yeah, it's nothing, just can't find my travel mug.'

'Oh.' Kat rifled in her own extensive kit bag. 'I think . . . Yes, here you go. I've got a Finchmere travel mug. Take it – I'll get another.'

'Thanks!' Filling the mug bearing the copper outline of Rufus, Rav smiled at Kat.

'I'd better be on my way, too.' Louise wiggled out of the bench seat and her gaze swept around the assembled company. Suddenly full of gravitas, she intoned, 'As almost all of you know, several sinning souls need my prayers this morning.'

Nell's blood ran cold at Lou's words. *Does she know something?*

Then Lou's eyes met Rav's, and their half-nod to each other made Nell's unease grow.

Chapter 11

Friday 7th July – 8 a.m.

James watched the artisans leave, amazed that one of them was wreaking so much havoc in Nell's and Rav's lives – yet you'd never know it. He had no idea who it was, from observation alone.

He wondered if he should have a better sense of people by now, if he was somehow missing cues or tells. The stalker might have firmly wormed themselves into Nell's inner circle, but it must be exhausting to play the part of a friend, or willing teammate. Maybe the character relished the acting?

He strode outside, and over the bridge towards the fete, comparing the view with the plan on the back of the day's programme. The showground was before him: the stands were open, displays arranged, and stallholders clutched their coffees and chatted to neighbours.

Passing the bedazzling maelstrom of the vintage fairground, he walked through the stands, and noticed how many of the wildlife groups were becoming familiar to him now, after joining a few of Nell's events. The *Graze!* stand was attended by their team of baristas, sending the scent of rich espresso through the food hall as they served customers.

A small crowd was gathered at Rav's streaming tent, with an impatient Kat looking for him. James frowned. *Rav had intended to come straight here, hadn't he?*

Glancing around, he noticed the Landy bumping over the field and saw Rav get out, to the obvious delight of his fans – Holly amongst them. As people pressed forward, taking photos, with those who had things for him to sign forming a civilised queue, Sylvia was in her element as crowd control. Bright as a beacon, dressed like she was at Royal Ascot in a scarlet summer dress, she was weaponising her headwear, tilting her mile-wide-brimmed summer hat to make people keep their distance from Rav.

It worked like a charm: the swarm of fans had to stand back, while Kat was able to dodge around and make sure the filming kept to schedule. In her white shirt, with emerald jacket sleeves folded back, she had a no-nonsense air as she oversaw Rav's welcome being recorded. James caught his closing words.

'. . . We hope today you'll find some inspiration to make your spaces – whatever they are – a little bit wilder.'

He held his smile, until Kat said, 'Cut. Great, Rav, we'll roll VT now, so you're out for a few hours. I'd better run to get the extra footage I need today. I'll see you at 9.30 in the event tent.'

'Fine!' Rav said, but she'd already darted off, lugging her kit.

With a shy smile at Rav, Holly departed for the courtyard, and James saw Rav force his smile a little wider as he welcomed the visitors. Then he looked alarmed.

Tense, James vaulted forward, ready for any action needed – then realised what had worried Rav and drew back, chortling inwardly.

A knot of three giggling girls approached Rav, all wearing Finchmere T-shirts with the slogan on the back: *Walk on the reWild Side*. One of them clutched a book, another held a spare T-shirt and one was empty-handed, her low-cut top knotted high above her abs.

She was nudged by the friend holding the book. 'Go on, Nat. *Do* it!'

Nat needed no further encouragement as she leaned towards Rav. 'I don't have anything for you to sign . . . except this.' She presented her cleavage with a giggle. 'But if you sign me there, I'll get it tattooed!'

Avoiding looking at where she was pointing, Rav leaned back and then, with an awkward chuckle, reached out for the book her friend was holding, signing it with a flourish of his green Sharpie. Then he signed the other friend's T-shirt.

Meanwhile, Sylvia moved in, with her signature millinery manoeuvre, making the trio step back. She slid a spare programme across the table and murmured to Nat, 'Might I suggest he signs this instead? As delectable as our Rav is, you may not feel the same about him in a year or two. Or even . . . tomorrow morning.' Her wink let Nat concede without losing face.

Relief made Rav overly cheerful as he signed it and passed it to her. 'Here you go!'

Nat pouted. 'At least give me a selfie!' Leaning across the table, she pushed her face near Rav's and snapped a picture. 'Mmm. Very nice.'

James could practically feel Rav's relief as the young women darted off, laughing. But James couldn't share the feeling. He was too worried about what one other fan might do.

As he headed to the courtyard, the morning sunlight drenching Finchmere's downland in a golden glow seemed to be trying to convince him that a glorious summer fete was too idyllic for danger. But James knew that the real danger was letting that deceive you.

It was hard to ignore, though, as the wildflower meadow blazed down the slope, dotted with beehives – although the Perspex-sided demonstration hive was notably unattended. The Artisan Courtyard was buzzing with visitors enjoying pastries from *Graze!*.

As he checked Holly's workshop, he noted how inviting this place looked now. So different from the looming impression the buildings had yesterday, when he'd been desperately searching for Nell, knowing something was wrong, but not how to save her.

Now, the workshop window had been expertly boarded after his vandalism – presumably, by the resident carpenter – and cleverly turned into an informative chalk board: *Join today's workshop at 2.30 p.m. – all welcome!*

Last night, SOCOs had found nothing helpful in there. Realising that the hatch had been blocked with the massive sculpture, and obscured by the strewn sawdust, they'd focused their fingerprint lifting there, and then visited Holly to take her prints, saying they were needed for exclusion purposes following a break-in, although nothing had been stolen.

After finding only Holly's and Rav's fingerprints on the sculpture, James knew that Nell's assailant had worn gloves. With no fingerprints on Rav's phone either, when they must have keyed in his passcode, James knew they had been meticulous about wiping the device clean.

The hatch itself had offered nothing useful, as it was cluttered with fingerprints from Nell, Rav and, presumably, a host of contractors. There was no other forensic material to go on – no material, blood, footprints, tracks – other than blood and hair from Nell on the steps. Given they couldn't do any more tests, Nell had asked that the workshop be fully available for the fete, free of the ominous signs of a police investigation.

Yet the investigation was still very much in progress, even if it was concealed.

Back at the station, Ed Baker was scouring the letters, hoping to uncover a clue. Today's assessment of Nell's house fire would give James more direction – even if the knot in his stomach tightened at what they might find.

DI Ashley Hollis and DS Hesha Patel were spending their day off keeping the Finchmere team under surveillance. James felt no guilt whatsoever about leaning on his team in their own time. He was too desperate for something – anything – to give him a lead.

He waved at Ashley, relieved to have her insights, as she walked over, relishing an almond croissant. 'There are worse ways to make overtime on a day off.' She beamed through the flaking pastry. 'Remind me of our expense account?'

'Zero.' James smiled back. 'But I owe you. Least I can do is buy you breakfast.'

Turning, Ashley regarded the courtyard and the bustle of the crowd. 'This is good, being this busy. We'll see our stalker under pressure to perform at work, while Nell takes a front-and-centre role, which we can assume our stalker won't enjoy.'

'I know what you're going to say.' Foreboding swelled in James. 'Forcing their hand? Pushing them to do something even more precipitous than a gruesome parcel, possible arson and a direct attack? There's only one way this is going, Ash.'

Licking her fingers, she nodded with a detachment he wished he shared. 'Yes, you're right. Escalation. More extreme.' She raised her eyebrows. 'So, we just have to be ready for it. Pre-empt whatever we can. Don't we?'

Friday 7th July – 9.30 a.m.

Backstage at the event tent, Rav was already sweating. And he wasn't even in the spotlight, being scrutinised on stage, yet. This would have been quite enough pressure on any other day.

At least Nell would be – *safely* – right beside him, on that beautifully set stage flanked with stunning enlarged photos of Rufus the Highland calf, and the downland estate through the seasons: the green haze of spring; gilded summer florals; the ruby-bronze of autumn; and frosted winter wonderland.

They may have narrowed down the stalker to one of the artisans, but even if James had the exact suspect under the closest surveillance, the stalker could still use this platform to make a scene . . . Perhaps if they wanted to make some sort of point – with maximum drama . . .?

Beside him, Nell's fawn-like, worried expression whacked him right in the heart. He hated the thought that she'd be sharing that fear – because of him.

He reached for her hand and held it gently. She stared down at it, then looked at him with a long, level gaze, before leaning in and kissing him tenderly. 'You OK?'

Nodding, he smiled. 'Only if you are.'

As she returned his smile, Rav saw Zeus sitting at the back, along the row from another man, whose black jacket gave away that he was on Conor's security team. That was clever: security would be expected, and obvious officers would make it easier for Conor's incognito guards to blend in.

Holly, Bea and Erin had taken seats near the front of the packed tent, while Gigi and Noah had seats near the exit, ready to oversee the arrival of picnic hampers at lunch. Ashley, James and Hesha were scattered amongst the crowd, but there was no sign of Lou.

Now, Sylvia's confident tones rang out from the stage. 'A warm Finchmere welcome to all of you. You are a very select group of Rewilding Champions – loyal *Following Finchmere* enthusiasts who want to learn more, locals who want to get more involved in our work, or specialists who can share know-how of rewilding reality. So let me hand over to our own experts, Dr Nell Ward and Dr Aravindan Kashyap.'

The applause was deafening. Suddenly hating his crutches for how vulnerable they made him feel – and *look* – Rav threw them aside and staggered the three short steps to the library-style armchair on stage.

His legs shook, and he felt drenched in sweat. But his nerves and discomfort were drowned as the audience went *wild*. Standing, they whooped, cheered, applauded, the sound overwhelming. He grabbed the armchair gratefully and fell into the generous seat.

More whistles and cheers followed, making Nell's arrival distinctly anticlimactic as she took her seat. The look Nell gave Rav, turned away from the audience, was full of love and pride at his achievement. He saw at once that she'd understood why he'd done it. But she turned a serious face back to the crowd, then smiled to cover her nerves.

'Thanks for that amazing introduction, Sylvia,' Nell said. 'We have a film that sets out our rewilding journey so far, and then we'd like to celebrate how *you've* been rewilding your spaces with our *Go reWild!* awards.'

He and Nell hadn't had a chance to review the highlights video, so Rav watched it with interest. A few shots had Nell showing the more unvarnished side of ecology: falling over, being bitten. Rav recalled having had just as many mishaps, but his soundbites were framed with stunning scenery.

Rav knew Nell shied away from those pieces to camera – which he couldn't blame her for, given her past experiences. And he knew Kat's choices were made in strict response to analytics, showing the audience more of what had been well-received from ratings, rewatches and comments. Despite Nell laughing, being a good sport about authentically showing the hard work involved in habitat restoration – and the rare species it meant Finchmere was now famous for – Rav felt his fame was unfair, and wished Nell would be more comfortable claiming the limelight that he thought was rightfully hers.

Then, *maybe*, she wouldn't be the one with this horrible threat hanging over her.

With all eyes on the screen, Nell turned to scan the tent, and Rav sensed something scheduled wasn't teed up. She exchanged eye contact with Sylvia, who gave a slight nod.

Rufus's birth – the first Highland calf on the estate – and his first unsteady steps got a ripple of '*Awwws*,' and the video's final frame of the fete's set-up brought them up to date.

'What a journey!' Sylvia beamed, steering the segment. 'And thank *you* for being part of it! Rav will answer your Finchmere-related questions now, while Nell leaves us briefly to make sure that our *Go reWild!* awards are ready.'

Rav frowned at the improvisation, wondering what was wrong. Sylvia held up the microphone, showing she was ready to pass it to audience members. So he smiled, bracing himself to field questions – alone.

The first barrage of questions was a blur, as he watched Nell head to the display end of the tent, then pause to send a text. He realised a dark-haired female fan was monopolising the microphone as she quizzed him, reading from notes, voice quavering with nerves. Sylvia practically had to prise it away and turn to the next person, who was waiting patiently.

Rav didn't even know how he managed to answer the next few questions. His stomach was churning as he watched Nell frown, and then – despite all their agreements to stick together, to be able to look out for each other – walk out of the tent. *Alone.*

Friday 7th July – 9.45 a.m.

Nell couldn't believe Louise was running late. They could host the awards without her, of course, but she was named on the programme, and she was popular with locals, given her habit of so thoroughly inserting herself in all community activities.

Brimming with annoyance, Nell texted Louise, then looked around for someone she could ask to go and look for her. Outside, as soon as she was clear of the tent and wouldn't disturb anyone inside, she put a call-out on the site walkie-talkies, so estate staff would keep their eyes peeled for an errant vicar.

A Landy stopped beside her, and an event team member dashed out, delivering something across the site. As Nell looked at the Land Rover, then glanced back at the rapt audience, hanging on Rav's every word, she realised she'd have a few minutes to dash over to the church. With only her left foot bruised and swollen, she could manage an automatic.

Within seconds she was bouncing over the field. Reaching the stone bridge, she waved at the security officer who counted guests in and out, making sure no visitors strayed from the chapel to the house.

Parking at the chapel, Nell eased herself out. The church's heavy oak door, framed with wildflowers, was closed, and Nell frowned. The door was supposed to be open, as a welcoming invitation.

Unease shivered over Nell. Her instincts fired, warning her not to push the door open, not to walk into the dim hush of the sacred space.

But she did, though her prior experience made her tuck her hands inside her shirt sleeves so she could push the door open without leaving fingerprints – and without rubbing anyone else's away.

Inside, squinting at the light, slanting shadows from the high windows, Nell paused. The crisp, green fragrance of fresh-flower arrangements rushed to meet her on the cool air.

But then another scent assaulted her. One that was hideously familiar: metallic, piercing, dreadful.

The silent chapel stretched ahead of her, every pew perfect for hiding someone.

Even with a bruised foot, she moved methodically, soundlessly, like any competent ecologist surveying a habitat. Then – as she moved so the aisle was no longer obscured by the pews – she saw the lumpen shape on the ground.

A broken vase of flowers lay on the floor, the water spilled, stems scattered across the flagstones. Beside the flowers was a body.

Nell fumbled for her phone, texting James: *Chapel. Please hurry, someone's hurt.* Then she turned on her phone's torch.

This didn't look like an accident.

Is whoever did this still here?

It took all of Nell's training (with a little help from her tender ankle) not to run towards the body and check it. If she did, she might be attacked, too. And Nell was all too aware of how much of a target she was.

So she proceeded with caution, her muscles twangling, desperate to run.

Passing the pews, Nell swung the torchlight to illuminate the narrow spaces, looking on the benches, on the floor, her phone nearly slipping from her sweaty grip. Her skin prickled with the need to keep alert on every side, all around her, all at once.

Her heart hammered loud enough to warn anyone who might be lying in wait. She tried to hold her ragged breath and move with stealth. Pressing on, she checked the next row, then the next.

Carefully, she stepped around the broken vase and flowers. But she paused, hunkering down to look for prints in case anyone had walked through the spilled water.

Nothing.

Standing again, Nell moved closer to the body, that dreadful smell growing stronger, the primal warning thumping through her head.

Nell made herself scan the nave, and around the altar, making sure the assailant wasn't lying in wait.

When she was sure there was no one else there, finally, Nell crept to the body.

She was slumped, as if fallen from the first pew, hands clasped, as if in prayer.

The back of her head was bloody, her dark hair matted. Her blood, now clotting in the wound, had drenched the pew, the kneeler, and her white surplice.

Chapter 12

James sprinted towards the chapel – *towards Nell*. She'd sent a second text, telling him there had been a murder in the chapel. He clung to the hope of an accident, but Nell had seen too many now for him to have any room for doubt.

As he ran over the tussocky fields, away from the main tent, the view of Finchmere House bobbed ahead of him, looming closer as he showed his badge to the guard at the bridge, then veered off towards the small church.

He paused at the door, where he collected himself and pulled an ever-present pair of forensic gloves from his pocket, preparing to walk into a crime scene.

Pushing the door open, he heard Nell's gasp before he could make her out in the gloom, then he heard, 'James. Thank God.'

'You OK?'

'*I* am,' Nell said. 'But Louise isn't.'

James watched where he trod, his senses on high alert for any clues, concerned not to trample evidence or contaminate the scene.

'I've called an ambulance, but I can see there's nothing they can do. She's Louise Brimstone. Our local vicar. You'd have seen her at breakfast.'

He was alongside her now, and saw the woman slumped beside the pew. He checked her pulse, then nodded at Nell. Unease nagged at him and he thumbed over his shoulder, whispering, 'Just going to check everything out. Then I'll call it in.'

He didn't need to look far for the weapon. An ornate candlestick, taken from the altar, was on the ground, against the pew, like it had been dropped and then rolled there. The end was bloodied.

Shining the light from his phone, James saw strands of dark hair, which would likely be a match for Louise's.

The broken vase suggested there had been a struggle. Or it had been broken afterwards to give that impression. There were no convenient footprints, though.

He checked the pews, around the altar, in the pulpit. A hand-written sermon was on the lectern, as if Louise had been practising. The space around the organ was clear and James crept towards the vestry.

Taking a breath, he pushed the door open, peered around it . . . *Nothing.*

Various cupboards took up the space. The largest held robes; the smaller two contained vases and bowls, and items for the church, including the locked collection box, which hadn't apparently been touched.

An ornate, carved door led out to the side of the chapel, but it was locked. Walking back, James darted outside and walked a circuit of the building, seeing no one.

Back inside, he called his office, and DC Ed Baker answered. 'Hi, Ed. I'm at Finchmere House's chapel. There's been a—'

'A development?' Ed's gruff voice had a hopeful note. 'Found the stalker?'

'No. We've got a murder inquiry. Can you mobilise SOCO at the chapel?'

'Sure. It . . . It isn't Rav?' As jaded as Ed may be, his voice brimmed with horror.

'No. The local vicar, Rev Louise Brimstone. I'd like you to join me for interviews.'

'I'll be right there. I can bring Rav's phone, too. I think tech are done with it.'

As James hung up, he glanced at Nell. 'I'm going to need an incident room.'

He sat down, a hollow gnawing in his gut.

We should have prevented this. We were all here, vigilant and ready. Is this a separate threat that my team needs to address? Or is this the work of our stalker, taking an unexpected turn?

As he glanced at Nell, another worry gripped him. *Did our*

distraction with Nell make it easier for the killer to strike? Or are we dealing with someone ruthless enough to kill someone, just to throw us off their tracks?

Knowing what the forensic officers would need, Nell called her mother.

Imelda answered at the first ring. 'What's happened now?'

Nell got straight to the point. 'Mum, Rev Brimstone, Louise, has . . . been murdered. In our chapel.'

'Murdered—?' Her mother's shock rendered her speechless for a few seconds. Then, 'How? Are the police—?'

'Yes, James and the Scenes of Crime Officers are already here. I'll set up an incident room in Finchmere Hotel.'

'OK. Can we do anything to help? Do we know Louise's next of kin?'

'James will notify them. He'll have to, under the circumstances. But please could you send someone over with some clothes for me? Some jeans and a long-sleeved shirt, ideally. I . . . I found her, so I need to stay here and be swabbed and hand over my clothes. But I can change in the vestry.'

'Consider it done. Are you OK?'

'Yes, I'm fine. But I'm not sure what we do about our event. Louise was due to co-host our awards, so we either need to cover that and keep it running, or we need to make a careful announcement and cancel.' Nell winced.

'Leave that to me. I'll step in to help Rav. We must do our best to keep things running, given the effort everyone's made to be here and to bring the event together.'

As the minutes drew out, Nell waited out of the way as the SOCO team swarmed the chapel, in blue booties and hooded suits.

She'd already spotted the sermon that Louise had left on the lectern, and had snapped a quick photo of it while James had been on his way over. She'd also taken photos of Louise, the fatal wound, the bloody candlestick, broken vase and altar.

A knock on the vestry door told her someone had arrived with clothes, and Nell was swabbed and sampled by a kind officer. Because Nell had checked if Louise had a pulse, the officer had needed to clip and collect Nell's nails, swab her DNA, and take her clothes. The macabre routine was becoming familiar to Nell now, but that didn't dilute the terror she felt.

Shivering, Nell climbed into the clothes she'd been brought, glad the shirt hid the scratches along her arms.

Once she had changed, James stuck his head around the door and handed her Rav's phone. 'Tech have done their magic. Our hypothesis was correct. The voicemail was made via this phone, and most likely used AI.'

It was a horrible reminder that she was also in the sights of someone willing to do harm. The ambulance bore Louise's body away without fanfare, in quiet dignity. But through all of it, Nell's mind swirled with worry about who could have done this. To Louise, of all people, who was so . . . involved in her community.

Well, if Nell was honest, that may have been part of the problem. Had Louise got a bit overinvolved? She could be quite puritanical, and made no effort to hide it.

But that couldn't be enough reason for someone to *kill* her.

Nell could barely believe it. There'd been no sign of this coming. As she confirmed the meeting room that James could use, her memory crackled with Rav's words from when he'd interviewed the artisans. He'd mentioned a couple of them had argued with Louise. *Zeus, wasn't it? And Noah?*

Were a few cross words enough? And *if* it was one of them, why today, of all days? How could they have managed it, with so much going on, and their own stands to look after?

Especially as Louise had said she expected a few people popping in this morning to see her. It was a massive risk, wasn't it, to try to get away with it?

Who would take a risk like that? And why?

Friday 7th July – 11 a.m.

Settling into the hotel's massive meeting room, James perched at the end of the polished boardroom table while Ed checked the alignment of the camera, ready to record the statements.

He glanced at James. 'I've asked Kat to come over and give her statement first. Nell told me that Kat was recording something with Louise, so she would have been with her for a while. She may have seen others that we can ask, to help us narrow down Louise's time of death.'

James nodded. 'We know she must have been killed between 8 a.m. and 9.30 a.m., according to Nell's timings. And probably towards the latter end of that, I'd say. Louise's wound was fresh and rigor mortis hadn't set in.'

A brisk knock on the door was followed by Kat striding in. 'Hi. I'm Kat Martin.' She glanced from James to Ed. 'I'm the creative director and film-maker for *Following Finchmere*. Rav's channel.'

Rav's, eh? 'And did you see Reverend Louise Brimstone this morning?'

'Yes. She asked me to help her film some content today.'

'Do you have the recording?'

'Of course.' She rummaged in her rucksack. 'It's saved on my laptop.' Setting it on the table, she clicked to the file and played it.

A stunningly framed shot of Louise filled the screen. She stood at the front of the chapel, with wildflowers blooming around her, a shaft of sunlight illuminating her face.

Her smile was a little too wide. 'Hey there, chaps and chapettes! The sustainability work at Finchmere includes the chapel – as you may see from the wildflowers grown from our confetti. And our new solar panels, carefully positioned so we don't block our bats in the belfry, ensure a warm welcome to anyone, anytime.' She spread her arms. 'All souls welcome.' Her smile froze into a rictus grin and her eyes darted sideways. 'How was that?'

'Let's try once more,' Kat said, out of shot. 'Just a little looser. And hold the gaze into the camera with a friendly smile for just a couple of seconds at the end, OK?'

'Gotcha!' Louise rolled her shoulders.

'Ready? And we're going in five, four . . .'

Three seconds later, Louise fixed a grin at the camera. 'Welcome!' James and Ed watched Louise rehash her statement.

'Better. We can certainly use that, thanks, Louise. I need to run now—'

'What time was that?' Ed asked.

'I went straight there from Nell's breakfast meeting, detouring a bit to collect my time-lapse camera from just over the bridge. Louise was already at the church. Before I could start filming, I had to set up the camera. I'd chosen the door for our location. It was stunning, with the flowers, and the light was just right. I was getting set up there, when Gigi came over. She went straight in to see Louise, stayed probably a few minutes – maybe ten or so – then left.'

'What sort of mood was she in?'

'Hard to say. She was in a hurry, and she looked preoccupied. But . . .' She grimaced.

'But?' James kept the hopeful note out of his voice.

'Well, when she left the church, Gigi didn't walk towards her stand at the fete, or the courtyard. I guess that doesn't *mean* anything. She could have had deliveries or something to get from home, or needed to see someone else. But . . . you know.'

Her shrug conveyed that she wasn't convinced of any good reason to distract Gigi from her post as the fete opening approached.

'So did you film when Gigi left?'

'No. Bea turned up. She looked . . . *glum*. But she never looked happy around Louise.'

'Do you know what she was talking to Louise about?'

'No idea. She was upset when she left. But she had something more about her than usual. A determination. Like she might have been . . . *angry*?' Kat raised her eyebrows.

'And Louise looked pretty riled up, too, when she came outside. I got her to rally and shoot those two takes. I couldn't spare any more time. Even though I'd got everything set up for Rav's filming, I wanted to be there to direct it, so I dashed over. And after that, I had to run off for more content shots.'

James nodded, recalling seeing Kat do exactly that.

She tilted her laptop towards him. 'These are what I filmed this morning, if you want to see them. They're raw footage because I haven't had time to edit them, but they're time- and date-stamped so you can see when I recorded them.'

James glanced through the files, seeing the misty morning that he recalled, then the golden morning light over the wildflower meadow lazily buzzing and fluttering with insects; there were also shots of the sunrise behind Finchmere House and more shots of the fete beginning to thrum with excited visitors.

He nodded. 'Is there a way you can send that to me?'

'Sure. I'll compress it and send you a link to my OneDrive.' She attached the file to an email, then hesitated. 'I can give you copies of all the footage if you like, including interviews from the past few days?' She reached into her rucksack. 'Here.' She passed James a clear ziplock bag with a few memory sticks in it. 'I always make copies – that's all the B-roll for the weekend, organised into categories, in case a link fails and I need to put out some footage.'

She sent the link to the email address James dictated, while he picked up the bag. 'Thank you.' Opening his email, he chose a file to watch, so he could make sure the link worked and the videos played.

As he clicked to play the recording of Bea's interview, the screen filled with a golden haze of humming wildflower meadow: a vision of lazy summer. 'We're delighted to have the famous Bea of *Bea's Bees* join us today,' Rav said warmly.

Bea looked shell-shocked, and Rav nudged her, eliciting a slow beam. 'Great to have you, Bea, and great to meet your bees. What are they doing at this time of year?'

Bea gazed at Rav, lost for words for a moment, and James saw Nell hastily fill in. 'Just standing here, amongst these wildflowers, we can hear the bees, busy gleaning nectar. So, what's going on inside all your hives, Bea?'

Gathering herself, Bea said, 'At this time of year, we're in the second – or main – nectar flow. The first is in the spring – with nectar from fruit trees and hawthorn – but *this* time of year, the nectar sources are typically clover and willowherb, and we're lucky enough to be amongst these wonderful wildflowers. We can open the hives and see if any frames have been filled with honey yet.' She held up a suit, looking at Rav. 'Fancy helping me?' An unmistakable blush swept across her cheeks, and she shot a pained look at Kat.

'Cut. Let's do that again.'

In the take that followed, they both took the suits. Rav needed Nell's help to get into his, one shaky leg at a time, while he gripped his crutches. Bea shot Rav a solicitous glance, as if she wanted to help, but restrained herself.

Once Bea had prised open the top of the first beehive, they leaned in, fascinated.

'I'll take off the cap and make sure they're calm.' Bea puffed the lavender smoke and lifted off the outside collar of the hive. 'Now I'll take a look at the frames inside.'

Gently, she lifted one of the vertical frames, undulating with bronze bees on honey. With a soft brush, she swooshed the docile bees from the frame and examined the cells.

'This one isn't full yet.' She turned the frame, bulging with honey on one side, but empty on the other. 'I'll put this back so they can fill up this side, too.' Pushing it back, Bea drew out another frame. 'Rav, would you like to brush this one?'

'Sure!' Taking the brush, he swooped it down, the obliging bees taking flight, swarming lazily around their heads. 'They're so cooperative, aren't they? What do you reckon to this frame, Bea?'

'This looks full on both sides and capped off.' Bea placed it under the cover across her wheelbarrow. 'We'll keep that away from the bees.'

They continued until they'd checked all the frames, finding only one more that was full and capped, which Bea stashed with the first.

'We only ever take a small amount from the bees, because this is their food resource, and we mustn't deplete a hive. The honey I extract here, harvested from Finchmere's wildflowers, is used by *Graze!* to make their delicious summer honey cake.'

The scene cut, and James sat back. Bea's infatuation with Rav oozed from her.

'Nice footage, don't you think?' Kat asked. 'I wanted it to feel completely immersive, to show Bea's work in the best light.'

'So, after Bea left Lou this morning, you headed straight off?' James checked. When she hesitated, he couldn't help leaning forward. 'What?'

'Well, it's probably nothing. But you ought to know anyway. Otherwise, you'll think that Bea was the last to see Louise. And she wasn't. Because, as I was leaving the chapel, *Zeus* was heading over. And *he* didn't look very happy, either.'

Chapter 13

Nell's instinct – after finding Louise so brutally killed – was to locate Rav, hug him fiercely, feel him close to her.

Her clamouring thoughts pounded in her head. She couldn't make sense of this. *Why* would Louise end up killed? And so . . . so *violently*? Why would anyone want to hurt her?

As awful as all this was, one question kept bubbling to the surface. *Are the stalker and the murderer the same person? If so, why was Louise suddenly a target?*

If there were two threats, what was motivating the killer? Would they strike again?

If there was just one threat, did that mean the person who had her in their sights wouldn't stop at just burning down her house and attacking her – but was also prepared to kill?

Gulping, Nell cut her thoughts off.

In the Landy, she headed over the fields, then slipped into the main tent.

Rav spotted her instantly, his shoulders dropping and a smile appearing as he concluded the discussion with the panel of experts. On the screen behind him were the final images of a fellow rewilder's presentation: a fledgling white stork taking its first flight. It must have gone well, judging by the enthusiastic questions flooding from the audience.

The golden rosettes pinned to the competition entrants told Nell that Rav had also fielded the *Go reWild!* awards while she'd been away.

As she loitered at the back, the Q&A rolled on for an agonising half an hour until, *finally*, Sylvia announced that everyone could move outside, and continue any conversations over their *Graze!* luxury picnic hampers. They'd aimed for an informal, relaxed lunch to keep the conversation flowing and enable everyone to socialise, including their artisans, who could share their experiences with enthusiasts.

Now, Nell had to socialise with someone far too dangerous, far too close for comfort.

Trying to push the fear aside, and doing her best to ignore Rav's and Sylvia's questioning glances, Nell circulated. Out of the corner of her eye, she saw Rav tuck his rucksack inside the tent, out of the way, as he chatted to the nearest group.

She homed in on folk who had won prizes from their *Go reWild!* competition to drum up conversation. Seeing an intense-looking young man in black and camos flicking through his *ReWilding Yearbook* prize, she moved in.

'Hi! I'm Nell, nice to meet you.'

'Hi. I'm Sebastien.'

'I see congratulations are in order!' She nodded at his book. 'What category did you win?'

'Oh, thanks. Wild Garden category.'

'Oh, yes!' Nell recalled the entry at once. 'I *loved* your study of your garden transformation. Stunning photographic record of turning that ornamental pond into a natural one, with those glorious native plants and the biodiversity it's nurtured. Incredible work. And such gorgeous shots of those azure dragonflies around the yellow-flag iris.'

'I've recorded Daubenton's bats at night, feeding off the water. It's amazing to see.' The man shot her a shy smile. 'I'm experimenting with night-vision cameras now.'

'Ah, then let me introduce you to Kat.' Nell beckoned to her as she rushed past. 'She's our talented videographer and may have some good tips for night filming.'

Extricating herself as he asked Kat's advice, Nell turned to the next group of people.

She saw Rav was doing the same, in demand and under pressure to keep up easy conversation. He was doing well – she was sure only she would notice the tension around his eyes, the worried tug at his lips, the tendency for his brow to fall into concerned creases when he wasn't making a concerted effort to smile and look fascinated by whatever someone was telling him.

The hour dragged, and Nell just didn't think she had the endurance to host the safaris. With the dread that now came with using her phone, she ran the gauntlet of sending a text to her land manager, asking her if she could cover it, so that she, Rav and Sylvia could step back. The few minutes until the end of lunch dragged, but Nell managed to keep smiling as she spoke to a few more guests.

At last, Sylvia announced the afternoon options: join a *reWild Side* Safari, explore the stands and meet the artisans, enjoy the fairground or join a bat-box workshop. Nell was relieved to see the crowd disperse, and the artisans return to their work.

It felt like a weight that had been crushing her chest eased and she could breathe again.

With everyone out of sight, Nell dragged Sylvia and Rav into the main tent.

'Nell? What happened this morning?' Rav asked, worried.

'And where did Louise get to?' Sylvia frowned. 'Why did you disappear for so long?'

Sinking onto a seat, Nell handed Rav his phone and said, 'Louise has been murdered. In the church. Someone attacked her with one of the massive candlesticks from the altar.'

'You . . . *What*?' Rav gasped. 'When?'

Sylvia clapped a hand to her mouth. 'Dear God. *Why?*' she asked.

'I wish I knew.' Nell shot them a sidelong look as they sat beside her. 'I really do. Because *then* I'd know if it was related to Rav's stalker. I'm just running every theory I can think of at the moment.'

She felt sick at how something so insidious and unknown to them was taking over everything and – if the stalker *had* killed Louise – causing so much senseless harm.

Rav frowned. 'There's no obvious connection, though, is there? I can't imagine how it could be related. I've only met Louise recently.'

'Yes, you and probably your stalker,' Nell pointed out. 'And you *have* been having mysterious conversations with her, arranging secret meetings.'

Rav's eyes darted to her and a flash of unease made Nell's skin prickle.

'What's all that been about?' she asked. 'More to the point, what might someone have overheard and *assumed* it could be about?'

Rav shifted on his seat. 'Weddings,' he mumbled. 'I don't know much about the general protocols. I . . . I asked her to keep it a secret from you. For now.'

A flash of pure love blazed through Nell's heart – but fear followed in its wake. 'How easily could someone have overheard you asking her those things? Lou wasn't exactly discreet. Do you think someone could have got the wrong idea?'

With a pained grimace, Rav shrugged. He sank his head into his hands.

Sylvia patted his arm. 'You weren't to know, Rav—'

'I was, though. With Nell being attacked, of *course* I knew I had to be more careful.' He rubbed his face and gazed at Nell with agonised, bloodshot eyes.

Sylvia filled in the silence. 'We need to try to be practical about things, don't we? There's an undeniable heightened risk now, isn't there?' Her face was stricken as she glanced at Nell. 'What was James's advice?'

'He's brought in a SOCO team to inspect the scene, and he and Ed have probably questioned our site team by now. They're using a meeting room in the hotel. We'll cordon the church off from visitors, which will be easy enough. We already have a gatekeeper on the bridge, so we can just reserve that route for family or police.'

'Good.' Sylvia approved. 'And what about you two? This is a huge amount of pressure. If you need to step back and let me and the team step up—'

Nell shook her head. 'No. I cannot respond by backing off from my responsibilities.' She was amazed how assertive her voice sounded, considering the quaking fear she was hiding. 'I cannot show that someone's succeeded in impacting my life like that.'

'But your *life* is at risk, Nell—' Rav sounded desperate to convince her to step back.

'Yes, exactly.' Nell gazed at him. 'So I need to fight for it. And you have to help me.'

With a defeated sigh, Rav rubbed his face again. 'So should we . . . pretend we've broken up? Would that help?'

Nell took his hand. 'I'm not doing anything to compromise the way I live. As far as I'm concerned, the sooner we flush out the perpetrator – or perpetrators – the sooner we and everyone around us are safe again.'

Their heads snapped up as someone walked into the tent. Nell's tension ebbed at the sight of DI Ashley Hollis, but it left a nauseous uncertainty in its wake.

'Ashley? Has something else happened—'

Ashley shook her head. 'No, just wanted to check how you're doing.' Her kind smile reached her hazel eyes. 'My Family Liaison Officer roots may be showing.'

Pulling up a chair, she sat with them. 'You're probably discussing whether the murder is related to the stalker? I'd say yes, it certainly could be. So we'll proceed with that in mind, but we can't afford to let an assumption narrow our investigation. We'll do our best to cover all bases, OK?'

As they nodded, Rav's phone beeped. Everyone stiffened, as if expecting bad news.

Rav opened the text, smiling at first, then dropping his phone like it had burned him.

Picking it up, Nell saw the photo of Rav's younger sister, Aanya, leaving his parents' house in Richmond.

Your sister looks nice. Do you think she'd want to be my friend?

Friday 7th July – 1 p.m.

James put out a call to ask for Zeus to be sent over to give a statement. He was thankful that Hesha was quick off the mark, scouting the grounds and escorting him to the hotel. Now, James was face to face with the smooth guy with the soothing southern accent; the recording had started and formal introductions had been made.

'Hey! What's this all about? How can I help you good officers of the law?' Zeus splayed out his long legs, pointing shining brogues towards James.

His olive tweeds seemed a little much for the summer heat, but the flashy cerise lining made James hide a smile. Not many could pull off that combination with so much aplomb.

'You may be aware that there's been a murder. Here. This morning. And we're asking—'

'What?' Zeus sat up sharply, his eyes wide. 'Who?'

'The Reverend Louise Brimstone.'

'Wh . . . *What*?' His alarmed glance flashed from James to Ed and back again. '*Louise*? How? Why?' His bald head glistened with sweat. He took a monogrammed handkerchief from his pocket and dabbed himself.

'And a witness says that you saw Louise, shortly before she was killed. Can you tell us why you took the time out of the morning's preparations, for a busy fete, to see her?' James asked.

The hand holding the handkerchief lowered, and Zeus's tone hardened. 'We just had something to discuss.'

'Which was?'

'Well, it was something and nothing, really. Not important enough to concern you.'

'Really?' James gave a disarming smile. 'Everyone was so busy finalising set-ups, putting finishing touches to stands. The chapel's across the river from the fete, so you'd have needed to make an effort to go there. That doesn't add up to an *unimportant* chat.' He narrowed his eyes. 'It would be something significant, surely? Urgent, even?'

'Well . . .' Zeus exhaled. 'You have a point. It wasn't a major issue, but it was something I wanted to settle between us. I hate bad blood.'

He grimaced. 'It was like this: Louise wanted me to supply the wine for Communion. That's *every week*. She seemed to think I could give it to her for free.' He turned his palms up. 'I just couldn't do that, Officer. A donation of a few cases for an event, sure – with the right publicity, that's a deal I can do. But a bottle or two *every week*, with no PR, just ain't sustainable. I was concerned that if I *did* agree, she'd expect the same deal for all the other churches in her parish. Louise wouldn't accept no for an answer. And when I made a joke about no one turning my water into wine – *well*. She thought I was speaking sacrilege. She just . . . *went* for me.'

'Give me a timeline here,' James asked. 'When did she first ask, and when did she, in your words, *go for you*?'

'Oh.' Zeus frowned. 'She asked me a coupla weeks ago. I said I'd think about it. I always try to consider things, especially if there's a local synergy, y'know? So, when she next came over, that woulda been last week, I confirmed that sadly I could not help her out. She wasn't happy. Then she came back over yesterday, and that was when she went at it.'

'Meaning?'

'Meaning she hurled a few "choice words" around. Not the kind of attitude you'd expect from your kindly pastor. I don't care to repeat them.'

'I'm asking you to. For your statement.' James nodded at the camera.

Zeus squirmed, hiding his discomfort by crossing his legs. 'Something about me not supporting the estate – which I did *not* appreciate. She attacked my character. But I was more concerned about the sense that she was attacking my business and my prospects here. I mean, I love this place. I didn't want her taking a complaint to the family. I . . . I'm not proud of myself, but I warned her off. Said something like she better not take it further. I can't recall the exact words. But that was the gist.'

'So when you went to see her, on that very busy morning of the public event that you'd put so much effort into starting off perfectly, was that to make sure that Louise didn't – or couldn't – take it further?'

Zeus leaned forward, his eyes narrowing. 'I don't care for your insinuations, Officer.'

'I'm not making insinuations, Zeus. I'm asking you questions.'

'I wanted to see her to clear the air. I didn't like the bad feeling. And I knew that this weekend I'd have to walk into a tent and do some judging with her. Those contests were meant to be light-hearted fun, getting the locals involved, celebrating their efforts. I just didn't think we'd set the right tone if there was tension. You can tell, can't ya? When folks are arguing. I didn't think that was right. I wanted to appeal to Louise. I thought if there was some event on her calendar, I could supply something for that. Goodwill, to soften the blow.'

'Soften the blow.' James pursed his lips and studied Zeus, wondering if he was only too aware how Louise had been killed; if these words had unwittingly given him away.

'Sweeten the pill. Whatever you Brits say.' Zeus threw his hands up, sitting back.

'Did it work?' James asked. 'Did you manage to resolve things?'

Zeus shrugged. 'I can't honestly say that we were best buds. But I hoped it had, y'know, smoothed things over a little.'

'Where did you have this conversation?' James asked. 'In the chapel?'

'Oh no. In her little, you know, *office*.'

'The vestry?'

'Yeah. She was in there, talking to herself, when I arrived.'

'Talking . . . to *herself*?' James frowned. 'Are you sure there wasn't someone else in there with her?'

'I'm sure. Unless they jumped inside that big cupboard of hers.'

James couldn't help glancing at Ed, wondering if someone had done exactly that. *So she hadn't been alone?*

'If there was a person in the cupboard, that would be useful for you, Zeus. You'd have a witness for your statement. Few have such an advantage. So, try – if you can – to recall any details to help us find the person who can confirm your words.'

Zeus's gaze dropped to the table. His eyes rose again as his shoulders climbed into a shrug. 'Wish I could remember something. But I can't, that's the truth.'

Ed scrawled a note and passed it to James. *Rehearsing her sermon?* James looked at Zeus. 'I'm sorry you can't recall anything else. What about the time you left her?'

'Oh, sure, I remember that. About a quarter before nine. I had to hurry back. I hadn't wanted to be too long.' More sweat beaded on his forehead.

'Well, that helps us with the time of death, since you were the last person to see her alive.'

'Oh?' Zeus looked at him, then Ed. 'But I wasn't the *last* person to see her. That was Holly.'

'Holly?'

'Sure. The *Wood Whisperer*, she calls herself. She was heading in to see Louise as I was rushing back.' He heaved a sigh of relief and flashed James a dazzling smile. 'So *that's* why you got your panties in a bunch. Thought I was the last one to see her? No, Officer. It surely weren't me. As the very lovely Holly will confirm.'

James frowned, unwilling to let his suspect off the hook too easily. 'Nothing stopping you waiting, watching – then going back.'

Chapter 14

Rav was pacing on his crutches, his stomach churning. This was all too much – too fast. 'I can't believe this. They've hurt you already, they might have killed Lou . . . and now . . . Now they're watching *Aanya*. At least here, we have Conor, James, all this protection. Aanya has *nothing*. Nothing like *any* of that to keep her safe.'

He doubled over, bile rising, shaking uncontrollably, fearing he'd throw up. Impotent rage, the guilt of feeling somehow responsible for this horrendous situation and pure fear roller-coastered through him. He could be here for Nell, to help look out for her – but he couldn't also be there, to help his little sister. Looking out for her was in his DNA, and now he was bringing a deadly threat to her door.

Looking up at Ashley and Nell, he nearly sobbed. 'What do I do?'

Ashley's calm hands steered him back to his seat and she crouched in front of him, looking right into his eyes.

'This is a shock, I know. But let's be logical, OK? Knowing where your family lives, and deciding your sister would make a good friend, is your stalker letting you know how well they know you and your life. How they'd be *perfect* for you, if only you'd realise.'

'But . . . what if they attack her, too? I can't—'

'I *highly* doubt Aanya is in any danger, because she's never going to be a rival for your romantic interest, is she? That's why Nell was subjected to an attack – and maybe also arson. Because she's a threat to whoever's stalking you.'

Rav's stomach twisted as he looked up at Nell. Bile burned again.

'So, what we'll do with Aanya,' Ashley angled herself to regain his eye contact, 'is I'll call her right now, and talk her through what's happening. I'll explain what she needs to look out for, in case anyone is following her to take more photos, or tries to orchestrate meeting with her, OK?'

Rav managed to nod as he tried to focus on her words.

'If Aanya spots anything, she can call me, any time. I'll talk to her local officers, too, so they understand the threat level and she'll have police nearby who can respond quickly, if needed. And by *that* I'm thinking more along the lines of it helping us to apprehend the stalker as quickly as possible, *not* because Aanya will be unsafe. OK?'

He began to absorb what she was saying, the panic lessening, but still roiling, still making him sick to the depths of his soul.

'And, actually, this may help us.'

He glanced at her. 'How?'

'Because she'll be able to tell us when this photo was taken. We'll be able to ask our suspects what they were doing at that time, on that date.' Her eyes gleamed, like she was a lioness catching the scent of the hunt. 'That, combined with asking about their whereabouts during Nell's attack, might just be the breakthrough we need.'

'Yeah. Maybe. Thanks, Ashley.'

She squeezed his hands. 'You're freezing, Rav. You're in shock. Let's get a warm drink into you. And think about what I've said: we'll get a plan in place straight away. If you give me Aanya's number, I'll call her right now.'

Once he'd shared Aanya's contact details with Ashley, Nell nudged him. 'Let's go for a walk and get a tea or a coffee.'

He shook his head. He couldn't face the courtyard . . .

'Go up to my office,' Sylvia suggested. 'Just take a minute somewhere no one will find you. You can raid my posh coffee. Maybe even break out the emergency madeleines in the cupboard.'

Nell nodded. 'That sounds good, thanks.' She tugged Rav's hand. 'We can look out at the fete and check how the footage looks, so we can get a sense of how the event is going.'

With a brief smile, Rav stood. He needed to move, to purge the panic. As they headed up the hill, towards the house, he felt like he was scaling a mountain. The exertion of navigating rough fields on crutches was exhausting.

The stone bridge was cordoned off with a chain and a clear 'No Entry' sign. But the team member charged with guarding the route waved at Nell and unclipped the barrier chain so they could pass. Rav managed a friendly nod, but limping this far, fuelled by adrenaline while still fighting shock, had drained him.

Sitting in the window of Sylvia's office, he watched the distant activity – stands thronged with visitors; Land Rovers touring habitats; the flashing colours of the fairground – and was glad of this respite.

Nell passed him a coffee and a cake, and turned on the TV to their YouTube channel, to see what was streaming.

The screen filled with Holly, in her element teaching attendees of all ages and abilities how to make a bat box, each putting their own stamp on it.

Sitting down, Nell groaned when she saw the next interview on the screen: her piece on the large blue butterflies, her image at the wildflower meadow filling the screen. 'Such a shame we left it too late. A week before, we had those glorious swarms, remember?'

He nodded. It seemed like years ago they'd been preparing these. He leaned in to watch, listening intently.

'I'm on Finchmere's chalk grassland, which has been restored by grazing our Highland cattle out here, on this stunning purple carpet of wild thyme, which can *now* host an incredible population of large blue butterflies. These butterflies became extinct in the UK in the seventies. While they've since been reintroduced, they're still very rare, and have protected status. However, don't be fooled: this rare butterfly may be delicate, and breathtakingly beautiful – but it's deadly.'

Stock footage of a swarm of large blue butterflies filled the screen as Nell continued, 'Large blue butterflies are rare partly because of their very short life as a butterfly, and partly because of their life cycle. *All* butterflies are sensitive due to their life cycle. As eggs and caterpillars, they're vulnerable to microclimate changes and depend on certain plants. But large blue butterflies' needs are even more complex – and their beauty belies their ruthless, murderous nature. It all starts when their eggs hatch and butterfly larvae, caterpillars, feed on the flower heads of this wild thyme.'

The next shot showed Nell gesturing at the verdant carpet – bright, with delicate amethyst blooms. 'If two eggs hatch on a plant, one caterpillar will eat the other – starting out their life with murder.'

Rav noticed that when Nell looked at the habitat instead of the lens, her shoulders relaxed.

'But it's when they reach their fourth development stage – or larval instar – that they get really devious. They drop from the plants to the ground and perform the ultimate honeytrap. Using chemical cues from their "honey gland", they trick worker red ants *Myrmica sabuleti* into thinking they're ant grubs. Completely deceived, the willing ants carry the caterpillars – who feign death – right into the ants' nest.'

Nell turned back to the lens. 'But here's where it gets really deadly – once inside the nest, the caterpillars betray the ants' hospitality with mass genocide. While they keep the ants sweet by secreting a sugary liquid for them to consume, they also feast on them – one caterpillar will gorge on two hundred ant grubs – growing rapidly, before turning into a chrysalis. With true Stockholm syndrome, the ants will care for the pupa, and ward off predators. A year later, the beautiful large blue butterfly emerges.

'So, ecosystem balance is key: the thyme needs to be near a red-ant colony which, in turn, needs the right conditions to survive. For that, we can thank our Highland cattle. They graze grass short enough to get the soil *warm* enough for these cold-blooded ants to thrive. Speaking of our Highland heroes, here's an update on how our new calf, Rufus, is doing.'

A VT of the heart-melting Rufus having a check-up by his vet followed, with plenty of close-ups of his shaggy fringe falling into adorable big brown eyes.

'That was *brilliant*.' Rav beamed.

Nell shrugged, uncertainty flickering. 'Look how adorable Rufus is. Even Sylvia thinks Kat's right to focus more on our young livestock than the ecology. She'd have done my piece at the right time, if she'd been more focused. But I seem to be the only one bothered about it.'

She glanced at the TV, now showing Rav and Rufus in split screen as their respective fringes flopped into their eyes in slow motion. 'See!'

'Oh, ignore all that stuff,' Rav said. 'Kat has a good eye for the silly, entertaining stuff. Your ecology work is the heart of it.' He glanced at her. 'Actually, I thought your piece was especially close to the bone right now. About honeytraps and deception, disguising deadly intentions to get close to a target.'

Nell shot him a glance. 'Yes, that thought did cross my mind as I was saying it. That's how I feel, to be honest. Like this person's a parasite, feeding off our lives.'

'The problem is that parasites are very successful.' Rav shot her a concerned look.

'Only when the hosts don't have the sense to turf them out.' Her smile made her look braver than he felt.

His nausea churned as a text beeped – then he sighed in relief when he saw it was from Ashley: *Just spoken to Aanya. She understands that she needs to be vigilant, and she has my number and a contact at her local station to call.*

Then another beep. *Bro? Just had the low-down from Ash. You OK?*

He replied: *I'm fine, just want you to be alert. Ash gave you contact details, right? And you'll keep a lookout?*

Yeah, no biggie. I'm OK. How's Nell and all the house stuff? You doing OK?

We're OK, but this is serious, Aans. Just be aware. You may see something helpful.

Knowing Aanya was all right, and had backup, made him feel a little better. He'd expected her to play it down, but she *could* be sensible when it mattered, and she wouldn't want him to think she was worried. Reassured, Sylvia's pastries were starting to look more tempting. He managed to eat, but couldn't stop wondering why on earth someone would hurt their local vicar. Guilt churned at the sinister turn everything had taken.

He turned to Nell, who was on her second madeleine. 'Do you have any thoughts on who might have had reason to kill Louise?'

Maybe the puzzle of it would occupy their minds, focus them on solving something proactively instead of feeling so helplessly reactive.

Of course she'd nod!

'Go on,' he urged.

'I was thinking about those arguments you mentioned Louise had. With Noah and Zeus. Can you recall what they were about?'

Rav dredged his memory. 'She accused Noah of predatory behaviour. Towards Erin.'

'Oh?' Nell was immediately curious. 'Did you agree?'

Rav gave an uneasy shrug. 'I'm not sure men are as attuned to it as women.'

'Ugh. That's a cop-out, Rav. You know it is. Good men call it out. What would you have to see, exactly, before you spoke up?'

'Hang on, I haven't done anything here! And I didn't notice anything . . . untoward.' Rav held his hands up as if fending off an attack. 'Believe me, I'm carrying enough guilt for everything that's going on. *Including* the state Erin got in.'

Nell shrugged, making no apology, so Rav continued, 'Lou also told Zeus he'd need to take responsibility for something and address it – or she would.'

'Any idea what?'

'No . . . but we could . . .' He tilted his head. 'We could go and speak to him? Ask some leading questions. See if we find out anything?'

Nell nodded. 'We'll need to be careful.'

Drawing out her phone, she found her photos and turned the screen towards him.

He winced at the images of the scene of the murder. 'Poor woman.' As he scrolled slowly, he saw the close-up photo of a letter, then realised it was the draft of a sermon.

'Did you read this?' He stared at her. 'It's a message, isn't it? Not a very subtle one.'

Chapter 15

Friday 7th July – 1.30 p.m.

Across the table, Bea was looking even more doleful than she'd seemed at breakfast.

'I'm sorry to share the news that Reverend Louise Brimstone was found murdered this morning.'

She didn't look shocked as she nodded, so the news was already spreading.

'I understand you were one of the last to speak to her.'

Bea's eyes lifted to meet his, and James saw shrewdness in their gentle depths. 'But not the last, Officer.'

'No, I know that. But I think you had one of the more . . . acrimonious conversations.'

'Acrimonious?' She folded her arms. 'No, I wouldn't say so. Difficult, perhaps. It was about my grandmother's funeral. So I was naturally upset.'

'I'm sorry for your loss. May I make a note of her name?'

'Irene. Irene Camberwell. She worshipped at the church all her life. She didn't know Louise all that well, as she's relatively new to the parish. But that's where she went, and where our family is. So it was important to her that that's where she's laid to rest.'

'Was Louise opposing that, for any reason?'

'No. Of course not. We just have the usual arrangements to make. And it's just me now. It's a lot to think about.'

As Bea left, her head bowed as if she was already in a funeral procession, James considered his next interview: Holly. He pulled up the footage that Kat had given him, as a starting point.

The recording began with her lovingly sandpapering a flat slab of wood with intriguing black spidery lines. As she ran her long fingers over the piece, it looked silkenly tactile.

Rav stepped into frame. 'Hello, Holly Blue, of *The Wood Whisperer* video-channel fame – can we interrupt your work for a moment?'

James noted how convincingly Holly could feign surprise. '*Rav!* And *Nell!* Thanks for dropping by. You've caught me in the middle of an important rush order. I'm finishing a set of charcuterie boards for our friends over at *Graze!* so they can use them for the fete this weekend.'

'And how beautiful they are.' Rav traced the dark veins along the board. 'This is spalted beech, right?'

'Yes.' Holly looked pleased that he recognised it. 'So delicate. The fungus growing on the tree creates the pattern. I love the marks you find in nature. I always want to bring those out in my work.'

'Well, that is why you're called the *Wood Whisperer*, isn't it?' Rav said. 'It's your talent of reading the wood to craft the most exquisite pieces.'

'Oh!' Holly's gaze dropped to her work. As she caressed the gleaming board, she shrugged. 'I love it. I know it sounds daft, but the wood seems to speak to me.' Looking at her extensive array of pieces, she added, 'It's been a dream to move into a workshop like this. I could barely move in my last place. Here I've got room to work on a few projects at once.'

'We're glad you're here!' Nell said. 'Especially as you're generously sharing your talents at Finchmere Fete. We're delighted that you're running some workshops for us.'

Holly's face seemed to flicker with annoyance at Nell leaning in, before she smiled. 'Ah, yes. I'll run several workshops, every day of the fete – the times will be in the programme you'll receive at the gate on arrival. Everyone's welcome – no skills required. I'll teach you everything you need to know and take you step by step through building a Kent bat box. Super simple, stylish and an easy way to enhance any area for wildlife.'

'That's fantastic!' Rav sounded enthusiastic, and James couldn't blame him – even he had good reason to have a soft spot for bats now. 'So, of those who join you, *some* may leave with a new skill – but *everyone* can take home a bit of Finchmere rewilding spirit.'

As they all held their smiles for the camera, the scene cut. From the recording, James expected Holly to be a convincing performer when he conducted his own interview.

Now, as the young blonde woman sat across from him, she shivered with nerves in the cool meeting room. Her widened, artificially lashed eyes made her look even more shell-shocked at the news about Louise. Even as he wondered if Holly's wiles were working on him, James found himself softening enough to get her a cup of hot, sweet tea.

As she wrapped her hands around the mug, she shook her head. 'I can't believe it.'

'I know this is awful news.' James used his gentle coaxing tone, even though he questioned if this was a carefully cultivated act. 'Are you up to answering some questions?'

With a gulp, Holly nodded. 'I'll . . . I'll try.'

'We have reason to believe that you spoke to Louise shortly before she died.'

Another nod, and another gulp.

'Did you have much to get set up this morning? Ready for the fete?' James asked.

Holly frowned at the change of tack. 'Well, no. I'd already set everything up. My demo today was only in the afternoon, parallel with the safari, after lunch. I just had to be in the event tent for the conference section. Which was at nine thirty.'

'That didn't leave much time to squeeze in a meeting with the vicar. So why go then?'

Holly shrugged her shivering shoulders. 'Louise can be hard to . . . pin down. She flits about the parish like a butterfly. For once, I knew where she was, so I went to see her.'

'And what did you need to talk about?'

'She'd . . .' Holly swallowed. 'She'd asked me to do a commission for her.'

'Oh? Of what?'

'Er . . .' Her long lashes fluttered. 'Um. She wanted something sculptural. For . . . um . . . the church. Something in keeping with the setting, the sustainability theme. But impressive. Like a talking point. She said she'd leave it to me. Maybe I'd have some divine inspiration.'

'Oh.' James raised his eyebrows. 'That seems a pretty open-ended brief.'

Holly blew on her tea and sipped. 'Yes. But not totally unusual. People often want something interesting but don't know exactly what that is. And some commissions that are too prescriptive . . . Well, if I can't find exactly the right piece of wood for it, they might have to wait some time.'

'So had Louise asked you over? To talk about the commission?'

'Er . . . yeah. Yes. Exactly. She asked me.'

'And what budget had she set for this work?'

'Er . . . About five hundred pounds. As a rough estimate.'

'Oh?' James couldn't help feeling surprised that Louise, who'd been described as trying to score free Communion wine one moment, was willing to splash a few hundred quid on a sculpture the next. Something about these accounts didn't add up. 'Did you provide a written estimate for her?'

'No. Um . . .' She bit her lip.

'Why not? That's the usual process, isn't it?'

'I . . . didn't have my order book with me. I said I'd draft it later for her. After the fete.'

'You don't do that electronically? On your phone?'

'I made notes. But if someone's placing an order, I'll do a few drawings. I find that easier in a sketchbook.' Unconsciously, she touched the pencil pinning her artful, messy bun.

James frowned. 'So you didn't take your order book, even though she'd asked you over to request a commission.'

Holly shrank in her seat. 'Not every enquiry becomes a commission. People are often surprised how much the work can cost, and some things never go further than the initial chat.'

'So how did you leave things? With Louise?'

'Just that I'd look through my timber, sketch out a few ideas, cost them up and get back to her a few days after the fete.'

She blushed and James took the cue to press for more information. 'And?'

With a sigh, Holly admitted, 'Look, if I'm honest, I wanted to push the budget a bit. I couldn't think of anything suitable when I looked around the church for ideas but – as I was leaving – I saw those wildflowers around the door, and it struck me: a beautiful wooden arbour outside the church. An arch of intricately carved entwined blooms, like everlasting flowers. I could imagine it being a gorgeous piece for wedding photos, and that's what the chapel is becoming known for. It looks stunning in spring and summer, with the wildflowers – so I thought my installation might echo that and bring interest in autumn and winter.'

'How much would that have cost?'

Holly's cheeks flushed again, her neck flaming. 'Well. You'd have to add on a zero, I reckon. I thought maybe I could build up to it. Maybe see if Nell would come on board, too. They've got money to burn, haven't they?'

James bit back his instinctive defence of Nell and her family. Instead, he shrugged, letting the awkward silence hang.

'Don't blame me for making the most of an opportunity. I depend on commissions for my livelihood.' Now, Holly met James's gaze, her chin lifted, a touch defiant.

He couldn't help wondering what this apparently delicate flower might be capable of.

'So, you were the last person to see Louise alive—'

'Me?' Holly frowned. 'No, I wasn't.'

'Oh?'

'As I was leaving, at what must have been about 9 a.m., I saw Noah skulking around the back of the church. I was thinking about the sculpture and scanning possible locations.'

'How did he seem?'

'He . . . Well, he turned away. Quickly. Like he was annoyed that I'd seen him.'

James frowned. If Noah *had been* there, if he *had seen* Louise, he *must* have been the last person to have seen her alive.

'And where were you on Wednesday evening, Holly?'

'Wednesday?' She frowned at the change of tack. 'In my workshop, probably. Been putting in some long days to get the boards ready for the fete, between other commissions.'

'Anyone else here, who could corroborate that?'

She shook her head, worry flickering.

'And what about Thursday afternoon and evening?'

'Yesterday? Oh, I finished early. I'd got everything done and it was just nice to have an evening off, ahead of the fete madness. I shut up early and went for a walk. I needed some fresh air and exercise after being at the bench all week.'

'With anyone?'

'No . . . on my own. In Pendlebury. Along the river.'

As James thanked Holly for her time and she left, Dr Saunders walked in.

'The team have finished taking samples now, James. There's a lot of blood but I fear it will all be the victim's. There's very little blood spatter, suggesting one single, killing blow. That'll mean little to no chance of blood spatter on the killer's clothes.'

'Shame.' James winced. 'Disposed garments or a change of outfit would have been helpful. Have you got anything else to go on?'

'Well, given that it looks spontaneous, we're hoping for fingerprints on the candlestick, but there are about a million on there, so we'll have a lot of exclusions to make. We'll have to track down cleaners, wardens, flower arrangers and churchgoers. Perhaps we could start with the list of people who spoke to her today?'

Ed offered. 'I can get onto that. I've got the names and have seen most of them now.'

As James nodded, Dr Saunders added, 'We've got Louise's iPhone, so I'll pass that to the tech team. And here's a copy of her latest sermon. Thought you might like a read.' She passed him the handwritten sheets inside the labelled, sealed, clear plastic bags. 'Quite Old Testament for such a modern vicar.' She arched an eyebrow. 'I'll leave you to it and get on with the post-mortem. See you back at the ranch.'

James barely said goodbye; he was already gripped by the sermon.

None of us are perfect. [Smile. Look around the audience]

Not even me! [Pause for laughter]

[Pace, as if deep in thought, like this idea is just occurring to me]

But the temptations of sin are everywhere, aren't they? They say the devil has the best tunes. Villains in movies have the best outfits and the fastest cars. It's easy to covet something that someone else has earned. Or be lazy or greedy when work seems too much. It's cool to be cruel, yeah?

Or is it? [Hard stare]

[Pace a bit more] Lust can destroy a loving marriage in seconds. Pride and greed can destroy hard-earned goodwill, ruin businesses, livelihoods, homes. Envy overvalues the superficial and devalues those things of substance. These sins aren't called the deadly sins for nothing. Because all of these are toxic, ruinous to the soul who harbours them, completely destructive to lives and the innocent caught up in their ripple effects.

And don't just take my word for it. In Mark 7:20–23, Jesus says: 'For it is from within, out of a person's heart, that evil thoughts come … [Hard stare – right at them] … Sexual immorality, theft, murder, adultery, greed, deceit, lewdness … All these evils come from inside and defile a person.'

In John 8:34, Jesus also said, 'Very truly I tell you, everyone who sins is a slave to sin.' And, in Romans 6:23, He decreed, 'For the wages of *sin* is *death*.'

Chapter 16

Friday 7th July – 1.45 p.m.

'Do you really think this sermon could mean Lou was killed by someone else? *Not* the stalker?'

Nell heard hope in Rav's voice, and recognised the depth of desperation he felt, as they went downstairs in Finchmere House's lift.

Yet, she was heartened to see him rally, driven to work out what had happened to Louise. 'It sounds possible. If she's making a point about sins and transgressing, then yes, someone *could* have wanted to kill her to hide something.'

Rav nodded. 'I wonder what Zeus did that Louise disapproved of?'

Walking outside, she said, 'Let's find out.'

'What are you going to ask him?'

Nell shrugged. 'I'm just a concerned employer, aren't I? Wanting to ensure he's OK.'

'Right. Let's see if that works, then.'

They fell into silence as they made progress across the bridge and the fields, then weaved through the crowd filling the courtyard. The hammering from Holly's barn and general chatter clamoured around them as they headed towards the tasting rooms for *Finchmere Estate Vineyards*.

The group listening to Zeus spilled out through the vast glazed doors. Whether they were squashed inside, or straggling outside, they were all captivated by Zeus's patter.

'The floral notes of a chalk downland are so delicate – so distinctive. You can taste the warm soil, the verdant grasses, the very *blooms* of the vetch and the thyme.'

Generous samples were passed around, and Nell wondered if Zeus's quota had anticipated such a large gathering. Then she wondered if he'd *have* such a large gathering if he weren't being quite so liberal with the wine.

'Now, imagine that bouquet in the heady effervescence of our sparkling wine!' He held aloft another bottle, popped the cork above his head, and the crowd cheered. 'This is a very special bottle, one of only a thousand bottled to mark the milestone occasion of Rufus's birth. A zestier version of our Classic Reserve, this is the Rufus Special Reserve Gold.'

He displayed the bottle's navy label, embossed with a copper outline of Rufus's shaggy head. 'Once you've had the delight of either of these tantalising your taste buds, you'll never celebrate with anything else.'

When he caught Nell's eye, his wide beam faltered. Turning, he poured small samples into the lined-up flutes, then let the crowd surge forward to take them.

'If our wines have delighted your palates today, remember we have some bottles available at a very special Finchmere Fete price.'

Skirting the crowd, he moved to the door to speak to Nell. 'Hey! *Look* at this interest. This is swell.'

'Yes. Very good. All things considered.' Nell patted his arm in sympathy. 'I'm sorry about the morning's news. Are you OK?'

'Me? Of course.'

It was true – he didn't seem to be affected in any way.

'Didn't you know Louise well?' Nell asked. When Zeus shook his head, she shrugged. 'Oh, I must be mistaken. Just . . . People had mentioned that she sometimes popped by to see you. And you said, only this morning, that you'd have liked to see her let her hair down. It sounded like you were acquaintances, at least. So I wanted to pass on my condolences, if she was a friend.'

'I'd pass the time of day with her, sure. But she wasn't exactly a target customer. And I was just teasing her, this morning. I was trying to build a rapport, given we don't really know each other. At all.' His tone was firm.

Nell grimaced, making her tone conspiratorial. 'Little overfamiliar, then, weren't you? If you didn't know each other? I thought you were friends, and you were teasing her. But it sounds a bit different if you don't really know her.'

'Oh. My bad.' Zeus flashed that grin again, but it was rueful this time. 'I'm trying to adopt your dry sense of humour. Forgive me if I don't get the tone just right. Nothing meant by it.'

'Well, look, I just wanted to pass on my condolences. Especially given the ... circumstances. If there's anything you're worried about, or upset, I'm here to help. OK?' Nell held eye contact until he frowned.

'Did ... Did Louise say anything to you?' he asked. 'Before she died?'

Nell nodded. 'Louise said quite a lot to me, actually. Anything you want to clarify?'

He held her gaze for an uncomfortably long moment, but she refused to look away.

Finally, he said, 'No. Nothing I can think of. Just wondered if *you* were worrying. Or upset. This must be difficult, for you and your family. And I'm sure you knew Louise far better than I did. So, my sympathies.'

'Thanks, Zeus. And I'd better leave you to your customers.' Nell stepped back, letting Zeus turn to the crowd again. Instantly, he switched back to his easy bonhomie, as he answered questions and handled purchases.

She and Rav headed away from the bustling courtyard. Clear of the crowds, they sat on the bench under the shade of the copper beech, where she asked, 'Convinced?'

'Not at all. Why would he ask you if Louise had said anything? Guilty as anything.'

'But of which deadly sin?'

'Let's go through them.' Rav nodded towards Nell's pocket and she took the hint to check the photo again.

Reading from the list, she said, 'I'd imagine the sexual morality, adultery and lewdness were aimed at Noah, surely, since you heard Louise accusing him of being predatory. So that leaves theft, murder, greed and deceit.'

'Oh, God.' Rav stared at her. 'Well, you've hit on it, haven't you?'

She frowned. 'I have?'

'Her sermon is directed at more than one person, isn't it? We know of two – you've just summarised Noah's sins. And we know she had an issue with Zeus over something. But what if there are others? You said it yourself, what if Louise had stacked up specific transgressions that she was on some kind of crusade to address?'

Nell saw the horrified look shadow his face as he reached for her phone and checked it. 'Yes. Look.' He turned the screen towards her, so she could see the photo, reading through the cracks that had splintered the glass during Nell's fall. 'She's included murder.' He stared at Nell. 'What if someone's killed *her* now to cover up *another* murder?'

He handed the phone back but before he regained his grip on the crutches, he ran his hand through his hair – telling Nell exactly how fearful he was.

Then he gave an agonised groan. 'And you've just suggested to Zeus that you know what Louise's concern with him was. If *he's* the one on her list who's guilty of murder – and he killed Louise because she found that out – that means you've just put yourself right in the firing line.'

Friday 7th July – 2 p.m.

As James skirted the fete, walking over the fields to the courtyard café to speak to Noah – who'd pleaded being too busy clearing up after lunch to come over to the meeting room at Finchmere Hotel – he had a feeling Gigi would join them, despite their workload.

He knew it was a dubious tactic, to question them in their workplace while they were flat out. But lying under questioning took mental effort. A suspect distracted with work would have less brainpower to spend on any cover stories they might cook up – and that improved his chances of getting to the truth. When it came to investigating murder, James was quite happy to use any ploy available.

Approaching the café, he had to dodge the queue of customers stretching across the courtyard, despite everyone recently having had lunch. People must be buying treats to take home, or grabbing an extra coffee as they visited the stands. Inside, the two baristas fulfilled orders for drinks, pastries, cheese, charcuterie, hampers and condiments with great dexterity.

As he and Ed pushed their way towards the back of the café, Noah's warm smile at a customer faded. He flung a tea towel down on a counter and stomped over.

A third barista finished cleaning a nozzle on the coffee machine and seamlessly moved into Noah's space, completing the order, while Gigi appeared from the storeroom, her hand covering her mouth, as if she was worried.

'Noah, Gigi, thank you for speaking to me, when I know you're so busy.'

'This timing is far from *parfait*.' Gigi sat, making it look like a magnificent flounce. 'Our delighted visitors wish to take a taste of Finchmere home, and we need to satisfy them.' Her spiky gaze followed a barista with a man-bun taking a massive box of coffee from the storeroom to the counter.

'I only need to speak to Noah – for now,' James reasoned. 'So I don't need to keep you both from your customers.'

Gigi shifted, and a flash of irritation clouded Noah's features.

With an elegant shrug, Gigi countered, 'You say *for now*. So you will probably need to speak with both of us eventually. So. Let us get this over with.'

'I see.' James kept his tone level – but he wasn't convinced Gigi was here for altruistic reasons, from the hot, sidelong glances she shot at her husband. James attempted a disarming smile. 'I only have a few routine questions. Thank you for helping us with our inquiries.' He gestured towards the camera that Ed had set up, and which was already recording, and made the formal introductions.

Then James turned to Noah. 'As you may know by now, this is a murder inquiry. We have reason to believe that you were the last person to have seen Louise Brimstone alive.'

'No.' Noah shook his head, clamping his hands into his armpits as he folded his arms.

'At approximately 9 a.m. Just as the fete was opening.'

Gigi's sidelong glance at her husband was tense.

'No,' he repeated.

'You were seen near the church, heading inside to speak to her.'

'No.'

Gigi had settled back in her chair, looking uber-casual – *too* casual – as her assessing gaze flicked from James, to Ed, to her husband.

Sensing they had reached an impasse with Noah, James switched tactic, without warning.

'And what did you speak to Louise about this morning, Gigi?'

'At the breakfast meeting at Finchmere House?' She shrugged. 'Nothing.'

'No, when you went to see her at the chapel. What was so important that you had to speak to her about today – of all days?'

'*Bof! Rien!* Nothing.'

'It can't have been nothing,' James pressed. 'Not on such a busy day. So, tell me. If you don't, it's only going to look suspicious, isn't it?'

'It was a minor issue,' Gigi insisted. 'But Louise had got confused. I didn't really have the time to speak to her, you are right. But I could see she was getting herself . . . agitated. I thought it was a . . . a . . . *kindness* to take a few moments to put her right.'

'Oh?' James inched closer on his chair, his tone warm, inviting. 'Very good of you. And what was it that she was so agitated – *wrongly*, I realise – about?'

'Like I said. A minor matter.' Her chin lifted.

Noah's heaving chest told James he was onto something. *Did Noah know why Gigi had gone to see Louise? Were their two visits related?*

But Gigi pursed her lips, shaking her head. 'It is not relevant. I assure you.'

'That's for me to determine, Gigi. And if you don't willingly tell me, then I'll be diverting resources from my investigative team to find out. Because usually people show *kindness*,' he echoed her sentiments back to her, 'enough to be transparent when it means helping a murder inquiry.'

'She had the wrong idea about something private. To do with me. I could easily correct her, put her mind at rest. She was worrying for no reason.'

'And what was that wrong idea, Gigi?'

'I have put those thoughts to rest, Inspector. I do not care to raise them in someone else's mind. Let that be enough.'

James could see he wasn't going to find out this way. So he changed tack again, hoping to catch Noah off guard.

'Where were you on Wednesday evening?'

'Uh . . . Wednesday?' He glanced sideways at his wife. 'I can't remember, I'll need to check.'

'We were at home, weren't we?' Gigi said. 'Checking hampers. Together.'

'Ah, yeah.'

'What about Thursday night?'

Gigi frowned and side-eyed her husband.

'Home early, for a bit of a relax,' Noah said. 'And then I just had this nagging feeling I needed to check some stock.' He hugged Gigi. 'We both did, didn't we?'

'Mm-hmm.' Gigi's lips set in a line. 'We have so much to keep track of, for this event. Don't we, *mon chéri*? It gets quite exhausting.'

James glanced between them, sensing the discord. 'And where were you, at 9 a.m. this morning, Noah?'

'Um . . .' Noah turned to Gigi again.

'If you assert that you weren't speaking with Louise at that time, perhaps you can tell me where you actually were?'

'I . . . I was getting our stand ready to open. In the food hall.'

James held eye contact with him for a second – recalling that Noah hadn't been on that stand when he'd walked through the showground – and Noah had to drop his gaze.

'My officers, who are currently checking everyone's whereabouts, will be able to confirm that, will they?'

'Or . . . Or . . . I might have been here.'

Gigi shot her husband a sharp glance. 'You were here, *mon chéri*. Remember? You were checking the stock, worrying that we hadn't got enough for such a busy weekend. You were pacing about, counting boxes. You gave me quite the headache!' Gigi rolled her eyes. 'My husband is a worrier, Inspector.'

'And you, Gigi? What did you do after you spoke to Louise?'

'I came back here. As you said, we had a busy day ahead.'

'You came straight here?' James pressed. 'No detours on the way?'

'Yes, I came straight back here.' Gigi uncrossed then recrossed her legs, as Noah shot her a tense glance.

'Good.' James terminated the interview with an amiable smile as he stood, but he didn't want to leave them feeling too complacent, so he added, 'How lucky that you both have staff who can account for your every move. Especially if someone was wrong about seeing you near Louise immediately before she was killed. And *especially* if Louise had concerns that you needed to silence.'

As he and Ed pushed past the customers again, and out to the courtyard, James realised how good it was to pull fresh air into his lungs, out of the tense atmosphere in the café.

Leaving Ed to inveigle his way to the front of the queue to question the baristas and see if their versions of events matched Gigi's and Noah's, James crept round to the back of the café, where the deliveries were made, tiptoeing over the gravel. He held his breath as he listened.

Gigi's growl had a manic note to it. '*Imbécile! Qu'est-ce que tu as fait?*'

'I haven't *done* anything, Gigi. That's all you, isn't it? But you know bloody well what I've been thinking. You've known all along. Let's just hope that bloody detective doesn't think the same, eh?'

Chapter 17

Even here, sitting on the bench, set away from the fete, passers-by spotted them.

A group of fans approached, saying, 'We love *Following Finchmere!*'

'Thanks for an amazing day!'

'We saw Rufus! *So cute!*'

'Will you sign this for us, Rav?'

With a brief nod, he reached for the book and signed it quickly. 'Hope you enjoy the book. Thanks for coming.'

He drew his rucksack towards him like a shield, opening it as he half-turned away, towards Nell, to ask, 'Do you want some water?' hoping the group would take the hint and move on.

Thankfully, they did, and Rav peered into his bag to find his water bottle.

But he saw something else. A picture.

'Um. Don't react but—'

'What do you mean, "don't react"?' Nell demanded, twisting around to stare at him.

'Yeah. Like that. That's perfect.' He pulled out his water bottle, but stared at the picture, committing it to memory.

'Someone's put something in my bag.'

Nell gaped, looking around.

'Again, excellent work on the not-reacting front.'

'*How?*' Nell insisted.

'It's a paper copy of a photo of us. But I mean it. If this is from the stalker, then they could be watching us. Our reaction could be feeding their sick obsession. So *please* just play it cool.'

'OK.' Nell nodded and took a long sip of water, gazing around the fete as if they were just enjoying the view, having a quiet moment.

The photo had felt instantly familiar, yet somehow it looked different.

Taking a long gulp of water, he gazed around like Nell had done. But he wasn't looking at the view. His mind's eye was fixed on the image he'd just seen, recalling every detail.

'It's that black-and-white photo of you and me, taken after we'd done the first full estate-wide survey to see the results of the first round of rewilding work. Remember?'

It wasn't a glamorous photo, but it was one he loved. It marked a vital milestone: their surveys had proved the success of their ecological enhancements, through the incredible diversity of birds, invertebrates and mammals – especially rare species. Their elation shone through the mud that streaked their faces after weeks of hard work.

The photo's placement by Imelda and Hugo in Finchmere's hall had marked another milestone for Rav: its inclusion with other family pictures had shown him that Nell's parents saw him as part of the family. That quiet, meaningful gesture – that had meant the world to him – had now been exploited by the person trying to harm those very relationships.

Emotion choked his words. 'The . . . copy of the . . . picture, in my bag, has been . . . vandalised.'

'Let me guess.' Nell leaned back. 'My eyes have been poked out?'

'You've been cut out entirely.'

Savage cut marks had sliced Nell out of the picture, even carefully tracing around Rav's arm to ensure that all of him – and none of her – was in the photo. The act to remove Nell was pointed and vindictive.

She blew out a long exhale. 'This doesn't really change anything, does it? We already know that I'm a target. We know it's someone here and that they'd accessed the house.'

Rav heard her voice shaking, however hard she may be trying to sound nonchalant. 'But I *am* concerned that they've got close enough to you today to be able to slip this, unnoticed, into your bag,' she said. 'When we've got the place crawling with security on high alert.'

Her brows gathered, making her gaze fearful.

Nodding, Rav tried to look unruffled as he voiced his darkest terror. 'That's what I'm thinking. And if they can get close to me . . .'

He couldn't finish the sentence. But he could vow to himself to keep her safe. Whatever it took.

Noticing the brief lull in customers at Zeus's tasting room, James took the opportunity to see him while Ed was still questioning the baristas at *Graze!*.

From across the bar, he asked, 'What were you doing on Wednesday evening, Zeus?'

Zeus frowned. 'Couldn't say. Lemme check.' Pulling up the diary on his phone, his smile faded. With a swallow, he shoved his phone away. 'Working, most likely. On my own.'

'And Thursday evening?' James asked.

'I was home, taking advantage of an early finish, ready for today.'

James waited a beat. 'Sure? Nothing you want to add? Anyone who can confirm your whereabouts?'

'Nope. No one.'

With a frown, James left him. A career in detecting did wonders for your upside-down reading skills, and he'd noted Zeus's diary entry: Meeting Chuck and Ryan.

If he's got alibis, why the hell would he lie?

As he strolled towards the main tent, Ed caught up.

'You were right about Noah and Gigi.' Ed panted as he fell into step with him. 'Their four baristas in the café, and their other two baristas in the food hall, were very shifty about where their employers had been. No positive confirmations from any of them to say that Gigi and Noah were checking stock.'

'Can we rely on that? Or could they have been too busy to notice?'

Ed shrugged. 'They did all caveat that the morning was hectic: they had their own items to check, lots of preparation to do, so they could easily not have noticed.'

'Great.' James wondered where he might find a statement he could depend on.

But Ed shot him another sidelong look. 'Even so, and this is just policeman's nose, the things those baristas said just . . . Well, they didn't ring true to me.'

Agreeing, James checked his beeping phone. Rav's text flashed: *The stalker's left something in my bag. I haven't touched it. Could one of you just pick it up and investigate? We're sitting on the bench near the courtyard. I don't want to create a fuss in an obvious way because it's a copy of the photo that's in the hall of Finchmere House.*

James's blood ran cold.

Conor may be overseeing the house security, but they were a team, and James had overall responsibility for strategising their approach in response to a criminal.

And this was *proving* that their adversary believed they could outwit the police. Right under their noses.

Yet James had to concede that the stalker was right – they *had* managed to outwit them. No one – none of his team or Conor's, nor Nell and Rav – had any idea who it was.

Scanning the grounds, James spotted Rav sitting with Nell, and headed straight over, finding an innocuous excuse. There was no obvious audience, but he couldn't afford to risk anything. This person was apparently everywhere, yet completely invisible. 'Hey, Rav, we're looking for a tow rope. Don't suppose you've got anything we could use?'

'Oh, sure.' Rav's smile was tense as he played along. 'There's a couple in my kit bag, there. Take the whole bag and use whatever you need.'

'Thanks, mate.' James hefted the surprisingly heavy backpack, strode towards Finchmere House and asked Ed, 'Can you call in a SOCO team to the house? We'll meet them there.'

As much as James was trying to sound like he had things in hand, he was inwardly alarmed. This was a major failure. The artisans might have been in the house for breakfast, but there was no way they should have had an opportunity like that.

He had no idea what their adversary would do next – but he did know that every success was making them bolder.

Friday 7th July – 3 p.m.

Nell's hand was nearly crushed from how hard Rav was squeezing it. 'This isn't a bad thing, you know?' He sounded like he was trying to convince them both.

She raised her eyebrows at him.

'Hear me out. They're showing more and more of their hand, aren't they? And . . . Look, I have an idea. It might be crazy, but still, it may get us a little bit closer to the truth.'

'Go on.'

'How about I find a few more reasons to speak to the artisans? I could do a couple of interviews. Kat has asked for more, so that's easy enough. And you team up with James to get the inside track on what the police have found. We can then compare notes and get to an answer – hopefully the culprit – sooner.'

'I don't like the idea of you interviewing alone—'

'What if I go with Kat and also take Erin? She's desperate to do more filming.'

'Won't that put her in the stalker's sights?'

'Only if she's an idiot. After the other night, I think she'll be too embarrassed. Besides, I think we're onto something. If Louise *was* tracking transgressions, then I want to use that excuse to dig a bit more.'

Nell knew he was counting on tweaking her investigative interest enough to make her concede. When she scrunched her face up, unable to resist the idea, he beamed.

'I knew you'd go for it. We have a free couple of hours today, don't we? Farewells to visitors shortly, with an early finish so stallholders can reset for tomorrow. Then drinks at the bar this evening. In between, I'll see what I can get Kat to agree to, filming-wise.'

Nell sighed. 'Worth a try.' She fixed Rav with a hard gaze. 'I don't like it, but I do see your point about trying to accelerate what we can find out.' She stood. 'Speaking of that farewell to visitors, they'll all be assembling in the tent for the parting words and gift bags.'

They headed over in silence. Sylvia was ready, despite the concern under her bright smile, with rows of bags lined up. All they had to do was hand them out and thank everyone for coming.

Nell didn't even mind when Erin inveigled herself onto the team and helped; if it made the farewells go faster, all the better.

As they watched the last of the guests stream towards the exit, Nell turned to the artisans – wondering who amongst them was wreaking all this awful havoc – and forced herself to smile.

'Well, today went . . . far better than any of us could have hoped.' Even if one of them was guilty, all the others had put on a brave face, after hearing about Louise and being questioned by James. 'Louise wasn't just a huge driver of community events, she was a real champion of the work here, so I hope today we might have made her proud. You all deserve a well-earned early finish today. And I hope I'll see you to say thank you tonight, and to raise a glass in Louise's honour, at the hotel bar.'

Before anyone could move off, Rav lunged towards Kat. 'Hey, Kat? Could we fit in some more filming today? I've got a few ideas.'

Nell saw the ears of Erin, Bea and Holly prick up as they stared at Rav, expectant.

'Great! I hoped to get some words about today with our artisans.' Kat smiled at the assembled team. 'I thought we could use them as teasers for tomorrow and Sunday. So yes, Rav, let me know what you'd like to do.'

At the general nods, she continued, 'Did you have anything else in mind?'

'Yes. Depends on who's free, I guess.' Rav shrugged. 'I was just thinking that some extra interviews could be good to fit in while we have some time – a workshop with Holly, where I make and put up a bat box could be fun. Or seeing Bea's honey-extraction process.'

'I'm free,' Bea spoke up, surprisingly quick off the mark for one usually so placid and deliberate. 'Now, if you like?'

Kat nodded. 'Great. Give me a minute to assemble the kit and we'll head over.'

'I'll join you,' Erin said.

'Oh, great idea, Erin, thanks!' Rav gave no hint he'd been expecting her to volunteer.

As Erin shot Rav an adoring smile, dread roiled in Nell's stomach.

Friday 7th July – 3.30 p.m.

James was relieved at how fast the SOCO team had arrived. In the hall of Finchmere House, he'd immediately spotted the photo Rav had mentioned. In it, Nell and Rav looked dishevelled and muddy – clearly having just completed some extensive ecological work – and also utterly radiant.

As an officer processed Rav's bag, photographing everything, dusting for fingerprints, bagging and labelling every item, James saw the copy of the photo, and how Nell had been hacked out of it.

Around him, the taped-off hall was dusted for fingerprints, searched for any samples. But the space was immaculate, with everything polished to a high shine. He knew they'd find nothing.

He fought to hide his despair, unsure if they were looking for a stalker and a killer, or a stalker who had already escalated to murder.

How the hell am I going to find them, before they do anything else?

His dark thoughts were interrupted by his phone ringing, and he recognised the number of the Fire Investigator.

'James? It's Jackie. I've got that update you wanted. You're not going to like it.'

Chapter 18

Rav tried to keep the conversation going as he limped alongside Bea, Kat and Erin.

He couldn't help noticing the sidelong glances that Bea kept shooting Erin, so he'd been trying to make introductions and find common ground. But Erin was being typically difficult.

Just what I need.

'Erin and I used to work together at EcoLogical Solutions. She's been doing some training at Finchmere, and the occasional bit of presenting.'

'Yes, I've seen that.' Bea's tone was a little starchy. As Rav's questioning glance flicked at her, she mumbled, 'I've seen all your episodes.' She eyed Erin. 'Erin's a bit more . . . outgoing on camera than Nell.'

'I think cameras make Nell quite self-conscious.' Now Rav said it out loud, that was hardly surprising. Nell's ordeal with an ex-boyfriend, who'd circulated an intimate video of the two of them, had been a traumatic violation of her privacy. Rav winced at the memory of it, and his unhelpful reaction. Deciding deflection was best, he teased Erin. 'Whereas Erin's never been hampered by modesty.'

With a grin, Erin pushed him playfully. It was gentle, but enough to send him off balance, rolling on his ankle, and he swallowed the swear word as he hid his wince.

'Rav and I have always had really great chemistry,' she was saying to Bea. 'Haven't we, Rav?'

She turned an angelic smile towards him, but he was still too intent on holding in his grimace to correct her.

Ahead of them was the two-bar chestnut paling fence that Bea had mentioned. He managed to double over and slide through the gap, then manhandle his crutches through.

Erin jumped over, nimble but noisy, which irritated Rav, given they were both ecologists and used to moving silently in woodland. But they all had to wait as Bea made heavy weather of the manoeuvre. She looked embarrassed as she straightened up and pointed ahead of them, as if relieved to distract them.

'We're here. This is my place.'

As they passed the ancient, gnarled yew – with its signs of recent pruning to supply Holly with wood – and pushed through the pink blossoms of the vast camellia bushes marking the woodland edge, a fringe of wildflowers led into the cottage garden, which was frothing with bellflowers, lady's mantel, forget-me-nots, roses and lacecaps. The blooms led to the unexpectedly large detached, timbered and tile-hung cottage.

'I'll take you over there.' Bea pointed at a neat outbuilding. 'It's the extraction room.'

A higgledy-piggledy brick path wound through spires of hollyhocks and lupins. As they walked past, grazing the fragrant stocks, phlox and drifts of lavender, the flowers' scent flooded the air with sweetness.

A narrow stream formed the far boundary of the garden, its bank smothered with nettles – more than enough for Gigi and Noah to forage for their new cheese.

When Rav spotted the white pitched-roof hives scattered amongst daisy-headed rudbeckia and cobalt stars of borage, which were fuzzy with lazy honeybees, he realised Bea's care for her garden was an extension of her love for her pollinators. Her work had started here, before Nell's family had granted her the use of Finchmere land.

Bea looked delighted at his obvious admiration. 'Borage is ideal for my bees because it refills its nectaries every few minutes. So, they literally can't get enough.'

Taking the opportunity to pause, he leaned on his crutches, not wanting his exhaustion to show. He scratched around for something to say. 'Miraculous, isn't it, that borage is so good for bees? Considering it would make humans ill.'

Surprise flashed over Bea's face. 'Yes. The transformations along the food chain that we don't even think about. You have to be careful; unlike borage, the nectar from some plants remains toxic to humans. I read somewhere that whole armies – like the one for Pompey the Great, I think – have been struck down just by the honey they ate. Imagine getting drunk and delirious, then the gastro issues . . . and then death. From an unassuming little pot of honey. It's fascinating . . '

She glanced up and shot Rav a self-conscious smile. But now his observations of her gorgeous garden were more analytical.

With a prickle of unease, he realised there was an abundance of deadly specimens masquerading behind deceptive, beguiling beauty: the dependable-looking yew bore heart-stopping taxine; deadly digitalis hid in every part of the elegant foxgloves; powerful opiates like morphine lurked in the delicate poppies. The graceful mauve bells of larkspur and columbine would scatter fatal seeds, while the spectacular passionflower rambling over the door contained alkaloids that would produce cyanide.

His eye continued to assess the garden, following the dusty-pink clematis climbing over the terrace's pergola, as it blended with the golden honeysuckle to thread along the haphazard hedge that ran along the quiet lane at the front of the house. In the hedgerow, between the hazel, hawthorn and elder, Rav saw something else was lurking.

Erin must have followed the same sight line, as she asked, 'Oh! What's that, in your hedge, Bea? Blueberries? *Yum*. Oh, no, is it blackthorn? I wish I'd known you had some. I'd thought about entering sloe gin in Nell's precious produce competition.'

'Oh jeez!' Rav laughed. '*Erin!* You should know better! Don't go foraging until your botany improves! It's far too early for sloes. Look closer. Those single berries are flatter, see?' He pointed, not wanting to touch the plant. 'That's *Atropa belladonna*. Fatal.'

'Or medicinal, depending on your point of view,' Bea said. 'I know it seems so delicate. But it's powerful.'

As Bea bestowed on him a smile that was clearly intended to reassure him, Rav attempted to divert the conversation. 'Huh, I don't recognise that plant, Bea? The shrubby one, in that sunny spot, that looks like miniature sweet chestnut with a spike of flowers?'

'Oh, that?' Bea shrugged 'That's a castor oil plant.' She walked towards the house, beckoning him and Erin to follow.

As the scientific name for it needled his memory – *Ricinus communis* – Rav recalled that the whole plant, especially the seeds, contained deadly ricin.

He couldn't help gaping at Bea as she led them inside, oblivious to his reaction. Her idyllic garden was crammed with deadly toxins.

And he sensed Bea was only too well aware.

Once Rav had gone, Sylvia had sidled up to Nell and squeezed her arm. 'I'll oversee the clearing up and winding everything down today. Everyone knows what they're doing. It'll be a military operation.'

'Thanks, Sylvia. I want to catch up with James, if I haven't already missed him.'

'Good idea.'

As Nell sent him a text, she wondered where they could meet. Assuming he was still at the house, she made her way over there. Finding no Land Rovers free as the teams around her went into overdrive, she walked as briskly as her sprained ankle allowed, purging her jangling nerves.

By the time she'd reached the guarded stone bridge, James had replied:

Meet you at the hotel bar in 30? If you've got time, we should head over to your house from there.

It was a good suggestion, to meet away from prying eyes. The thought of going home filled her with dread. She couldn't bear to face the devastation again.

She checked her pocket for her own car key, headed towards the mews garage and eased herself into her electric RS Audi.

Reaching the hotel a few minutes later, she parked in one of the reserved bays beside the entrance and headed along the path, around the circular drive with its ornamental fountain. Unexpected raised voices made her stop, and listen.

They came from beyond the entrance, towards the screened

side of the hotel. Men yelling – and she could detect an accent . . . *American?*

Reaching for her walkie-talkie, Nell radioed in. 'Hi, this is Nell. Call for security to attend the hotel's front entrance. Sounds like some men having a disagreement, and I don't want things to escalate. Over.'

Hoping she'd have backup soon, Nell headed over to see what was happening.

The trellis screen, planted with fragrant jasmine, disguised the bins and recycling point in more ways than one. The smell of cigarette smoke hit Nell as she rounded the corner.

Three men were there: two golden-tanned blond men were facing her, their expressions angry, while the third man had his back to her. But he was unmistakable, with his bald head and tweed suit.

'Zeus?'

He wheeled around on the spot at the sound of her voice.

'Is everything OK here?'

'Nell . . . Dr Ward . . . Lady—'

'What's going on?' Nell interrupted his uncharacteristic stuttering, as her worry mushroomed.

'Lady Beaumont!' one of the blond men said in a Californian drawl. 'Finally, we meet.' His disarming smile bared blindingly white teeth. In his pastel linen jacket, he and his colleague, wearing a short-sleeved shirt, looked like out-of-place tourists.

'Isn't for want of trying,' his colleague said, offering his handshake. 'You're a most elusive woman. I'm Ryan Goldstein, and this is my colleague, Chuck Garrod.'

Warily, Nell shook their hands, seeing how it made Zeus wince. The names were oddly familiar and she took a moment to recall them. 'Ah. You're the vintners from Napa Valley . . .' Were they Zeus's former colleagues? Associates? As she looked at them, their chests heaving, their glances aggressive, she wondered what their history was.

'We scheduled a meeting with you,' Ryan said. 'But you pushed it out into next week.'

As Zeus cringed, the two men stepped towards her, like they were squaring up to her now. Taking a step back, Nell wished she'd cancelled their meeting, rather than postponed it. Maybe they wouldn't have hung around, hassling her team, if she had.

'I asked what's going on here,' she repeated, sounding calmer than she felt.

'I'm sure Zeus would like to put you in the picture.' Ryan circled Nell, walking towards her, making her turn to face him, then back up.

'Yeah, that's right, isn't it, Zeus?' Chuck clapped a hand on Zeus's shoulder, his grip so hard that Nell could see his knuckles whiten.

'If you've got a complaint to raise, this isn't how you should go about it—'

'Well, as you know, we requested a meeting,' Chuck pointed out, releasing Zeus's shoulder with a forceful push that made him stagger towards Nell.

'Yeah.' Ryan sneered. 'Going through the proper channels hasn't gotten us anywhere.'

'So now we're having to rely on our . . . natural resourcefulness,' Chuck said. His too-white shark-like smile made Nell's hackles shiver. With rising panic, she saw she'd been cornered.

Her heart hammered as she scanned the distant driveway. No one was close enough to hear if she yelled. In fact, she realised with a plummeting heart, the place was deserted.

Where are security? No one's replied. Has anyone heard?

'Not on my estate, you're not.' Nell squared up to them. 'There's no place for behaviour like this here, whether you're on business or as a guest. So, your stay is over. Kindly leave.'

The two men looked at each other and burst out laughing. 'We're guests of the hotel! You can't throw us out! We're not the issue here. Aren't you at least a little curious why Zeus is so silent?'

'You're going to quietly go up to your rooms right now, and pack, then leave within the next ten minutes. Understand?'

'But you don't have any grounds to throw us out!' Ryan looked incensed. 'You didn't hear what was going on. We've paid good money, we could sue—'

'You'll receive a full refund.'

Zeus glanced at her, his body language twitchy, breathing heavy. He expected trouble.

'You're not listening, lady. You need to know what we have to say, believe me.'

'Not like this, I don't. And you'll go. Now.' Nell took a step closer to them.

'And how are you going to make us?' Chuck asked, stepping towards her.

Nell nearly buckled in relief to see Conor lurking in the background, assessing before he moved in. For his benefit, Nell repeated her request.

'As I said, you're going to go to your rooms, pack, and leave within ten minutes. Starting now.'

Conor nodded at Nell, radioed in for backup and moved in. As he clapped both men on the shoulder, he made them jump, their eyes bulging.

'Let's go, shall we, gentlemen?'

Chapter 19

Friday 7th July – 4.15 p.m.

In the small whitewashed outhouse, Rav was struggling to look at ease in front of the camera, as Bea went through her process of slicing off the wax and placing the honey-filled combs into the extractor.

He was grateful for the whirring spin of the machine as Bea cranked the handle, hoping that Kat's focus of the camera on the noise and movement might distract from his discomfort.

'How long does it take to spin all the honey out of the combs?' Erin had to raise her voice above the rattling, and Rav hoped that the footage wouldn't be a pain for Kat to edit.

'Hmmm.' Bea's nose crinkled as she thought. 'These frames will only take about twenty minutes to spin. So they should be pretty much finished now.' She let the spinning wind down and checked the combs. 'Yes, these all look empty of honey. Which means we can start to drain and sieve it to remove all the impurities.'

She opened the tap at the bottom of the extractor, lined up over a strainer, and the thick golden liquid oozed out.

'Ah, I see the wax collecting there, on the sieve,' Rav said.

'And the best part is seeing the seasonal variations, as well as the differences you can taste, depending on the plants the bees have taken their nectar from. I've got some samples, which show exactly that, over here.' As she pointed, her hand brushed Rav's shoulder.

'Oh, sorry, Bea.' Rav pointedly moved aside, wondering if her move had been deliberate.

Unbothered, she gestured at the array of honeys of different shades, all immaculately labelled with season, flowers that had provided the nectar source, and which hives they'd come from. They were lined up below an apothecary cabinet of dried herbs, berries and flowers, all sending spicy green scents into the air around them.

'I made these jars of honey so that I could provide some tasting samples at the fete, as well as selling some. You can try them, if you like?'

When Erin held out her hand in eagerness, Bea turned back, selecting samples with care and finding tasting swizzle sticks. Eventually, she turned back to them, presenting a tray of options.

Bea twirled a clean sample stick in the first jar for Erin to try. The honey was a rich bronze and aromatic.

'Mmm. It seems complex, deep somehow in flavour.'

'Exactly.' Bea smiled. 'Now try this.' She offered Erin a sample from a second jar of pale gold honey.

'Mmm. Yes, I can taste the difference. This is sweeter, a bit lighter?'

With a beam at Erin's reaction, Bea explained, 'It's the difference between summer and spring. It's really noticeable, isn't it? I always list what plants are in bloom while the bees are producing the honey, and you can start to taste the flavour profiles of the flowers.'

Rav feared Bea would turn to him and offer the same taste test. After seeing the deadly plants hiding in plain sight, behind the beautiful blooms of her cottage garden, he just couldn't bring himself to try any. Instead, he leaned forward and provided the link Kat was waiting for, to draw the segment to an end. 'And anyone can taste the seasonal differences if they find you at the fete, then, Bea?'

As she nodded, Rav concluded, 'This has been a fantastic insight into how you produce such delicious honey.' He turned to the camera. 'And it's just one of the many delights people can have fun exploring at Finchmere Fete.'

He held the warm smile for a few seconds, until Kat said, 'That's great. Thanks, all.'

As Kat dismantled her kit, Bea studied the stacked jars of honey. 'I keep trying to persuade Noah to sell some of my honey alongside his cheese.' She ran her fingers along the descriptions, before selecting a golden jar. 'This should be perfect. Summery and floral to offset the richer notes of the cheese.' She hugged it to her chest and moved towards the door.

Rav followed, with Erin, who fanned her hand at her throat. 'Bea, can I get a quick drink of water before we head back? That honey was delicious, but—'

'Oh, sure.' A wince flitted across Bea's face. 'Um . . . Take a seat on the terrace and I'll bring out some drinks.' She hurried outside, leaving them to pack up and wait for her.

Moving slowly, Rav made his way on his crutches out to the garden. Kat followed after a few moments, having packed up her kit with an efficiency born of practice. But Erin had bounded ahead and was heading towards the house.

As Erin wandered in through the kitchen door, calling, 'May I use your loo, too?' Rav heard a glass break and Bea's scream.

Hobbling quickly, he peered inside through the kitchen's latticed window, while Kat dashed past him to the door.

Bea had frozen, turned away from the sink, gaping at Erin, who'd come to an abrupt stop near the doorway.

Erin was staring across the kitchen, at something Rav couldn't quite make out.

'I'll bring the drinks out.' Bea strode across the room, shooing Erin outside so forcefully that she hurriedly backed out, making Kat stumble backwards, too.

Once both women were over the threshold, Bea slammed the door shut. Erin turned to Kat, stunned. 'I only wanted to quickly dash to the loo. I didn't expect *that*!'

Kat's gaze flicked from Erin to the window, where a tense-looking Bea was sweeping up the broken glass.

'Did you see it?' Erin hissed at Kat in disbelieving glee. 'On the fridge? Oh my *God*!'

At the lack of reply from Kat, Erin leaned back to see if Bea was still occupied, then she held up her phone, zoomed in and snapped a photo. Sniggering, she headed over to the table, sitting on one of the wooden chairs.

Rav joined her, curious. Then Kat did, too, saying, 'It's fair enough, Erin. Maybe Bea just doesn't like people traipsing through her home? Some people are very private.'

'Yeah, and I can tell you why,' Erin spluttered, showing them the photo she'd just taken. 'She clearly doesn't get many visitors. Not to be putting psycho things like *this* on display!'

As she turned her screen towards Rav, that prickle of dread shivered over him again.

Bea's fridge was smothered with pictures. At first glance, it looked like a montage of her friends, cut out from printed photos.

Then, with his stomach churning, his heart *thundering*, Rav realised that all of them were of him.

Chapter 20

Rav couldn't have hobbled back to Finchmere any quicker. He just wanted to get himself – and Erin and Kat – out of that uncomfortable, odd situation.

If he overthought it, he'd find himself laughing at the absurdity that he should feel in any way disconcerted about Bea. Quiet, unassuming, apparently sweet – she was absolutely the opposite of threatening.

But who cuts out hundreds of photos of a person they barely know and smothers their fridge in them?

Kat kept silent, but she hadn't missed a nanosecond of the drama, while Erin looked half-horrified, half-delighted at the cruel reveal of Bea's crush. Her thirst for gossip would carry this back to Nell, the artisan team, Sylvia – everyone – though her scandalised side-eye did all the talking for her. He'd have to find a way to rein that in.

Because neither Kat nor Erin knew about his stalker. Or what they'd done.

His shiver was involuntary but, as soon as it passed, he felt like an idiot again.

Is Bea just a lonely woman with a crush? Or does she really have it in her to be the stalker who'd sent threatening texts, disembowelled a rat, attacked Nell in the cellar? And maybe also burned down our home?

He just couldn't believe that.

And, if Bea's crush *was* harmless, if his stalker *was* someone else – who seemed to be in the frame of mind to do something . . . drastic, then he couldn't risk provoking them even further by letting them think an innocent person could take the blame.

Even so, his blood iced as he remembered James saying that women were accomplished at masking.

Despite this uncomfortable, possibly damning, discovery, since they were all returning to the courtyard to film Kat's teasers for tomorrow, all four of them were now walking back *together*.

I should tell James. Even as he thought it, his eyes slid towards Bea, who looked mortified and vulnerable – stumbling over her own feet, embarrassment making her clumsy – and he just couldn't bring himself to make the accusation.

Poor Bea! Rav had to laugh at himself. He forced small talk. If nothing else, it would make the time pass faster. 'That's a lovely home, Bea. How long have you lived there?'

'All my life. My mum passed away, then my gran, just . . . Just recently. But not unexpected.' She attempted a smile. 'So now it's just me.'

'I'm sorry you lost them both so young.'

Bea's sad smile flitted through her mortification. An overwhelming sense of loneliness radiated from her, and Rav could only feel sympathy.

'Still, at least I have my bees. To keep me busy.'

Acknowledging that she was rallying, Rav shot her a smile, then wondered if his empathy was misjudged.

Bea could certainly have taken a quick photo of the picture in Finchmere's hall, when she'd come over for any one of the artisan meetings. She had opportunity – for that and everything else.

What if their other theory was correct? That the stalker and Louise's murderer were one and the same? Would Bea have a reason to kill Lou?

He *had* to remain cautious. He'd be cordial, but ensure he didn't lead Bea on, or fuel false hope: just neutral small talk. He searched for a suitable subject. 'Did you plant the garden yourself?'

'Oh yes, that's all me.' Her smile was a little less tense now, and Rav saw he'd hit on something she'd talk about happily.

'How did you get started?'

'It was a smallholding when my grandparents had it. Left over from the war. Granddad was proud of his vegetables and chickens. He died when I was quite little. Granny and I gradually planted it. It was our project. She took me to buy seeds at the weekend, we'd plant them in the seed trays, nurture them in the greenhouse, and then choose where to plant them.'

'Ah, that sounds like me and my grandmother.' Rav smiled. 'We used to garden together. That got me into botany and, from there, ecology.'

'Oh, how nice that we have that in common!'

Rav inwardly cringed. *Great.*

'I love all the stages of gardening. From planning it all out so carefully – when you prepare the ground and plant the right seeds at the right time – and then, when it all comes together perfectly. Exactly as you planned.'

'Uh-huh.' Something about her quiet delivery made the back of Rav's neck prickle, and he had to resist the urge to shudder. He almost sagged in relief as they reached the field near Bea's wildflower stand and, keen to escape, she made her excuses and dashed away.

Unable to hold in her reaction any longer, Erin spluttered with laughter, which made Bea turn back, blushing bright red, before scurrying on. Unaware, Erin clung to him, chortling.

'Oh, God! Rav, you're priceless! Seeing her mad super-crush and then keeping up small talk about her *gardening*!'

'Yes, well, let's be discreet about that, shall we? Gossip isn't kind. We're the only three who saw that, so I'll know who'll've been blabbing if this gets out.'

Through the tears of mirth streaming down her face, Erin looked surprised. 'My, how very gallant.'

'I mean it. Bea's lost her family. No need to make her feel isolated at work, is there?'

'Oh, well, if you *will* be sick-makingly soft-hearted about it . . .' She rolled her eyes.

Knowing Erin was trying to save face, Rav forced a grin. 'You know me.'

'Yeah.' She nudged him, a touch too conspiratorially. 'I do.'

Wondering if he was imagining everyone being overfamiliar, he told himself to get a grip. Hoping to make the most of the remaining couple of hours of filming, he turned to Kat. 'Where to next?'

'Let's go to the Artisan Courtyard and get some final words on today from Holly, Zeus, Gigi and Noah. If they'll give me some teasers for tomorrow, I can splice in shots of the busy day and use them as signposts for visitors to the fete over the weekend.'

'Sounds good.'

Within minutes, Kat had set up a chair at a bistro table, with the backdrop capturing the great view, and tested the lights and sound.

Rav turned, at the sound of fast footsteps crunching over gravel, to see Zeus come into the courtyard: he was out of breath, and swinging his jacket jauntily over his shoulder, at odds with his grim expression.

'Hey!' Zeus's welcoming tone sounded a little forced. 'What brings you two back here?' He hung his jacket over one of the chairs at a different table, then looked askance at Erin. 'I thought you'd had your fill of Finchmere's finest? But, here you are, back for more!'

'Oh, not today!' Rav spoke for both of them – firmly – holding up his hands. 'Your generosity has already proved too much for us.'

'Yeah, well, I better be careful.' Zeus glanced towards the tasting room, looking a little hunted. 'A few visitors today also enjoyed my generosity a little too well. The sales they generated may have been sky-high – but now I'm all out of samples and if I give any more away, Nell will think I've got some kinda side-hustle going.' His easy laugh made them join him, but he eyed them carefully, and Rav had to wonder why he was being unusually awkward. 'So, what are you here for?'

'We just popped back for any closing remarks on the day, Zeus,' Kat clarified. 'No obligation, but if you want to film one, I'll use it as a teaser over the weekend.'

'Love it!' Zeus grinned. 'Give me a moment, I've got a leftover glass of fizz inside.' Sauntering into his tasting room, he emerged moments later with a flute of sparkling rosé.

Taking his place before the camera, he waited until Kat counted him in. 'Well, what a great day! I just want to raise a toast – of the finest Finchmere Reserve, of course – to all the wonderful visitors who joined us for the first day of Finchmere Fete. I'm looking forward to making merry over the rest of the weekend with even more new friends. Come join me at *Finchmere Estate Vineyards*.' He raised his glass towards the lens and held his dazzling smile for a beat.

'Perfect! Thanks, Zeus,' Kat called out.

As Zeus headed back to his barn, Gigi walked over to Rav, an unsettled expression on her face as she checked her back pocket, then forced a smile.

'Ah, you are here to film the teasers? You can have my thoughts on the day. Happy exhaustion!' She managed a smile, but Rav could feel tiredness – or was it worry? – rolling off her.

Over her shoulder, he spotted Noah rounding the corner, just as Bea ran up behind him. She tapped him on the shoulder and offered the jar of honey she'd chosen.

Rav couldn't quite catch their exchange, but could see that Noah shook his head. Bea wilted, but Noah didn't seem to want to leave it at that. He stepped towards Bea, making her back away, and raised his voice. 'Just leave it now, will you? I've said no, and I mean no. I know that Gigi went along with it for the cake and the nettles, but I don't want to sell any old random crap alongside my quality produce. Got it?'

As Noah strode away, towards Zeus's barn, Bea crumpled. Her whole body sagged before she stumbled away.

Rav got up, trying to see if she was OK, but took a while to untangle himself from the seat and limp over, and by then she'd dashed away. With a heavy sigh, he turned, but caught Noah accosting Zeus, who was walking out from the stockroom end of his barn, holding a box full of bottled wine.

'Hey, Zeus, I heard a couple of guys at the hotel mention you earlier. They were wondering if you're going to call on them. Is that where you're headed?'

'Oh! No, I'm just reorganising stock right now, ready for tomorrow. But I know who you mean. I can drop by when I'm done today. Thanks for the heads-up, man.'

Returning to the table, Rav heard Noah's hurried footsteps crunching behind him.

'More interviews? I better get an agent at this rate!' he joked. 'Or are you here for some well-deserved refreshments?'

'It's our closing remarks,' Gigi said. 'Do you have any?'

'Oh, I'll give you some closing remarks, mate! Abso-bloody-lutely knackering! Will that do?' He stood up straight while Gigi shook out her hair and rolled her eyes, before Kat hit record.

'We've had a bundle of fun at Finchmere,' Noah said. 'It's been mind-blowing to see the response to our food . . .'

'. . . And a delight to see that *our* favourites are *your* favourites.' Gigi beamed.

'We're looking forward to doing it all over again, all weekend long. Whatever you fancy, you'll find it at *Graze!*,' Noah concluded.

'That'll do very nicely, thank you both,' Kat said.

As Kat checked the recording, Gigi pulled her phone from the back pocket of her jeans and sat down. As she did so, Rav spotted a note fall out, which landed under her chair. He was about to point it out, when he recognised the handwriting. Saying nothing, he hoped Gigi wouldn't notice and he'd have a chance to read it.

He'd missed what Erin was saying. '. . . Embarrassed, but you were so kind. Thank you so much.'

'Ah, *petite*, we know the feeling, eh?' Gigi was smiling and stood up to hug her.

Noah moved in to hug Erin, too.

'And thanks for the food and the coffee, Noah.'

Noah's hand landed low on Erin's back, brushing, and then cupping, her bottom, and she pushed him away, outraged. 'What the—?'

'Sorry, sorry!' Noah raised his hands and stepped back. 'Innocent mistake!'

Rav began to protest, but Erin was vocal and forceful, and needed no validation from him as she loudly accused Noah, 'That was absolutely *not* an innocent mistake. You actually *cupped* my bottom!'

'You're hysterical! Why would I . . .?' He half-turned towards Gigi, who'd paused on her way back to the café, and was now slowly walking back.

Rav noticed Holly emerge from her workshop, gripping a chisel.

'Hysterical?' Erin yelled. 'You've got a bloody nerve! Feeling me up, then gaslighting me.'

A laugh exploded from Noah. 'Good luck getting that to stick.' He held his hands up as Gigi stopped beside him. 'I've got a gorgeous wife, here. Why would I go chasing girls like . . . *you*?'

'Good question. You should leave this creep, Gigi. You're worth a million of him! And I hope you get chucked out, assaulting women at your place of work!'

'What did you do?' Gigi demanded. As Noah shrugged, Gigi shoved him. '*What* did you *do*?'

'She's deluded! Claiming all sorts of nonsense! *She* hugged *me*, if you recall!'

'That was sexual assault, right out in the open, in plain sight and everything!' Erin's breathing was rapid with shock and fury. 'And I'll report it. Creeps like you need to know you can't get away with it. How many others have you tried it on with? *Eh?*'

Erin was now yelling at his retreating back, as he hurried off. Gigi stared at Erin for a moment and then, shoulders slumping, turned to follow her husband into the café.

Erin glared at Rav. 'Can you believe it?' She drew in a long breath, steadying herself.

'Are you OK?' Rav asked. 'Do you want me to do anything?'

Erin's chest and shoulders were still heaving at the violation, her cheeks red with outrage. 'No. I'll deal with it.'

As she glared in Noah's and Gigi's direction, Rav leaned down, his phone in his hand, and reached for the note. Under the table, he unfolded it, photographed it and refolded it, and then sat up, blinking as the blood rushed to his head.

'I wish I could convince Gigi she doesn't have to put up with a husband like that,' Erin said.

'She dropped this – you could return it to her . . .' Rav put the note on the table, and Erin needed no further encouragement.

Grabbing the piece of paper, she ran over. 'Hey! Gigi!'

Erin was discreet as she passed Gigi the note, but she clearly had plenty to say. Rav felt relieved that Noah hadn't seen, despite him peering out of the window as he wondered what Erin was saying to his wife.

Glancing at the photo he'd taken of the now familiar handwriting, Rav read: Hebrews 13:4, Proverbs 6:26, Ezekiel 9:10, Psalm 50:21, Isaiah 47:11.

Wondering what the verses would say, Rav pocketed his phone, noting Gigi's tense body language as she – and a stern-faced Noah – watched Erin walk back to the table. Both of their gazes brimmed with suspicion and concern.

Is Gigi worried that Erin read her note?

Even if she had, its meaning wasn't obvious. So a brief glance wouldn't necessarily be revealing . . . Noah, on the other hand, was obviously terrified of whatever Erin intended to do about the assault.

With a too-familiar slither of dread, Rav realised that Erin had just made it abundantly clear, to both of them, that she wasn't the type to keep quiet.

Chapter 21

Friday 7th July – 5.30 p.m.

With her nerves jangling from the encounter with Zeus and the two men, Nell had waited for James. The thought of his arrival made her feel a little better – right up until he sent a text: *Sorry, Nell, held up here. Can I meet you at the courtyard so we can head off sooner?*

Zeus had raced off before Conor had extracted the Californians, clearly unwilling to divulge whatever was at the root of the incident. Even if Zeus had got involved in some kind of scandal, that was so far down her list of priorities right now that she couldn't bring herself to care.

Nell hoped a walk back to Finchmere, along the river, might calm her down. It was lovely on an evening like this, but the journey turned out to be quite a trial. Her injured foot was bearing up well, but she'd been on it all day now, and it was throbbing. Hopefully, she'd arrive when Rav was completing the filming, and they'd be able to take a moment together. As time had gone on, Nell had become more and more twitchy about where Rav was – and *how* he was.

Approaching the courtyard, she passed Bea, who was red-faced and crying. Nell had stopped her to ask if she was OK and Bea had shaken her head, muttered something about 'that bastard Noah' and then dashed off, making Nell wonder what on earth had happened. She'd hesitated, wanting to make sure Bea was all right. If her priority hadn't been finding Rav, Nell would have followed her, to see if she could have got to the bottom of whatever was wrong.

As she approached the barns, Nell saw that Zeus had got there before her, despite not knowing the quick route along the river. But he hadn't hobbled part of the way. Noah was talking to him and, although Nell couldn't hear what they were saying, it looked like

Noah was having the same effect on Zeus as he'd just had on Bea. Once Noah had left, Zeus dumped the box of wine bottles he'd been holding on the floor, and sat on a stack of pallets, rubbing his head.

Pausing to rest her foot, Nell wondered whether she should speak to him or not. But she knew she wasn't in the best frame of mind to listen to what seemed to be an involved story. And Zeus might be overwrought, too, given the long hours of prep the fete had taken, and the shocking murder of someone they all knew.

She'd give him some space, and pick a time to visit when he might be more inclined to confide, so she could find out what was happening.

As she hobbled onwards, she was sure she heard more raised voices. *Not again.* But as she stopped to listen, the noise had passed.

When she finally reached the courtyard – and immediately spotted Rav, perfectly all right and sitting with Kat and Erin at a bistro table – relief rolled through her.

Even though she ached to head straight over to him, she kept her distance. Deciding to check in with the teams and thank them, she popped into *Graze!* with compliments at the ready – then halted at the sound of Gigi and Noah in the middle of a row.

'How *dare* you!' Gigi's accent was thick with rage.

'Don't you think *you're* part of the problem? Or even the bloody cause?' Noah yelled.

Hesitating, Nell wondered if this had anything to do with Louise's death, and she couldn't help but listen – until the couple stormed into the café from the storeroom.

'And another thing—' Noah was saying to Gigi, before stopping dead, and bringing his anger into check. 'Oh . . . Nell . . . Hi.'

'I just wanted to say thank you for today. I hope it's been good for you and the business. But I won't keep you. I know it's also been stressful – and with Louise, of course . . .' She swallowed. 'Anyway. Thank you for all you've done.' Backing away, she managed an appreciative nod.

Out in the courtyard, Holly was giving her final remarks to camera. Nell noticed that her eyes kept sliding towards Rav, a slight blush appearing on her cheeks.

Was she Rav's stalker? She'd have had access to Finchmere today . . . Slinking into the shadow of the barn, Nell watched, wondering if she'd notice any giveaway signs.

Sure enough, once Kat thanked her, Holly moved over towards Erin and Rav. Nell expected Holly to appeal to Rav, asking another favour. Instead, she spoke to Erin.

'I saw w-what happened . . . with N-Noah . . .' Holly stuttered.

Erin nodded. 'He better not try it again, or I'll knee him in the balls. See how he likes being manhandled.' Then her eyes narrowed. 'Don't tell me he's done the same to you?'

Nell saw Holly's nose wrinkle. She hesitated, then forced out the words. 'Yes. He . . . um . . . He kept popping over . . . to my workshop . . . and . . .'

Disgust made Nell's lip curl as she realised what the two young women were talking about.

It was clearly painful for Holly to share this, but Erin was oblivious, and fired up with indignation. 'Oh my *God*!' She jumped up, eyes wide. 'What did you *do*?'

'Well . . .' Holly took a backward step, looking like she wished she hadn't shared this confidence.

Erin frowned, moving forward. 'Yes?'

'What *can* I do? I work here.' Holly shrank away from Erin's ire.

Nell's heart sank at that. Surely, Holly knew she could bring any concerns to her? That she'd take them seriously?

'You can bloody stand *up* for yourself! Jeez. What's *wrong* with you?' Erin waved towards Holly's workshop. 'And in there, you're surrounded by weapons, for God's sake. You've no excuse not to defend yourself. Bloody hell. He'd be a eunuch by now, if I'd been in your position.'

Rav's hand moved to his lap, in subconscious protection, clearly at a loss as to how to diffuse the situation, or address Erin's victim blaming. Then Holly changed the subject, turning to Rav. 'I've, um . . . I've been thinking about what you said, Rav . . .'

Her pained glance at Erin suggested she wished she could ask Rav this privately. But Erin wasn't getting the hint – or rather, she was refusing to get it and, instead, seemed to be enjoying Holly's awkwardness.

'You mentioned doing the bat box earlier.' Holly's faint blush was growing. 'So, um . . . I was wondering . . . Would you be interested . . . in doing something else, like a bigger project? You know . . . together.'

'Maybe.' Rav glanced at Kat. 'Depends on the content, I guess. But I'd be up for a discussion about it.'

'Oh really?' Holly's face lit up. 'I was hoping we could co-present—'

'Now, hold on,' Erin interrupted. 'Rav already has enough superfans trying to monopolise his airtime. He doesn't need any more. After Nell, it's always *me* who co-presents.'

Nell couldn't help gaping at Erin's audacity. Her words weren't completely *un*true, but they certainly overstated Erin's role, and her tone was distinctly proprietorial.

Nell had to wonder if Erin's former feelings for Rav been stirred by their recent work together. And when Nell caught the sly smile on Erin's face, she knew she was right.

Friday 7th July – 6 p.m.

When James spotted Nell, lurking in the shadows between the barns in the courtyard, watching and listening to the artisans, he didn't know whether to be impressed with her irrepressible curiosity or worried for her.

So he didn't give her away, and instead hung back and texted her.

He felt a pang at how the vibration made her jump, the obvious breath she took before looking at the screen. Her shoulders dropped, then she turned and headed towards him.

As they got into his car, James asked, 'Are you OK, going back to your place?'

Nell scrunched her nose. 'No. But I assume you've got a good reason for it.' She looked at him, her face stricken. 'I don't feel ready to go back and pick over it all. Not yet.'

'I know.' James's tone was gentle. 'But I think you should understand the findings.'

Nell side-eyed him. 'Maybe you'll make me feel better about it by sharing how your investigation is going, then?'

He had to smile at that. Then he sighed. 'Not much to report. Well, not as much as we *need*, given how things are escalating.' He tried not to let his worry leak into his expression.

'So why the house visit, then? Is there news?'

James nodded, pulling into Nell's open gateway. He waved at someone sitting in the car already parked there. As they all got out, he made the introductions.

'Nell, this is Jackie, the Fire Investigator. Jackie, this is Nell.'

'Hi, James. Nice to meet you, Nell. Sorry it's under these circumstances. Right, I've completed your assessment today. Usually, I'd send in my report, but given James's investigation, I passed on the findings straight away, and he suggested I talk you through them.'

'OK . . .' Nell shot them both a questioning glance.

As Jackie gestured towards what was left of Nell's burned, disintegrating barn, she was forced to turn and look at it.

Last time she was here, she hadn't known about the stalker, or any threat, and she hadn't been attacked. Now, that was a constant sinister undercurrent, drowning out every other thought. The need to be even more careful, even more private, clamoured like a warning burst of birdsong in her head.

All this – just when her home had been destroyed, and that dereliction had revealed all her inner, private life. All the things she kept behind such tightly closed doors were out in the open, ruined, ashen, her whole life horribly exposed.

'James tells me you're a scientist, Nell, so I thought you'd appreciate understanding the investigation. Let me show you our key finding.'

James saw Nell swallow and clamp her lips as she followed Jackie, their footsteps crunching over charcoaled remains as they walked round to the back of the house.

Peering through the window, something Nell spotted in the desolation of her living room made her shoulders shudder as she held back sobs.

Putting his arm around her, James watched as Jackie pointed towards the ravaged bookcase.

'We look for a blackened smoke plume pattern to tell us where the fire originated – and we found it below that small window on the west side of the house. See it?'

Nell nodded.

'From here you can just about make out the plume. We went inside, of course, but we haven't officially declared the building safe for you yet, and you can see enough from here. The plume has a V-shape, where the flames chase the available oxygen. And the *angle* of that V can tell us if a fire has been started with accelerant, or not. A wide V indicates a slow burn. A sharp V with a deep point shows the flames raced towards oxygen – and a fire that fast needs accelerant.'

James stared at the distant wall, the faint pattern, knowing Nell was doing the same.

When her shoulders shook, he knew she'd registered what he had: the deep point, the steep sides of the V.

The sign of arson.

Nell could barely hold in the clamouring terror: someone had been here, creeping around in the shadows, watching her in her house for the right moment to set fire to it – destroying the sanctuary of her home and, very probably, hoping to kill her.

The invasive nature of it, the cold deliberation, was such a personal and total violation.

For a moment, she couldn't seem to breathe. It was like she'd forgotten how to inhale. She staggered, leaning against James, her body shaking as she heaved and heaved but couldn't fill her lungs.

'OK, Nell. Take it easy. I know this is a shock. I thought you needed to see it first-hand, and have a chance to hear Jackie's assessment and ask any questions.'

James rubbed her back, and Nell tried to push him away, mortified at causing a scene, at showing any weakness. It had become necessary for her survival to build up a shield to hide how she was feeling, and now the brittle carapace was cracking, she felt like she was being robbed of any dignity.

'Nell, your reaction is totally natural, you know. Even if this had been an accident, the loss is huge. And, of course, there's so much more to deal with here.'

Through the fog of emotion, Nell heard James trying to reassure her. She heard a quaver of grief in his voice and glanced at him.

His trembling smile, the rallying nod, showed her that he shared a little of her sense of loss, and the hopeless desperation that whoever had done this hadn't stopped. They'd attacked her, and they may already have killed someone.

So it was even more important that she listen now, find any clues that might pinpoint who this was. With her mind sharpening at the thought, she managed to draw in a steadying breath, and nodded.

'Sorry.' She gave a shoulder-lowering exhale. 'This . . . This was just such a shock. To know, for sure, that someone really intended to hurt me. But thank you, for the chance to understand what happened.'

She knew her sidelong glance at James gave away her itch to look for clues – then wondered if she imagined the corner of his mouth twitch as he squeezed her hand.

'So, we've concluded that the deep V-shape plume shows us the fire was started with accelerant,' Jackie picked up her assessment again. 'If that small window was open, it's feasible that the arsonist could have used it to get the accelerant – lighter fluid, we think, via a hose or a soaked rag – inside.' She shrugged at James. 'But that's your part of the investigation.'

'Did you leave the window open, Nell?'

At the question, Nell's fear engulfed her all over again, as she pictured all too vividly someone doing exactly what Jackie had described. Now, it seemed like the fire was back to being her fault again, and her quashed emotions roller-coastered. She bit her lip. 'It was such a hot night. I locked all the others, but that one's so small I thought it was safe to leave open.'

'So your gates would have been locked,' James mused, as he paced to view the east side of the house, looking along it to the driveway. Then he turned to look at the fields and downland at the back of the house, and pointed. 'But it's possible someone could have gained access across the fields at the back and got in through the hedge, if they were determined enough.'

'Well, I've reinforced the hedge with thorny species, as a deterrent.' She walked towards the bottom of the garden, thinking that those thorns would be perfect for snagging something of whoever had pushed through it. Just like surveying for badgers, when she'd follow a mammal path to a patch of brambles and test the hairs snagged to see if any amongst the rabbit, fox and deer belonged to a protected badger.

'So what would you do first?' Jackie asked.

'Work out access and egress,' James said – in exact unison with Nell. They looked at each other, and gave a short laugh.

'Go on, then,' James challenged. 'Where do you think they got in?'

Thinking of the area like a survey site gave Nell some element of detachment, and she clung to it.

First, she looked around the area outside the window: she could see exploded shards of glass glinting between the blackened grass, where the arsonist had definitely been. She imagined containers of lighter fluid in some kind of bag, opened and unpacked silently in the dark, and wondered if anything might have inadvertently been pulled out, which might give away the perpetrator. No such luck.

Eyeing the garden, she assumed they wouldn't have been bold enough to stroll across the lawn; they'd have slunk around the edges. Nell traced the route back to the hedge along the bottom of the garden.

She already knew that a narrow mammal track, made by a regularly visiting fox, led across the lawn from a sparse patch in the hedgerow. Nell headed towards that patch now, to check it. That was where she'd get in, if this were a site she had to survey.

Stopping some distance away, she crouched, scouring the ground before trampling over anything that may be evidence – exactly like James's SOCO team would.

He joined her. 'See anything?'

'Not yet.' Nell was working carefully from this side of the hedge towards it. Now her gaze followed the soil under the tangled branches.

Drag marks. Her heart hammered.

'See those? This is where they must have got in, dragging a bag through,' she said.

'Probably containing the fuel,' James confirmed what Nell was thinking.

She scanned upwards, the wicked needles of blackthorn and hawthorn criss-crossing, like a miniature medieval fortress.

Nell realised she was holding her breath, in case an exhale dislodged any crucial evidence, and made herself breathe, cautious and shallow.

Beside her, James was just as intent.

She was desperate for some identifying scrap of material, something to reveal who was so intent on all this destruction . . .

With effort, she pulled her thoughts back from that dark spiral and kept searching.

With a sigh, James eased himself back onto his feet. 'Can't see anything. I'll send SOCO out, just in case, but I won't get my hopes up. This person's very forensically aware. I blame all those true-crime podcasts.' He offered Jackie a handshake. 'Thanks for your work today, and for taking the time to talk us both through it.'

But Nell couldn't give up yet. Methodically, her eyes scanned every nanometre of the twigs and twines.

And then she saw it.

'James?'

'What?' In an instant, he dropped to the ground to see what she'd found.

She pointed at a flower head.

'Oh. Well, yes, that's nice. But I thought you had some evidence . . .?'

'It *is* evidence. *Look* at it.'

'It's just a little bud . . . Flower. Whatever the right botanical term is.'

'Yes. But should it *be* there?'

James frowned. 'Part of the hedge, isn't it?'

'No. The hedge is a hawthorn, blackthorn and hazel mix. This flower head isn't any of those. And it isn't growing – it's snagged on a thorn.'

James pulled on a pair of gloves and passed some to Nell. Once she was wearing hers, and at his nod, Nell gently lifted the flower head off the blackthorn spike.

Nell knew exactly what this was, and where it had probably come from, but a hunch wasn't enough. 'Do you have a pencil?'

Behind them, Jackie lunged forward, holding one out. 'Here you go.'

Studying the tiny lobed, trumpet-like corollas arranged around the head, Nell used the pencil's sharp point to lift a delicate petal.

She smiled at the minuscule, flat blue dot which was tinier still than the pinpoint of the pencil beside it.

'Bingo.' She turned to James. 'This doesn't help us identify who left it here, but it *does* confirm our suspicions. This is a flower head of wild thyme – and I know *this* exact flower is from Finchmere because this,' she separated the petals with the pencil nib again and showed James the tiny blue egg, 'is a large blue butterfly egg.'

The triumph of finding something briefly quelled the flash of bile in her throat as she pictured the route the arsonist had taken. Someone she trusted had skulked in the shadows, intent on harming her.

James nodded. 'So now we have actual proof. Whoever set fire to your home had been at Finchmere that same day. It's definitely one of your team.'

Chapter 22

After taking Nell back to Finchmere, James was desperate to set his SOCO team to work at her house, in case more time and specialist equipment yielded anything else to go on.

At the station, the team confirmed they'd got no fingerprints, other than Rav's and Nell's, from Rav's rucksack – and not even the cleaner's fingerprints from the hall in Finchmere – so James was relieved to have another line of inquiry to follow. It kept the momentum of the case going, even if he was frustrated at having nothing leading him to the perpetrator.

Yet.

Around him, he saw how hard the team were working, heads down, hot on any sniff of a trail. Joining their industry, he made coffee for them all and set up the incident board, even though it was depressingly bare.

He'd resigned himself to more agonising waiting, but then jumped as the office door flew open and a tech officer barrelled in. 'Sir? We've got into Louise's iPhone and thought you might want to take a look.'

'Fantastic!' James reached for it and checked the messages. Looking in her emails, he found nothing contentious. Some were from the bishopric and there were a few emails about the upcoming funeral of an Irene Camberwell – he knew from Bea's statement that this was her grandmother – along with correspondence from the doctor who'd provided the death certificate.

Scanning Louise's texts, he saw a few addressed to some clergy colleagues. One of Louise's last messages to Rev Shirley Abara was a shocked face, so he clicked on it. But it was only in response to

Shirley sending a photo of herself enjoying a bottle of wine as she sat on a balcony, the glassy wall beyond revealing a few hundred more identical balconies of the upscale hotel. The photo's background showed an illuminated cityscape and an epic bridge – a span of white supports fanning out like rigging for a sail.

Peering over his shoulder, Ed pointed at the picture. 'Looks like Trinity Bridge. In Manchester.' He glanced at James with a shrug. 'I've got family there. That's a distinctive landmark, and that hotel's pretty swish.'

James wondered what had prompted Louise to respond with a shocked face. He squinted at the bottle of wine and recognised the Finchmere label. Maybe that was why Shirley had sent the photo.

Had Louise been quite ... puritanical?

He opened her photos next. The latest ones showed the chapel brimming with flowers earlier that day. Then he saw the video.

Clicking on it, James stared at the screen – showing a still photo with a 'play' symbol in the centre. As Ed squinted over his shoulder, James tapped the triangle, watching avidly for any clues.

'Hey there, peeps!' Louise grinned at her camera in what was clearly the vestry. 'Welcome to All Saints of Finchmere, open to all souls. Join us on Sundays for a rousing, affirming service and refreshments afterwards with our welcoming community ... No. That's rubbish. This is meant to be about all the eco stuff. No hard sell.'

She raised her eyes heavenwards. 'But don't hold back now, will you, Lord? Give me a sign that we'll grow our congregation. That I can meet the diocese's commitments. And not always be the one lagging behind. Help me lead this community away from all this ... *sin*.'

Shaking her shoulders, Louise let out a sharp exhale. 'OK. Hi! Welcome to All Saints. You might notice something different about our cosy chapel, and that's that we're warmed by the solar panels on the roof—'

'Louise?' A woman's distant voice cut the filming off abruptly. James sat forward, holding his breath. *Did they actually have a recording of one of Louise's last conversations?*

'Shhhh-*sugar*.' Louise's head jerked round. Her phone dropped to the side and James prayed that the footage wouldn't cut off.

With a view of the vestry's ceiling, James could hear the echoing footsteps approach.

'Oh, hi, Louise. Have you got a minute?' Now James recognised the voice: Bea. Who'd said in her statement she'd talked to Louise about her grandmother's funeral. 'I just wanted to address some of your questions about the service for Gran.'

'Oh . . . Good!' Louise sounded oddly breathless. 'Do you want to pray with me, then?' A shuffling step made it sound like she'd moved towards the door.

'No. No, I don't, Louise. What I *want* is for you to stop asking such awful questions and just get on with the actual funeral. This is where Gran worshipped, and this is where she wanted to be laid to rest. And *I* just want to make sure her wishes are honoured.'

'Yes, and it's *just* you, isn't it, Bea? Since your mother died.' Louise's tone had a strange edge to it, making James glance up at Ed. He raised his eyebrows.

'Don't start all that again, Louise. You're . . . *deluded*! You *have* to let it go. God knows, I'm having to, however upsetting it is, if I'm going to do what's right by Gran.'

'But I can't let it go, Bea. That's the point.'

'OK.' A step suggested Bea had moved closer. 'I'm going to make this as easy as possible. For both of us. Will you – or will you *not* – host Gran's funeral?'

'I've told you my condition, Bea. It's simple. I will – *if* you pray with me. *If* you confess what you've done.'

'You need to get something straight, Louise. You're forgetting who you are. You're *not* God. You're *not* the one who bestows forgiveness. You're just a busybody.'

Bea's footsteps faded away, but Louise's gasping breaths were audible. The view on the screen swooped around the vestry as Louise picked up the phone, but then she must have tapped the button to stop recording, either accidentally or deliberately.

James glanced at Ed. 'So, Louise reckoned Bea needed forgiving for something. The question is, what?'

* * *

Rav wished Nell had found an excuse to cancel the drinks with the team at Finchmere Hotel's sleek navy-and-copper bar, as he limped there.

Apparently, it would be too awful to let the team down and renege on her promise, though. And *apparently* – inspired by the artisans he was hosting – bartender Merlin had created a special menu of cocktails for the occasion, and he'd be crushed if he didn't get to show them off.

Bloody fine set of priorities that is . . .

While Nell had gone to the bar ahead of him, with some of the group, he'd been waylaid by Sylvia, who'd had the smart idea of asking him to sign the prizes that would be given out over the weekend. That way, he'd have more opportunity to absent himself from parts of the fete, if the attention was too much or if other dangers surfaced.

Nell wanted everything to run as usual – and Rav could understand her reasoning. He didn't want to feel that someone else was controlling their lives either. But after the day they'd had, honestly, he just wanted to make sure that Nell – and now Aanya – were both OK, and retreat to the sanctuary of home.

Not that we can now . . . Despair swelled through his chest.

His time didn't feel like his own. There was always an obligation to put first. Now, worse than that, he had to make a *point* of putting the obligation first, in case taking a break looked like a chink of weakness, ripe for exploiting.

So here he was, neglecting his family, his own needs, to socialise with people he didn't want to talk to – one of whom was his stalker *and* intent on harming Nell, and one who was a murderer, unless the two were the same person. As he limped onwards, rushing right into the situation despite himself, he swore heartily under his breath. His stomach thumped with foreboding at courting fate like this.

He hurried through the shadowy woodland in the dimming summer light, then across the field, and down the hill to the hotel. He could still appreciate the approach, over the sweeping lawns and garden shrubs, which looked stunning in the first hint of sunset. The already twinkling lights of the orangery's terrace and the spa hotel beyond drew him towards it.

At least the manicured lawn was easier to navigate than the tussocky field. It enabled him to move a little faster. Even though he was rushing, his tread was silent; it was ingrained to be quiet in any habitat. He'd mastered it, even on crutches.

So, when he heard a twig snap in the shrubbery beside him, he froze.

Turning, he felt like prey scenting the still summer air for an unseen predator. His senses screamed: *RUN!*

But he couldn't, could he? Even though the hotel was almost within reach of a concerted sprint, he just wasn't up to it.

So, he'd have to face it. Whatever it was. *Who*ever it was.

His heart pounded so hard that blood surged through his chest and through his arms like a tsunami, his body nearly buckling.

He stood there, upright only for his crutches, wondering what – *who* – was following him. And why.

His head jerked round as leaves rustled – *seizing* his attention, making him peer up towards the dark woodland, and into the scattered copses across the field, to see what had disturbed them. *Just the breeze? Or something else?*

Beads of sweat on his forehead began to trickle, stinging his eyes. An echoing scream made him *leap* out of his skin – until he realised it was a distant fox.

Despite his rising adrenaline, he made an effort to control the panting, trying to hold his breath so he could listen.

As sweat slicked down his back, the silence around him grew ominous, threatening, making him feel small, and uncomfortably vulnerable.

The sensation of weakness fired through him, igniting impotent rage. '*Come on*, then!' he yelled towards the shrubs. 'Stop skulking about and *show* yourself, you sodding coward!'

He found himself brandishing one of his crutches like a great sword, trying to cover his fear with bravado. He was gasping now, and pacing on his crutches, as if weighing up his invisible opponent.

As the breeze stirred the leaves around him, Rav didn't know where to focus. He began moving towards the hotel, head swivelling until he grew dizzy, as he tried to keep all angles around him in view.

He was beginning to think he'd imagined it, when he caught a glimpse of something moving on the edge of his peripheral vision. A distinct person, moving past the hedge.

He didn't think. He didn't stop. He just *raced* on his crutches – even though his arms were burning, shaking, his legs on fire, his heart *thundering* – to get inside the building.

James couldn't bring himself to go home. Without any more leads to follow up, he felt scratchy and restless.

So, he turned off from his usual route and headed instead to Cookingdean, until he reached the vicarage. The whitewashed, double-gabled house gleamed in the evening light, and he noticed Ashley's Mini Cooper parked outside.

Buoyed at the thought of seeing her, and finding out more about her day and any other developments, he hurried in, pausing only to greet the constable standing guard outside of Louise's home. Handing him the flask of coffee he'd brought, and pulling on the protective hooded suit, gloves and booties, James ducked under the tape.

'Ash?' he called.

'James?' She walked into the wide Victorian hallway, from one of the two rooms off to each side, her protective gear rustling. 'Itching for a lead, too?' she asked.

'Yep. How far have you got?' He glanced around. The decorative floor tiles led to the stairs, then the kitchen beyond.

'Not much yet, I'm just taking it all in. SOCOs haven't been here yet. Considering she had an early start on her last day, she was meticulously orderly.'

Walking around the house, James saw what Ashley meant. Upstairs, the bed sported hospital corners; the bathroom was splash-free and lemon fresh, the glass shower door squeegeed clean. Even the linen cupboard was full of precision-folded towels and bedding, grouped into sets and then ordered by size, the curved side outwards so there were no loose edges dangling over the shelves. It looked like a display at a spa, not the contents of somebody's cupboard.

Back downstairs, he peered into the dining room, with its polished table and dust-free ornaments, then glanced into the sitting room, where the magazines were stacked neatly on the gleaming coffee table. He found Ashley in the modest but immaculate shaker kitchen.

'Looks like she barely lived here,' she said. 'Do you think she was staying with someone else?'

James opened the dishwasher. 'What did Saunders reckon Louise had for breakfast?'

'Umm . . .' Ashley checked her notes. 'Muesli, coffee, protein shake.'

'Bingo.' James pointed at the mixer cup, mug, cafetière, and bowl with a crusted edge of dried cereal, then closed the door. 'So, she's just unusually tidy.'

'Well, I feel like all my life choices are completely inadequate.' Ashley grinned. 'I'll be going home to an unmade bed, and all the breakfast things on the side because I grabbed my toast as I was running out the door and ate it in the car.'

'Well, you know where you'll find cleanliness.' James clasped his hands in prayer.

Ashley eyed him. 'You think that really was her mantra?'

'She does seem pretty puritanical. The unusual thing is that it looks like she actually lived by those values, instead of enjoying judging others while not applying them to herself.'

'So, you think she was genuine?'

James nodded. 'I'm starting to think she was *evangelical*, actually.' He moved to the fridge for a closer look at the photo stuck on it.

It was Louise – a few dress-sizes larger – with her arm slung jovially around a young, undeniably handsome, man who was clearly a colleague, in surplice and dog collar.

On a hunch, James checked the fridge, full of salad and fresh vegetables. Not a carb or a sinful food in sight. 'That could be why,' James mused. 'There's no zealot like a convert. She's fanatical about running and healthy living.'

'Yes, you sometimes see that in people with addictive behaviours, especially those in recovery, morphing bad habits into good ones. Excessive exercise is fairly common.' She glanced at him. 'You're thinking that, in this case, the same applies to moralising?'

She peered at the photo. 'Who's the man? Do we know?' When James shook his head, Ashley read the notice board at the edge of the shot. 'Rev Wo— somebody? At Ambledown Parish. That's local, isn't it?'

'Local-ish. It's few miles away. She probably knows several of the local clergy.' James moved on to the room he hadn't looked into: Louise's study. Her roll-top writing desk, set into the bay window that overlooked the garden, had items neatly filed into labelled sections: Sermons; Research; Parishioners; Diocese; Archive.

With gloved hands, Ashley reached for the folders in the Parishioners section.

James pondered which to select, and found himself drawn to the Archive section, wondering if there'd be any hints of old news.

'Well, this is full of health updates about various members of the congregation. Notes to make home or hospital visits, to include prayers for them at the next Sunday service. And there's marriage banns to read and upcoming christenings.'

Ashley leaned across to pick up Louise's diary next. 'Yep, this is full of corresponding appointments. See? "*Hospital visit: Woodwhite*" here cross-references with "*Prayers: Woodwhite*" here. Loads of similar lists.' She whistled. 'She was one busy bee. Her days are *crammed*. Services across several parishes, meetings, group talks, community events. Here, visiting The Priory with Rev W. She never stopped.'

'Hmmm . . .' James scanned the pages he had selected. These were all five years or older, and he was starting to think he wouldn't find anything useful.

'Here's the notes for Mrs Camberwell's upcoming funeral.' Ashley read from the diary. 'Wasn't she Bea's grandmother?'

James's head jerked up. 'Yes. What does it say?'

'There are notes on what to include in her eulogy. But she'd underlined the meetings. Appointment with undertakers, a meeting with Bea. And a consultation with the doctor who wrote the death certificate. Which looks like it wouldn't have been the first.' She glanced at James. 'That's unusual, wouldn't you say?'

'Yes.' James recalled the recording between Bea and Louise, and wondered about the confession the vicar had insisted on.

As he set his folder down, a page flicked over. And he saw the surname again, this time in a newspaper cutting from March:

> APRIL CAMBERWELL, much loved daughter of Irene and mother of Beatrice, sadly passed away at home. Service to be held at All Saints Church, Finchmere. All welcome.

'I'll ask Ed to get hold of the death certificate for Irene Camberwell. Looks like we should also get the certificate for her daughter, April,' James said, sending the email. 'And we'll need to make that a priority.'

'Good. Something doesn't feel right about that, does it?'

'Hopefully, we'll know more soon.' James took photos of the notes. 'We'll need SOCO to bag and label this.' He tucked the pages away and, just for the sake of completion, took out the Research folder while Ashley skimmed the Diocese file.

He started at the unexpected sight of a familiar name. The letter, from Gatekeeper, Wall & Brown solicitors, was brief but assertive.

> The recent donation of £500,000 to the Cookingdean parish upon the death of Mr Blue is contested on the basis of Mr Blue's obligation to his sole surviving daughter failing to be considered.
>
> Since attempts to reach amicable agreement with the will's executor and beneficiary, Reverend Louise Brimstone, have been unsuccessful, notification is therefore given to commence legal proceedings on behalf of our client, Holly Blue.

Chapter 23

At the loud clatter, Nell jumped round, shocked to see Rav stagger into the bar. He looked like he'd been scared to death and hadn't slept for a week.

Stomach lurching, she hurried to the bar, meeting him there.

'What the hell's happened?' As Nell reached for Rav, Merlin gave him an appraising glance and poured him a double brandy, then moved away to serve another group of guests, to give them privacy.

'Nothing *happened*. Not really.' Rav gulped his drink. 'Well, no, that's not true.' He wiped his mouth. 'I think someone followed me – and no, I'm not sure who, and no, I don't know why.'

Nell was grateful for the background music and the chatter of a busy bar to ensure they weren't overheard. But she whispered anyway, as she slipped an arm around him and pulled him close. 'Did they threaten you?'

He shook his head, but his gulp told her he'd been afraid, even if he wouldn't admit it.

'Any signs? Clues about who it could be?'

'It was a man. Broad. Heavier tread than a woman. I caught sight of him amongst the shrubs, near the hotel, like he was on a stakeout. But he was in shadow.' He shrugged and finished his drink.

'I'll ask the hotel manager to send me – and James – the CCTV from tonight.' She fired off the email and glanced at Rav. 'You never know, it may show something.'

They both managed to smile as Gigi came over to fetch some more cocktails for her six baristas. 'Hi, Rav! You must try one of Merlin's creations. They are,' she made a chef's kiss in Merlin's direction, making him smile in delight, '*magnifique!*'

'Allow me, Gigi.' As Merlin finished her drink order and added garnishes, he twirled a tray, transferred the vintage cocktail glasses and followed Gigi back to a large table to deliver the drinks.

Rav had managed a half-convincing smile at Gigi's recommendation. 'Yeah, OK. Not a strong one, though. That brandy has left a lasting impression. And I feel like I need to have my wits about me.'

'Well, I'm on mocktails.' Nell smiled at him. 'Same reason.' Seeing worry flit across his face, she added, 'They're delicious. And Erin's on them, too. She's *driving*.' Nell grinned. 'I think she's saying that so she has a reason to lay off the alcohol after yesterday. She and I have been enjoying the Bilberry Forager.'

He glanced over his shoulder at Erin, peering at the laptop screen.

'Kat's showing us the footage that didn't make the cut,' Nell explained. 'She put together a blooper reel. It's pretty funny.'

Erin, draining her glass, nearly spluttered at something on the screen; Gigi and the team of baristas laughed at whatever mishap they were viewing, which must have involved Erin, as they all grinned at her or nudged her.

Nell was amused that Erin, who wasn't usually very good at laughing at herself, was playing up to the attention of the good-looking barista with the man-bun.

Seeing the camaraderie, Rav clearly rallied, and nodded. 'Sounds good.'

With sixth-sense timing, Merlin glided up, towel over his shoulder. 'What'll it be, folks? Same again, Nell? Or do you want to try something different? Would you like to see the full menu, Rav?'

Merlin pushed over a wooden coaster with the QR code etched like a scorched brand. Using it, Rav pulled up the online menu on his phone, showing the various drinks moodily backlit and artfully garnished, lined up along the polished copper bar. As well as the Bilberry Forager, there was a Rose Bellini, a Bea's Knees – which was a gin and lemon concoction made with Bea's honey – along with a Meadowsweet Spritz, a Blackberry Mojito, Strawberry Pina Colada, and a Country Garden cocktail fizzing with Zeus's elderflower cordial, lemon thyme and wild bergamot.

'I'm tempted by all of them!' Rav said.

Nell peered over his shoulder. 'They look great on there, Merl. I hope you'll keep these on for a while.'

'I'll have a Forager, please,' Rav said.

Nodding, Nell said, 'Same again for me, please.'

'Fine choices. Coming right up.'

Merl muddled the crushed berries, fruit puree and honey syrup, then poured the sparkling water to create the mocktail's graded colour. He added a jauntily angled skewer of three foraged bilberries, effortlessly replicating the picture-perfect version on the menu, and passed the glasses to them.

Kat joined them at the bar. 'Good to see you, Rav. Did Nell mention we've got some hilarious footage from today? You should get over there and take a look.'

'Yes, I will!' Rav sounded enthusiastic, and only Nell saw his smile fade when Kat turned to Merl. He seemed as worn out as her by the need to keep putting on a façade. 'Same again please, Merlin.'

Merlin started making the drinks, but then he saw Nell pick up their glasses as Rav began to limp to the seat.

'One sec, Kat, I'll be right back.' Whizzing around the bar, he took the drinks from Nell, saying, 'Allow me,' and brought them over to the table, then darted back to finish Kat's order.

As Rav sat, he was met with cheers from the team, and he soon saw why. The footage playing on Kat's laptop showed him in comic anti-glory: heaving a sigh of relief with wide eyes and puffed-out cheeks at an announcement going well, then comically raising his eyebrows; then a shot of him pulling a face; and then others of him variously shaking himself, looking around for something, frowning in confusion, counting on his fingers the points he wanted to mention, and then recoiling, wide-eyed with terror, from the fan thrusting her cleavage at him.

'Oh, that bit's priceless!' Erin laughed as Kat passed her a refill of her Forager. 'Play it again!' She settled back, sipping her drink.

Kat grinned and obliged, then settled back to sip her Meadowsweet Spritz.

'Nice choice,' Gigi said. 'The flower tastes a little like almonds, I thought?'

Kat nodded in agreement. 'They've all been delicious so far. You should ask him to do cocktail kits for the farm shop, Nell. They'll go down a storm.'

'Good idea,' Nell said, making a note to ask Merlin to talk to the shop manager.

All eyes were on the screen again as the footage played – until their viewing was interrupted by Noah, Zeus, Holly and Bea arriving.

'Look who we bumped into as we walked over.' As Zeus gestured at the young women, Noah's eyes flicked to Gigi. She arched an eyebrow and Nell wondered if Noah was trying to prove that he hadn't been alone with the young women. Especially if Holly had reason to complain about his behaviour.

Had Noah asked Zeus to make a point of saying they'd walked over together?

Bea and Holly smiled in greeting, and Holly asked, 'Anyone in need of a new drink while I get ours in?' She looked around at the choices on the table and raised her eyebrows. 'Wow, they look amazing. Any recommendations?'

As everyone recommended the drink they had, Holly laughed. 'OK, no such thing as a bad choice, it seems.' She joined the others heading over to Merlin, to order, and Rav shot an awkward glance in their direction. As Kat pressed play again, and the reel continued, he forced a cheerful expression.

When Noah returned, sliding in beside Gigi, his wide smile overcompensated for her frosty reception. The conversation she'd been having with the barista sporting the man-bun ended abruptly and he turned away, suddenly engrossed by the footage that was playing.

Holly took a seat beside Erin, as Zeus set down the drinks he'd carried over, placing Holly's Forager in front of her, beside Erin's.

He stayed standing behind Holly as Nell said, 'Now we're all here, can I say thank you again for today – and even more so for the rest of this weekend. And please could we take a moment to toast and remember our friend Louise.'

'Louise,' everyone said. Some raised glasses, some bowed heads, but a silence fell. And Nell wondered which one of the party wasn't remembering, but responsible.

After a long, sober moment, they looked at each other again, at a loss for words.

'Oh, play more of your blooper reel,' Rav said. 'Louise would have enjoyed it.'

As more footage played, Zeus looked bemused by the recording of unflattering shots.

On the screen, Nell was placing a small nest box, with no obvious entrance hole, into a wide plastic bag. She jumped as she was ambushed by Rav, who laughed and patted her arm. Nell looked annoyed, gesturing at the box, and Rav stood back, contrite.

With caution, she lifted the lid – and a whirlwind of ferocious rodent flew out, biting hard, sinking sharp, strong teeth into the tender spot between finger and thumb.

Her yelled expletive was covered by the comedy music as her face contorted with pain. She dropped the empty (yet heavy) nest box on her foot and winced. Yet she was cupping the mouse even as it attacked her – not flicking it off her hand – and she was rewarded by it urinating copiously.

'Oh, Nell! You would pick a yellow-necked mouse for your demo, wouldn't you!' Tears of laughter were streaming down Erin's cheeks.

'Warriors of the wood, they are.' Rav nudged Nell. 'You're not a real dormouse surveyor until you've racked up a few injuries from those chaps.' He glanced at Erin. 'Kat and I had been there for ages, waiting for Nell. We should have been quieter, because our disturbance would have scared it, and then it took all of its wrath out on Nell.'

As if making the point, the mouse gave Nell another nip on her hand before darting up her arm and across her shoulders. There, he deposited a dropping in a finale of further displeasure, then scampered onto the tree and disappeared into the undergrowth.

Picking up her drink, Erin's shoulders shook as she wiped away her tears of mirth at the catalogue of disasters wreaked on Nell by the moody mouse. She didn't see Bea fling her hands up, as if about to applaud, and bump Erin, making her Forager cocktail spill down her jeans.

Shooting to her feet, Erin dabbed her trousers as Nell passed her a handful of paper napkins.

'Oh, no! Erin! I'm so sorry.' Bea looked mortified as Erin cleaned up the mess. 'Here, have my cocktail. I haven't touched it. I'll go and get another.'

'It's OK.' Erin wiped her fingers as Merlin appeared, removing the soggy tissues and empty glass. 'I'll just get another Forager. I'm driving, so I'm not drinking.'

'One won't hurt, will it?' Bea said, offering her glass. 'I don't think this one's very strong.'

The fizzy, floral drink looked inviting and Erin hesitated. She glanced at Bea's face and said, 'Oh, go on, then. Thanks.'

When Erin took the glass, Bea smiled. 'Least I could do.'

As Bea left to order her replacement drink, Nell was relieved to see that the blooper reel had come to an end. Now, conversation ranged from the long day, the success of their respective stands – and then, inevitably, to Louise again.

'It's just awful,' Holly murmured, her eyes wide.

Bea nodded, sharing the shock. 'I still can't believe it.'

'Who would want to harm her?' Noah asked.

'Pff.' Gigi looked at her husband like he was a fool. 'She interfered with everything. She believed she had the right to judge. This does not win friends, eh?'

'Yeah, she could be a little intense,' Zeus acknowledged. 'Even so . . .' He raised his hands.

Kat's eyes flicked to the laptop. 'I probably recorded one of her last moments. She was so excited to be involved.'

'S-s-seriously?' Erin slurred. 'S-s-she was a total pain! Y-yet another s-s-superfan of R-r-rav. *Ugh.*'

Nell stared at Erin, apprehension prickling.

'Woo! I th-think that cocktail's stronger . . . than I-I thought.' Erin leaned across the table. 'I might be . . . s-sick.'

'Not again,' Zeus murmured, moving out of the splash zone.

If Erin's only just had a few sips of a real cocktail, she can't possibly be drunk. Not like this.

'Erin? Erin, look at me,' Nell demanded.

Squinting at her, Erin winced. 'Oof, my head.'

'Can you open your eyes?' Nell insisted.

But Erin shook her head, and sank back onto the table.

Nell reached across, felt her forehead – clammy – then her pulse, galloping like a racehorse.

With great care, she lifted one of Erin's eyelids, seeing the wide, dark pupil.

Relieved that Rav was already pulling his phone from his pocket, Nell nodded at him. 'Get an ambulance. I think Erin's been poisoned.'

Chapter 24

Friday 7th July – 10 p.m.

Rav listened to the emergency call handler, who agreed there was no time to wait for an ambulance, and was trying to fight the rising panic and ignore the horrified faces around him.

Nell had called Merlin over, asking him to transfer the drink Erin had sipped into a travel mug.

Rav held the phone to his ear with his shoulder as he limped outside, while Noah and Zeus carried Erin to Nell's electric RS Audi – blessedly parked in the reserved bay at the front of the hotel. As Erin was eased into the back seat, Nell scrambled in and Merlin handed her the cocktail.

Rav climbed in beside Erin so he could keep an eye on her symptoms and listen to advice from the call handler, while Noah jumped into the front seat.

When Nell glanced at him, he said, 'You'll need someone to help at the other end, won't you?'

Agreeing, Nell drove like a demon to Pendlebury Hospital.

By now, Erin's face was alarmingly flushed, her heartbeat through the roof.

'How's she doing?' the call handler asked Rav.

'She's very flushed.'

As Erin squirmed, she muttered, trying to speak but slurring and struggling to swallow. 'Turn out the l-l-light . . . Too bright.'

'Seems very sensitive to the light. She can't swallow easily.'

'Check her airway, please. Do it now.'

Gently, Rav tilted Erin's head back, his pulse racing as he tried to make sensible observations. 'Her throat looks swollen. Like it's closing up.'

Oh, God . . .

'Is anything restricting her neck? Can you loosen any tight clothing?'

Rav saw that Erin's shirt wasn't tight, but he undid the top button anyway. 'No. It's from what she's drunk. It must have been spiked.'

'Can you get a sample of it to us?'

'Yes, we're bringing it along.' A flash of appreciation at Nell's quick thinking sliced through Rav's desperation for Erin.

Her face was slick with sweat, and ghostly pale. He felt sick.

'Come straight to A&E,' the call handler advised. 'They're prepared for you.'

He willed Nell on, to fly down the twisting roads to Pendlebury even faster. Their eyes met in the rear-view mirror, and he saw the determined set of her jaw as she floored the accelerator.

'The doctors are ready for you,' the call handler reiterated. 'Sounds like acute poisoning.'

The assurance only made Rav's fear spike.

Nell may have broken every speed limit there was, racing there, but it had still taken an agonising twenty minutes.

As she screeched to a halt outside the emergency unit, Noah dashed out and ran round to lift Erin off the back seat.

Rav and Nell both clambered out, and saw the triage nurse tell Noah to seat Erin into the waiting wheelchair.

Within seconds, two doctors ran out to collect her.

Nell handed them the drink. 'She had a few sips of this. Just in case it helps.'

With a nod, they whisked Erin away, through the double doors.

The sudden silence – the stillness – felt *shattering* after the tense race to get Erin there.

'Bloody Nora!' Noah turned to them, shell-shocked. 'Hope she'll be OK.'

'Yes, so do I.' Nell eyed him, and Rav knew she felt as suspicious as he did about how solicitous Noah was being. 'Thanks for your help.' She shot him a warm smile and patted his arm. 'But I can wait here for her and keep you posted. It's been a long day, so if you need to get back . . .?'

'Oh . . . uh . . . sure.' But Noah sat down, staring at the doors.

'We could be in for a long wait, Noah,' Nell cajoled.

'Yeah, no need to keep Gigi waiting,' Rav said.

'Gigi?' Noah frowned at Rav. Then he ran his hand over his face. 'Yeah. You're right.' He got up. 'Looks like you've got things under control here. I'll go and get an Uber.'

Rav nodded, glad that he'd be able to speak freely with Nell, but also brimming with worry and the crushing weight of responsibility for Erin being in danger.

He leaned forward and gazed at Nell. 'Is this my fault, do you think? Do you think my stalker has gone after Erin?'

Her shrug was unconvincing. 'Maybe.' Then she heaved a sigh. 'There's no escaping it, is there? Erin is still quite possessive of you. She hasn't really ever got over you turning her down.'

Guilt churned, and Rav winced, knowing Nell was right.

'And all this presenting work isn't really what she came here to do, which was training.'

Rav turned to her. 'Are you upset that she's been presenting with me?'

'No . . . Well, not really. She's good at it, but we'd planned this project together. I'm already sidelined because you're such a star.' She smiled. 'Which I'm pleased about, despite everything. But I don't need Erin to elbow me out.'

A silence stretched between them, until Nell said, 'If anything, I feel guilty that I've known about the stalker and let Erin get more involved with you and the filming.' She glanced at Rav. 'We should have told her. Or we should have done more to protect her. I . . . I had a feeling something would happen. She just can't hide how she feels. I shouldn't have let her walk into danger.'

I've done the same. Pushing the thought away, Rav squeezed his eyes shut.

'That's not all I've been feeling guilty about.' Nell stared at her lap. 'Did you hear what Erin said in the bar? That Louise was another of your superfans? She *was*, wasn't she? Lou hung on your every word. And I'd wondered if anyone had noticed you two scheming about meeting up in secret. If Erin noticed, then I'd say that's highly likely.'

Desolation gnawed at him. 'So now you're saying I'm responsible for Louise's death?' Rav stared at her, shaking his head in horror.

This is a nightmare.

'*You're* not responsible. But your *stalker* may be. And we should definitely assume so, because otherwise we could be walking into more danger.' She hesitated, then said, 'Especially now that the fire investigation has been completed.' She took a breath. 'It was definitely arson. They got in through the hedge. And I found a thyme flower head there, with a large blue butterfly egg, so—'

'So the stalker and the arsonist are one and the same, and they're part of our team at Finchmere. No doubt about it.' Rav squeezed her hand, the worried look in her eyes tugging on his heart.

'And they'd have to be the same person who's poisoned Erin, from an opportunity standpoint alone – so it makes sense for them to also be Louise's killer.'

The thought made his breath catch. He couldn't even bring himself to wonder what else might happen to Nell.

'Unless . . .' Nell frowned.

'What?'

'Well, what if Erin found out something about Louise's murderer? Maybe it has nothing to do with you and your stalker, but Louise's killer covering their tracks?'

'Well . . . Maybe . . . It's possible.' Rav knew that was wishful thinking. He glanced at Nell. 'So . . . We need to work out who had the opportunity to poison her.'

'You've been with Erin all afternoon. Did you spot anything?'

He gave an agonised sigh. 'Yeah. There's been . . . a few shifty things going on.'

'*Like?*'

Exhaling, Rav tried to recall. 'Noah basically sexually assaulted Erin. Gigi saw, and both were pretty upset at that. Apparently, he'd done the same thing to Holly, but Holly obviously didn't feel able to say anything, and Erin wasn't very sympathetic. Plus, she interfered when Holly asked to film with me.'

Though Nell's jaw clenched, she didn't look as surprised as he expected. 'I'll speak to Noah. If that's how he's behaving, I'll have to fire him. I'll see if Holly and Erin want to file a complaint with the police—'

'Well, exactly. Creates a lot of problems for everyone, doesn't it? Something like that. Not least Gigi's income. *And* Erin returned some cryptic note that Gigi dropped. No idea what it means, but we can probably work it out – and, if it *was* significant in some way, and Gigi thought Erin had read it, then she might need to cover it up. *And* then there was Zeus, being tense. Not like his casual, charming self.'

'Yes, he was tense with me, too,' Nell said. 'He's having trouble with some . . . associates.'

'And . . . And then there's Bea.' He sagged, not knowing how to even broach this one. 'She . . . She's got pictures of me. All over her fridge.'

'What?' Nell stared at him. 'Hold on – *she's* your stalker?'

'Looks like it,' Rav said. 'They were cut out like . . . like the one taken from Finchmere House.'

Nell shuddered. 'So . . . has *she* done all this? Do you think she poisoned Erin?'

'Oh, no problem. Her garden's stocked better than a pharmacy.' Rav groaned as he recalled their afternoon. '*And* she gave Erin some honey to try. I thought she took a while to make her a sample. Now I think about it, she was right beside her apothecary cabinet of dried flowers and berries.'

Cold, creeping dread engulfed him as he realised he should have told James. Straight away. If he had, maybe Erin wouldn't have been poisoned.

Nell was staring at him, clearly thinking the same. She confirmed it when she asked, 'Did you tell James?'

When he shook his head, grimacing, she shoved his arm. 'What are you playing at? If she's your stalker, she's dangerous! Think about all the things that have happened! To me – and now Erin!' She seized her phone and sent James a hasty text. 'There. Let's hope James comes to the hospital and you come to your senses.'

She sat back in her seat, huffing.

Rav couldn't disagree. 'You're right. It's just . . . She doesn't seem . . . I don't know. I can't imagine her attacking you. Or setting fire to your house.'

'But you just imagined her poisoning Erin,' Nell pointed out. 'What if she brought something with her to the bar? Slipped something into her drink? She made Erin spill hers, didn't she, and gave Erin

184

her own drink as a replacement. So she could have been trying to make it look like Bea herself was the poisoner's target.'

'Or she could have actually *been* the target . . .?' Rav said. 'We can't rule it out.'

'If Bea's the stalker, why would someone else be causing her any harm?' Nell asked. 'It doesn't make sense. Whereas, if *she's* the stalker and poisoned Erin, she could be trying to deflect attention away from herself, or introduce uncertainty.'

'It doesn't stop anyone else spiking Erin's drink, though, does it?' Rav said. 'Or anything else she may have had today.'

With a sigh, Nell reached for Rav's hand, squeezing it. 'We'll wait here and find out what poison it was. Then we'll know how long it would have needed to take effect. And then we can work out who poisoned her.'

Distracting herself from the agony of waiting for an update from Erin's doctors, Nell peered over Rav's shoulder at the photograph of Gigi's note.

As she googled the bible references, the theme became clear.

'Hebrews 13:4 says: "*Give honour to marriage, and remain faithful to one another in marriage. God will surely judge people who are immoral and those who commit adultery.*"'

'So, Louise was trying to deter Gigi or Noah from playing away?' Rav asked. 'The next one's Proverbs 6:26.'

'Pff!' Nell exhaled. 'This one isn't mincing its words. "*For the price of a prostitute is only a loaf of bread, but a married woman hunts down a precious life.*"'

'So, Louise suspected – or maybe knew? – that *Gigi's* having an affair, then,' Rav said. 'Not very subtle about it, is she?'

'Ezekiel 9:10, and Psalm 50:21,' Nell murmured. 'Wow.' She glanced at Rav before reading aloud, '"*As for me, my eye will not spare, nor will I have pity; I will bring their deeds upon their heads.*" And, "*These things you have done, and I have been silent; you thought that I was one like yourself. But now I rebuke you and lay the charge before you.*"'

Rav widened his eyes. 'So this was . . . a warning? What the hell was she going to do?'

Nell looked up the last reference. 'Isaiah 47:11. "*But evil shall come upon you, which you will not know how to charm away; disaster shall fall upon you, for which you will not be able to atone; and ruin shall come upon you suddenly, of which you know nothing.'"*

They exchanged a look, and Nell grimaced. 'That sounds more like a threat to me.'

'So, what do we think? Noah's a sleaze, their marriage is an unhappy one, Gigi's having an affair, Louise finds out and gets all Old Testament? Even though Noah is trying it on with other women – not too discreetly – Gigi might feel trapped, with their joint business.'

'And even if Gigi was planning to leave, it's not really up to Louise to force that conversation, is it?' Nell fumed. 'What if she was in an abusive relationship, and a revelation like that could put her life in danger?'

'Speaking of which . . .' Rav jerked his head towards the double doors at the approaching doctor.

'You brought in Erin Everly? Are you next of kin?'

'Yes,' Nell lied. 'Sister. How's she doing?'

'She's . . . Well, she *is* responding at least. But we need to keep her in for more treatment. She's going to her ward now, so you can see her there. Don't stay long, though. She needs to rest.'

They stood aside as the porter pushed – a hopefully sleeping and not unconscious – Erin past them in her hospital bed.

Nell saw that Rav looked stricken as Erin disappeared along the corridor to her ward, but she turned back to the doctor. 'What was it that Erin reacted to?'

'Atropine. A dose large enough to kill her. *If* she hadn't had emergency intervention.'

Nell frowned, her thoughts racing. *Belladonna? Fast acting . . . If a drink of Erin's had been poisoned, it would have been best disguised in the Bilberry Forager . . .*

So it wasn't a surprise when the doctor said, 'There was no trace of it in that drink you brought with you.'

But his narrowed eyes, the cloud of suspicion, made Nell shiver as he stared at her, and added, 'So you should be aware that we've logged this with the police. Because this poison is a clever choice. The enlarged pupils return to their normal size as the muscles relax in death. And the toxin goes completely undetected in post-mortems.'

Chapter 25

James hurried along the hospital corridor, dreading what he'd find in the ward.

Erin's been poisoned?

Potential motives rolled automatically, his brain cross-referencing who could have killed Louise and also wanted to harm Erin.

Unless the two attacks are unrelated . . .?

He didn't even want to think where that would put the investigation. As he reached the ward, he spotted Rav and Nell sitting beside Erin's bed. It looked like Erin was in a coma. She had a ventilation mask over her face and a beeping machine alongside her.

'How is she?'

'Better than she looks,' Nell reassured him. 'She's had treatment. She just needs some time to recover. She'll stay in, under observation, tonight and tomorrow but, even once she's out of hospital, she'll need a lot of rest.'

James looked at them. 'Looks like you could do with some rest too. You both look exhausted.' He saw Rav ready to protest, and added, 'I'll get a police guard. So she'll be safe, and you won't need to sit with her all night.' Turning back to Erin, he asked, 'Do they know what poison it was?'

'Yes. Atropine. Belladonna.'

'Belladonna . . .?' James frowned. 'Where on earth do you get hold of that? Are we back in the Renaissance—?'

'No time travel needed.' Rav's tone was grim. 'It's growing in Bea's garden. Along with all the world's other toxins. If your team search, you'll find it in the hedge along the lane, camouflaging like it's blackthorn.' Rav googled and passed James his phone, showing the plants on the screen.

'Hmm. Can you send me that?' James asked as he fired off an email to Ed, after adding that a botanist must be included in the search team. Noting the email with the image arrive in his inbox, he appraised Rav. 'And how do you know about what's growing in Bea's garden?'

'We did some filming there today. Me, Kat and Erin.'

'And how did Erin get on with everyone?'

Rav held James's eye contact. 'Not well. Erin offended Bea. Went into the house when she was asked not to, openly laughed at her.' He winced, looking at Nell, and then back at James. 'She had pictures of me. All over her fridge. Erin saw it and made fun of it. You know how Erin can be.'

'What?' James stared at him. 'Like the one in your bag? You're saying she's our prime suspect to be your stalker? And you're just telling me this *now*?'

'Possibly. Yes. But she's . . . Well. She seems too . . . gentle.' He swallowed. 'Doesn't she?'

'No assumptions, remember? Did Erin know you have a stalker, Rav? Did she know there could be danger in making fun of Bea like that?'

'No.' Rav's face twisted in agony. 'But I will tell her. Once she's awake.'

'Make sure you do.' James let his unimpressed expression do the talking for him. 'Aside from Bea, has Erin had run-ins with anyone else?'

Rav shrugged. Then winced. 'Yes. Almost everyone. She had a . . . bit of an argument with Holly. Noah sexually assaulted her. Erin was very assertive that he'd behaved unacceptably. But when she found out that Holly had experienced the same behaviour, Erin was pretty brutal, telling her how she should have handled it.'

James felt his eyes widen. 'Did this happen at the courtyard?' Rav nodded, so James asked, 'Did Gigi see all this?'

When Rav nodded again, James raised his eyebrows – the list of suspects wasn't getting any smaller.

'Not sure if it's relevant, but Erin was plied with alcohol by Zeus, during the interview with him, Gigi and Noah. Gigi's barista took her some coffee and sat with her, but Gigi looked pretty annoyed at that.'

As he prepared to take Rav's official statement, James could easily imagine Erin blundering onto some clue about Louise's murder or igniting the stalker's ire.

And, if those two things were related – if Louise had been killed because of Rav's attention – then more people were at risk than James had initially thought.

Friday 7th July – midnight

As Nell drove them back to Finchmere, Rav was trying to remember what he'd overheard in the courtyard, when Erin had overindulged with Zeus, but he was struggling to recollect all that had happened in such a short space of time.

'I . . . I only caught snippets—'

'*Try*, Rav!' Nell insisted. 'We have to try to see where there's a link between Erin and Louise. Who would have wanted to kill both of them? Do you think Noah killed Louise because she'd threatened to report him for sexual harassment? Which would have risked his job and his marriage, as well as a criminal record. Do you think he tried to poison Erin for the same reason?'

'Maybe.' Rav grimaced at the thought. 'But this is complicated, isn't it, with Gigi and Noah having a business together. If the marriage is under threat, so is their livelihood, depending on how acrimonious the settlement would be. And even if the marriage is over, it doesn't mean you want someone else forcing your hand. If Lou and Erin were both exposing Noah's sexual harassment, that might actually be motive for Noah *and* Gigi.'

Nell didn't look convinced. She frowned as she steered along the dark, winding country roads. 'What about Zeus? You said he and Louise argued.'

She wondered if it was related to Zeus's associates. If it was, Louise could have stumbled onto something very unsavoury . . . Maybe even dangerous . . .

'Yes, but I've got no idea what Lou was upset about. She said something like Zeus needed to do something and if *he* didn't, *she* would. I don't know what exactly she was accusing him of doing. And then . . .' He frowned with the effort of recall. 'She rushed off. Like she was interrupted.'

'Oh? By whom?'

Rav felt the blood drain from his face. 'Oh no. It *was* Erin. When Kat was helping her after the interview.'

Saturday 8th July – 5.30 a.m.

James felt like the conductor of an orchestra as he oversaw the dawn search of Bea's garden. The team would move in as soon as it was light enough and, in the meantime, were being careful to get set up out of the line of sight from the property's windows: they would be prepared, but Bea wouldn't be forewarned.

From the path, their botanist had pointed at almost every plant in the garden, and SOCOs had already moved in to ensure they had photographed, bagged and labelled specimens of belladonna.

Clutching the expedited search warrant for Bea's house, James knocked on the thick oak door. After a few moments, it opened a crack, and Bea's eyes blinked at him, bleary from sleep.

'Beatrice Camberwell, we have a warrant to search your premises, as part of our murder inquiry.'

'What? Why?'

James pushed at the door, surprised to find resistance.

'No. I don't agree to this. You don't have my permission.'

'I don't need it, Bea.' James kept his tone gentle. 'We have to search. Erin's been poisoned, with something that grows in your garden. The warrant gives us the right to search your house and grounds, whether you consent or not. There's no need to make this confrontational. Let us search and, if there's nothing to worry about, you'll be excluded. *Won't* you?'

'No . . .' Her voice sounded like a sob now. 'No. Please.'

But when James pushed at the door again, it swung open, and Bea staggered back, crumpling and crying on the wide patinaed flagstones.

Behind him, SOCOs poured in, fanning out in a well-practised rhythm. The click of photos from the kitchen told James there was something to see. As soon as he walked into the old-fashioned kitchen, he spotted the pictures plastered all over the fridge.

So she hasn't torn down her montage of Rav.

Did she feel she didn't need to hide it, because she hadn't done anything to feel guilty about? Or was she so attached to it, so obsessed, that she couldn't bear to remove it? Worst of all – was she deluded or maybe mentally unwell enough that she believed what she was doing was somehow reasonable, and she was far better at masking than anyone was giving her credit for?

Moving closer, he saw that the print quality, paper and style of cutting looked exactly like the picture left in Rav's backpack.

He nodded at the officer. 'Bag those, please. We can compare them to the one at the station.'

Once the officer had done that, she moved to the recycling bin, and James held his breath as she drew out paper-towel roll centres, used paper bags, washed cans . . . and then cuttings of paper.

With careful precision, the officer lined up the cuttings on the counter. The grainy print was of Nell – the exact replica of the photo in Finchmere House – and it was the part that had been hacked out of the picture left in Rav's rucksack.

'Nice work.' James felt a surge of relief at the proof that Bea had planted the photo.

But this isn't enough to charge her with anything. I need something to connect her with Nell's attack, and the arson – as well as Louise and Erin.

Inviting Bea into the kitchen, he sat her on a wooden farmhouse chair and set up his iPad to record the interview. Once he'd stated the time and made the introductions, he asked, 'What can you tell me about these snippets of paper, Bea?'

She sniffed, half-sobbing, and shook her head.

He offered her a square of kitchen towel and tried again. 'It matches something I found somewhere else. Do you have any idea what that might be?'

Bea snivelled into the tissue, soaking it with tears and snot. But she gave a slight nod.

'Tell me about that, Bea.'

'It was sup-supposed to b-be a g-gift.' Bea's words came out in gulps. 'Ju-Just to sh-show I like h-him.'

'And what was that gift, Bea?'

'A c-copy of a p-photo. In F-Finchmere's hall. He . . . He always smiles at it. I t-took a photo of it with my ph-phone and printed it out.'

'Did you do anything else with it, Bea?' James looked pointedly at the cuttings, but it was lost on Bea as she blew her nose loudly.

'I c-cut Nell out.'

'Any reason why?'

'Obviously. I don't like her the w-way I like him.'

It sounded so logical, the way Bea said it, and James found himself nodding.

'I p-put it in his bag at lunch on Ch-Champions day.'

'Did you send anything else, Bea?'

She frowned, looking at him for the first time, confusion on her face. 'Like wh-what?'

'Anything. Letters? Messages? Anything.'

'No.' She wiped her nose again, misery tugging the corners of her mouth down. 'Just the photos on the fridge.' Her face flickered. 'It seems so ridiculous, when you have to say it out loud to someone else. He's just so . . . *lovely*. I just liked having him here, in the kitchen. Seeing his face. And then it just . . . *grew*.'

Her loneliness was so tangible, James reached out and squeezed her arm. She'd probably fixated on Rav – appreciating his warmth and friendliness – as someone to love after the losses she'd suffered. His sympathy couldn't prevent him asking her the crucial question, though.

'Where were you on Wednesday night and Thursday afternoon?' he asked.

'Here. At home.' She looked surprised at the question. 'Alone. I'm always alone.' Her voice trailed off as she stared out of the window.

Excusing himself, James stepped outside to log the findings on Bea on his iPad. An email from the manager at Finchmere Hotel flashed up. Ignoring it, he continued making notes – until his phone rang.

'James?' Nell's voice was breathless. 'You should just have had an email from the hotel. It's the CCTV footage from last night. Rav thought he was being followed by someone, and he caught sight of them skulking outside the hotel.'

'Oh? Did you get them on camera?'

'Yes! You'll have to watch it a few times to spot him, though. It was Zeus.'

'*Zeus?* Has he . . . shown any interest in Rav?'

'Yes and, well, kind of. Rav said he was a bit flirtatious during their interview about *Finchmere Estate Vineyards*. That could be nothing, though, with Zeus. That's kind of his style. But Rav did say that Zeus and Louise had heated words. He didn't hear much, though.'

'Hmm . . . I wonder why Zeus and Louise would disagree.' Remembering the photo on Louise's phone, James said, 'The only connection I have is a photo a friend sent her, enjoying a bottle of Finchmere wine in Manchester. How far afield do you sell it? Your food is all about staying local, isn't it?'

'Yes, we only sell produce within the county. No further. But Louise's friend could have bought it locally and travelled. Or had it as a gift. Why is that odd?'

James wished he knew. Despite the clues starting to emerge, he didn't feel like he was seeing the real picture.

Chapter 26

Nell felt dead on her feet. It took everything she had to keep her wide smile in place, standing before the expectant crowd, to announce the winners from the next round of competitions.

The morning had been an art form in disguising chaos – running the fete for their thousands of visitors while complying with the very active police inquiry.

According to James, after a few initial questions at her house, he'd taken Bea to the station to give her formal statement. She'd admitted to having a crush on Rav and being jealous of Nell, and she was responsible for the photo in Rav's bag. She'd snapped it on her way into the breakfast meeting in the morning, dashed home to print it off, and then placed it in his bag over lunch. A gift, apparently.

But James couldn't get her to admit to anything else. Not texts, dead-rat parcels, following Aanya, attacking Nell, nor arson. And certainly not murder.

Her claims of not poisoning Erin, though, hadn't been so easy to accept. It seemed too convenient that she not only had the plant right there in her garden, but she was also one of the few who'd recognise it – *and* know how to deploy its deadly properties.

So, Nell was trying not to bristle as she had to stand next to Bea, along with Holly, to fulfil her obligation of awarding the craft prizes to the expectant competitors. And it was all being captured on live-stream camera.

'Welcome, everyone!' Nell tried to make her tone friendly. 'It's been fabulous to see all the incredible talent on display here today in our craft section. And I hear that our judges, Holly and Bea, had some tough choices to make. I have the very great honour, though, of awarding the first prize for best woodwork item, which goes to John for his stunning spalted beech bowl.'

To the full tent's whooping applause, John collected the coveted rosette from Holly, who stepped forward to add her own comment.

'I admired the craftsmanship in this. The shape looks simple, but it's deceptive. The size and balance of this piece, and its gorgeous tactile nature, together with how you've worked with the natural pattern of the spalting in the grain . . . There is a real mastery of the craft. That's something I always aim for but don't always achieve. So congratulations, John, for a well-deserved first prize.'

The other prizes for woodwork were presented, until it was Bea's turn to award prizes for small pets. This was aimed at children, who by now were fidgeting and looking expectant.

Nell smiled at their bright faces, and rallied herself to give another warm-hearted speech. 'We've seen some gorgeous pets today. Thank you, all of you, for bringing them in and telling us how you look after them. I know that the judges would give you all first prize if they could. But we only have one first-prize rosette. And that goes to Lucy and her Angora rabbit called . . .' Nell did a double take at the prompt card. 'Casserole.'

Cheers and applause soared, and little Lucy had to have a nudge from her mother to step forward and accept her rosette, with sticky fingers and a gap-toothed, 'Thank you!'

Bea crouched to look the little girl in the eye. 'Casserole is a lovely little bunny. It's very clear that she enjoys lots of cuddles, and you're very good at handling her so that she feels safe. I saw that her hutch was beautifully clean, with fresh hay, and you know about the food she eats and when to feed her. When I look after my bees, I want to make sure they don't get poorly and that they have everything they need, and you're giving your little bunny excellent care. Well done, Lucy!'

As Lucy returned to the group of children, a few pressed in to look at her rosette before staring at Nell and Bea again.

As Bea presented the rest of the prizes, Nell noted that most of the children went away with something. Despite herself, she couldn't help smiling that Bea was such a soft touch. She wondered if her obsession for Rav had grown out of genuine loneliness.

When Bea touched her arm, Nell nearly jumped.

'Nell? I-I expect you've heard.' Bea looked ashamed, staring at her feet before eventually meeting Nell's eyes.

Nell looked at her, deciding to let her explain in her own words.

'I'm . . . *mortified*. I let a crush get totally out of control. And it affected my feelings towards you, too. It was immature and silly. Tragic, really. I'm sorry, Nell. For any concern or worry I might have caused you or Rav.'

Nell began to relent, prepared to accept her apology, until Bea added with a timely wobbling chin, 'I should have come to my senses much sooner. He's far too good for me. He'd never look twice at someone like me.'

Bea's overly self-critical self-deprecation made Nell suspect professional victimhood. Her hackles rose, and she wondered if this was another of Bea's tactics, to draw her in and manipulate – if Bea couldn't get Rav to fall in love with her, she'd entrap him with guilt, and make everyone else feel sorry for her while she was at it.

Given that Bea's obsession may yet prove to be far more destructive, Nell battled inwardly to remain neutral. 'Thanks for the apology.' Nell kept her tone level. 'Let's leave it in the past, shall we?' *For now*, she added, silently, though – since James had to consider people innocent until proven guilty, she should at least try to echo that principle.

With another wobbly smile, Bea moved off. Nell watched her leave, as avid as a hawk, and checked her itinerary.

Rav had agreed to spend the day at the streaming tent. With Kat there for at least some of the day, and Sylvia stuck to his side, Nell hoped that would be safe, if pretty dull for him, given how much he hated being cooped up and still.

She, however, had to present the Best Homemade Libation award with Zeus. The competition entries were lined up, and already the tent was full of competitors and onlookers.

When Zeus entered, his reputation meant he got a rapturous reception, as everyone whooped and applauded. Playing up to the crowd, he tipped a bow and fanned himself.

'Wow! Thank you for such a warm reception!' He stretched out his arms. 'I'm not surprised this award ceremony has been met with such good cheer, because this, of course, is the coveted prize for Best Homemade Libation.'

He turned to Nell, smiling, like they were hosting a TV show together.

She took the cue to add, 'Thank you all for your inventive selections of hedgerow wines, infused spirits and liqueurs, flavoured ciders and beers. I can tell you that you've made our resident expert, Zeus, one very happy judge!'

She expected him to dive in with the next soundbite, but he floundered, stuttering.

'H-hey! When duty calls, I'm . . . I'm happy to do my bit.' He flashed his smile at the crowd and, to Nell's relief, ready laughter rippled around the audience and competitors. But Nell noticed his smile falter; and his body was tense.

Zeus kept looking at a spot in the crowd, near the camera set up for the live-stream.

Maybe he's just nervous about being filmed?

But unlike her, Zeus was a natural performer, so that didn't seem quite right. Smoothing her frown into a wide smile, Nell continued, 'You produced tipples of everything, from sloe gin to bullace brandy.'

Pausing again, she expected Zeus to comment on the quality, but he'd stepped back, his eyes flicking from her to the crowd, and then towards the open side of the tent. He looked like he wanted to leg it from the podium.

Is someone here making him feel worried? Thinking of the Americans, Nell scanned the audience. She spotted Ashley and Hesha, and though she wasn't sure if anyone else would realise they were detectives, if Zeus *did* know, could the presence of police make him feel twitchy?

She couldn't work out what was wrong, but it couldn't be the competition: he'd come to Finchmere with an impressive résumé. He'd created award-achieving wines, as well as winning and judging highly regarded contests in the most esteemed vintner organisations. Appraising a few homemade concoctions couldn't possibly be a stretch.

With Zeus edgy enough for both of them, she widened her smile to announce the first winner. 'Zeus and I found the array of spirits and liqueurs *all* to be delicious – but the winner of our coveted first prize is Denise's delightful rosemary limoncello! Perfect on a summery day like today. Fresh, herby and zesty, we all agreed this was dangerously good.'

Denise stepped forward, amid cheers, to receive the golden rosette, and then Zeus continued with the second, third and highly commended prizes.

As the ceremony drew to a close, the crowd dispersed and Kat dismantled the cameras. It was then that Nell could see who'd been sitting beyond them, out of her sight line, but firmly within Zeus's: the two Californians who'd cornered her yesterday.

She tensed; Conor may have evicted them from the hotel, but that hadn't stopped them still gaining access today. The fact that two people, with nefarious intent, had circumvented their security so easily was an ominous sign.

Zeus's eyes darted towards the tent's open sides, like he couldn't wait to get away. Reaching for him, and shaking her head at his instinct to escape, Nell called for security on her walkie-talkie.

The last time she'd seen these men, Zeus had bolted to avoid explaining. Their pursuit was clearly far more personal; she couldn't afford to be fobbed off this time.

Once she heard that one of the security team was on their way, Nell turned to Zeus. 'I think you owe me an explanation. What's going on?'

Saturday 8th July – 4 p.m.

Rav was desperate to leave the film tent. He'd been stuck there all day and now he was jangling with cabin fever.

Seeing Nell driving over in the Landy made his heart leap and he scrabbled to his feet. 'Thanks for today, Sylvia. I'll see you tomorrow.'

She shot him a grin and a wave as he hobbled to the Land Rover and got in.

Without a word, he and Nell just looked at each other, gave a long sigh, then smiled. As she drove off, he fastened his seat belt.

'I'm glad today's over. Just one more day to go.'

'Mine was uneventful. How was yours?' he asked.

'I got an apology from Bea, which seemed like such a performative poor-me pity party, I'm almost certain it was an attempt at emotional blackmail.'

'I think she's just lonely, Nell,' he said.

'She may be. That doesn't mean she isn't manipulative. And I think she's very adept at that.' Shooting him a sidelong glance, she said, '*You* might be the proof of just *how* good she is at it.' She heaved a sigh. 'Plus, Zeus is having trouble from some former colleagues.'

'Oh?'

She shrugged. 'I still can't get him to tell me what it's about. But I have arranged a meeting with the two men, for next week. So I'll find out one way or another.'

'No such excitement for me. But I did get a text from Erin. She's at home.'

'Ah, so let's see her there, then.'

Nell turned towards Erin's place while Rav sent her a text warning of their visit. Soon, Nell was parking outside the Pendlebury Georgian townhouse, converted into flats.

As Erin answered the door, she managed a wan smile. Rav was alarmed at how pale she looked.

His worry must have shown on his face, as she waved a hand. 'I'm fine. Honestly. Any excuse to watch trashy daytime TV.' But her breathing was laboured as she walked to the sofa.

'I've brought those croissants you love,' Rav said. 'Gigi's made frozen ones so you can cook them fresh at home. They're amazing. I'll pop them in your freezer, but I'll leave one out, to defrost overnight.'

'Oh, thanks. That's breakfast sorted, then.' She was smiling when he walked back into the sitting room. 'But what I want to know is, who spiked my drink? I'm sure you two will have a hunch.'

'We're not sure. Yet,' Rav said. 'But you *do* need to know something important, Erin. And please don't treat this like a joke, because it isn't.' He sighed. 'I've got a stalker.'

Erin's eyes widened. 'A *stalker*?'

'They've been sending Nell hate mail, and me obsessive fan mail. They've met me in person, but I don't know who they are. They attacked Nell, that's how she hurt her ankle—'

'What did they do, Nell?' Erin's eyes were wide.

'They pushed me into a cellar, basically. Down a flight of stairs. And I think they intended to trap me there.'

Erin gaped, staring at them.

'Whoever it was may have killed Louise . . . and they may have poisoned you.'

'Bloody *hell*, Rav! *When* were you going to warn me? Didn't you think I had a *right* to know that some psycho was going to be jealous of your friends? And maybe harm them!' Her rant made her wheeze.

'I don't think they're targeting *friends*.' Rav cringed inwardly, but he had to say it. 'I think they're targeting anyone who is, or seems to be, more than a friend. So, Nell . . . and anyone they feel is too close to me.' He winced. 'They may have interpreted Louise's behaviour that way—'

'Or mine.' Erin looked indignant. 'That's what you're saying, isn't it? You're punishing me for being a bit . . . flirty. When you *know* there's nothing in it.' Her furious tone and the flush rioting across her previously pale cheeks contradicted her.

'I'm not punishing you for anything. You're a good friend, Erin. You know that. But I do have to let you know that there's a very real danger. One that's very nearly cost you your life already. I don't want to see anything else happen to you.'

Erin shook her head. 'I'm not letting anyone dictate who I can be friends with, or how I behave.' She glared at Rav. 'Neither should you.'

'I just want you to be safe,' Rav implored her.

'Well, I just want to flush the psycho out. Isn't that what *you* want? And you don't do that by hiding away under self-imposed house arrest.'

Chapter 27

As Nell headed over to Holly's workshop in the bracing morning air, she knew this was a long shot.

Yesterday afternoon, she and Rav had tried to convince Erin to keep a low profile. Erin was vehement in disagreement, threatening to visit Finchmere that evening, just to prove she wasn't afraid, wasn't going to be bullied. Nell wasn't sure how much notice Erin had paid to Rav's warning, but she had to hope something would sink in.

Nell had to admit that Erin's stubbornness reflected her own. But Erin wasn't listening to the risks. And Nell was infuriated, and afraid, that Erin was going to blaze in and make everything worse – for herself, and for her and Rav. *It would be really great if Erin would just grow up sometime soon . . .*

Trying not to spiral into worry about what Erin might do, Nell focused instead on why she was there, following up on the other issue that Erin had flushed out: Holly and Noah.

She hadn't had a chance to arrange a meeting with Holly, so today was optimism in action. Knowing that Holly was desperate not to fall behind with her commissions while she helped with the fete, Nell guessed that she might squeeze in any opportunity to work. But it didn't mean she'd be here on a Sunday, before the last day of the fete started. Even if she'd planned to come in, this might be too early.

Recalling Holly describe herself as a morning lark, Nell had thought this ambush was worth a try to get her alone. It would be her best chance to ask her if she needed any support to raise a complaint against Noah.

Graze! was open already, wafting delicious, tempting aromas. Nell's stomach growled as she thought about their heavenly almond croissants.

And then Holly walked out, bleary-eyed, clutching a coffee and a paper bag.

Waving and hurrying over, Nell fell into step beside her. 'You're here early!'

'Yeah, well, I can't afford to get even more behind with my commissions. Besides,' she shot a glance towards the café and lowered her voice, 'Gigi usually does the morning shift, so if I pop in early, I can avoid Noah.'

The unhappy slump of her shoulders at the mention of his name told Nell that Holly was enduring more than she'd mentioned.

'That's why I wanted to speak to you,' Nell said gently. 'I heard about what happened with Erin, and that it wasn't the first time Noah's been inappropriate. So I want you to know that I'll terminate his lease. He can't work here if he behaves like that.'

'Oh . . . Look, I don't want to cause any trouble—'

'You're not. *Noah* is. It's *his* behaviour that's objectionable. *Criminal.* No one is to blame but him. I just wanted you to be aware, in case you were inclined to complain to the police, and ask if you needed any support.'

Holly winced.

'Rav was a witness to him assaulting Erin,' Nell continued. 'And he's going to make a complaint on those grounds. So yours wouldn't be a lone word against Noah's now. And Erin has been so vocal about it, other people here might come forward, too. The police would see there's a pattern.'

Holly glanced at Nell. 'I didn't want to make a fuss. We all work here together. Isn't it . . . awkward? For you?'

'Nope. Not one bit. He needs to know it's unacceptable. It *is*, Holly.'

They'd reached her workshop, but Holly didn't make a move to open the door. Instead, she hesitated.

'Look, I'll think about it, OK? Thank you.'

'Shall I get the door?' Nell offered, realising Holly may have been dawdling in the doorway, frowning at it, because she didn't have a hand free to push it open.

'Wait—'

But Nell had pushed the unlocked, ajar door open, and stepped forward to flick on the light.

The smell hit Nell first. The high, metallic, drenching scent of blood. Mixed with sawdust in the cold workshop, it was like walking into a butcher's.

As Nell peered around, the familiar dust motes swirled on the air from the breeze wafting in through the doorway.

Then she saw the body.

It must have been a split second before Holly spotted it, too, because an animalistic scream ripped from her. 'Oh God! *Oh my God!*'

'Go outside and call an ambulance and police, Holly. Now!'

As Holly backed outside, her phone to her ear, Nell moved closer, numb with denial.

No . . . No . . . *Nononono* . . .

It can't be.

But it was. The lifeless body, slumped on the bench, was Erin.

Nell shook her head, rejecting the awful scene.

Erin – sprawled across Holly's wide workbench – had shockingly bright blood cascading from the horrific, gaping neck wound, coagulating in claret puddles on the floor.

So much blood.

The long, sharp chisel was embedded in her throat, and Nell saw there had been multiple stab wounds.

This was a rage-filled attack. Erin's killer must be covered in her blood.

Knowing it was pointless, yet having to hope, Nell reached out and felt for a pulse.

Defeat welled up inside her at finding nothing. She tried for a pulse in both wrists, then looked for signs of breathing, desperate for anything.

Erin's skin was still warm to the touch, which made her lifelessness almost senseless, like Nell expected her to sit up and for it all to have been an awful joke.

But her eyes told a different story: widened and frozen, they spoke of Erin being petrified by some dreadful terror.

A sob caught in Nell's throat at the thought of Erin's final moments being full of such terrible trauma.

What had Erin been doing here? Had someone asked to meet her? Or was she here early to prove a point after their conversation yesterday?

Emotions crashed through Nell like storming waves, as horror, guilt and concern became anger. But it made her rally, and she looked around for any signs of who did this.

With shaking fingers, she took quick, furtive photos, knowing Rav would want to help her look for clues. Eventually.

Rav . . . Oh God, he'll be distraught. There was no easy way to break this to him. She texted James, with the stark words: *Erin's been murdered in Holly's workshop.*

But for Rav, she had to be gentler: *Rav, I'm so sorry. There's been another . . . incident.* She sent the text, waited a few moments, then sent another: *I'm so sorry, it's Erin.*

Tenderly, Nell closed Erin's wide, terrified eyes, then pulled up a chair to sit beside her, so she wouldn't be alone.

Taking Erin's unresponsive hand, Nell clasped it between both of hers, as if trying to infuse life back into her.

Then she bowed her head and sat in silence. Waiting.

Chapter 28

Sunday 9th July – 6.45 a.m.

In Finchmere's refectory, Rav poured a mug of coffee, wondering where Nell had got to. Thirty minutes ago, she'd showered and then hurried out, calling to him as he'd stepped under the water. When he'd yelled to say he hadn't heard, the door had slammed shut.

Despite being certain that Nell would have fed Jezebel, Rav couldn't resist the headbutts and, even though he was sure this was her second breakfast, he found himself dishing up tuna and refreshing her water, winning delighted purrs.

Curling up beside him, Jezebel rested her head on his thigh as he drank his coffee. She'd been clingier with both of them since the fire, and Rav didn't stint on extra cuddles. They weren't doing him any harm either, at the moment.

He reached for his phone, about to check Nell's location to make sure she was OK.

And then the texts flashed.

Dread rose as he read the first . . . and then the second . . .

No . . . No . . .

He blinked, staring at the words, unable to accept them.

It *had* to be wrong.

He didn't realise that he'd knocked over his mug, coffee pouring over the table and onto the floor. He stood jerkily, unsure what to do, and the bench seat toppled backwards.

Groping for his crutches, he hobbled, then hurried to the hall.

Seeing a Land Rover outside the house, he clambered into the driver's seat.

Legs shaking, he drove over the grass, straight for the courtyard.

Pulling up, and limping around the corner of the workshop, he came face to face with Holly.

Mascara was streaked down her face as she shivered outside her barn door.

She shook her head, teeth chattering as she tried to speak. 'D-d-d-don't go . . . in.'

Rav paused and adjusted his crutches to clasp her arm. 'Are you OK?' When she nodded, he asked, 'Did you call an ambulance? The police?'

Once Holly nodded again, he limped past her, elbowing his way through the door.

He'd been braced for the sight, but not the smell, and he nearly gagged. As he crumpled in the doorway, Nell half-rose from across the workshop – blocking his view.

'Rav? I'm so sorry. You don't need to see her . . . like this.' She stood, setting Erin's hand down carefully.

'I do.' He moved closer. 'Because it's my fault, isn't it?' He heard his voice crack. 'Everything, *all this*, is all my fault—'

His words dashed away as he caught sight of her, lain across the bench, stabbed so . . . *ferociously*.

As he twisted away from the awful scene, devastation welled through him. He didn't fight back the sobs rising in his throat.

This shouldn't have happened to Erin. This *wouldn't* have happened to her, if he'd been better at protecting everyone.

He felt Nell gather him into a strong hug and he pressed his forehead onto the top of her head. Her scent was comforting, blurring out the pervasive stench of blood.

'I had a *warning*, though, didn't I?' he mumbled into her hair. 'When someone tried to poison her, I should have *made* her take things more seriously. I should have made her realise there was a real danger. I should have made her keep out of harm's way—'

'You did, Rav. She was as stubborn as both of us, in her own way. She wanted to be here—'

'I didn't do enough, then, did I? If I had, she wouldn't—' His whole body tremored as undammed grief poured from him. He felt his face crumple as sobs shuddered through his chest.

Nell pulled him close again as he wept. The pain in his chest didn't lessen with the outpouring. The agony just seemed to build. Time drew out, as they stood like that, until the door was wrenched open and James peered in, a SOCO team behind him.

'I'm very sorry, Rav, Nell. You know what I'm going to need you to do.'

Once Dr Saunders had processed Nell and Rav for evidence, and they'd both been given SOCO suits to wear in exchange for their clothes, now bagged for analysis, James steered them away.

With them sat in the courtyard, gulping the fresh air and trying to steady themselves, James asked Ed to take their statements, while he turned his attention to Holly.

He eyed the young woman, as she shivered and sobbed across the table from him, and he wondered how much was for effect, to evoke his sympathy.

Once he'd recorded her formal statement, he asked, 'Why was Erin here?'

'What?' Holly wiped a hand across her mascara-smeared cheek.

'Had you arranged to meet her?'

'N-*No*.' Holly frowned.

'Then why was she here?'

'I-I don't know.' She sat up, staring at James. 'It's nothing to do with me that she's . . . she's . . .' Holly gulped back a sob.

'Been brutally killed? In your workshop? With your chisel?' James finished for her.

'Yes . . . but . . . that's, well, that's . . .'

Leaning forward, James looked like he very much wanted to know what 'that' was. 'Did you invite her?'

'No!'

'Maybe you talked about something? Maybe you argued? And you got angry? I know you were angry with Noah, even if you didn't confront him.'

'No! That's not the case!'

'Well, that's not true.' James held her gaze until she looked down and stared at the table. 'I'm sure you don't mean to misdirect me, do you, Holly?'

Now Holly did look at him, her chin raised a little. 'You're right, I was angry the other day, with Noah. But I had no reason to be angry with Erin.'

Her cheeks flushed as she folded her arms around herself. As James watched the lie leaking from her, he simply stated, 'But you were. Tell me about that.'

'Pfff.' Holly shrugged and shook her head, trying to shut the questions down.

'Well?' James pressed.

'Oh, Erin's always got to be number one, hasn't she?' Holly rolled her eyes. 'She's . . . a bit . . . much. But just because I didn't get along with her, it doesn't mean I would have done anything to harm her.'

'And what do you think of Rav?' On a hunch, James changed tack fast, hoping for a genuine response, before she'd be able to cover her reaction.

'*Rav?*' She blinked, but her cheeks flushed again. 'He's . . . Well, he's great, isn't he? Very upset by all this, I'm sure.'

'Yes, I'm sure he is. He and Erin were close.'

'Not as close as she wanted to be.' She gave another defiant jut of her chin as she wiped her face.

'Possibly not.' James kept watching her. 'Maybe Erin came to your workshop to talk to you about something? Rav, maybe? Or something else?'

'No. She didn't.' Holly shook her head.

'Was there anything she might have wanted to discuss with you?' Holly's gaze slid over towards *Graze!*.

James seized the opportunity. 'Is this related to Noah?' As Holly's lips clamped, James pressed the question. 'What about him?' He ignored the beep of his phone and looked at her. 'Tell me.'

Her shoulders slumping, Holly leaned in. 'Noah makes me . . . uncomfortable. He's always in my workshop, offering to help. But actually he's . . .' She tilted her head at James. '*You* know . . .'

'I can guess.' James made his tone gentler now. 'But I still need you to tell me.'

'He makes it look helpful. But his hands are . . . everywhere. He'll come in when I'm working and I'm in the middle of something so

I can't stop and he'll . . . *leer*. Right down my top. It's horrible.' She shuddered. 'But what can I do? We both work here. If I complain, Gigi will lose out – and that's even if my complaint is taken seriously. And how could it be, when it's my word against his.'

'Nell would take that seriously,' James said.

Holly scuffed her shoe into the gravel. 'Yeah. Well, someone must have said something to her, because she asked me this morning. That's why she wanted to catch me on my own. To ask me in private. She was trying to convince me it wouldn't be just my word now.'

'And isn't that a good thing?' James asked.

'I-I don't know. Nell can't evict him without evidence, can she? That would mean I'd have to involve, well, *you*. And I didn't want that. I didn't want to upset my workplace. I just wanted to get on with things.'

'But since Erin had tried to address it . . .?' James pursued the link. 'Did you feel your hand was being forced?'

Staring at the table, Holly sighed. 'Fine for her, isn't it. She could swan off after the fete. Not like the rest of us, who work here all the time.'

'Erin isn't swanning off anywhere, now,' James reminded her. 'So, who needed to silence her?'

Holly couldn't hold eye contact. Then her head jerked round, to check the café, before she looked at James. Leaning across the table, she whispered urgently, 'Noah. *Noah* wanted to shut her up, didn't he?' She gave a half-laugh. 'And why not get me framed, even arrested for it? That would be convenient for him, too, wouldn't it? And, even if nothing sticks, my word with the police would be totally discredited if I did make a complaint in the future, wouldn't it?' Her wide eyes met his.

It wasn't entirely implausible. But something about her face was a little too earnest, a little too desperate. As he nodded, and concluded the interview, he checked his phone, but his mind was on Holly's words.

Noah might have wanted to silence Erin and perhaps discredit Holly. But why kill Louise? Did she know about his sexual assaults? His attack could have been spontaneous, in a flash of rage, if she'd threatened him.

Messages from the tech forensic team loaded, with the subject: 'Emails retrieved from Rev Louise Brimstone's laptop'.

James scanned the list as they loaded, noting colleagues, congregation members, community event organisers. He moved to the sent emails, and his search stopped at a name.

Noah Grayling.

He opened the email, and nearly jolted backwards at Louise's tone.

Noah, I'm putting in writing how utterly UNACCEPTABLE your behaviour is. I've seen you letching over Holly in her workshop. I've seen her trying to avoid you touching her, as you try to make it look accidental. Let me spell it out: your attention and your wandering hands are UNWANTED. If you don't stop your creepy behaviour, I'll go to the police.

Chapter 29

Sunday 9th July – 12 p.m.

Time lost any meaning for Rav, as the day stretched on. The courtyard had been excluded from the fete and cordoned off with police barrier tape, which meant the area was private and quiet, at least.

He'd stayed, sitting at the same table, unnaturally still, glued to the sight of the SOCO team coming and going, laying down the metal plates to step on as they took samples of blood, measured spatter patterns on the wall, took endless photos. They labelled everything with such care, such methodical diligence, that his heart nearly broke.

When the medic brought the gurney, he tensed, and the minutes seemed like aeons as, inside, Erin's body was transferred to it, emerging contained in a . . . He gulped. A body bag.

He stood up as the gurney was slowly, carefully, steered past him, his head low – not so much bowed in respect as hanging in shame. He felt like he was drowning in guilt. It crushed his chest, making it nearly impossible to breathe.

Sylvia approached, sombre in respectful navy, clearly in shock. Rav tried to smile, knowing it was a gesture, but couldn't manage it.

'I'm so sorry, Rav. I can't . . . I can't believe it. I keep expecting her to turn up with some outrageous comment.'

As she sat at his table, he remembered that Sylvia had been Erin's colleague, too.

'She had so much . . . potential.' Sylvia shook her head, her scarlet lips setting into a line as she watched the police work. 'I'm trusting James to find whoever was responsible.' She turned to look at Rav. 'Or you and Nell.' She reached for his hand. 'Are you up to it?'

He shrugged. He wasn't sure. This was . . . worse than a nightmare.

'You don't have a hope unless you stop thinking you're responsible,

211

Rav.' Her admonishment was kind. 'You're not. And there are things you can still do for her, as long as you don't let yourself be consumed with someone else's guilt.'

He swallowed, shook his head. 'I . . . I don't know.'

'No, but *I* do, my dearest Rav. You're resourceful and brave, and you and Nell observe so well. There will be something that you both see, I know it. But you have to make sure you don't get mired in that fog. Keep sharp. Now, more than ever. Promise me?'

He couldn't deny her insistent gaze, her expectant smile that showed that she had belief in him, even if he didn't.

His two words, 'I promise,' made the tension ease from her face and her smile warm a little.

'Thank you.' She sat back. 'I wish I could help with this, the investigation. But I know that if I keep the load off you and Nell, then you'll find something. I'm trying to do my bit to make sure the business side of things still runs smoothly.'

Holly stumbled past, clearly upset, and Sylvia beckoned. 'Holly, my dear, I'm so sorry for this awful shock. If you need anything at all, please just let me know, OK?'

As Holly nodded, Sylvia added, 'This courtyard is off limits to visitors now – obviously, with the police cordon up – but some space has been set aside for you in the craft quarter, on the way to the wildflower meadow. There's no expectation, of course, I just wanted you to have the option of somewhere to display your work and take commissions, if you wanted.'

Dashing the back of her hand across her face, Holly mumbled, 'Thank you. I'll . . . I'll use it. I can't afford to waste the opportunity. I'll set up after lunch.'

As Holly stumbled away, Sylvia looked around the courtyard. 'I've been working with James's team. Since they've cordoned off the courtyard, the fete team have made sure that any paths no longer direct guests here, and we've put up a couple of spare tents for *Graze!* and *Finchmere Estate Vineyards*. The baristas from *Graze!* are already there, getting set up, but I haven't found Noah or Gigi yet.'

She pulled out her phone, shooting a wary glance at Rav. 'I'm not sure if Nell's seen the press we've been getting?'

The headlines were typically unsympathetic: *Finchmere Fete worse than death*; *Finchmere puts the Fete in Fatal*.

'Imelda and Hugo are talking to the press team. They'll handle it. I just don't want Nell to get poleaxed by it. Have you seen her?'

'She's with James. Should be back soon.'

As they looked around, Rav saw James walking over, with Nell, still asking questions as he nodded in greeting and then sat down at the adjacent table.

Both Rav and Sylvia sat in silence, listening.

'Did you come here to talk to Holly this morning, Nell?'

'Yes. I wanted to know if she wanted to make a complaint. About Noah.'

'Along what lines?'

'I'd heard that Noah had been inappropriate with Erin, and that he'd behaved similarly with Holly. I wanted her to know that I was terminating Noah's lease here, and that if she needed any support to take things further, she could count on me. It wouldn't be her word against his, not with Erin's account, and Rav as a witness.'

James turned to Rav. 'Can I get a statement of what you saw between Noah and Erin?'

Rav nodded.

'Now?'

He knew his face had clouded at the memory. With Erin killed so savagely, the precursor to that harm filled him with wrath.

'It happened in the courtyard, right there. When she hugged him – just a friendly hug, nothing intimate – he felt her up.' Rav's lips curled in disgust – at Noah; at himself, for not making a fuss, not standing up for her, not letting himself be the target for Noah's retribution instead of her . . .

Then his mind cleared. 'Hold on . . .' Rav shook his head as he made the leap. 'Are you saying *Noah* killed Erin?'

'Rav, you know very well we don't have any evidence yet. I'm not assuming anything at this stage—'

James's caution couldn't stop the fireball igniting in Rav's chest. He pushed himself to stand, pacing on his crutches.

'I should have said something. I might have been able to stop it.

And now . . .' He choked. He couldn't face up to the consequences. He couldn't even say it aloud.

As he drew a laboured breath, he shot a hopeless look at James, then Nell. She was frowning, lost in thought. But the fact that she hadn't instantly disagreed with him was a stab in the heart.

He sagged onto the seat, gripping the pole of his crutches, mired in misery. So, when Ashley moved from the workshop to the café, and a few minutes later escorted Noah out, Rav fought to stand up again. He heard yelling, and it was a few seconds before he realised it came from him.

'You *bastard*! What kind of disgusting coward are you?'

He swatted something on his arm, until he saw it was Nell's hand, as she tried to calm him, quieten him. But that had been the problem, hadn't it? He'd been *too* silent.

And now, Erin was dead.

So was Louise.

Had Noah killed her, too? From the mists of his mind, he remembered Louise arguing with him, accusing him of predatory behaviour. She'd been so right, and now she was dead.

Outraged, he yelled again, 'Louise was right about you, you slimy *bastard*!'

Noah pivoted on the spot and stormed over to Rav. 'And you're a paragon of virtue, are you? Yeah, stick the knife in, mate, while *you* play away.' He was face to face with Rav now, spittle on his lips. 'That's how your type get away with it, isn't it?'

As Noah moved in, Rav knew what was coming: he gripped his crutches, clenched his abs and braced – letting Noah's shove meet a wall of immovable muscle.

Glad he hadn't staggered back, Rav met Noah's eyes as the man continued ranting, even more enraged now.

'You enjoy making trouble for blokes like me, then? How about I bring trouble to you?' He kicked one of Rav's crutches out from under him, and Rav nearly overbalanced. Quick as lightning, Nell grabbed him, steadying him, glaring at Noah.

Ashley seized Noah by the arm and pulled him aside. 'You can come with me quietly, or I can put you under arrest for threatening behaviour and take you to the station in handcuffs. I'm only giving you *one* chance – *this* chance – to choose the former, understand?'

As Noah was led away, he glared over his shoulder at Rav. Gigi, emerging from the café, looked stricken at Rav, spurring him to call to her, 'You don't have to put up with a sleazeball like that, Gigi.'

'Let's cool it with the shouting and the marital advice.' James tried to calm him down. 'Even if you are right.'

'Are you going to arrest him?' Rav demanded.

'He's cooperating with our questioning.' But as James used the tactful words, he gave one, pointed, nod.

It was enough to make Rav pause, his chest heaving. 'Good.' He ran a hand through his hair and looked around. 'Good. Thanks, James.'

But Nell still looked worried. He sat beside her. 'Sorry. Sorry for causing a scene.'

'Don't be. I know you and Erin were good friends. This is . . . so *horrific*. But you *do* need to know that it's not your fault.'

He shook his head. 'Don't. It doesn't make it easier to hear you lie about it.'

A look passed between Nell and Sylvia, making Rav wince. He didn't deserve their sympathy.

Taking his hand in both of hers, Nell gazed into his eyes. 'We'll find whoever did it, Rav. You know we will.'

He shook his head, as tears fell. 'Even if we do . . . This time . . . *This* time it won't be enough.'

Sunday 9th July – 2 p.m.

James had left Nell and Rav at the courtyard. They weren't in any state to do anything towards the fete today, so allowing them to sit somewhere out of the way of the visitors seemed to be for the best.

Kat had approached before James had departed, assuring both Nell and Rav that she had enough footage to use, and that they didn't need to do any pieces to camera. It was just as well; Rav had been utterly shattered by the shocking news. He couldn't have put on a game face today.

Now, at the station, James could only hope their investigation would push them towards an answer. He looked up, optimistic, as Ashley strode out of the interview room.

'Noah's still being held under caution. He's "no commenting" every question. But, reading between the lines, I don't think he has an alibi for any of his movements.'

'Oh?' James held on to the spark of hope that gave him a line of inquiry.

'Considering he and Gigi live together and work together, they manage to spend very little time together.'

'Quite a trick.' James frowned. 'But if he doesn't have an alibi, then presumably Gigi doesn't, either?'

'She seems to spend a lot of time looking after their team of baristas. So she always has someone to account for her whereabouts.'

James shrugged. 'An employee may have a few good reasons to provide an alibi, though . . .?'

'Always a possibility,' Ashley conceded. 'So we have SOCOs searching their house now, in case any blood-spattered clothes are stashed or have been destroyed somewhere, or any clean-up attempts have left traces of Erin's blood. And the tech team have their phones and computers.'

'Good. With luck, we'll hear something soon.' He paced to the board, reviewing the photos. Ed joined him and pointed at the picture of Louise with her vicar friend.

'That's young Rev Woodwhite. His wife's a friend of my sister. He had some sort of breakdown. Ended up at The Priory.' Ed shook his head. 'Poor chap. I think he's on the mend these days. Back in circulation now, though, so I hear.'

They both turned as Hesha walked in. 'Oh, a full house!' She smiled at the team. 'I've got an update from tech. You won't like it, but I'll tell you anyway. We checked the phone numbers of our suspects – Noah, Gigi, Zeus, Holly, Bea – to see if any of them were in the Richmond area on Wednesday, when the photo of Aanya was taken.'

'Why won't we like this?' James asked, already guessing. 'Inconclusive?'

'Exactly. Everyone's phone was at their home address, except Holly's and Zeus's – both of them at Finchmere, with no further resolution than that. So I suggest that the burner phone, which was being used to send those texts, was taken by the stalker, while they left their registered phone at home or work.'

'So they've got some good tech awareness, then,' Ashley said. 'Does that limit the group any?'

James frowned. 'Not really. Most people know that their whereabouts can be tracked by their phone. And this is a pretty tech-savvy group, isn't it? All using high-tech equipment in one form or another, or running their own YouTube channels and monitoring analytics.'

As Ashley nodded, James asked Hesha, 'What about Thursday? Any phone data for then?'

'Holly was in Pendlebury, near the river; everyone else was home all night, except Gigi and Noah, who were home, and then back at Finchmere at around 10 p.m.'

'That's a bit odd,' James mused. 'And what about this morning, at about 6 a.m., when Erin was killed?'

'Well, I'd appreciate some amazement that I've got that data from my now very good friend at the phone company. Everyone's phone was at home. Gigi arrived at 6.15 a.m., which is actually a little later than usual for her. Everyone else arrived at Finchmere at around 8 a.m. Except Holly, who arrived about 6.20 a.m.'

'Great.' James grimaced, glancing at the clock. 'I need something. We can't detain Noah for much longer without some solid evidence.'

Ashley checked her phone. 'Incoming email.' She glanced at James. 'SOCO, so hold your breath. They've matched the fingerprints on the candlestick to those of one of our suspects.'

James tried to be patient for the few the seconds – which felt like years – it took her to open the attached report.

Maybe, just maybe, this would be the clincher.

He knew, as Ashley frowned, that the chance to arrest Noah and detain him for questioning had just slipped through their fingers.

After she'd reread the report, Ashley stared at him. 'Huh. They're Holly's.'

Chapter 30

The day had passed in a daze for Rav. Unable to eat anything, those markers of time had been absent. Now it was dark, he found himself having to face either eating some food or heading to bed for a sleepless night.

He just couldn't bring himself to attempt any supper, however tempting Nell had made the cheeseboard, with all his favourite nibbles.

Restlessness overwhelmed him. He scrolled endlessly through his phone, rereading texts from Erin, scouring every line for clues that weren't there, convinced he'd see something *if only* he kept looking.

His search was interrupted by Kat's email flashing across the screen, outlining the stats from the fete and asking for a call to discuss what they'd like to do next, in case she needed to set anything up.

'Bloody filming,' Rav fumed. 'Doesn't she realise we have more on our minds at the moment?'

'I'll call her back,' Nell offered. 'She's only trying to do her job.' As Jezebel sat up, reminding them of how late her dinner was, Nell scratched her cat's chin. 'And yes, little poppet, I'll feed you, too.'

As Nell made the call on speakerphone, while going through to the boot room, Rav resumed his search.

It was almost by accident that he tapped Erin's name at the top of the column of texts, and her information loaded.

Along with a map.

He sat up.

A map of her current location – well, her *phone's* current location. *What if something's on it? What if the person who harmed her, lured her to the workshop with a text, then disposed of her phone? We'd know – we'd know exactly who's responsible . . .*

With his heart racing, he enlarged the map. They'd sometimes shared locations when they were surveying for work as consultants together. Erin must have forgotten to disable it.

The blessed blue dot showed that her phone was near the courtyard. The dot was large, without a specific pinpoint location, but it looked like it was in the woodland that curved around the workshop. Exactly as if Erin's killer had snatched her phone from her, then lobbed it into the bushes.

Rav knew he may not be able to find the precise location, but if he got close enough and called it . . . hopefully, maybe, it wouldn't be on silent, and he might be able to find it.

But Rav could also see that Erin's phone was on the last few ebbs of its battery. There wasn't enough for the charge to last the night. It was now – or never.

Itching with impatience, he urged Nell to finish her call, so he could tell her, so they could go *now* to find the phone.

As she came back in, still on the phone, she grimaced at him. 'Yeah, that's great news, Kat. We're really pleased that the streaming has gone so well . . . Oh? I think I lost you a bit there.' She sat, then checked her phone for signal, turning it off speakerphone and putting the handset to her ear. 'Is your signal . . . ? Oh, yes, I hear you now . . . Yes, the numbers really are incredible . . . Yep, we know that's all down to you . . . We're really pleased. Thank you. Yes . . .'

Seeing the call wasn't about to end any time soon, Rav lost patience and hobbled out to the Land Rover. There would probably still be a police guard at Holly's workshop, so it would be safe enough for him to go and take a look. If he dashed over now, he could check the phone – then hand it in.

He steered directly towards the courtyard, over the fields. But he had to limp to reach the woodland on the far side, beyond the buildings.

He hesitated at the sight of Holly's workshop, unlit and unattended. Maybe the team had processed everything already, and left the place locked and taped. But the lack of a police presence made him uneasy.

Trying to decide what to do, he sat in the cabin for a long moment. There was no movement around the barns.

Trying to be sensible, he sent Nell a text: *Hey Nell, I'm out by the barns, I can see the location of Erin's phone and I'm trying to find it, hoping for some clues on there.* Then: *I'll text James, so he knows.*

Taking a long breath, he wondered what to type to James. After starting and deleting a couple of messages, he managed: *Hi James, I'm still sharing the location of Erin's phone. It's at the back of the courtyard barns but the battery is running out, so it'll need finding asap. I'm there now to help, if someone can come soon.*

He waited in the dark, his breath fogging the Landy's window as he looked towards the woods.

Seconds felt like aeons. He checked his phone about six times each minute – and even that felt like superhuman restraint.

The place looked deserted. There was no point being spooked for the sake of being spooked. He could just go now and take a look . . .

As he got out of the Landy, he realised he wouldn't manage crutches, phone and a high-powered survey torch, so he made do with the light on his phone.

This wasn't like surveying; even a nocturnal survey didn't have this sinister threat wrapping around him, pressing in.

The beam bleached the undergrowth ahead of him, and he immediately found himself tangled in brambles.

His heart drummed like a rabbit's warning beat of danger as he unpicked his feet, heavy and clumsy in the darkness. Thorns clawed his jeans, ripping into flesh, making it hard work to pull himself free. Sweating with effort and fear, he jerked away from one cruelly prickled strand, only to stumble into the spiny grasp of another.

As he ripped himself free, he staggered backwards, dropping his crutches and landing on his back so heavily that he winded himself.

Shocked and shaken, he took a moment, listening to the night air rustling through the trees, the distant bark of foxes.

In the darkness, he felt for his dropped phone, his wrists clawed by thorns. Finding it at last, he shoved it in his pocket; then he gradually managed to bend his legs and push himself up to sitting. He groped around for his crutches and pulled himself to his feet, panting with effort. Leaning on them, he looked at his phone again.

His blue dot blinked – right near the location of Erin's phone. *I'm close.*

Beaming the phone's torch around the space, he squinted for the gleam of reflecting glass, or Erin's familiar red case. But he saw nothing. Dialling her number, hoping it wouldn't use up the last of her battery, he called her phone.

Holding his breath, he listened for her ringtone.

Nothing. Then . . . something faint, but close. The purr of a phone vibrating on silent.

The snap of the twig could have been him as he moved clumsily, his focused gaze following the methodical sweep of his phone's light.

Yes!

Catching a glint, he stopped, leaned over and reached for Erin's phone, threading his hand through nettles and bramble.

Just as his fingertips reached it, the woodland around him *shrieked*.

The blood-curdling, terror-filled screech echoed through the trees, across the courtyard.

What the hell was that?

In sheer panic, Rav dropped to his knees, shooting fire through his recovering limbs. His crutches clattered beside him, as he shrank into the shadowy scrub, seeking cover, protection.

From what?

He peered around, trying to see what had happened, trying to listen over his ragged breathing, his hammering heart.

Something told him danger – *real danger* – was close.

The silence pressed in, all the more terrifying for what it could hold.

He grappled with his phone, trying to turn off the giveaway light. His fumbling fingers took forever to switch off the glow.

Slowly, he stretched his arm out, trying to reach Erin's phone. The brambles ripping his shirt seemed louder than thunder.

Just as his fingertips touched the edge of Erin's phone, a nearby twig snapped.

Sunday 9th July – 9.40 p.m.

Growing ever more frantic, Nell searched the house for Rav, then dashed outside.

His text beeped, and Nell stared at the phone, not certain if she should trust it.

What if it wasn't him?

What if it was?

Her heart lumped in her throat as some instinct told her, *screamed* at her, that something was wrong, that Rav needed help, needed her. She stopped dead at the front of the house, seeing that one of the Land Rovers was missing.

So, he has *gone to the courtyard, then . . . The message must be genuine . . .*

Peering in the direction of the barns, she looked for telltale headlights. But, beyond the house, the surrounding estate lay in darkness.

She tried calling him again, but there was no answer, then she checked his location.

Yes, he was near the courtyard. Or his phone was. Could someone fake that?

Nell hung back, not sure if she would be running into a trap if she followed him.

But she had to go. Even if it was a trap, she couldn't risk leaving him if he needed her.

Her stomach churned and she fumbled in the hall sideboard for a Land Rover key, then hurried to the nearest one. As the vehicle bounced over the field, she managed to call James.

Giving him no chance for small talk, she barrelled in, 'It might be nothing, James, but Rav has been out on his own near the courtyard. He's not answering my calls. I'm nearly there. Please come.'

She nearly passed out in relief at his reply. 'Already on my way. See you in ten.'

She parked next to the Landy that Rav must have used. *So he* is *here?*

Thankful that her own Land Rover's arrival would be silent, Nell slipped out of the cabin, then reached into the flatbed for a torch. Instead, her hands found a billhook. Her fingers curled round the handle as she hefted the long, curve-bladed tool. The idea of having something to defend herself with was both a comfort and a dread.

Instead of giving her location away using the light on her phone, Nell let her eyes grow accustomed to the dark. This was how she liked being in woodland best . . . usually.

Now, though, she was reticent to leave the cover from the shadows of the barns. She scanned for movement, for any signs of anyone, listening intently as she held her breath.

Seeing and hearing no one, she inched along the building, her footsteps silent. Her apprehension grew as she saw Holly's unguarded workshop. Vulnerability shivered over her.

Fighting down her rising panic, she wondered again why Rav wouldn't answer her call. Holding up the billhook, she crept forward, towards Rav's location – which was seared on her memory – as long as he hadn't moved.

With the cover of the barn coming to an end, she looked around carefully, then crept across to the woodland, pressing her back against a tree as she peered into the gloomy forest. The rustling breeze distracted her, as she tried to listen for any sounds.

Not seeing anyone, and not hearing anyone, gave her no comfort. There were too many places to hide in the dark. Too many places to silently lie in wait.

But Rav was here somewhere. And he might need her.

So Nell moved as quietly as she could in the darkness, not daring to use her phone.

Knowing she was near where Rav should have been, she couldn't stop herself hurrying, desperate to find him.

Then she stumbled, sprawling into the undergrowth, the air forced out of her lungs.

Urgently, she reached in her pocket for her phone, tapping on the light.

It was like a laser beam against the deep darkness of the wood.

It was more than enough to illuminate the hand on the ground beside her.

In horror and fear, she scooted backwards, away from it. But she raised the light with her shaking hand.

Then, with rising, burning nausea, she saw what – or rather *who* – she'd tripped over.

The arm . . . the body . . . and the head, battered by the blow that had killed him.

Chapter 31

James raced across Finchmere's estate, the blue flashes from the police car washing the fields and then the woodland with icy light.

Parking inside the courtyard, he pointed his bright headlights towards the trees. Dashing out, he seized his baton and Taser, and strode into the wood.

'J-James?'

The voice was so small, he barely recognised it as Nell's. His feet were running before he realised, and almost immediately he saw Nell kneeling on the forest floor, blanched in the ghostly light.

Then he realised she was sitting beside a body.

'Have you called an ambulance?'

Nell nodded. 'I'm not sure how much the call handler heard, though. I had to whisper. In case . . .'

He nodded. '*Is* anyone else around?'

Nell shrugged, but it looked more like a shiver.

'Rav?' James almost couldn't bear to creep forward and to have confirmation. But Nell was in shock, so he didn't hesitate. He ripped his jacket off and wrapped it around her shoulders, then checked the body.

No pulse. But . . . this wasn't Rav.

James shone the torch on his phone at the side of the face that remained visible.

It was Noah.

James rocked back on his heels.

That . . . doesn't make any sense.

A sound in the bushes made James leap to his feet and spin around.

He saw Nell scrabble to her feet as he pointed his torch towards the sound, beyond the beam of his car's headlights.

He braced for an attack, reaching for his Taser, and glanced at Nell, only to see she was holding – *oh, bloody hell* – a *billhook*.

He prodded her arm and held up his Taser, eyeing her stout, sharp blade.

She glared at him, then stepped back. But still, she didn't lower her arm.

In the dark bushes, another ripping sound came, and then, 'Nell? James?'

As Rav stumbled into view, James lowered his Taser, almost weak with relief.

'Rav? Are you hurt?' Nell hurried to him.

'No. I'm . . . I'm OK.'

'Did you hear or see anything?' James asked.

'Yeah. Yeah, I heard something . . . *awful*.'

Only then did he see that he was standing beside a corpse.

'Oh . . . Oh, *God*. I think I heard . . . *that*.'

Sunday 9th July – 10.30 p.m.

Rav understood that James had to get a formal statement from him, and that he'd be considered a suspect after he'd yelled at Noah across the courtyard, shortly before being found lurking in bushes mere metres from Noah's dead body. But James was taking that formality very seriously right now as he recorded everything carefully. Rav tried to understand that he would have to, for both their benefit.

Beyond the courtyard, he could see the SOCO team swinging into action again, setting up their cordons and tents so they could process the scene, while Nell directed the ambulance to yet another body.

He shivered on the seat, discreetly away from the work, near the café. As Nell came and sat with him, Rav felt like a fool, recounting his terror. Especially as it seemed like he wasn't the target.

'So you were out here, in the first place, and on your own, because you were sharing locations with Erin's phone.'

'Oh. Yes. I found it.' Rav rummaged in his pocket and pulled out the red-cased phone. 'I was just looking, you know, idly, at her messages and saw that we were still sharing locations – and her phone was near the courtyard. So I guessed the . . . the . . . person who hurt her might have thrown the phone into the bushes.'

James took a bag from the SOCO team and placed the phone inside, labelling it. Then glared at Rav. 'I know you texted me, to let me know what you were doing, but you didn't wait for me or a member of my team to turn up and collect it properly, so we could look for any additional related evidence. Instead, you blundered all over the scene, eliminating our chance of finding something that might – *might* – have helped with a prosecution.'

Rav saw that James was really furious, and he couldn't disagree with the point he'd made.

As James took a deep breath, he admitted, 'I don't blame you for being desperate for answers. I am, too. I feel like the clock is running out while the body count is rising.'

'I honestly expected an officer to be here. I was planning to tell them.'

It was obvious that James saw right through Rav's half-truth, and Rav admitted, 'I didn't think about trashing evidence. I am sorry. Obviously, I'd never want to impede the case like that. I just thought—'

'I know what you thought.' Jame's voice rose in exasperation. 'You somehow imagined that Erin's killer would have texted her, inviting her to the courtyard, and if you found the phone and unlocked it . . . Bingo. There's the murderer. Our very tech-savvy, forensic-aware killer giving away their identity.'

Rav stared at his lap. He managed one last defence. 'Her battery was running out. We might not have been able to find it at all if I'd waited.'

James – shaking his head and folding his arms – made it obvious he wasn't buying it. 'You know enough, Rav, to know you've contaminated this evidence. And you put yourself in danger. Needlessly.'

Shame jolted through Rav. But at the same time, something rebellious fired him.

'I'm sorry, James. I'm sorry that I'm to blame for all this. I didn't mean to stir up anything *like* this when we started filming. I didn't want to put the people I care about in danger. And I'm sorry that I'm so bloody useless. So sodding *helpless*.'

He kicked out at his crutches and they clattered over, crashing into the wall of the café.

As Nell reached to grab them from her seat, Rav spotted the movement in the window of the café. It was barely perceptible, but the blind definitely swayed.

He pointed, worried that speaking aloud would spook whoever was inside.

Beckoning an officer, James directed the constable to the back of the café. He waited a few seconds for his colleague to get into position, and then hammered on the door.

'Police. Open up.'

The blind moved again, and this time Rav saw who it was: a stricken-faced, bare-shouldered Gigi.

As the door was unlocked and James pushed his way in, Rav glimpsed Gigi holding a shirt against her chest to preserve her modesty. Behind her, the barista with the man-bun was wearing only tiny briefs and body oil.

Back at the station, James was trying to get answers out of Gigi, while Ashley interviewed her companion.

They'd been invited in for questioning to ascertain if their affair had given them motive to kill Louise, in case she was threatening to tell Gigi's husband. James hadn't yet broken the news about Noah's death. He was trying to work out if Gigi might have had anything to do with it, and hoping she might give something away if she had to hold in the lie.

'How long has the affair been going on?'

A Gallic shrug. 'How British of you, to sound so disapproving.'

'Does Noah know?'

Gigi laughed. 'Of course.'

She hadn't reacted to James's use of the present tense.

'So, is yours an open marriage?'

'Well, I was open.' Another shrug. 'Noah, not so much.'

'Were you having more than one affair?'

'No.' Gigi looked thoroughly disinterested. 'Not at the moment.' She huffed in impatience. 'Isn't all this overkill? For an affair?'

'All what?' James asked.

'The team spying outside the café. This interview.' She raised her hands. 'Louise had an unhealthy fixation with my sex life. But she at least was invested in the sanctity of marriage. But you need only concern yourself with the law.' She leaned across the table. 'And I have done nothing illegal.'

'The SOCO team weren't outside your café because they were spying on you,' James said. It was his prearranged signal for Hesha to walk in, with a note, so that he could pretend to have just learned about Noah's death, and gauge Gigi's reaction.

At the soft knock on the door, he said, 'Come in.'

'Excuse me, sir.' Hesha duly handed him the note and left.

James took a moment to read it, grave-faced, before glancing at Gigi.

'Unfortunately, a body was found in the woods tonight,' he told her.

'A body?' Her brow was creased, her face bewildered with worry. If she was lying, it was convincing.

'I'm very sorry to tell you, Gigi . . .'

Her hand shot over her mouth.

'That the person we found tonight . . .'

Her eyes squeezed shut.

'Was your husband. Noah.'

At the confirmation, her eyes flew open. She took a couple of deep breaths, then rested her hands in her lap. Eventually, she nodded. 'So. It is over.'

James studied her. 'What? What's over?'

Gigi sighed. 'The lying. The sneaking around. The pretending. The oh-so-happy business together that could be a delight but felt more like a millstone, with the wrong partner.' She stared at James. 'You're sure it's him? Certain?'

James nodded. 'You can formally identify him, of course. But we are sure.'

'And he's definitely dead?'

James nearly choked at the unexpected question. 'Yes, Gigi.'

He gave her a moment as she looked up at the ceiling, eyelids fluttering, while she made sure tears wouldn't fall.

'So, now, is there anything you'd like to tell me? You mentioned Louise. Did she antagonise Noah? Would he have had a reason to harm her?'

'Oh, several. Louise was determined to tell my husband of my affair. But he already knew! He just didn't know who with. He would follow me some nights, trying to find out. He wasn't very subtle. What Louise failed to realise was that him knowing made no difference. It suited Noah to play the hangdog. Gave him a reason to beg affection from other women. You see, I am so heartless. So cold. I don't understand the attention he needs.'

Her nose wrinkled. 'Noah has always chased other women. It makes no difference how affectionate I am. I came to realise I would always be in the wrong. And here I was, trapped in a business with him. It is already so difficult to separate all these strands of your life – if one person refuses, it becomes impossible. So I decided to please myself. My affair began in rebellion, but then . . . something blossomed. And I wanted to protect it.'

She looked down at her lap, taking a breath before meeting James's eyes. 'And that was when I realised Noah was following me. He knew I had found someone special. He didn't know who. He was determined to find out. He wanted to destroy any 'appiness I had.'

James wondered how far Gigi would go to protect that. And to keep the business she'd built up with Noah, when divorce would only have granted her a share.

Would she have killed Louise, who was insistent on making her affair public?

Did she have any motive to kill Erin, who'd unwittingly flirted with Gigi's paramour? Or had her threats to Noah been enough to provoke an attack?

Because James could definitely see Gigi killing Noah; she looked positively relieved to be widowed.

Chapter 32

Monday 10th July – 10 a.m.

Nell got up quietly so she didn't wake Rav. When they'd finally got in from the ordeal in the wood, they'd been too distressed, too restless to go to bed.

It seemed like Rav was in shock. Nell had plied him with hot chocolate, hoping it would be warming and help him sleep.

He'd fidgeted all night and only fallen into a deep sleep with the first light of dawn. Jezebel had curled into the crook of his arm, her contented sleep calming him.

As if understanding she was providing much needed comfort, Jezebel didn't even stir when Nell got up, despite her breakfast tuna being thoroughly overdue.

So, Nell had left the curtains closed and crept out, to let him – and Jezebel – sleep in.

Because she couldn't.

Forcing herself to eat some toast, she wondered what on earth they could do to work out who the killer was – someone who was too dangerously close to Rav.

Had Noah been following Rav? Why, though? And why had he been killed? By whom? Something didn't add up . . .

She dredged her memory for anything that might give any insights at all, however minor, not wanting to leave any stone unturned.

'Here you are!'

Nell's head jerked up at his voice and she saw him limping into the refectory, with Jezebel twining around his ankles.

'Rav! I thought you'd be able to get some sleep this morning.'

His smile was thin, wan, his hair dishevelled. He was still in pyjamas.

'I'm tempted to go back to bed. But I woke and you weren't there and, well . . .' He shot her a sheepish look. 'I panicked a bit.'

'Oh, sweetheart.' As Nell kissed him, sat him down and moved his crutches, she noted that Rav hadn't used his wheelchair all week. And he was managing better than he realised. It wouldn't be long . . .

He took the coffee she poured him. 'Thanks. I just don't know what we can do for the best at this point.' He looked distraught. 'And I don't understand . . . the *pattern*, if you like.' He ran a hand through his hair. 'I don't know how to even *try* to keep you safe.'

'I know this is easier said than done. But you must stop feeling somehow responsi—'

'But this *is* all my fault, isn't it? None of this would be happening if it weren't for the filming. I feel like we wanted to start something amazing here but, because of me, it's turned into something that's wormed its way in and . . . and . . . it's turning everything rotten. It's spreading decay through everything. And three deaths, Nell. Three *people*.' He leaned his head on his hands.

Nell wrapped her arms around him until he gave a long, shuddering sigh.

She sat back to look at him. 'I think the only thing we can do now is to try to recall anything – anything at all – that we've noticed over the past few days and check it out or report it to James. Even if it seems minor, or silly, it could be a glimpse of something more.'

She was relieved to see Rav sit up straighter, run a hand over his haggard face. 'You're right.' He downed his coffee and looked for another.

As she refilled his cup, Nell said, 'Erin's time of death was about 6 a.m. We saw how tired she was the evening we visited. Someone persuasive must have encouraged her there to do something that early. But who, and to do what?'

Rav frowned.

'I thought Holly might have asked her, given the issues.'

'Or someone could have just seen her there early, waiting to meet someone else, and . . .' Rav cleared his throat. 'You know, opportunistically. Who might have been lurking around?'

Nell frowned. 'Well, Zeus is up to something shady, I think. I'll talk to him today.'

Rav nodded. 'I think I need to speak to James about Bea. Something about her has been nagging at me.'

'Shall we get on with it and compare notes afterwards?'

Rav nodded. 'Sounds good.'

At the thought of taking action, Nell saw resolve and determination set his jaw, and smooth out the furrow of fear and doubt on his face. Rav's shoulders squared and he pushed himself up.

'Can I refill your coffee? Have you eaten?' he asked.

As he topped up her mug and then dug into some cereal, Nell just hoped that whatever he spoke to James about today wouldn't set him back again.

An hour later, with Jezebel fed, Rav on his way to see James and her meeting with Zeus arranged, Nell was scouring LinkedIn. If the Californians were fellow winemakers, and had worked with Zeus before, surely there'd be some connection she could find.

She went off on a tangent when LinkedIn suggested she might also know colleagues, like Gigi and Noah, and Kat.

Nell had read their bios before she'd hired them, but took a quick glance now.

Kat's bio included some stunning stills from her work at Finchmere, and beforehand. As a freelancer, she'd worked all over the country, becoming more local in the past five years. Flicking through habitat pictures, Nell paused at one that was unexpectedly familiar – a fairly nondescript photo of a small barn. Hardly anyone, except for an ecologist, would know what they were looking at: a purpose-built bat barn for brown long-eared bats, usually built as a replacement when a loft space was developed. This bat species was fussier than most, with their need for internal flying space to warm up their flight muscles before they'd venture outside. The small barn was similar to those whose construction they'd overseen when they worked at EcoLogical Solutions.

Nell recalled with a pang the last one Rav had overseen, in Ambledown, when Erin had come into the office and returned his trousers, borrowed after she'd fallen in Little Smitington pond. The shock of Erin's death hit her all over again. It just didn't seem real . . .

With a heavy sigh, Nell clicked on the bio for *Graze!*. Noah's and

Gigi's photos were from their New Zealand days. Noah was leaner, rugged, with rough-and-ready stubble, his shirtsleeves rolled up his forearms. Tanned and working the land, his younger self looked at peace, with a windswept Gigi beaming beside him. In one photo, Gigi was uncharacteristically messy, smothered in blood, with a newborn lamb in her arms, looking at Noah in total awe.

With growing sadness, Nell clicked on Zeus's impressive bio. Over the years, he'd grown from competition winner, to award recipient, to esteemed judge, with an increasing list of memberships to professional associations.

Nell followed every one of these, to see if any were linked to the Californians. She clicked on every award, every association, every competition. Methodically, she followed links to websites, searched galleries and scanned photos.

And then she saw one of the Californians: Ryan.

The photo was a group shot of competition winners and judges for Napa Valley's Prestige Award. Ryan's face was small, amongst the back row – but there was no mistake.

Nell took a screenshot, then continued the search.

The prior year's photo clinched it: Ryan was there again. With Chuck. *And* Zeus.

Monday 10th July – 1 p.m.

At the station, James's heart went out to Rav. It looked like he'd aged a hundred years and, even though he clearly had something important to bring up, he was struggling to find the right way to say it.

'First of all, can I be clear that I don't know if any of this is fair to the person concerned. It's just a few throwaway comments that could be completely innocent.'

He glanced at James, who nodded. 'Of course. But at this stage, any ideas are worth following up. And better for a suspicion to be investigated and proved wrong, than ignored and then a murderer goes free. Or kills again.'

Rav nodded. 'It's about Bea. I know you've searched her garden, and her house. And you found the pictures.' He winced. 'After you interviewed her, Nell said she apologised – but that something about her apology seemed . . . manipulative. That was the word Nell used.'

'Oh?' James leaned forward, his interest brightening. 'Go on.'

'Before Louise was killed, she came over to speak to Bea, about her grandmother's funeral. And Bea looked furious about it for some reason.'

He glanced at James. 'I'm sure I'm not making any real sense. But anger, or irritation, aren't usually the emotions you're experiencing when you're arranging a funeral.'

'Well, it can be surprising. Especially if there are a lot of family opinions in the mix—'

'That's the point, though.' Rav leaned forward. 'She doesn't have any other family. It's just her now, isn't it?'

James frowned. 'Yes, you're right.' He glanced up, wondering if Ed had followed up the enquiry into the death certificates, which Louise had questioned so many times.

Rav swallowed again and James's radar tweaked. 'What?'

'Nell and I saw Louise's sermon. The one she'd left on her lectern—'

'*Rav!* For—'

'Yes, all right, I know. We didn't touch it. She just took a photo. But hear me out. It sounded like Louise had made a list of sins, and that she was pointedly going through each one, turning her sermon into a personal message. And *one* of those sins – one of those *messages* – was about murder.'

James managed not to gape as he realised he'd missed the clue entirely. He beckoned Ed over. 'Ed, what did you find out about Bea Camberwell's relatives? Did we ever get those medical reports?'

Ed's frown was not encouraging. 'Er . . . Let me look into it. I might need to make a phone call.'

While Ed searched his emails, found nothing and did indeed have to chase it up with a phone call, James made a pot of coffee. Not that he needed anything to make him feel even more jittery. By the time he'd made the drinks and taken them through, Ed was looking happier.

'They've emailed them over now,' he said, taking his drink. 'They'd put them together for sending, but the email was sitting in their draft folder. I've forwarded you a copy so we can both read them.'

Under Rav's hopeful gaze, James sipped while he read the first report aloud. 'Irene Camberwell, aged seventy-two; Cause of death: Heart failure; Certifying registered medical practitioner: Kim Glanville.'

Then he checked the second, for Bea's mother. 'April Camberwell, aged fifty-one; Cause of death: Heart failure; Certifying registered medical practitioner: Kim Glanville.'

He raised his eyebrows at Rav. 'Both mother and grandmother died of heart failure, four months apart.' He glanced at Ed. 'And the doctor – the *same* doctor – didn't think that was a strange coincidence?'

'Apparently not.'

James was pleased to see Ed already tapping in the search for Dr Kim Glanville's details. The doctor had a few things to answer.

Chapter 33

Monday 10th July – 2 p.m.

Nell called Zoe, Finchmere's Business Manager, before she spoke to Zeus. If there was something dodgy about his references or reputation, then this would be a task for her to handle, with her appropriate HR training.

But Zoe surprised her.

'I'm so glad you called, Nell. There's a problem in our accounts. I'm just rechecking the figures now, but perhaps we could meet before we speak to Zeus?'

Now Nell waited, drinking yet another coffee, in Zoe's office. Zoe looked up from the spreadsheet on her screen and nodded.

'We're missing just over ten thousand pounds' worth of stock. Let me show you.'

As Nell drew up a chair, Zoe took her through the columns.

'Here's Zeus's intake, in terms of raw product. We obviously know the volume we'll make from processing the grapes so that we order enough bottles, forecast sales and ensure we'll meet agreed deliveries.'

As Nell nodded, she moved to the next column. 'But here's the outgoings. Far lower than expected. The key deliveries are met – to our flagship shops and local restaurants – but other, more flexible, orders have been sent fewer bottles than usual.'

Nell pointed at another row of figures. 'This is the delta, isn't it? The amount set aside for samples and schmoozing.'

'No. That's my calculation. You're right, it *does* show the delta – the amount missing. But the hospitality budget is already *fully* accounted for, here. See?' Zoe pointed at another row. 'Yet orders are still too low.'

'Maybe his hospitality budget wasn't enough, given the extra samples for the fete?'

Zoe scrunched her nose. 'Not unfeasible. But he and I discussed that. He added an additional quantity to set aside specifically for the fete.'

Recalling Erin's tipsy state after a tasting with Zeus, Nell sighed. 'He *is* a bit heavy-handed with the free samples. It's lovely, of course, to feel like you have a generous host. But *not* if it's actually damaging the business.' She shot Zoe a firm stare. 'And that does seem to be what you're saying?'

'Yes. That's exactly what I'm saying. Because, without those sales, our overall profits have dropped – to *way* below forecast. If we continue like this, we'll be running at a loss by the end of the year.'

As soon as Nell agreed to discuss this with Zeus, Zoe went into overdrive. She phoned Zeus, and then confirmed in writing, with an email, that she needed to have a meeting to make some critical enquiries.

When Zeus saw both of them walk into the barn, his confident smile dropped, until he tried to cover it with a beam of bravado. 'Hey, this must be my lucky day! Both of you here to talk to. Please,' he gestured at the comfortable bar stools, 'take a seat. How can I help?'

As Zoe outlined her findings, Zeus raised his hands, the smile intact again. 'Hey! Come on, guys! You know how it's been! You did *such* a great job, creating such a buzz around the fete, that of *course* we had record numbers. And *all* of them were keen to try our famous wines. Who could blame them?'

He turned to Zoe. 'And I know you allowed a very generous amount for samples for the fete. But we didn't expect such glorious sunshine.' He glanced at Nell, chuckling. 'No offence – but California this ain't!'

Zoe remained stony-faced. 'There's no reasonable way you could have burned through that set hospitality budget, Zeus. So I'll need to ask you to leave – today – while I have my assistant run a full stocktake—'

'What?' His eyes darted from Zoe to Nell. 'There's no need. Look.' He dashed behind the bar, fumbling through paperwork. 'I've got full details here. You can take this.' He took a breath, then smiled. 'Save yourselves the bother.'

Taking the paperwork, Zoe scanned the barn. 'Thanks, I'll compare our stocktake to your records, so that is helpful.'

As Zoe closed her folder, Nell asked, 'Zeus, is there anything you have to say? This may be your best opportunity to speak to us, if there's a problem.'

He stared at the ground, chewing his lip, then looked at Nell.

She felt him wavering.

'Is this to do with the two Californians?' Nell asked. 'Ryan and Chuck?'

As Zeus gave a half-laugh, half-resigned sigh, Nell held the silence, glad that Zoe did the same.

After the weighty moment dragged out, and seeing that Zeus didn't know how to put words to the problem, Nell pulled out her phone. She found the photo of Zeus with one of the Californians and showed it to him.

'I can see that you've crossed paths with them before. Given what Zoe's just shown us, I think I can guess what's going on. Are you bootlegging, Zeus? Have you done that to them, and now they're coming for what they believe you owe them?'

Zeus stared at the floor, his ultra personality folding in on itself, like he burned to disappear.

'Were you already doing that here? Or did you have to, to pay them off?'

A sound like a whimper came from Zeus.

'Were they threatening to expose what you'd done? Is that why they wanted a meeting with me?' Nell paused, remembering their remark that following the proper channels had yielded nothing, and she wondered if a transatlantic police inquiry for something like this would be a non-starter. It sounded like Chuck and Ryan were only too willing to take matters into their own hands. How desperate would that have made Zeus?

He stared at the floor for an age, in silence. When he looked up again, defeat was carved across his face.

'You're not gonna understand, Nell. You're not gonna relate to a young kid, with well-meaning parents, but poor. Real poor. Where you don't even know about jobs like this. You know about welfare, or working in a shop. Or stealin' and dealin'. But you don't even know there's a *life* like this.'

Nell sat back, signalling that she was listening.

'I . . .' He blinked rapidly. 'I wanted more. I saw my parents scraping by and I didn't want that. I got a sports scholarship, and it got me into college, and it showed me another world. I was enough of a jock to get some classy dates and go to some fancy places.'

He shot a wary glance at Nell. 'I was so far out of my depth, though, in those types of places. I was watching people spending more than a month's wages – a year's salary, in some cases – on just one bottle of drink. It seemed . . . Well, the extravagance of it seemed almost offensive to me. But there I was, and I had to play along. I kinda poked fun, to begin with, describing the wine. Kinda felt like I had to, to keep me grounded, you know? But folk didn't think I was making fun. They thought my descriptions had flair. And I was with the kind of people who open doors. Before I knew it, I was in training. A sommelier, a buyer, a producer, a competition winner. A judge!'

Shaking his head, he gave a short laugh. 'It couldn't have been a better career path if I'd planned it. But still I . . . I wanted more. So I . . .' He grimaced. 'I started siphoning off the produce. When you have a discretionary hospitality budget, it's one gift of a grey area.' He jerked his head towards Zoe. 'Unless the accountant's on the ball.'

He raised his chin. 'So, you *will* find a deficit. It's about seven . . .' He squinted at Zoe. 'Eight thous—'

'Try ten, Zeus,' Zoe interjected. 'Given the circumstances, honesty's best, isn't it?'

'And your former colleagues knew about your bootlegging?' Nell confirmed.

Wincing, Zeus admitted, 'Yeah. I thought I'd covered my tracks when I left, but they found out. Then my whereabouts became a little less anonymous thanks to how successful your channel has gotten. I was nervous as all hell, knowing what would be coming, when I had to join in with the filming.'

He studied his hands. 'Once they found out where I ended up, there was no peace. They wanted their money back, and I knew they weren't making empty threats.'

'And when did that all start?'

'On the Wednesday, before the fete. They arranged to meet me. I could hardly say no, could I? They knew the timing, with the fete coming up, would pile on the pressure. I knew they were staying at the hotel. And they kept turning up at the fete events, to let me know the threat was real.'

'Is that why you were hanging around the hotel?' Nell asked, recalling the CCTV footage. 'Or was that after I'd asked them to leave?'

His eyebrows flashed. 'Yes, it was after that conversation. But I'd seen Noah since you'd thrown them out. He told me they were asking for me, and I didn't know if he'd seen them before or after you'd had those words. And I didn't know what they might have told Noah. I didn't need trouble from him, on top of everything else.'

Nell nodded.

'So, I . . . I hung around outside the hotel. I'm sorry to say that I spooked Rav, when he was on his way for those drinks at the hotel bar. I never woulda wanted to cause him any distress. I'm sorry for that. But I'd been hoping to catch them, to . . . I don't know. Draw a line. Persuade them to stop. Somehow.' Zeus looked shamefaced.

'But you must have known they'd arranged to meet me,' Nell said. 'I'm pretty sure they planned to tell me everything.'

As Nell studied him, she ached to ask what sort of persuasion Zeus had planned to use. Would he have stolen more from her family to pay them off? Or worse?

If Louise had worked out what he was up to, with evidence from her friend's photo – who would have been able to tell her where she'd bought the wine – then that must be why she had argued with him.

She'd threatened to expose his sins of deceit, greed and theft. And, in doing so, threatened his livelihood, reputation and – judging from Chuck and Ryan's reaction – maybe his life.

If that was the case, had Zeus's sins already gone beyond stealing?

Chapter 34

Monday 10th July – 3 p.m.

James was finding it impossible to hide his frustration with Dr Kim Glanville.

'You're seriously telling me that two women, dying in the same house, in identical circumstances, with the same person – Bea Camberwell – calling for an ambulance . . . And calling *late*, in *both* cases, didn't ring any alarm bells?'

'My job is to diagnose, Detective. The police would have been called, too. If alarm bells *should* have rung, don't you think it should have been with your team members?'

'But they wouldn't necessarily have seen April Camberwell, and realised that she had had the same recorded cause of death just four months before. Whereas *you* would.'

Now, Kim was openly irate. 'You're as bad as that vicar. Rev Brimstone. She kept emailing me about this, too. Why do you expect *me* to have an encyclopaedic memory, but not your *colleagues*? Have you any idea how stretched healthcare professionals are? How large an area I cover? How many people that involves?'

James dialled back the confrontation, out of professional sympathy. 'Yes. Yes, I do have one or two ideas about that. What can you tell me about your conversation with Rev Louise Brimstone?'

Kim frowned. 'Um. She sent me several emails, where I repeatedly replied that there wasn't any cause for concern.' She folded her arms. 'Frankly, I was annoyed at my competence being called into question. It wasn't warranted.'

'I can understand that, too.' James saw that empathy was getting him further than playing hardball. 'But – now that I'm asking you to consider the coincidence of the similarity of Irene's and April's deaths – do you, as a healthcare professional, have any reason to think it's odd?'

'It's certainly a coincidence, yes.' She glanced at James. 'But, *unlike* the police, doctors don't necessarily view that with suspicion. After all, many health conditions are hereditary. So, if a daughter dies for the same reason as her mother, then it's probably down to genetics. Not only likely, but causally related.'

'And is that the case for heart failure?'

Kim sighed. 'Congestive heart failure *does* have some hereditary elements, yes. Such as complicating factors, and things that make it more likely you'd have the condition. For example, you'd be at higher risk if you have diabetes, or coronary artery disease, which does run in families.'

'So, what did you make of Bea being slow to call for help?'

'Shock can do that. Or people trying to give medical help. Or not realising how serious the condition is. Maybe she wasn't there when it happened. Do you have a statement?'

James didn't want to admit that he hadn't been able to find one. He wasn't even sure any had been taken.

'It's inconclusive.'

'Uh-huh.' Kim's eyes narrowed. 'I see why the pressure's on me, then.'

'Is it possible any substances could provoke these symptoms?'

'Certainly.'

'Like?'

'Almost anything: ibuprofen, ketamine, cocaine, alcohol, arsenic . . . Pick your poison.'

As James looked at her, he was afraid that was exactly what had happened.

An hour later, James and Hesha were sitting in Bea's garden. He was trying not to think about all the deadly substances around him, masked by their beautiful blooms.

'I'm sure you understand, Bea. I don't want to do this,' James said. 'But I must follow every lead I have. I need to know what happened, with your mother and your grandmother.'

Bea's lip trembled, but she said nothing.

'Let me put this to you completely straight, Bea, OK?' James gazed at her, desperate to appeal to her loyalty to Rav. 'If Louise's suspicions were well-founded, then, frankly, you had motive to kill her. *If* I need to, I can launch an investigation today: I have the warrant to perform the toxicity tests that weren't conducted at their times of death.'

He thought he caught a faint gasp but, still, she said nothing.

'And, *if* I need to do all that, then my team is going to have all that extra work. And I'd rather they were focused on who's stalking Rav, and who's killing people *now*.'

At the mention of Rav, her hot gaze met his and he saw her eyes were welling with tears.

'So, Bea? Can you help me? Can you save me any work here?'

Her shoulders shuddered with the sobs she was holding back. A tear fell, streaming down her cheek, and then a torrent followed.

But she nodded, and James's pulse sped up.

Hesha leaned across the table, passing her a tissue, squeezing her hand. 'We're listening, Bea.' Her tone was gentle. 'Go ahead.'

'It . . . It was so awful.' Bea mopped her face and took a breath. 'My poor mum tried so hard. Really, so hard. My gran was lovely. But she was also stubborn and proud and cantankerous, so it was hard for her as she got more and more dependent. And it was hard for Mum, too.'

She blew her nose on the soggy tissue, and Hesha passed her another.

'Everything became worse when Gran got dementia. The awful thing was, we didn't realise for a long time. We thought she was just getting more and more bad-tempered, and you can't blame someone for that, when they're getting more and more infirm, and their life is shrinking – and what they can *do*, what they can *enjoy*, is shrinking, too. Sometimes she didn't eat, and we didn't recognise that as a symptom, either. Sometimes she'd say hurtful things, and once she actually hit my mum. It was totally out of character, and that was when we realised.'

She took a breath. 'It was enough to make it unbearable for Mum to care for her, and Gran refused to go into a home. Her doctors didn't recognise the signs or diagnose her with dementia, either. As far as they were concerned, Gran had full capacity, and her decision was to stay at home. But *all* the burden was on Mum.'

She paused for breath as more tears fell.

'I don't think I can do justice to what that really meant. Day after day, Gran would lash out when she was angry. It wasn't her, we knew that – it was the disease. It's so wicked, it's like a parasite, leeching out the person you love. But it still hurts to hear those things, to see them like that. And it's hard to shake that off.

'And *that* day . . .' She took a long shuddering inhale and stared at James. 'That day I came home and found Mum . . . There was a note.' Her face crumpled and her body convulsed with sobs at the pain of reliving that moment.

'She'd used the passionflower plant in the garden to distil some cyanide. She'd poisoned herself with it. She wrote me a letter, saying . . . Saying sorry . . . That she couldn't cope.'

Bea buried her face in the tissue, pouring out her heartbreak. 'I hate that she thought she needed to do that. I'd have done anything to help. I thought I *was* helping.'

More anguished sobs made Hesha reach out and rub her arm in gentle comfort.

They let Bea cry out the memory of it all. As her sobs subsided, her breathing steadied.

'By the time I found Mum, it was too late to help her. That was obvious. And when I saw the note, I panicked. I had to destroy it; I couldn't risk just hiding it. I know it's an outdated view, but I was terrified that if Louise knew Mum had committed suicide, then she'd refuse to conduct her funeral. And Louise is pretty black-and-white when it comes to behaviour. I knew a funeral at Finchmere's All Saints Church would matter to Mum. And to Gran. Once I'd burned every scrap of her letter, I phoned the ambulance.

'And then there was the funeral, and all the sympathy.' Her shoulders shuddered again. 'I didn't deserve it. I felt like a fraud. It was all my fault. If Mum could have leaned on me more, she'd still be here.'

She stared at her hands, screwing up the tissue. 'I hate to say it but I resented Gran, too. And I knew it wasn't her fault. Of course it wasn't. And the day-to-day care was . . . Well, that was OK, until she'd do or say something mean.'

Squeezing her eyes shut, Bea shook her head. 'I tried to follow Mum's example. I tried to do the right thing. Then, one day, I was trying to help her see the garden. I hoped she'd remember how much joy it gave her. That it was something we'd done together. And when I got her to the window, she grabbed a paperweight from her bureau and threw it at me – right *at* me – and the look on her face was just . . . Well, it unnerved me.'

As Hesha squeezed her hand, Bea swallowed. 'So I did what Mum did. I used the passionflower, I made a concoction of cyanide, I gave it to Gran and then I waited to make sure it had worked before I called the ambulance.'

She heaved a long, shuddering sigh, like the weight of confession had exhausted her.

'Louise might have had suspicions, and she might have been a busybody, but I didn't kill her. I couldn't do that.'

James looked her in the eyes, reminding her that she'd just confessed to exactly that.

But Bea shook her head. 'No, James. It isn't murder. It can't be. Not when the person they are – the person you know them to be – has already died.'

With Bea arrested, James was at a loss where to turn next.

Fortunately, Hesha wasn't. 'Sir, I think we should interview Holly. I'm guessing she'll be at home, since her workshop is out of bounds.'

James noted that Holly's flat, on the edge of Pendlebury, was in the less salubrious part of town, where housing was cheapest. The block where Holly lived was past its best, poorly maintained, its lift out of order. Their climb up the graffitied stairwell was accompanied with a flickering light and a whiff of urine.

When they knocked on her door, Holly only opened it a crack, on the safety chain, then let them in. She wore overalls and held a hammer, her hair pinned up in typical style, with a pencil.

Her place was sparse, but neat. Mismatched furniture suggested hand-me-downs or second-hand bargains. As James saw the items were all good quality, he realised they were probably pieces she'd repaired. Everything was cared for, clean, in good condition. A dust sheet was spread on the floor, under a makeshift bench that Holly had set up, to contain a work area; the air was scented with beeswax and fresh sawdust.

'Have you lived here long?' Hesha asked.

'Too long. What do you want to speak to me about?' Holly perched on the floral armchair opposite them, her arms wrapped around herself.

'You explained to me yesterday – after Erin was found, killed, in your workshop – that her response to Noah's assault was very different to yours.'

Holly's head snapped up and she stared at him.

'You told me it was because you worked there, didn't want to cause problems,' James added.

'Yes.' Holly's chin lifted. 'I thought I'd be marked as a troublemaker at best or end up losing my job at worst. It was my choice to keep quiet about it. That's not unreasonable, is it?'

'Not at all,' James said. 'But Rev Louise Brimstone was also raising the issue, wasn't she?'

'Was she?' Holly blinked rapidly. 'I-I didn't know that.'

'Sure,' Hesha conceded. 'You might *not* have seen her watching from afar, like a guardian – or maybe avenging – angel. Or the emails she sent, warning him off.'

As Holly gaped, Hesha leaned forward. 'But Erin's response was very public. No plausible deniability there. Did you feel angry that Erin didn't share the barriers you felt stopped you from seeking justice, Holly? That she was in a position to challenge Noah?'

Holly's shrug was unconvincing.

'And, more to the point, that her challenge could drag you into it? Endanger your position? Another type of violation, without your consent?' Hesha's tone was kind, sympathetic, despite the insistent words.

Referring to Rav's statement, James winced. 'Sounds like she was pretty blunt and unsympathetic when she told you to stand up for yourself. More than a hint of victim blaming. It would make anyone furious, I imagine.' He gave her a level look. '*Did* that make you angry? *Did* you stand up for yourself, when Erin came to your workshop?'

'What? *No!*' Holly looked horrified. 'I didn't see Erin. I've no idea why she came to my workshop. I don't *want* trouble at work. That's the whole point! It's too important to me.'

'Why is that?' James asked, glad to have got to the crux of their questioning so quickly.

'It's ... It's just ... It's the one good thing I have. And I'm just starting to make a go of it—' She clamped her lips, and James noticed they were trembling. 'And now that I've *finally* built up a set of commissions, I can't even use my workshop.' Her voice cracked, like she was on the edge of crying. She raised her hands at the work around her, in despair. 'This is hardly ideal working conditions, is it?'

'You don't have another workshop? Or a garage? Or a friend's place?'

When Holly shook her head, clamping trembling lips, he asked, 'Why didn't you mention that to Nell? She'll have another spot you could use in the meantime, surely?'

'I ... I don't want to ask anything that makes her think I'm a pain. I can't risk losing that lease.'

'That's up to you, Holly, but I think she'd accommodate you somewhere, and it wouldn't be a problem. Really.' He turned to Hesha. 'Have you seen Holly's work? I saw some at the fete. You'd love it, Hesh. Original pieces, exquisitely made.'

'I'll have to check it out.' Hesha smiled at Holly. 'But it must take a while to get established, I imagine. It can't be the easiest way to earn a living.'

'No.' A wince flashed across Holly's face.

'And that must sting, when you know it could have been made so much easier,' James said.

'How *did* you feel when your parents left half a million to the church, instead of you?' Hesha asked.

Holly did a double take at the provocative, unexpected question under Hesha's apparent warmth.

'I ... Well ... I ...'

James sat back, letting Holly fill the silence, knowing Hesha would do the same.

'I mean . . . How would *you* feel?'

'Oh, I know how *I'd* feel, Holly. So you can feel free to be honest here,' James invited.

'Well. It was their choice, wasn't it?' Holly's chin lifted, but her lip tremored. 'I suppose they had confidence I'd be OK. Or they wanted to encourage independence.'

'But it was *half a million*, Holly. *Everything* they had to leave,' Hesha pressed.

Holly dashed a tear away as she stared at the wall. Following her gaze, James saw the large damp patches, and he knew resentment had spread through Holly like the black mould speckling along the wall.

'I was . . . upset. Confused. I didn't know anything about it until the solicitor gave me their will. I mean, it was awful enough to lose them both in a car accident. Both of them.' She stared at James, like she was still in shock from it. 'Just like that. And we were *close*. So if they'd *really* planned to do that then I just don't know . . . I don't know why they didn't *tell* me, or explain.'

'Do you think they were . . . persuaded?' James asked.

Holly shrugged – but it turned into a nod. 'Yes. I am worried about that. It can happen, can't it?' Her face darkened. 'People get involved with . . . organisations. End up being pressurised into doing things.'

'But you can contest the will, can't you?' Hesha said.

Holly's face grew wary. 'Ye-es.'

'And of course, you'd be furious with whoever you thought responsible for . . . What was it you said? Pressurising them?'

Holly's eyes darted between them.

James pretended to consult the notes on his iPad. 'And that was Louise, wasn't it?'

Holly's mouth opened, then she clamped it shut.

'But of course, contesting a will can take time,' Hesha mused. 'Might not be successful. And, at best, might only gain you a portion of the whole amount of money. And *if* you felt it was rightfully yours – and *if* you also suspected your parents had been duped into betraying you – you'd be angry with the person you thought was responsible, wouldn't you?'

James nodded, as if conversationally agreeing with Hesha, before turning to Holly. 'Something else to make a person rightfully furious, I'd say. Is that why your fingerprints were on the candlestick used to kill Louise? Did you stand up for yourself there?'

'No! Of *course* not! I was upset with Louise . . . I didn't understand . . . but I wouldn't *hurt* her.' She looked confounded. 'I . . . The *candlestick*? Maybe I . . . Maybe I moved it? When I was thinking about the commission Louise asked for? I walked all around the church before I thought of the carved flower arch.' She shook her head, like she hadn't even convinced herself.

'But you weren't there to talk about a commission, were you, Holly? You were demanding what you believe is rightfully yours. So if you touched that candlestick that day, it wasn't because you were considering where a commission might go.'

'Which almost certainly wouldn't have gone on the altar anyway,' Hesha added.

'Did you threaten her?' James pressed.

'Even if I did,' Holly raised her chin, 'threatening isn't killing.'

As they left the flat, Hesha lowered her voice. 'I hadn't thought she'd be able to summon the rage for attacks like those. But it's all bubbling under the surface, isn't it?'

Walking to the car, hearing the repetitive bash of hammer on chisel echoing through the estate, James had to agree.

Chapter 35

Rav sighed at the endless text messages rolling in from Kat.

Hey Rav! just checking what you'll need from me this week? Usually I'd do field pieces but . . . with everything . . . I don't have a brief.

Then: *Just wanted to give you some options if you wanted to keep things going?*

And then: *I have a few ideas, needing low input from you or Nell, that I can run, if that would help?*

And now: *Just need your go-ahead . . . Happy to step back if that's more appropriate right now. Can you let me know?*

He knew that Nell had tried to ensure that Kat felt appreciated for her work, but she clearly had uncertainties about what she was expected to do next.

Glancing across at Nell, he knew she was itching to discuss their findings from the day, now they'd swapped updates. So was he. But Kat wasn't going to be put off with a text. His body felt too leaden to move, but he had a feeling she should have the courtesy of a meeting, in person.

With a sigh, he said, 'I think Kat needs some confirmation of workload for this week. She's not taking any notice of our messages, saying that we need to take a break from filming for a while, is she? I think she needs a catch-up, face to face. If I go now, I can get it over and done with. And you could fill James in on what you've found today. He might even be willing to swap notes? I can meet you at the station, after I've seen Kat?'

Nell hesitated. 'You're right. But I'll see Kat. I'll be quicker. See if she wants to grab a drink at the Foresters, since it's halfway between Finchmere and her place.'

'Ugh, James already thinks I've overstepped his investigation,' Rav complained.

'All the more reason for you to go and be helpful, then.'

He gave her a sarcastic salute. 'Fine. I'll text Kat and let her know about a meet-up at the pub, and then I'll head over to the station. See you there. Don't be long.'

As Rav sent the text to Kat, Nell kissed him.

His phone beeped. 'Yep, she can get to the pub,' Rav confirmed.

Nell headed out, climbed into a Landy and wound down the country lane.

The country pub glowed in the evening light, with most tables outside already taken by groups appreciating the downland view.

She ordered a Coke and took one of the snugs inside, with a view of the door, and waited.

Rav, she saw from the blue dot on the map on her phone, was well on his way to Pendlebury police station. And she only had to wait a few minutes before Kat turned up.

At the door, Kat scanned the pub, looking a little breathless.

Nell felt guilty for making her rush. Especially as Kat's top was unusually low-cut, and she was wearing makeup, like the meeting was interrupting a rare night out.

At least, if Kat's going out after this, then we'll both want to keep it short and sweet.

As Nell waved, Kat walked over.

'Hi, Nell. Can I get you a drink? Or Rav?' She glanced around.

'No, I'm fine for a drink, thanks. And Rav isn't here, it's just me. I'd have ordered for you, but I wasn't sure what you'd have.'

Nodding, Kat turned towards the bar and ordered, then joined her with a mocktail.

'Thanks for meeting at short notice,' Nell began.

'You're welcome. I just wanted to talk over what would be needed over the next few days.'

Kat's glances around her made Nell feel unsettled. But she replied, 'First, let me apologise. Rav and I haven't been as communicative as usual. It's been . . . fraught.'

'I can imagine.' Kat stirred her drink with the metal straw, staring at Nell.

Nell couldn't hold eye contact. Something about her critical, searching gaze made her uneasy.

'So, just for the moment, the filming needs to take a back seat.'

Disappointment flashed across Kat's face before she managed an understanding smile.

'Only temporarily,' Nell assured her. 'And, let's be honest, you've been working flat out. You *deserve* a break. Rav and I thought you'd appreciate that.'

'Well, that's kind. But let's think *strategically*.'

Irritation twitched at Kat's tone, and the inferred criticism that she hadn't thought strategically about this – and that any disagreement would draw out the meeting for longer than necessary.

'We have, Kat.' Nell forced a smile. 'But right now just isn't the right time. Rav and I have both lost a colleague and a friend.' She winced. 'As well as the other deaths. And we're not just dealing with our . . . *personal* grief. We need to be respectful to how others feel, too.'

'I understand.' Kat nodded, her face softening with empathy. 'And I'm sorry if I've not recognised that enough. I am very sorry for your loss.'

'Thanks, Kat.' Nell searched for a way to tactfully conclude the conversation, and escape. 'So I hope that makes our position on the filming clearer—'

'Well, no. It doesn't.' Kat glanced at her. 'I understand, *of course*, the need for a momentary . . . reprieve. But how long will that be? And, in the meantime, what do you want to do with the channel? We don't want to have built record numbers with the fete, only for that to fall off a cliff, do we? Not with your – or, really, Rav's – star on the rise.'

'Well—'

'And I haven't had a chance to share my ideas yet. All the things I could do to keep things going until you feel . . . *able* to return to presenting.'

'How about you email those ideas?' Nell suggested. 'Then Rav and I can discuss—'

'Oh, you know they come to life when we all discuss them, Nell. Let's talk them through—'

'No.' Nell stood up. 'No, Kat. I can't get into a discussion now. And honestly, I've said all I can for the moment. I'm interested in your ideas, they're always great. But email them so I can give them proper consideration and work out how we'll keep the momentum up, even while we're . . . We're dealing with everything. OK?'

'I'm sorry.' Kat stood up with her. 'Sorry if I . . . If I . . . overstepped. It's just been so hectic with the fete planning, keeping ahead of the filming schedule, at all hours, then the fast turnaround on editing and splicing in the live-stream. It's all been a bit . . . *intense.*'

Nell immediately felt terrible. Kat had been under more pressure than anyone to ensure the publicity was impeccable. She'd poured so much effort, over so many long days, into making the event a success.

With a sigh, she nodded. 'I know it's been a massive amount of work. What you've accomplished is incredible. Please don't, for one moment, think that we don't appreciate it. But circumstances have rather overtaken things now.'

As they stared at one another, across the polished oak table, a waiter delivered a bowl of chips, some olives and nuts. He grabbed two bundles of napkin-wrapped cutlery from the stack on the bar, and put those on the table, too. 'Anything else?'

Nell shook her head, glanced at the nibbles, then at Kat's pleading expression.

'I thought if you – and also Rav – could just give me ten minutes, just hear my ideas, then we could make sure we don't lose the benefit of all our work.'

Against her better judgement, she found herself sitting down. 'OK. I'm listening.'

At the station, Rav had found James and summarised what he and Nell had found.

He knew James was feeling less officious about his transgressions when he made him a cup of dodgy station coffee and led him to the incident board.

'It seems like Holly, Bea and Zeus have been more focused on keeping their own secrets than stalking.' Rav studied the board. 'Did everyone have an alibi for Noah?'

'Gigi's alibi is the member of staff she was having an affair with.' James sighed. 'And, as dubious as that is, no one else has an alibi at all.'

'So everyone had an opportunity, then. And Holly and Gigi both had motive.' Rav frowned. 'Nell mentioned that Bea was upset with Noah, but doesn't know why. And Zeus had a strange conversation with Noah, which she thought was about Zeus's bootlegging.'

James raised his eyebrows. 'Right, so let's assume those are enough to be a motive. For now, at least.'

Rav sipped his coffee, thinking. 'We need to see if we can recall anyone doing something suspicious.' He frowned, then raised his eyebrows. 'I don't suppose Kat gave you copies of her B-roll footage, or the VT she recorded, did she? There might be something caught on there that shows someone doing something out of character?'

'Yes . . . We *do* have some footage. Hang on.' James scanned the evidence list on his computer and pulled up a file. 'Kat gave us this. To show us what she was filming when Louise was killed. By way of her alibi.'

As the video loaded, he pulled on a pair of latex gloves and opened the box on the desk. 'And, in here, is the bag of memory sticks she gave me, of the B-roll she'd recorded.'

He passed Rav a pair of gloves and, once he'd snapped them on, passed him the ziplocked bag, with four memory sticks inside.

Opening the bag, Rav took out the sticks and read their neat labels: 'Winery + workshop'; 'Fete'; 'Scenery + bees'; '*Graze!*'.

He joined James, and drew up a chair to watch the screen, his eyes flitting everywhere, trying to catch anyone on the edges of the frame who might be acting suspiciously.

The film was unedited, the shots separated with blank footage. Time-lapse shots of the fete being set up culminated in the sunrise of the first morning, over the wildflower meadow. The field of thyme, near Bea's apiary, buzzed with insects in the glowing morning light. The footage of people arriving, the stands thronging, then crowding with people, filled the screen.

As the footage ended, Rav sagged back against his seat. There was nothing obvious.

But something . . . *Something* nagged at him.

It seemed to be more about something Nell had said.

James put in the memory stick, and the footage of Nell's interview filled the screen.

A thought, buried at the back of Rav's mind, sparked. It was Nell's comment when she'd been watching her interview back with him in Sylvia's office: that Kat had left it too late to record any butterflies alongside her piece on them – their short adult life-cycle was over.

'Would you play that first piece of footage again, please, James?'

'Sure.'

Rav leaned forward, staring at the screen. And then he saw it. But he had to be sure. 'Can you tell me exactly what Kat said when she gave you this?' he asked.

'Yes. She offered it as her alibi. This is what she'd been filming when Louise was killed.'

'You're sure she said filming, not editing? She hadn't selected and put these shots together, but it was her continuous filming from that exact morning?'

'Yes, exactly. It isn't an edit. You can see that clearly enough. She specifically described it as raw footage that she hadn't yet had time to edit. And yes, she said she'd filmed it that morning, to show that she couldn't have killed Louise, and that it was even timestamped to prove it.'

'Could you play it again?' Rav asked. 'Then, can you pause it . . .' He waited for the thyme field to fill the screen. '*There!*'

James peered at the screen, and Rav smiled, knowing he wouldn't see it, despite the evidence being clear as day.

'That's proof, James. Firm proof – of who the killer is.'

'I don't get it. We've got purple flowering something-or-other. Stunning morning light. A little white beehive.' He glanced at Rav, as if asking if that was a clue.

'Yeah, all true. That's not the evidence, though.'

'A lot of bees. Lot of insects in general.'

'Oh, yeah,' Rav agreed. 'Too many.'

James frowned. 'What do you mean?'

'The butterflies?' Rav pointed at them. 'An actual swarm, if you look, of large blue butterflies.'

James squinted. 'That's all these?' He ringed a section on the screen. 'And over here? And these?'

Rav nodded. 'And that's proof that if Kat said she was filming this on the morning of Louise's murder – which she's confirmed by timestamping it as being recorded on that *exact* day – then she's lying. The adult stage of the life cycle for those butterflies is restricted to only a few weeks, which is limited by temperature. And that very small window of time had passed by the Friday of the fete.'

James was frowning, and Rav knew he'd need more substance.

'You'll see for yourself if you compare this footage with Nell's interview, which was filmed on the Thursday *before* the fete. By then, Kat had left it too late, and there were just one or two butterflies left. Certainly not a swarm like this.'

James played the comparison footage, staring at the screen. When it was over, he nodded. 'Yes, you can see the difference. But couldn't the butterflies have had another lease of life? A surge of adults emerging?'

'No.' Rav shook his head. 'The period was over for the microclimate at Finchmere, at least.'

In the box was the bagged thyme flower head that Nell had found at her place.

'May I?'

At James's nod, Rav tipped the flower out, pointing a gloved finger at the petals, the tiny blue egg just visible. 'They lay their eggs when they emerge – see? And the whole cycle starts again. Once this egg hatches, the caterpillar will dupe the poor ants into taking it in, while all along it's going to predate them.'

James shivered. He looked almost convinced.

'Since Kat's footage was timestamped, then she must have deliberately altered the setting to make it look like she filmed it on Friday morning, instead of when she really did – which this species shows *must* have been several days previously.'

James stared at him. Rav appreciated the confidence he was showing by not asking if he was sure, but he confirmed it anyway.

'I'm *sure*, James. Kat's my stalker.' He shivered. 'She's the killer.' He felt the burn of fear and sickness rise from his gut. 'And she's with Nell.'

Chapter 36

Monday 10th July – 7 p.m.

Conditioned into excessive politeness, Nell knew she should leave, but she was still listening to Kat's ideas.

She hated to admit it, but they were brilliant. Kat's suggestions meant they could fill a few weeks' worth of episodes, giving her and Rav some space from thinking about producing content. They could take the time off together that they so desperately needed.

She drained her drink and nodded. 'These are great, Kat. I like how you're thinking about extending the interview, it's really smart. Rav will love this.'

'I hope so.' Kat smiled.

Feeling like she'd been a bit inconsiderate earlier, Nell added, 'I really appreciate you coming up with a solution. Thank you. Being given some time off, able to take a step back . . . Well, it's just what Rav and I need.'

'Well, it's my job, isn't it? To anticipate, and understand. I know what's needed.'

Something in her tone made Nell glance at her.

The two women gave tense smiles across the table.

'And you – and Rav especially – have built up such a fan base. It inspires loyalty. You have to make sure you keep them happy.'

'Well, I want to make sure Rav's got some time to recover from all these awful losses,' Nell said.

'Yes, we must look after our star,' Kat agreed.

'Mmm.' Nell noted the proprietorial edge, and tried to joke. 'Maybe I can even take Rav on the holiday I keep threatening him with.'

'Holiday?' Kat leaned forward, avid. 'Where? When?'

'Oh,' Nell stuttered, grappling to find an excuse. 'No idea. Just a few weeks away.'

'But you *can't*!' Kat hissed, eyes flashing as she leaned across the table, low and taut like a provoked rattlesnake.

The way she turned like that, that flash of danger, sent Nell leaning back in her seat. Her heartbeat galloped.

It took all her control to keep her breathing normal as she eyed the steak knife, still wrapped in the napkin, on the table in front of Kat.

Oh God . . .

Poor Erin. Poor Louise. And Noah . . .

Her eyes flitted to the far door of the pub. The place wasn't packed but there were enough people here that surely, *surely*, Kat wouldn't try anything.

'You may be right,' Nell said lightly, standing. 'It's hard to fit holidays in at the best of times. Just wishful thinking on my part. It won't happen.'

'So, Rav isn't joining us?' Kat looked around, almost panicky. 'I thought he was coming?'

'He . . . He can't tonight,' Nell said. 'But I'll tell him everything you said, and he'll probably want to say thank you himself. He may have a few ideas to talk to you about.'

She moved out from the table, forcing herself to smile, holding herself up with sheer will on legs of jelly.

'No, that's not good enough.' Kat stood up, blocking Nell, her eyes wild. 'I want to see him. Now.'

'OK, fine.' Nell edged around her. 'Let me call him, then.'

Aching for escape, her eyes strayed to the door, and she nearly sagged in relief at the welcome sight of James walking in with Ed. And then desperate fear gripped her heart as she saw Rav following them, searching for her.

Nell had to fight to control every rioting nerve in her body just to stay upright, unreactive, breathing normally, as she locked eyes with James.

Within a nanosecond, James sauntered to the part of the bar nearest their table.

She rationalised away her fear: *If James is here with Ed, then Rav knows. Somehow, he's worked it out.*

She hoped Rav would stay out of view. Kat had the brittle air of someone on the edge of doing something precipitous, and the sight of him might just drive her over it.

Over Kat's shoulder, Nell saw Ed nudge James, and the two officers moved in.

'Kat Martin, you're being arrested for the murders of Reverend Louise Brimstone, Erin Everly and Noah Grayling, the attempted murder of Dr Nell Ward, the arson of Dr Nell Ward's home . . .'

At that, Nell's initial relief as James read Kat her rights, turned to churning nausea. She gripped the table.

For a moment, it looked like the situation would be contained, resolved . . .

But, as Ed moved to take the handcuffs from his belt, time seemed to slow. Without warning, Kat's hands thrust out, faster than lightning, shoving Ed aside. As Ed stumbled against James, sending him reeling, Kat grabbed Nell.

The shock of it, and Kat's unexpected strength from endlessly lugging heavy kit around, pulled Nell off balance. She found herself standing, Kat's arm locked around her chest – then something cold, sharp, at her neck.

Her eyes slid sideways, scanning the table in dread: Kat's steak knife wasn't there.

'Back off!' Kat yelled next to her ear, the pressure of the knife at her neck increasing. 'I don't care if I hurt her, do I? So you better back right off!'

Ed held out his Taser with both hands, ready to use it. 'You don't want to do this, Kat. Trust me.'

Nell saw the patrons in the pub freeze, staring at the unexpected scene. The expressions of incongruent horror would have been absurd, funny, if she hadn't felt the hands at her neck tense.

Kat pushed the blade – just a little, but enough – and Nell felt a warm, worming trickle. 'I'm deadly serious. Back off.'

'It's over, Kat,' James said. 'We've got evidence. We know everything. So the best thing now – the *only* thing now – that *you* can do is not to make this any worse.'

But Kat shook her head. 'You'll have to try harder than that.'

Nell could see James assess the situation. She knew that they were *threatening* to taser Kat – rather than *actually* tasering her – because it would risk her being injured. Very probably fatally stabbed in the throat. A result that would delight, not deter, Kat.

Perfect.

Kat knew she had the advantage. 'Taser me. It'll just kill *her*, won't it?'

Rav limped forward, into Kat's view, making her gasp. Her arm muscles tightened around Nell. The vicious blade bit Nell's throat.

'Is this what you want, Kat?' Rav asked. '*Really?* More deaths? More harm to the people I care about? Because I promise you, if you harm Nell, there's no depth to the hatred I'll feel for you. And that's *all* I'll remember about you, *forever*. Not your great work, not the dazzling ideas you've had, not the fun we've had building this – *together*.' He gave a sad shrug. 'It's up to you.' He looked like he was turning away, walking away.

Nell realised he was inviting her to follow. Luring her away.

Kat whimpered. But the fight had drained out of her. '*Rav!* Please!'

Letting go of Nell, and dropping the knife on the table, Kat moved to follow Rav as he walked to the door.

Swooping in, James pushed himself between Kat and Nell, who'd staggered back.

Seizing Kat's arm, James steered her towards Ed, poised to make the arrest.

Without warning, Kat roared, grabbed the knife again and swung it wildly at James. It sliced sideways, towards him – the swoop of her arm stopping dead as the blade slammed into James's body.

Everyone froze. The onlookers in the pub gasped, making Rav turn round.

His face contorting, James's hand flew to his side.

Kat stared in horror, as James lifted his palm, smeared with bright blood. Shoving Ed, she made a dash for the door.

But Ed blocked Kat's move, tackling her like a rugby player, and then wrestled her to the floor.

James stared at his bloodied, shaking hand, and then at Kat. She squirmed on the ground as Ed wrangled her, like he was trying to catch an eel as Kat writhed, kicked and slid around from Ed's grip.

Grabbing a pile of paper napkins, Nell thrust them at James. He clamped them over his wound, just as Ed managed to cuff one of Kat's hands . . . and . . . then . . . the other.

Sweating, Ed got himself and Kat scrambling to their feet, holding her firmly with one hand as he called for an ambulance. He looked at James, assessing him. 'You OK?'

'I'm OK,' James said, his hand still clamped to his thigh. 'I think . . . Yeah, I'm OK.'

'Ambulance.' Ed paused, listening, then said, 'This is DC Ed Baker. My DI's been stabbed in the Foresters pub on the Nye Road.' He looked at James. 'Where are you injured?'

'I'm fine, Ed. It's . . . superficial.'

'Where, James?' Ed nodded towards his phone and the questions from the call handler. 'They need to know, in case it's deep, or nipped any organs.'

'Definitely not the case,' James said. 'No need to make a fuss.'

'James!' Ed asserted. 'They need to know where.'

'My buttock.' James groaned. 'OK? She hasn't so much injured me as given you lot ammunition. And it still really bloody hurts!'

But Ed had enough loyalty not to look amused in front of Kat. 'Serious offence, that, assaulting a police officer.' Grim-faced, he dragged her towards the door, talking into the phone, 'The injury site is the gluteus maximus. Pressure's been applied.'

Twisting in his grip, Kat's face was stricken as she passed Rav.

Handing James more napkins as he leaned against the bar, Nell glanced up at Rav.

His face mirrored her sheer relief: they were both OK, Kat had been caught, and their torment was *over*.

The door creaked as Ed hauled Kat outside, but Rav's eyes didn't stray from Nell's. His face shone with pure love as he gazed at her.

As soon as Ed had wrangled Kat through the doorway, Rav dashed to Nell, pulling her into his arms, kissing her face, her head, holding her close enough for her to feel his heartbeat hammering though his chest.

'God, I was terrified.' He lifted her chin to gaze at her again. 'I'm so glad you're safe.'

He leaned in to kiss her again, but she smiled at him, feeling her eyes brimming. 'You haven't realised, have you?'

'What?' He stared at her. 'What is it?'

'You just practically sprinted over to me.'

As Rav frowned, she added, '*Without* your crutches.'

Chapter 37

Nell waited while Rav spoke to Erin's parents at the wake. He'd spent a lot of time on Erin's eulogy, and he'd been visibly relieved that it had been well-received. His fond descriptions of his and Erin's mishaps on site, especially the borrowed trousers incident, had even raised some affectionate smiles.

Now, Nell shared her own stories of Erin. But she couldn't drag her eyes from Erin's picture – a bright, vibrant shot of her laughing.

With a stab of guilt, Nell acknowledged that she'd always found Erin to be a total pain. But she'd been so vitally alive, so impossible to miss in the office, on site, *anywhere* – that to think of her being gone was just . . . unbelievable. The hug she gave Erin's parents was heartfelt.

She was also pleased to see that James and Ashley, along with Ed and Hesha, had made time to attend the funeral service.

But there was a sense of unfinished business between them. James still needed a formal statement from Nell to outline the missing details of the case, so she turned to the officers, anticipating the question.

It was Ashley who approached her. 'Nell? Rav? We were hoping you could both attend the station, in an hour or so?'

Nodding, Nell said, 'I know. I'll be ready to make a statement.'

'Yes. That. But . . . something else, too. We've got a little surprise planned for James.'

When she told Nell what it was, Nell bit back a grin and offered to host a champagne reception, at Finchmere instead, to mark the occasion in style.

Friday 14th July – 5 p.m.

James did a double take at his Chief Constable arriving. In dress uniform, no less. He straightened his tie, glad to still be in the smart suit he'd worn to the funeral, even if the wound dressing under his trousers rustled.

Is she here because of the case? Shuffling the files on his new standing desk, he craned his neck to try to catch what Val was saying. He was horribly aware that there were gaps in the details that pinned this case together – until Nell arrived to make her statement.

Which would at least be soon. Heading for the door, he thought he could make sure the interview room was ready.

'Ah, James. Good. We have somewhere to be.'

Ushering him out to her car, Val offered him a round cushion to sit on.

'Oh, come on!' James said. 'I'm not afflicted with piles. I've just had an unfortunate . . . incident.'

'It's not mandatory.' Val's reply was starchy at his reaction. 'I was only thinking of your comfort.'

Glaring at her, he eased himself onto the seat, and found the cushion did help. 'That's actually very thoughtful, thank you.'

She didn't reply, but he had a fleeting sense that her focused stare out of the window as she drove was hiding amusement.

While Val was tight-lipped about the destination, she was keen to talk about the case. 'I'm glad the team took stalking so seriously. You can see how drastically things can escalate – and how quickly it turns from a threatening danger to something deadly.'

James shook his head. 'Three deaths, Val. That's not a good result.'

'You caught the perpetrator, James. And that *is*. Stalking's complex.' She shot him an appraising look. 'We should have a retrospective, write up a paper and share what you've found. There could be something in that experience that might help other cases. Especially around reporting and prevention. Our hands are tied on pre-emptive action; you and the team were resourceful in getting around that.'

James frowned as they turned into Finchmere's drive and pulled up by the house. 'Have I forgotten something?' he asked. 'What's all this?'

But still no answers came. Inside the hall, Ashley, Ed and Hesha stood to attention, serious in dress uniform, along with Nell and Rav, just as formal, still in their smart funeral attire.

'Is . . . Is everything OK?' James asked. His mind searched, frantic in case he'd overlooked some important occasion.

'Good question, James. Are *you* OK?' Ashley asked, making the team snigger, then snap back to being serious again.

Nell led them through to the library and handed round glasses of Finchmere sparkling wine. *Still*, James had no idea what was going on.

With everyone standing, ready, Val spoke. 'Detective Inspector Clark. We're here to acknowledge the danger that officers put themselves in, to protect the public we serve. And sometimes the peril we take upon ourselves can lead to injury. *When* it does, we recognise that bravery, that call to courage. And so today, DI James Clark, we recognise you.'

James was taken aback, momentarily touched and lost for words. Then he frowned. These sorts of acknowledgements usually took place at an annual event, not a one-off with your team. And not in a friend's house . . .

He assessed his teammates through narrowed eyes, wondering what they were up to.

'In addition to the Service Medal you'll get at the National Police Chiefs' Council's annual Police Public Bravery Awards . . .' Val began, smiling as James gaped at her, 'we wanted to add our own particular appreciation, with our own award. For *posterior*-ity.' She nodded at Ed, who passed her a small trophy.

'DI James Clark,' Val intoned, 'you are the *first* – possibly *only* – proud recipient of our new Award Recognising Service in Extremis.'

Ohhh . . . James groaned, shaking his head at Val's perfectly deadpan face.

He took the trophy, styled as two globes pressed together, which looked suspiciously like shining golden buttocks, with the award's initials underneath.

'Right. Yep. Thanks, all!' James admired the trophy, then raised it in mock-appreciation. 'I knew the minute it happened that it would make me the butt of all the jokes.'

'Ha!' Hesha looked delighted. 'That's not all!'

As Ed led the singing: '*For he's a jolly good fellow . . .*' Nell slipped outside and brought in a cake, the sparkler standing upright in it blazing in the room.

As the cake was placed before him, James saw that it was a shapely bottom, with criss-crossed plasters in icing at the site of his wound, and the fiery sparkler nestled safely between the cheeks.

'Couldn't leave this case on a bum note, could we?' Ed chuckled.

'Do you want to carve?' Ashley handed him the knife with an affectionate smile. 'X marks the spot? We wanted to make sure you could put any trauma of the attack *behind* you.'

After they'd all eaten too much cake, Nell made her statement with Rav, James and Ashley as they sat together in the library.

With the tech team now in possession of Kat's cameras and laptops, Nell and Rav would be able to confirm the real dates of filming, and the tech team would be able to verify if the recordings had been edited.

James had rewatched Nell's interview with Kat, filmed on the Thursday, with barely any large blue butterflies, and made notes as he'd compared it to the footage Kat had claimed to film a day later, on the Friday. The data showed that the difference was obvious.

'I'll need to verify that with an independent specialist,' James said. 'And I'll get the meteorological data, too, to show the daily temperatures.'

'I can make a recommendation,' Nell said. 'But it's probably better that you find an invertebrate specialist on CIEEM's website. You can search for any experts there, based on the skills you need.'

She saw James write that down. With the formal part of her interview over, James turned off the recorder. But they all remained seated.

'That was a lucky piece of evidence,' Nell said, 'considering how many times I asked to record the piece when the butterflies were out. And considering how many times I tried to explain the confined adult period.'

'Just think yourself lucky Rav didn't ask to film that segment, or repeat your explanation.' Ashley shot her a wry glance. 'She'd have paid attention, then.'

Nell met the wry glance with raised eyebrows, seeing how fragile the opportunity to convict Kat had been.

'At least Rav spotted it. Or I dread to think what would have happened in the pub.' Nell shivered, and Rav's arm around her tightened.

Glancing at Rav, then Ashley, Nell asked, 'When Kat played the voicemail of Rav to get me to the courtyard and pushed me in the cellar, do you think she was just trying to get me out of the way, or actually kill me?'

'Either.' Ashley met her gaze levelly. 'She'd already burned your house down, knowing that Rav was safely out of the way. And it would have suited her if you'd been killed then. The gruesome rat in the post didn't make you back off. It was all ramping up at that point. Dead, or retreating, or split up from Rav – any of the above would have delivered the result she wanted: Rav, all to herself.'

Rav shuddered.

'We need to study stalker behaviour much more, though,' Ashley said. 'This might make a good research paper.'

'That's what Val suggested,' James said.

'Oh, good.' Rav raised his eyebrows. 'I'd hate the experience to go to waste.' But his tone was agreeable, and Nell knew his scientific mind was already pleased about improving the data to help future cases.

'I still don't understand why Kat would go after Noah, though?' James asked.

Nell shook her head. 'I don't know either. We'll never know for sure, will we? Just that Noah was furious with Rav after their face-off in the courtyard. Could that have been it?'

'Maybe,' James mused. 'But Rav also spoke up about Gigi that morning, right when Noah was being taken in for questioning. Right after Noah seemed to call Rav's own morals into question.'

He leaned back in his seat, deep in thought. 'At that point, I'm sure Noah knew that Gigi *was* having an affair, but not who *with*. Gigi knew Noah sometimes followed her, to try to find out who she was seeing. She was keen to throw him off the scent.'

'Oh, no.' Nell gaped at him. 'You think she deliberately flirted with Rav to make Noah think they were having an affair? And *that* led to Noah perhaps planning to harm Rav? And, ultimately, Noah's murder?'

'Maybe,' James said. 'If Noah had followed Gigi to the courtyard, and saw Rav lurking about, he could have followed him. And why *else* would he be in that part of the wood, at that time? If he was about to attack him, and Kat *saw* that, she may have attacked Noah to protect Rav.'

Nell shivered. 'That means Kat had tabs on Rav's whereabouts almost all the time.'

'Well, Rav was pretty open with sharing his location via his phone. So it wouldn't have been challenging for Kat, would it?'

'No.' Nell frowned. 'I thought Kat was a bit quick to get off the phone to me that evening. I'd been trying to end the call a million ways, and I thought it would be easy because the line was patchy . . . Ohh!' She stared at James. 'Because she was probably sitting in her car. *Ugh*.' She shivered again. '*Watching* the house.'

Nell had to pause and take a deep breath. *Poor Rav*. She reached out and took his hand. He gripped hers.

'And Kat killed Louise partly out of jealousy,' James said.

Rav winced and buried his face in his hands. 'God, this is all so, so awful.'

'Yes, but *partly* is the operative word,' Ashley pointed out. 'We discovered that Kat has form. When she was freelancing as a videographer and living in Ambledown, the local vicar, Rev Woodwhite – who just happened to be fairly young and fairly handsome – asked her to help with some social media pieces. Kat formed an obsessive attachment to him, and he ended up having panic attacks.'

'He was treated at The Priory for a while,' James added. 'Louise happened to be a good friend, and she'd visited him throughout his treatment. So, it wouldn't have taken much for her to put that connection together, and realise who Kat was.'

Ashley nodded. 'If she *had*, Kat would have lost her job – and her proximity to Rav.'

Gaping, Rav said, 'Lou mentioned him! When we were doing the interviews! She told Kat she should introduce her to him.'

'So that was the trigger, then.' Ashley raised her eyebrows. 'Until that point, her methods when trying to kill someone were a level removed. Maybe the fire would kill Nell, maybe Nell wouldn't be found in the cellar in time. But for Louise, suddenly Kat was desperate enough to make a direct killing blow.'

As awful as these revelations were, Nell wondered if they might just lessen the terrible guilt still gnawing at Rav. She recalled why he'd been so keen to talk to Louise, and after all this, she wondered if he'd ever want to bring that up again. A bleak sadness, like mourning, settled in her heart.

But James was pressing on. 'Louise, of course, had made herself enough of a thorn in everyone's side. She made no secret of the fact that she'd uncovered everyone else's. And that muddied the waters for our investigation.'

'Quite,' Ashley said. 'I still feel sorry for Holly – with the problems with Noah, and fearing for her place at work if she made a fuss. Then finding her fingerprints on the candlestick, not that long after the discovery that her parents had left all their earthly goods to the church. It all put her firmly in the frame for all three murders, especially given how she was struggling – yet determined – to get by, literally carving out her own path with her craft.'

Nell grimaced. 'I wish she'd confided in me. I'd have helped her. Same for Zeus: if I'd known he was struggling, we could have worked something out. He didn't need to steal from us. I hate the idea that he was being blackmailed, and did more damage as a result. *And*, that it could have got him arrested for Louise's murder because she'd found out about it and was pressuring him to own up.'

'Of all our suspects, I feel sorry for Bea, if I'm honest,' James said. 'What a desperate state she must have been in, with her mum committing suicide and her gran with dementia, and then Louise probing into the tragedy.' He glanced at Rav and Nell. 'We had to arrest her, for what she did to her gran. She'll be at the mercy of the CPS, and judge and jury now.'

'She's got strong mitigating circumstances,' Ashley said. 'I hope they'll be taken into account.'

'We can't say the same for Kat,' James observed, his expression grim. 'We know that jealousy was her motive for . . . harming Erin.' He glanced at Rav as he chose his words with care.

Rav nodded. 'Erin always was a bit overfamiliar with me. I . . . I felt sorry for her, knowing I'd rejected her, but with us still having to work together. So I tried not to keep rebuffing her. I knew she'd never go too far. It was just her trying to save face.'

'Hmmm.' Nell wasn't so sure of that. But she'd never protested because she'd felt as guilty as Rav that their relationship made Erin so miserable, and that Erin was forced to bear it on a daily basis at work. Nell had known that she and Rav leaving the consultancy to work at Finchmere full time had helped. Until Erin had asked to join them there for training – hoping it would be with Rav. Nell had just been waiting for enough time to pass for Erin to find her peace with the situation. Until then, she'd tried to ignore Erin pushing things, playing for Rav's attention.

'But Kat didn't know your history,' James said. 'She just read the situation as Erin flirting, and Rav going along with it.'

Nell nodded. 'Even if she'd known that, I don't think it would have made any difference, though. Kat saw Erin's closeness with Rav as a threat.'

'Erin ruffled other feathers, though,' James said. 'While it looked like Holly could have killed all three victims, Erin's reaction to Noah made us think he was the prime suspect for a moment. Especially with Erin being killed in Holly's workshop, making it seem like Noah had met her there and attacked her, to take revenge on both the women complaining about him, as well as Louise, who'd threatened to go to the police about him.'

'Zeus was concerned that Erin knew about his bootlegging,' Nell added. 'With Kat being there when Louise accused him, that was another useful cover.'

Rav nodded. 'Bea had been distressed by Erin barging into her home – she was so fiercely private for obvious reasons. And when Erin saw the pictures on the fridge, she openly made fun of Bea having a crush. Which, together with Erin flirting with me, would have been especially provocative.' He grimaced. 'No wonder Kat tried to poison Erin with belladonna from Bea's garden. It put Bea straight under suspicion.'

'Kat took full advantage of that, didn't she?' Nell said. 'All those disagreements were a gift.'

'I'm certain she got Erin to the workshop on the pretext of filming something,' Rav said. 'She wouldn't have needed to risk sending a message, she could just have popped round to see her with a get-well gift and a ploy of keeping her in the loop, asking her to be there early. Kat loved a bit of dawn filming, to get that incredible light. It wouldn't have been unusual.'

'Kat would have had a busy day on Wednesday, though,' Ashley said. 'Getting to Richmond for late afternoon to photograph Aanya, ready to send that photo to Rav later, leaving her own phone safely at home so it didn't give away her location.'

'That would have been quite easy. Nell and I left early on Wednesday, for some time out together before I went to see my folks. So we didn't see who was around. And, with all the B-roll Kat had already recorded, she had more than enough material to be able to take the whole afternoon out.'

'And later that night,' James added, 'maybe around 3 a.m., Kat would have crept through the fields to set Nell's house alight.'

'Ugh. I can't bear to even think about that.' Rav shuddered. He gripped Nell's hand.

With Bea arrested and under investigation, Zeus sacked for gross misconduct, Gigi leaving the country with her barista, and Holly finding new premises since her legal dispute had promised a favourable result, Nell had to admit that she hadn't envisaged all this when they'd planned the fete.

Or the three deaths: an employee, the local vicar – and their friend.

She glanced at Rav, still weighed down with guilt and grief. She knew it had changed things for him, too. Maybe for them both.

Unless she took matters into her own hands.

Chapter 38

Saturday 15th July – 8 p.m.

Rav protested as Nell gently took his crutches away from him: she was intent on persuading him. 'Just try. Let's just try one walk. All-terrain – see how you go. We don't need to race.'

'I don't know if I can manage without them. What if I get stuck? It'll be dark soon.'

She knew he was worried at letting her down, looking weak, being helpless.

'So?' She shrugged. 'We won't be far. You can lean on me. We can take our time. And I have a torch.' She nudged him. 'And I've timed it perfectly. It will be romantic. We can have our first walk, holding hands, watching the sunset, in more than *two years*.'

'Two years, twelve weeks and one day.' He stared at his crutches as Nell set them aside.

She nudged him for tracking the time so closely, and his face softened at her smile as she leaned in to kiss him. Taking her arm – less for stability and more for closeness, for the novelty of it, how special it felt after all this time – they made their way across the terrace to the barn and the orchard.

'I see our barn owls are busy raising two chicks, from the live feed on the website.' He grinned at Nell. 'Nice to know our nest box is in good use, year after year, isn't it?'

She smiled and squeezed his hand. It felt so good to be holding it again, walking shoulder to shoulder with him, her arm around his waist, his arm around her shoulders, pulling her close.

'Oof. This is harder going. Bit slower here.' The uneven ground made them both take more care.

As they headed towards the woods, she knew they'd naturally

272

gravitate to that spot where their photo had been taken, when the first rewilding survey had been completed. Now, leaning on that five-bar gate again, they drank in the view, seeing the effects of their work around them in the species-rich plants, the thriving habitats, the diverse and rare fauna.

Their shared silence was deep, interrupted only by the sounds from the forest.

Nell wondered if she should leave more time, for Rav to get over the grief of the past few days. But it already felt like they'd been waiting forever. She sensed he needed something ahead of him, to look forward to.

Leaning close, she smiled and kissed him. The way he kissed her back, wrapping his arms around her, told her the moment was right.

Nell nudged him towards the woodland beside the gate, where Rav had taken charge of the dormouse surveys. He'd been entranced by them, delighting in any opportunity to see one in the fur. But now, other opportunities awaited.

As they approached the woodland edge, Rav frowned. 'Is that box new?'

Biting back a grin that he'd spotted it straight away, she shrugged. 'Let's check it.'

She pretended to search her pockets, feigning surprise at finding a large plastic bag, and handed it to Rav.

Gently, he blocked the hole against the tree with his hand, as he held the box while Nell unclipped it. He lowered it into the bag and carefully – slowly – opened it.

Nell watched his face as he frowned, did a double take. 'What's this?'

He held up the neat, black jewellery box, handing it to Nell. 'Do you think someone's lost this?' He re-clipped the box to the tree, bundled up the bag and stuffed it in his pocket.

'No,' Nell said, waiting for him to look at her again so she could hand it back. 'I think the right person's found it.' She was gratified at the perfect timing, as the sky streaked golden and scarlet, the evening birdsong echoing around them.

He eased it open, frowning at the contents. 'What's this?'

'It's tungsten, because it's precious and the strongest metal on Earth. Like someone I know.'

His eyes locked on hers and his indrawn breath told her he'd finally realised what she was doing.

'Rav, you're the most incredible person I've ever met. There's no one else I'd want to share the rest of my life with. Would you make me the happiest person in the universe, and marry me?'

'Yes.' His eyes shone as he gazed at her. 'Yes. A million yesses.'

Her heart somersaulted as he pulled her close and kissed her.

'And I think we should take a leaf from our dormouse's book.' She glanced at him. 'We need a new nest, don't we? One we've chosen together.'

He hugged her again, kissing her. When he eventually released her, he laughed. 'I have to say it: you're brave.'

She frowned at the unexpected comment. 'Why?'

'Brace yourself, is all I'm saying.'

When she prodded him, he pretended to relent, and she knew he was teasing her. 'For a full Indian wedding in Delhi? I mean . . .!' He exhaled through puffed-out cheeks.

'Hang on!' Nell looked at him, not sure if he was serious. 'We'd have it here, surely?'

Laughing, Rav looked at her. 'Good luck with that. I'm Number One Son, remember, with a force of nature for a mother, who'll have centuries' worth of cultural expectation on her shoulders. It's going to be massive. It's going to be beyond our control. It's going to be parties for days.'

'Wow . . . Well . . . that sounds like fun!' Nell was already adapting to the idea, whether he was teasing or not. 'We could have two, then. One wedding with your family, one here for those unable to travel, maybe? And maybe some guests will come to both?'

'Are you asking for the best of both worlds?' Rav raised his eyebrows. 'Or double the trouble?'

The Nature of Crime

Nature never fails to amaze me with its ingenuity – not least how some species can get away with activities that could be considered downright criminal.

Just like the stalker in this book, parasitic species can adopt a variety of guises to dupe hosts into not only enduring their presence but even welcoming and protecting them – even as that same interloper methodically destroys their resources, their home and often the host themselves.

The large blue butterfly is a perfect example of exactly this type of parasite: its caterpillar rewards its host of red ants with a sugared secretion from its honey gland whenever the ants do what it wants (a type of social conditioning called operant conditioning, similar to awarding a gold star for homework!).

It also cunningly imitates the ants' chemical and acoustic signals (called aggressive mimicry or chemical camouflage) so that the ants carry the caterpillar safely into their nest. Here, the ants protect it – even as the caterpillar gorges on their young. The caterpillar escalates its ruse here, using auditory mimicry to imitate the queen ant, overriding the ant's defences of its young as the caterpillar feasts on at least 350 ant grubs during its (up to) ten-month stay. The caterpillar metamorphosises into a pupa, then finally emerges for just four-to-seven glorious days as a butterfly.

I found it fascinating to compare the butterfly's survival tactics to classic patterns of stalking, especially in how some stalkers can identify and grow closer to their target, insinuating intimacy as they wreak destruction, while so convincingly masking their intentions.

Many plants also disguise their poisons behind their beautiful appearance – seemingly innocuous and innocent, yet deadly. While plants may typically have developed toxins as a defence mechanism rather than offence – as a deterrent from being eaten – they are no less potent and, as Bea points out, can heal as well as harm.

The story Bea referred to, about an entire Roman military column being defeated by just a pot of honey was too good to pass up: Legend has it that the legionaries were poisoned with a hallucinogenic honey produced by bees living along the Black Sea coast. Those soldiers who consumed it were rendered defenceless to an attack.

The ambush was masterminded by King Mithridates VI of Pontus: The Poisoner King of the Third Mithridatic War, who the Roman Republic faced as Rome expanded across Anatolia between 73 and 63 BCE. The king was obsessed with poisons and had developed a tolerance to several through regular consumption of sub-lethal doses (which is still known as mithridatism).

Made from the nectar of a rhododendron species, the honey contained high concentrations of grayanotoxin, a neurotoxin which caused hallucinations, nausea and loss of coordination in small doses – with larger amounts able to cause serious heart complications.

Despite his victory, Mithridates did not win the war, and his kingdom was destroyed by the Roman army. When the deposed king tried to kill himself, his immunity to poisons thwarted his attempt. But it's another cautionary tale that something apparently sweet may hide darker secrets!

One species that isn't considered sweet by everyone, however, was a hero in this story. It may seem unlikely that rats and mice can chew through (uncured) concrete and brick, but they can and do. Due to their diet, rodent incisors are tough – more than half as hard as pure diamond on the Moh's scale – and continuously and rapidly grow. So rats and mice need to grind their incisors down frequently to prevent them growing too long. In this case, a rat chomping on the wall in the bat hibernaculum was a lucky break for Nell.

While Rav and Nell lose much in this book, they also make some gains: their rewilding work is a salute to many successful and inspiring projects across the UK where habitats have been able to flourish, enabling rare species to thrive. This considered habitat management is, in itself, a focus on the delicate balance of nature – and one species that relies on exactly this type of management is that dastardly large blue butterfly.

The butterfly's fragile life cycle – from its tiny blue egg laid on a specific plant *Thymus drucei*, which in turn must be grazed by a specific animal (longhorn cattle – hurray for rewilding!) to ensure the earth is maintained at a certain temperature so that a certain ant species *Myrmica sabuleti* will nest there – is an exemplar of nature's fine tuning.

It's because of that delicate life cycle that butterflies are both so valuable and so rare – their life stages as herbivores, insectivores and pollinators make them important – yet their sensitivities make them perfect indicator species to alert us to issues endangering not only their conservation but the status of their whole ecosystem.

Poor habitat management, habitat loss, pesticide use and climate change are key concerns for the fate of our habitats and species; and those champions who rewild our spaces and protect nature – and the value it brings all of us – need support to continue their essential work.

And, if the scale of the challenge ever seems too steep, remember: just when the caterpillar thought the world had ended – it became a butterfly.

Acknowledgements

I'm so thrilled to work with the fabulous team at Embla Books, who consistently delight and amaze me with their talent and dedication: Emilie Marneur, Jane Snelgrove, Katie Williams, Vishani Perera, Danielle Clahar-Raymond and Emma Wilson, thank you for your incredible support and your brilliant, creative ideas. You are all a total joy to work with.

Thank you, Martina Arzu and Emily Thomas for your skilful touches that have made all the difference to this manuscript – and for making the editing process so much fun!

I'm indebted to the eagle eyes of Daniela Nava, Jon Appleton and Lucy Littlejohns – your precision and attention to detail is tremendous and I always learn something from you!

Katie Fulford (most marvellous agent in the universe) and the ace team at Bell Lomax Moreton – thank you a MILLION for your insightful advice and support on this journey.

Lisa Horton, thank you for yet another delicious, characterful cover, and for adorning this butterfly with ominous skulls – which, as it happens, is very fitting for the deadly large blue butterfly!

And huge thanks to Chelsea Graham, Emma Kiesling and the fantastic audiobook team who weave total magic when they bring a book to life with Kristen Atherton's sensational acting talents and captivating narration. It's a real privilege to work with you.

While inspirational brunches with Erin and Nigel, and motivational cocktails with Brenda, Julie, Alan, Bruce and Bob might become treasured rarities, I hope for many more with Jo, Rachel, Esther, Sabrina, Mark, Matt (and Lauren, in a few years' time!).

Mum and dad, thank you for reading the drafts, as always. You can always be relied upon to give your honest opinions, whether I want them or not (and, to be fair, whether they're book-related or not). Naturally, they are cherished and never ignored ☺

Ian, my stunt-co-ordinator partner in crime, thank you for joining me, jumping off a balcony for this one. The realism is important. (Though we should probably increase our insurance.)

And for those who have taken the time to read – thank you, and I sincerely hope you enjoy reading this as much as I've enjoyed writing it.

About the Author

After spending sixteen years as an ecologist, crawling through undergrowth and studying the nocturnal habits of animals (and people), Dr Sarah Yarwood-Lovett naturally turned her mind to murder. She may have swapped badgers for bears when she emigrated from a quaint village in the South Downs to the wild mountains of the Pacific Northwest, but her books remain firmly rooted in the rolling downland she grew up in.

Forensically studying clues for animal activity has seen Sarah surveying sites all over the UK and around the world. She's rediscovered a British species thought to be extinct during her PhD, with her record held in London's Natural History Museum; debated that important question – do bats wee on their faces? – at school workshops; survived a hurricane on a coral atoll while scuba-diving to conduct marine surveys; and given evidence as an expert witness.

Along the way, she's discovered a noose in an abandoned warehouse and had a survey derailed by the bomb squad. Her unusual career has provided the perfect inspiration for a series of murder mysteries with an ecological twist – so, these days, Sarah's research includes consulting detectives, lawyers, judges and attending murder trials.

About Embla Books

Embla Books is a digital-first publisher of standout commercial adult fiction. Passionate about storytelling, the team at Embla publish books that will make you 'laugh, love, look over your shoulder and lose sleep'. Launched by Bonnier Books UK in 2021, the imprint is named after the first woman from the creation myth in Norse mythology, who was carved by the gods from a tree trunk found on the seashore – an image of the kind of creative work and crafting that writers do, and a symbol of how stories shape our lives.

Find out about some of our other books and stay in touch:

X, Facebook, Instagram: @emblabooks
Newsletter: https://bit.ly/emblanewsletter